Dec 15, 1998
Dear Evelyn —
To God be the
Glory! Enjoy the
Journey & Love —
Nikki

$235.52...

Every Two Weeks in Corporate America

$236.52…

Every Two Weeks in Corporate America

by Mikki Rogers

A pragmatic and thrilling fictional yarn, which depicts uninterrupted interplay and volatility in the workplace…

In our professional lives, if we are one of the chosen few to make it to the top, through the glass ceiling applying our personal drive, dedication, constancy, hard work and intelligence, which logic says should dictate stability and advancement, we run into a brick wall around the next corner. Corporate America is overrun with people who will trample over any person to get what he or she wants. Some people have no real respect for themselves, so it is physically impossible for them to have a revering thought to anyone else. Fair treatment and promotions based on merit are more the exception rather than the rule. We run as fast as we can only to be given more and more tasks and with each task unreasonable demands, making big companies bigger and richer taking little for ourselves and our families. But, what choice do we have? It literally becomes a vicious cycle for which there is no way out.

Toney Chambers is a classic example of an intelligent thoroughbred who has been down that road, through encounter after encounter displaying all of the classic attributes of a winner, but who happened not to have "the look" that mainstream Corporate America readily accepted. Smart, dynamic, personable and driven, she rises to the top under the suppressive actions of supervisor after supervisor and even subordinates, who intentionally test her resolve. One day a fair-minded manager saw in her what she knew she had all the time and she rose. The trials that she experienced during those assiduous days could have put most human beings in a destructive phase, but instead she was steady, while she rose and maintained.

Perilous, original and suggestive, this anecdote will keep you engrossed with vivid pensiveness of ones own personal predicament.

Also by Mikki Rogers:

HOMEGROWN...Back in the Day

Coming in spring 2001

SOUL IN THE STREETS

Editor

Moses Norman, Ph.D.

Typing changes of Dr. Norman's editing by:

Ms. Bridgett Phillips

Photography Credit: Artistic Images
Art Terrell, II

This book is dedicated to my Mother

Mrs. Nina Reece…

She is my beacon

FOREWORD

In **"236.52...Every Two Weeks in Corporate America,"** her second novel, Mikki Rogers, a refreshing new talent in the literary world, produces a compelling, thought provoking and well written expose' on the subject of professional advancement and associated problems in Corporate America.

With Chicago as the major setting for this contemporary, fictional work about a female executive who climbs the corporate ladder of the computer industry, Rogers adeptly paints insightful descriptions that make the characters, but especially the central ones, believable, if not recognizable. From humble beginnings in rural Kentucky just outside of Lexington, Toney Chambers, the novel's heroine, goes east to attend and graduate from Howard University, prior to making her entrance into Corporate America. Destined to succeed and compelled to achieve, she rises to the rank of Vice President of Prophecy Computers worldwide, but not without consequences. Grant Parlarme, her soul mate and confidant, is a lawyer by profession, and he helps her to operate in the "real" world.

A moving work, with interwoven reflections of Toney Chambers' past and present experiences, the plot gains momentum with the emergence of Jim Surrant, a Regional Vice President for Prophecy Computers, whose cavalier and chauvinistic expressions are obvious and recurring. Antagonistically, he battles Chambers, his female boss, for her position.

Evocations of a series of negative events, which suddenly, and with a mesmerizing effect, impact seriously the lives of Toney and Grant, add mystery and intrigue to the novel. The ending is both poignant and surreal, making the entire novel by Rogers one that you will want to read continuously from cover to cover.

John S. Epps, Ph.D
President and CEO
Epps and Associates

Words From A Friend

It is of notable consequence that we understand that in the corporate arena, what one knows or the talent that one has does not always dictate success. Oftentimes, there are complicated factors involved that have nothing to do with our ability. To survive in this arena, it is important to have the attitude that we will do whatever it takes, without compromising ones beliefs or integrity. We must always understand that there are those of our color and not of our kind, and those of our kind and not of our color, so never let your guard down. Remember, success is a journey and not a destination, and is determined by the obstacles that we successfully overcome and not by the position that we hold. So, be focused, work hard, and stay one step ahead.

Thomas W. Dortch
President
TWD & Associates, Inc.

Words from the Author

This story is based on fiction. The story line is from the creative mind of the author and any references to any person or persons, places or actual events is purely coincidental. The purpose of the story line is to give the individual who reads this novel a sense of authenticity; respective to the events that take place in the periods indicated in the story.

For additional copies of this novel…

Send **$17.95** for Deluxe Paperback, plus **$3.50** shipping and handling to:

Creative Novels, Inc.
Post Office 57273
Atlanta, Georgia 30343

Distributed by Baker & Taylor Books

ISBN # 0-9663541-2-5

First printed in the United States of America by
Otto Zimmerman & Sons Company, December 1998

Published by Creative Novels, Inc.
Atlanta, Georgia

Book design and composition by Mikki Rogers

VOICES....

Massive mahogany double doors revealed voices from board members of a major American oil company off the Chicago shoreline speaking of the business at hand. The meeting was lead by the Chairman of the Board in an orderly manner with only murmurs of conversation audible to other employees. In the initial stages, the assembly was methodical as the executives took care of business. As the meeting approached closure the voices became pointed and nasty by the time that they started with the last of the agenda items. This item addressed internal candidates vying for a mid level management position, vacated unexpectedly by a Caucasian male whose resignation from the key post left the executives scrambling to fill the position. If the position were left vacant for an extended period of time, it would yield a major lull in revenue generation for the company. They had to move swiftly. It was revealed that the former employee had tendered his resignation to the Corporation in order to join another firm. In his exit interview, the individual stated initially that his resignation was solely for advancement, which was offered by the new firm. He reluctantly admitted toward the end of his exit interview, however; that many of the employees in the company were not content with the internal politics. He also said that the standards of the corporation were questionable and hinted that he was uncomfortable with the unfair practices of management and how certain members of the staff were being treated. That was the undeniable reason that he decided to leave. As the board reviewed the list of candidates, they realized that many of the employees on the list were well qualified for the position and had more than paid their dues, worked diligently, and remained loyal to the corporation. They also realized that neither of the individuals on the list had "the look" that was necessary. Due to corporate policy, the position had to be posted for five business days to determine any inside interests from employees who qualified. The interested candidates with tenure submitted their names, which made up the list in hand. When the names of the internal candidates were read, the jeers and insults shouted out became loud and unprofessional, filling the air with laughter and sarcasm. Two of the three individuals applying for this newly vacated position were African American and would be considered only if all other employees were dead, according to one of the executives. Others joined in with loud jeering.

"Who do those niggers think they are? And, the fat trailer trash wants a promotion too…please! As if we would allow either one of them to sit along side of us…How dare they!" shouted Mr. Smithers.

"We certainly do not allow gorillas in this boardroom," said Tom Hallon with the sharpest edge on his words.

"Yeah, we have no bananas today," Tom continued as they all laughed so loud that the passers-by outside the boardroom doors stopped and stared in disgust shaking their. . . .

WHY MUST WE ALWAYS BE IN FOR THE FIGHT OF OUR LIVES?

Eight blocks away down Lakeshore Drive light rain was falling. One looking at Lake Michigan could see a horrible storm headed to the city in the form of dark skies quickly consuming the region and coming on fast. The winds gusted to a terrific force in an instant, pushing the waves hard onto shore. In a matter of seconds the weather turned threatening. The current of the lake became fierce, forcing strong waves, as high as ten feet tall to push violently at the shoreline of Chicago.

A *raven*, which somehow got lost from the flock in the torrential rains, found himself fighting to find shelter from the storm. As he flew against the winds, just about out of breath with his wings so tired from the struggle, he saw the Chicago skyline within his reach. It appeared to be an endless effort. He reflected that this was no more than the struggles that he had endured all of his life; so, he had to keep going . . . he just had to. This is as it always had been, a matter of life and death, but because things had always been a struggle for him, he was prepared for the fight. He felt that he could reach deep down inside and pull more strength in order to keep going.

The raven continued to fly with everything he had inside facing the odds of the storm. It seemed as if he could actually touch the first of the tall buildings on Lakeshore Drive. Only a few more feet...just a few more minutes and he could rest. Was the skyline a mirage? Did it look closer than it actually was? Was this just a storm or maybe a dangerous weather front? Maybe this was the remnance of a hurricane? He was too tired to fight it if it was a hurricane. That would be too much.

"Please guide my way," he uttered to an invisible force in the universe. "Help me to reach safety from these horrific winds," he whispered as he fought the elements.

Just as the last of those words left his beak, he realized that he was seconds from shelter. A window ledge of one of the tallest office buildings in the Chicago skyline was at his wing. Even though he would still be outside in the storm, he would at least be out of the direct reach of the strong winds, which had uninterrupted access to him. The wind had been cutting him to shreds. Nearly blinded by the rain and wind, he landed on the window ledge. As he got his bearings together, he noticed that he wasn't alone. His eyes cleared as he got settled. He realized that a pretty dove was comfortably nestled in the corner of the same ledge. The dove was very manicured and well kept, but had obviously gotten lost in the storm. The dove had also, from its appearance, found shelter before the worst of the storm started. The raven began to get its composure together as he uttered thanks for safety, not addressing the presence of the manicured dove.

"Thank you for once again showing me the way," he said as he bowed his head.

Just as the last of those words left his beak, he heard telephones ringing in the distance...

ONE

'Focus. I should focus more.' She thought to herself as she sat at her desk listening to the other party on the telephone. It could really make a world of difference. As interesting as her life had or had not been, she knew that she should focus more. Or, did focusing cause her daydreaming? Her name is Toney Chambers. Quite a name, right? Her name reflected a very strong person to most of the people that she had met over the years. She had come a long, long way as a woman and a professional, in her limited years in the workplace. She hadn't started out strong though, not at all. But, she was much stronger now. Conditions insisted that she become stronger or loose all of the battles that really counted along the way. And, she was strong in all the ways that mattered, but as she traveled these roads there had been several bouts with impending darkness caused in part by strangers and in part by her self.

As she sat talking on the telephone, behind a huge specially designed desk, which was located in an enormous opulent, well appointed office…it began to come to her.

"Vanessa, I'll talk to you over the weekend. I'm still trying to get back to Lexington for the holidays, but that may not be possible. I know that's several months off, so we'll have to see."

As she paused to allow for a response from the individual on the other end of the line, she responded, " I love you too." Toney concluded.

In a matter of seconds, the conversation on the telephone was over and she hung up. Toney just sat there. Several minutes came and went; she appeared to be going deeper and deeper into a trance and had begun to daydream again. She had been through so much over the last eighteen years since she left Lexington for college and ultimately graduating from Howard University. She had done well, but at what costs, she thought? Her office was adorned with three very thick oriental rugs to match the theme of the decor along with two sitting areas formed by supple sofas and chairs as well as rich accent pieces. This was truly an office of a successful person.

"Buzz, buzz."

The lady in the semi trance, seated at the big desk responded to the intercom of her telephone.

"Yes Sonjia," she answered as she tried to shake off the trance.

"Toney, your conference call operator is on line two and she's setting up your call," said Sonjia, Toney's secretary.

"Thanks Sonjia," she responded.

"Would you ask the operator to ensure a roll call once all the parties are on board?" she asked in a respectful yet authoritative tone.

"Yes ...no problem," Sonjia answered while they both hung up the phone.

Toney continued to sit there waiting on the completion of the conference call ritual, partially still in her day dreaming state as she gazed at the expensive art work that garnished the walls of her office, as well as the elaborate systems installed there, all for her benefit. She was a fairly light skinned, very attractive woman, who was intensely well manicured and well dressed in a seriously professional Saint John two piece navy blue ensemble, navy Bruno Magli shoes along with her Rolex watch and ring, two karat diamond stud earrings and all the signs of success.

Toney was the Vice President of Prophecy Computers Worldwide. She reported directly to the president of the company Charles Corbin and was responsible for keeping all of the remote hardware offices in the United States and abroad in a flourishing revenue-generating mode. She had nine Regional Assistant Vice Presidents, who were mostly white males, reporting directly to her. The hierarchy of the company was setup with the Board of Directors, President, Vice President, Regional Assistant Vice Presidents and Remote Managers. This conference call was a weekly call that reviewed all of the statistics as they related to the monthly forecasts and how they stacked up to the annual forecasts of each location under their direct supervision. She wanted to make sure that they were on target weekly to ensure that all of the individual investors were satisfied with the company's performance. Toney had a staff of thirty-seven people right outside her door, who hinged on her every word. Sonjia Belleu, her assistant, was the office manager and was in charge of running the day to day operation of the office for Toney... Manny Matthews, Corporate Director of Public Relations and his assistant, June Morgan; Imogene Peay, Director of Operations Worldwide and her assistant Barbara Oliver; Freddy Talbert, Corporate mail distributor; Simon Sane, Corporate Controller and his assistant Shirley Seaton; and others all in the Vice Presidents area. The forty-fifth floor was hers. She was clearly in charge.

As she sat there waiting on each Regional Assistant Vice Presidents to chime in to the call, she continued to daydream about how she got to where she was. She had come from humble beginnings in a rural area in

Lexington, Kentucky, almost fifteen years before. She moved to the Washington, D. C. area to attend Howard University after studying very hard in high school. Her major in college was Business Management with a minor in Computer Science Management, then a totally new field on the horizon. She was a mediocre student in her first year of college. That was way off the mark for her because she had gotten the highest marks possible in high school. Her low grades early in college were due largely to the excitement of moving from a small rural area to the big city. When she arrived on the campus of Howard University, the other young girls laughed at her because she had no style and appeared to be a true country bumpkin. But, as the weeks turned into months, she met some of the other young folks from similar rural surroundings and they befriended one another. Week by week, each of them became more and more familiar with the new environment and became more and more accepted by other freshmen and eventually by upper level students. After several months on campus, they all frequented fraternity parties, went to football games and other campus and non-campus related activities. By that time, it was more a continual party than anything else. By the time she buckled down to her studies, she was becoming a sophomore in college and had begun to recognize that this college game was serious stuff. She had partied intensely at first, almost as if she was trying to make up for lost time; her grades were suffering and suffering badly. She hadn't understood exactly how serious things were, though, until one of the counselors at school sat her down to help her get direction. She also hadn't realized it at the time, but she would never be able to thank Ms. Singleton enough because she was the single entity that helped to chart Toney's future. The fact that her future would be an uphill ascent, at best, hadn't presented itself at that point. The years ahead would be the only indicator of what she would be up against as she began her ascension to the top. She hadn't counted on the obstacles that were ahead. To say she was naïve in those days would say it best. Toney was a woman of moral values, taught to her as a child through the years just before she left Lexington, Kentucky, to start her adult life. She was a woman of principle and was determined to use her mind and to work hard. But, she had been taught not to compromise her self worth, dignity or integrity. She thought many times over the years long and hard about it, and she still couldn't understand how some women could compromise themselves. How could they allow themselves to be used in inappropriate ways and look at themselves in the mirror the next day?

As Toney continued to sit there shuffling papers, while she waited on her conference call participants, she thought about the years leading to this time in her life. She had been richly blessed in her limited time in the workforce; even though, there had not been the customary merit raises or promotions for her. Her blessings came in the form of being able to catch on quickly and to get the job done and to be extremely successful in each level of work for which she was hired. Not many African Americans ever got a fair shake unless they were the Uncle Tom types who did everything they were told, never having a mind of their own or an independent thought, which could be voiced with confidence. She had to fight for every single thing she got. How sad that in most every case, it had to be that way. But, she realized that that was the way corporate America had been set up. She was determined not to settle for it in her personal career and to do what was necessary to get ahead. She vowed that she would fight to her last breath, if that was what it took....

Beep.

"Ms. Chambers, your roll call," Sonjia announced.

"This is the A T & T operator, Ms. Chambers, I am ready for your roll call now.

"Okay," Toney said.

"Mr. Buchanan?"

"Here,"

"Mr. Anthony?"

"Here"

"Mr. Surrant?"

"Present."

"Mr. Michaels?"

"Yes."

"Ms. Anson?"

"Here."

"Mr. Walker?"

"Present."

"Mr. Bukura?"

"Here."

"Mr. Dunham?"

"Here."

"Mr. Bradley?"

"Present and accounted for boss." he said sarcastically.

As everyone chuckled.

The operator said, "Ms. Chambers, all of your parties are on the line."

"Thank you operator."

Toney got down to business.

"Good afternoon everyone. Please keep in mind that this is not the normal nine a. m. time slot for our weekly conference calls. That is still in effect. This call was rescheduled because of a conflict I had with Corbin, so this will be the only time change. Thank you for joining me."

"I have eleven items to review. The first agenda item is regarding the broadcast fax that was sent out by Miss Belleu earlier in the week. These items have to do with the financial forecasts year-to-date and how each of your regional responsibilities stacks up to the forecasts. The action plans submitted by each of you during the last quarter of 1997 have been broken down into monthly statistics. Because this is the second month in the third quarter 1998, we need to measure where you are and what still needs to be accomplished by year end." She said in a very smooth and authoritative manner.

"This report is due to me at the end of the month. Have each of you collected the data needed to have your information to me in time?"

A collection of "Yes" responses were given.

"Item number two. The average buying rate is off pace in four of the six areas of responsibilities for Southern California, Mr. Surrant. And from the reports that you've submitted there are funds unaccounted for. We have had this discussion during one of the earlier first quarter conference calls and I thought we were all acutely cognizant of the seriousness of this issue. The Board of Directors are reeling because 1997 was such a bad year and we assured them that 1998 would be a completely different story. The expenses are out of hand, the future system sales are off pace, and your average buying rates are significantly lower than the targets, which you put in place. There is no excuse for any of you to have all three areas in such a funk."

Surrant stumbled in his response. He was infuriated that a nigger was speaking to him in this manner, especially a woman.

"Well, we have put some alternative action plans in place?" Surrant stammered.

"And the missing funds, I'm sure that they can be accounted for. It's in the numbers somewhere, but we'll find it."

He was in a defensive posture all the way around as Toney interrupted,

"The only thing that matters to me is that these numbers are up to par by the mid year meeting here in Chicago and most certainly by year end, Surrant."

She continued, “And there are two others of you, Michael’s and Buchannan, who are not far from where Surrant’s group is at this point. I want this remedied immediately. Do what you have to do, but get the numbers in line.”

A sense of quiet came to the speaker line of Toney’s telephone…Over the next thirty minutes they reviewed several other items. More than half way through the call they wrapped up the business at hand.

“Finally,” Toney said.

“Next and last item. We have developed eight ‘key segments’ regarding overall regional efforts, which we all agreed to. I assigned this task to each one of you with the understanding that you were all responsible for all of them and that we all had to reach an agreement on them before they could be submitted to the Board. Have each of you completed the input for resolution?”

Tyler Anson spoke up first, “Toney, my input has been completed. I’ve tried several times to get at least two of my counterparts together to discuss theirs, but we have all been running in different directions.”

Toney responded, “Thanks, Tyler, I can certainly understand how busy all of us are, but remember we all have this deadline and the Board wants no excuses.”

Jim Anthony chimed in…”We’re all here together now, so let’s just review each item until we are all satisfied with our findings and then we can move forward.”

Each participant embraced the idea. Toney gave Anthony verbal kudos as she instructed them to work on this issue, while she just listened in and took notes periodically. This particular item took many components of information from each member of the group and while they continued the conversation, Toney drifted back into her day dreaming mode ...

She thought, 'How on earth did I get here, especially in light of all that has happened?' She recalled that Surrant really wanted her job. He said so to her face. He made a lewd suggestion directed at her while they were at the last Corporate meeting in Dallas during the summer of 1997. He knew that the post for which he was jockeying was being sought after by many of the seniors. The short list of candidates was Jim Surrant, Chad Williams, an employee who had since left the company, and Toney. When the announcement came toward the very end of the national meeting last year, the look on Surrants face said it all. He was incensed. While many of Toney's other counterparts faked their congratulations to her, many of them were sincerely pleased in their acclamatory remarks. But, she knew that Surrant would become bitter after she took the position and a handful to manage.

She thought to herself, 'I guess I could have anticipated his snide remarks from that point on, but she had high hopes that the problem would simply fade away in time.' Nevertheless, over the past year he had gotten worse instead of better. 'But, Surrant had better be careful,' she thought many times to herself...he probably hadn't realized it but he had really been bordering on insubordination many times, but Toney had chosen not to deal with it.

Part II

Toney's earlier years were questionable as they related to her humble beginnings. Her situation back then was a far cry from where she was now. She grew-up on a farm near Lexington, Kentucky. She was a loner of sorts and very shy. She was always very bright and studious. She had a clean and innocent look about her. Her teachers all through school took special time with Toney, because they saw great promise in her. Whenever she was given a new subject or course of action, she caught on quickly. Through her early school years she was quiet and rather mousy in her appearance. As she walked through her early and midlevel school years and through high school she developed a following which made her kind of popular, only because she was such a brainiac. Many of the students befriended her so that she could help them to achieve passing grades too. Toney had natural instincts about learning and had realized early that education inspired her. She wanted to achieve more in her life than the farming community that she was so accustomed to and knew that if she really worked hard and applied herself, she could eventually see the world that she was learning so much about.

In Toney's senior year, with the help of her senior guidance counselor, she completed all of the forms necessary to apply for tuition assistance from the U. S. government to make sure her financial needs would be met to attend college. She knew that with her high academic achievement she was a sure bet for a scholarship, but wanted to make sure that she had enough backing to go all the way through school; so she applied for government grants as well. She had been named valedictorian of her class, and as graduation approached, she toiled over the speech, which she had the honor of giving to her fellow classmates and others. On the day of her graduation, she was proud to wear an all white cap & gown, mostly because she had no real idea how to dress or to make herself look on the outside how she felt on the inside. She was beaming with pride and excitement. She knew that her life was about to change dramatically and all for the best. After this important offering to her schoolmates, their families and other supporters, she would make her final mark on the community from which she grew into a young woman.

On the big day it was sunny with just a hint of summer approaching. As the gentle winds brushed through the trees and into the faces of the youthful and joyful graduates, they all marched into the gymnasium paired up two by two, first the girls and then the boys. The school's principal started the program and one item after the other led the schedule along. The Valedictorian was introduced. The audience was made up of mostly sophomore and junior students as well as the families of the other graduating seniors. Most of them knew Toney, and although she was quiet and extremely shy and unassertive, they seemed to all have a great deal of pride in her educational accomplishments as they gave her a huge round of applause. Toney very awkwardly, and not very sure footedly, made her way to the podium to begin her address. She thanked the audience sincerely for their applause as she appeared to be as much a shrinking violet as always. She had the knowledge to speak the right words but hadn't come into her own with any measure of confidence because she was still so shy. After thirty seconds or so, Toney began her address…

"The years have been kind to all of us as we have grown into young adults. We have had the good fortune to have dedicated and loving parents, strong and determined teachers who would not allow us to be defeated. And, even though we are poor in terms of money, we are rich in all the ways that really count. We have been blessed to have had the opportunity to learn and grow with one another. Now that we embark upon a change of seasons, our time is now. We have been properly prepared to pursue new trails to blaze and new territories to explore. We thank God for his guidance to this milestone in our lives."

She continued for the next six minutes, holding the audience spellbound, listening to each and every word as she concluded:

"At this time we must only look back, if there is something to gain from doing so. We will hopefully keep our eyes on our futures, looking and marching straight ahead to the beat of our own drummers and being mindful that we can only get out of life what we put into it. Hard work and determination will be our tools for whatever trade we chose for our life's work, keeping God as the cornerstone of all that we undertake. Remember that the 'haves' are separated in this society from the have 'nots.' We must each determine what it is that we want to have, what will fulfill our personal lives, while not dwelling on what someone else has. For what makes them tick may not be of any interest to us."

God bless you all!

Toney's standing ovation was awesome. She seemed to have, in that instant, developed a small amount of self-confidence. She marched off the stage and took her seat with her fellow classmates. Her eyes locked with Vanessa's. She smiled slightly at her one true friend with whom she was graduating, Vanessa Donavan, who was seated directly behind her. The principal thanked Toney and asked that she stand for one more round of applause. She did so, shaking noticeably to those people who were seated closest to her. And, finally she quickly took her seat again as she tried hard to regain her composure and to remove herself from the attention of the others. The program continued. The final ritual was performed. Each of the graduates marched up on the stage to accept their long awaited diplomas. Once they were all back in front of their respective seats still standing, they were instructed to be seated again together. The principal stood once more to bring the entire senior body to their feet again. They all turned to face the audience and were instructed to take off their caps and toss them into the air. This marked the finale and that they were all finally official high school graduates. This was a day that Toney and her classmates would remember forever.

PART III

The summer was hot and hazy. There wasn't much for anyone to do other than the norm for them. Sundays were spoken for. As families, they all attended Greater Spiritual Baptist Church and afterwards each family had a huge dinner, then prepared for the beginning of their week. The younger kids played in the yard each day, but Toney wasn't use to having anything more to do than to read books for relaxation after she finished with her chores. Her books took her to far away places throughout the entire world - in her mind. She was determined that one day she would see that world in person. The only other distraction that she had was when some of the other students came over to her house for tutoring lessons. The number of students had been recently reduced to those who had to go to summer school.

Most of the parents in the area worked the land or had other jobs to make ends meet. They still pursued their Saturday evenings at the Elliott's, Big Helen's and Mr. Charles' farm just down the road. The Elliott's made a living from entertaining all of the local adults. They offered some of everything. It was a juke joint of sorts. In one room of their farmhouse, they had a crap game going on with Big Helen taking all bets and getting ten percent off of every throw of the dice. And, in another room, activity included the card table, where people played their tonk or poker. There was a room allotted just for music, drinking and dancing. Mr. and Mrs. Elliott also sold fried chicken and fish dinners to their regulars. For many of the people in this particular farm community, this was the routine highlight of their existence. But, they still looked out for each other and worked together to keep a close knit life. The biggest thrill in any of their lives was to actually go into downtown Lexington to the movies, the Piggly Wiggly or to the five and dime store to shop - what they really called "stepping out." So, the Elliotts' house was the distraction that all of the adults needed to break the monotony.

On the weekend of the July 4th holiday there was the big cookout at the Elliotts' farmhouse picnic ground. Everyone in the community was there. The day was filled with loud talk and drinking. The younger people engaged in games. The young adults were grouped in several pockets talking about this and that, just to pass the time. Around seven Toney and her parents headed home. They prepared for church and their regular Sunday dinner. Toney had been noticeably jumpy for the past few weeks, because each day she ran to the mailbox to see if there was any response from the colleges that she had applied to. The following Tuesday, Toney received a letter from Howard University. She ran back into the house screaming, "Mom…Dad, here's a letter from the college. I wonder if I got in?"

Dorothy came walking toward Toney at a very fast pace.

"Open it honey. Let's see what they're saying."

"I'm afraid. Mom, I'm afraid to open it." Toney said jumping up and down.

"Calm down Toney. You've got to open it to see what it is." Her mom said with patience.

The excitement of the college's response was heart stopping. She had been accepted at her college of choice, which was number-one on her list. She would be headed that way in September. She had always been shy and had a long way to go to becoming like those people she had read about in big cities all across America. Toney knew that she wouldn't want to be left to live and die in this small town ritual that she saw her parents stuck in.

Toney had already begun to give some thought as to how she would pack. She knew exactly what she wanted to take with her to the college campus in the Washington, D. C. area. She didn't, however, have that much, but wanted to make a good impression, which just thinking about it made her nervous. Was she putting the cart before the horse in thinking about clothes of all things? She really didn't think so because she was so used to planning each and every step that she took, which was second nature to her. She also knew that she was making herself sick inside with the anticipation of this new step in her life. She wondered would she be accepted? College was such a huge step for her. She daydreamed as she did often about the caliber of young people that she would meet. She had selected Howard because she felt that other young people much like herself would be there. She knew that she needed a great deal of life's lessons and a more formal education before she could take on other segments of society. She definitely wanted to be well prepared. She thought about her hometown and the schoolmates that she had just left at the high school. They accepted her only because she was smart and needed her to help them with their schoolwork and eventually graduation. The only person who had ever accepted Toney for herself was Vanessa Donavan. She was a cheerleader for the high school, and what a pretty girl she was, both inside and out. She was about five foot five, and had filled out early in her teens, having large supple breasts and shapely hips and big legs with a tiny waist line. Her hair was down her back, and she was one or two shades darker than paper bag brown. All through her junior and senior years, she always had all of the jocks chasing her, but even though she was pretty she was shy just like Toney. That's why they were drawn to each other in the beginning. Vanessa wasn't especially bright, but she tried hard and when they became friends. Toney tutored her through the eleventh and twelfth grades, so that they could graduate together. She was really the only true friend that Toney had. The difference between helping Vanessa and the others was she never asked for the help or wanted Toney in her life for what she could give her. One day a couple of years before, they just started talking and the relationship bloomed from that point on. Vanessa wasn't fortunate enough to be going to college. She barely got out of high school with her grades. Thank God they became friends because by her own admission, she would have had to repeat the eleventh and maybe even the twelfth grade.

The summer rolled by rather slowly. It was much warmer this year than last. Many nights after the days had passed, Toney took her bath and put on her pajamas, which were much too small for her (but in her mind she had to wear what she had). She tossed and turned because of the heat and finally decided to get up and go out on the front porch into the moonlight to cool off. That special night while she was sitting there, a feeling came over her about what she would be doing the following month. She was three weeks away from the start of her new journey. It was frightening to her to say the least, but she fought the feeling with the thought that she would not stay on this farm for the rest of her life. She looked up at the moon, instantly thinking of God, fell into a kneeling position, and went directly into a long prayer:

"God, thank you for loving me and giving me all that you have. I'm afraid of the future, because I feel that it will bring mostly uphill battles for me. But, I am acutely aware that I cannot let that stop me. I only ask that you keep me lifted up and I promise that I will remember your word when times get hard and it appears that I have lost my way. Please give me the strength to go forward. I promise that I will do the very best that I can in Your Name always. And, please keep my parents safe while I am away...as well as Vanessa....Thank you, Amen."

With the end of her prayer, she got back to her feet and went in to bed. She drifted off to an immediate peaceful sleep **...**

Toney faded back into the conference call. The regional folks were hard at a debate about the particulars of the moment.

"If I headed up this area, I would intrude on the strongest sales people in all of the major cities. It would be my intent to hire them at absorbent salaries and take all of the business potential from the competition. We would then be assured of our direction. Winning at any cost is what I'm all about," spewed Surrant!

Toney chimed in, "It is my feeling that we must maintain an ethical position at all costs, and if we continue to apply proper business practices, business will be ours as well," she said in an unruffled manner.

A moment of silence was upon them, and then ten to fifteen seconds later, Toney reiterated, "And, while I'm Captain of this ship, this is indeed the way that we will move forward."

The conference call was then concluded with the agreement to get back together on another call at the regular time the following week for more updates before the big meeting to be held at the Corporate Offices in three weeks.

They all hung up. Toney collapsed back in her chair, with feelings that fatigue was pulling her down. It was more a mental thing for her than anything else. The mental gymnastics that Surrant always tried to play on her was wearing her down, but she couldn't appear as if she couldn't handle him. After all, he was a loudmouth, and she had to continue to remind herself that all he wanted was her job. She took a deep breath, which appeared to give her a lift, opened the bottom left hand drawer of her desk to grab her purse. She retrieved her comb from her purse while simultaneously pulling her hand-held mirror from her middle drawer. She leaned her head back as she gently combed her hair, which was slightly in disarray from the busy afternoon. She freshened her makeup before standing up to leave for the day. She had had enough. Besides, if she left now, she could make her dinner appointment on time. As she opened her door to the outer area of her office, her secretary, Sonjia Belleu, gave her the remaining messages that had come in while she was on the telephone. Toney breezed through the messages and handed Sonjia two of them to call back for her, asking that the callers reschedule with her for tomorrow. The rest could wait.

"Goodnight Sonjia. Be careful going home. I'll be in at six in the morning, Okay?" Toney said as she walked away.

"Okay, Toney. I hope you and Mr. Palarme have a great time at dinner tonight. And, Toney," Sonjia said softly with a calming effect, "Everything will be alright."

Toney smiled as she left, turning to Sonjia, to say, "God has never let me down yet...after all he sent you to me, didn't he?"

Toney left the office and called for the elevator. While she was waiting, she ran into Freddy Talbert, her mail person. He was a character. He was always quick with the fast and loose comments, which provoked humor and light heartedness.

"Hi Miss C." Freddy said quickly.

"Well hello Freddy." Toney responded smiling while thinking of some of his recent fast and witty comments.

"I haven't seen you all day today. You've been locked away in that ivory tower that you call an office, huh?" Freddy continued.

"You got to get out more often, you know? You're looking real, real good though." he said flashing a big smile and giving Toney a once over.

"I got one more piece of mail for Sonia and then I'm outta here. Have a good night." he said in his fast quick-witted way shoving himself into the door of the outer office and disappearing through to the other side. Just as quick as he appeared he was gone. The elevator came. She rode down to the lobby, waived at Marvin, the security guard, walked out onto the street and hailed a taxi. She got in, reciting, "Vidi Vini Vicci's on State Street please."

TWO

He fought himself constantly without even knowing it. Jim Surrant, Jr., one of the Regional Assistant Vice Presidents for Prophecy was responsible for the entire West Coast region. He lives in Southern California in a rich community called Manhattan Beach. Jim was accustomed to a very high standard of living, due to his upbringing. His father Jim Senior was an affluent businessman in the old days in the Baltimore, Maryland area. Jim's father had left Jim and his two sisters, Saundra, named for his grandmother, and Barbara, who was named after their mother, extensive trust funds to be administered after his father's death and once the children came of age. At the time of Jim Senior's death, Jim Jr. was barely seventeen. Jim was angry about the death of his father. He felt that he had been cheated out of the leadership and nurturing that he needed to become a complete man, and from that point on he felt he was on his own. Jim Jr. became the only other male member in their immediate family overnight. Jim Jr. knew that his father's death tore away from the natural fiber of his family and felt that it was never the same to him again.

As Jim drove down the Freeway in his two-seater black Mercedes headed home late that night, he was still strongly shaken up, directly in light of the conference call from earlier in the afternoon. He reviewed the entire day in his mind and even the last part of the evening. He and his secretary, Holley, had been the last ones in the office, because the conference call had made it necessary for them to make a commitment to stay late in order to finish the intricate items of the tasks at hand. He knew that the next step that Ms. Big Shit would take would be to follow-up on him and his shortfall from his region. Each Regional Assistant Vice President was accountable for offering the results of the telephone meeting, which took place today. Ms. Big Shit had to do it, he thought. It was clearly her responsibility. It would be a clear-cut case of covering her own ass and if he were in her shoes, he knew that's what he would have to do. The implications of the shortfall challenges summarized by Chambers had the spotlight, of his inability to be effective, shinning directly on him and his computer stores and remote offices. He knew that he had to clean up everything before Chambers had the rug pulled out from under him. He also knew that it was just a matter of time before she had him dead to rights. It was a damned shame that it had to be this way. Jim felt that he was doing the best that he could under the circumstances, and anyway, he just knew that he was better suited for Ms. Big Shit's position than she was. He thought about it a lot, and if he were the big boss it would be different.

Immediately after the conference call that day, Jim stepped out of his lush office to get the attention of his secretary, motioning for her to step into his office.

She rose from her desk after completing the call that she was on and immediately followed him.

"Yes, what is it Jim?" she asked as she stepped inside.

"Do you have plans for tonight," he asked, "I could really use your help," closing the door behind her?

"No. What did you have in mind?" she teased.

"Come on, Holley, I'm serious," Jim stated.

"Nothing that I can't get out of, what do you need?" she said as she took a seat in one of the two-armed chairs located in front of his custom made tabletop desk.

"We're in a real bind and the hammer may be coming down on me real soon, so I have got to get it together." he said nervously trying to disguise his temperament.

"Whatever I can do to assist you, I'll do it. You know I'm here for you anytime." she said tenderly.

"Please pull all of the reports from each of the store locations in our region and the remote business offices. We have to go over them with a fine-tooth comb this evening. There has to be something that we've missed. We simply can't be that far off the mark and that much down in our revenue figures. I've got to find the areas where we can make up the difference or at least find some of the obvious errors," he said in an almost defeated tone, while still trying to maintain some sense of strength.

"I'll get right on it, Jim." Holley said getting right to it.

Holley got busy at once going about her way to retrieve all of the material needed. She wanted to conduct the research in as much detail as possible. After about twenty-five minutes of gathering the documents, she returned to Surrant's office. One by one they laid out all of the documents on his boardroom table and began the painstaking task of reviewing each of them. In between careful review of the first five documents, Holley fielded telephone calls or departmental questions having to do with today's challenges until the interruptions became to costly and time consuming. They were not getting through enough of the information as timely as they needed to. At this rate they would be here until tomorrow, Jim thought.

Jim finally said, "Holley, get one of the other girls to sit at your desk to be a buffer so that we are uninterrupted. We need to get through as much of this material as we can tonight."

"Okay," Holley said stepping outside of the office soliciting Jocelyn, the Director of Business Development's secretary to take over her responsibilities for the remainder of the day.

"Jocelyn, will you help Jim and I out and answer the telephones while we take care of this project?"

Jocelyn said, "Sure, are there any special instructions? Am I to hold all calls?" she asked.

Holley responded with authority, "Yes, all calls. We are not to be interrupted unless it is a case of emergency."

Once Holley returned to the office and closed the door, Jocelyn and two other secretaries in close proximity looked at one another and their faces said it all. There had been whispers about the relationship between Jim and Holley. It was so obvious to all of the office workers because of the way Jim leaned on Holley for everything. It was almost as if Holley ran the operation single handedly. Office gossip had taken what they thought amounted to a torrid affair and run away with it. The secretaries waited each day to see what else they could see. They knew that it was only a matter of time before it all came out, and they wanted nothing more that to be there when the shit hit the fan.

After two uninterrupted hours, Holley finally found one of the big errors. It was one that added up to Two Hundred, Fifteen Thousand Forty-Five Dollars and Seventy-Eight cents.

"That is awesome!" shouted Jim. "I knew I could count on you, Holley. I just knew I could. Let's continue the process. There has to be more," he said to her in a revived tone.

After three more hours of constant searching, they discovered one other small error adding up to another Fifty Thousand Dollars. It appeared that they were still down over a quarter of a million dollars, but Jim felt that they could make that up in a couple of weeks with no problem.

Jim and Holley completed the tasks at hand. They were exhausted and decided to enjoy a celebratory cocktail together.

"I'm plum tuckered out." Holley said taking a seat on one of the office sofas.

"I'm tired too. Maybe these drinks will rejuvenate us." Jim said pouring them the drinks.

It was already nine thirty five. They had both put in a day and a half already since they started at six thirty this morning. They initiated conversation about the day and before they knew it they were undressing each other with their eyes.

Holley, a strawberry blonde, with large breasts, a tiny waistline and big legs, stood about five foot-seven in her bare feet. She wasn't a spring chicken anymore, but was very good looking and was still in search of a break to get ahead. She had just turned thirty-five years old last month. She landed the job at Prophecy about two years earlier after attending classes at the Los Angeles College for Word Processing, which was all she needed to get her foot in the door of a fortune 500 company. She had strong common sense and was also knowledgeable about how to handle herself in most cases. Her educational opportunities were limited to high school, where she was just above an average student and was only able to obtain menial jobs after that. But, she was on a mission now. Holley's concept about life was to make sure she put her best foot forward now, because she didn't want to see herself in ten to fifteen years with limited accomplishments. She moved to California about ten years earlier with high hopes of being discovered for the movies, much as over fifty percent of the population of Tinsel Town had done. She was conditioned to access most situations quickly and was poised to learn Jim's quirks after studying him for the first few months that they worked together. So, she used what she had learned and managed over the last two years to work well with him anticipating his every move. She made sure of that. Her plans were unfolding nicely as she made herself indispensable to him. They had become close over this time and had flirted back and forth with one another much in a joking manner. The last six month had proven to be the proof of the pudding regarding their mutual interests in one other, and that made both of them realize that they were really attracted to each other. They had engaged in serious conversations about the expectations of a relationship between them. One night late in the evening after they had worked on a deadline together, Jim asked Holley if she wanted to grab a quick bite to eat. Jim's wife and kids were out of town at the time and he didn't want to go to his big lonely, quiet house until later. Holley accepted. Jim took her to a fancy candlelit restaurant, which happened to be just a block down from their offices. With no real plans to do so they ended up in a steamy conversation about sex and eventually were off to a motel about fifteen minutes away. It was purely unexpected, but much to their pleasure and it was what they both wanted. Periodically, after that, they had dinner and drinks and sex and eventually it was a routine for them to do it two or three times a month.

This particular night, Holley looked extra good to him. After a couple of sips of his cocktail, Jim walked over to the sofa where Holley was seated. He leaned down to give her a quick kiss on the lips. Holley responded by kissing him back in a sexy manner. One thing lead to another as he ran his hand through Holley's hair, while still coddling his drink with his other hand. Then he began stroking her face and eventually her breasts all in one motion with his right hand, pulling her up out of her seat toward him. She seemed to be expecting all of this. They kissed a long wet sensuous kiss as she gave in completely. Her compliance taunted him. He became instantly erect. Since they were alone, they let all of the inhibitions down and quickly undressed one another. They were standing in the middle of his office naked, grinding against each other with their tongues simultaneously going down the throats of each other. Jim grabbed for Holley's buttocks as she hopped up on him putting her legs around his waist. He walked over to the sofa while they continued to kiss and slowly lowered her down until her backside reached the edge of the couch. She slowly reclined back on the couch putting her feet on the piece of furniture sitting near the area, opening her knees revealing her private area. They began making love right there on the sofa in his office. What was Holley after? Was she going to settle for just being his fling? She had really begun to care for him as more than her boss, but for the time being she was satisfied with the situation the way it was. They continued for over thirty minutes. They completed their sex act and tip toed off to the wash room right there in his office for a quick clean up, and then they got dressed.

A few minutes later he asked her as if nothing had happened, "You ready to go?"

She smiled and said, "Sure, if you are."

He walked her to her car and gave her a quick kiss on the forehead. She got in and started her engine, putting the car in gear then turned to look up at him, smiled and drove off. He sauntered to his car only a few feet away, which was parked in the only reserved spot in the garage. Then it appeared that he started to feeling like he was the king and drove off. It was after midnight when he arrived home. Everyone in his family was sound asleep. He slipped into the shower to completely get the smell of Holley off his person, put on his silk pajamas and slid into bed beside his wife. She woke-up slightly, turned over and moved under him as they both got settled and eventually drifted off to sleep.

Jim, his wife Joanie, and their two children, Jim, III, who was twelve years old, and Marge, who was ten, had a home, which amounted to an estate. The nearly million dollar home had eight bedrooms and eight bathrooms alone, not to mention the various other specialty rooms in the house. They had a live in maid, Amy and groundskeeper Juan who also had their residential quarters on the estate. The family was living mainly on the monies from Jim's father's estate and hadn't had to depend solely on the earnings from Jim's job to carry them through.

PART II

Joanie and Jim met during their college days. She was a petite, cute, very shapely blonde cheerleader, while he was the starting quarterback for the football team. He had gotten his scholarship for athletics. Academia was certainly not his strong suit because Jim's father's money bought him out of each and every scrape that he managed to get himself into over the years. Joanie attended an all girls' college in the Clemson area. Some of the girls from Marymount College were the cheerleaders for Clemson and cheered at all of Clemson's football games. From the moment Joanie saw him standing on the sidelines that fall afternoon, six-foot five with his dirty blonde hair, blue eyes and the physic of a god, she had fallen desperately and deeply in love with him. Jim noticed her too, but had a bad reputation with the girls of being a guy who loved them and left them. He thought that there was something very different about Joanie and that there would be no possibility at all that he could get the attention of a prim and proper girl like that. She was innocent, sweet and appeared to be very giving. She had grown up in a St. Louis suburb. Her parents were blue-collar workers who worked hard to make ends meet and to put enough money aside to send Joanie to college. Joanie Compton was an average student but gave her studies all she had inside. Winning a partial scholarship was a coup for Joanie and helped as her parents had saved over the years to assist in sending her to college. This helped to finance the remaining portion of her four-year college. So, there she was in her sophomore year and making the most of this time in her life, when she met the guy of her dreams. She wasn't the strongest girl in the world, but she had a constitution for survival. This had been demonstrated by her determination to make her grades good enough to be accepted into the college of her dreams. She had never really been tested to the limited, though, so she wasn't aware of her inner strength or that her inner strength would ever come into question. She just moved along each day, stringing one day to the next, hoping for the best.

Jim wanted to get to know Joanie, after a couple of encounters at the football games. On the third occasion during the home game against Auburn, they were on the sidelines while the Clemson defense was on the field doing their jobs. Jim wandered over to the cheerleading squad to ask Joanie out for pizza. She was reluctant to take him up on his initial offer, but feared that she wouldn't get another chance if she said no. So, she reluctantly accepted. The next weekend, there they were out on a date. His demeanor was awkward and clumsy, but the mere fact that he was giving it a try spoke volumes to the people who had come to know his antics all too well.

He had been a cad of a boy through his teen years and in to his young adult phase, knocking down any and everything in his path as he grew. His father had spoiled him rotten, and Jim truly believed that the world was his oyster. Jim's attitude was putrid to the core. He rarely got into his studies, if at all. He drank, cursed and ramroded his way through high school and four years of college. The fact that he was the quarterback of the football team at this highly rated college would prove, as some people saw it, to be his undoing. It was so difficult for his counselors and professors to contain him while he was in class. He was sarcastic and very disruptive. They saw that he was personally hurting and had reached out for him so many times, but it was a laborious task and it was impossible to reach him. The mere fact that he was so valuable to the school as Quarterback of this high-ranking collegiate team meant that he was off limits to constructive criticism by the people who saw what was happening to him. So, for over four years, he lived recklessly and was not forced to achieve academically. Maybe Joanie was just what the doctor ordered for Jim.

Before he met Joanie, Jim had numerous clandestine meetings with various girls in the area. He was, on a couple of occasions, locked up for forcing himself on two girls. But, the charges were dropped because of his father's connections and no words were ever spoken about either situation again.

Jim and Joanie had eloped right after college. She was so afraid of what her folks would do when they found out. This was not like her at all. But, she had always been easily influenced. This topped anything that she could ever do to bewilder her parents. But, she was in love, so she had to go for it. On the afternoon after she and Jim said their vows, Joanie called her mom and dad to break the news to them.

"Hello," her mom answered in a domesticated voice.

"Hi, mom, is dad there?" she asked timidly.

"Hi, baby, how are you?" her mom asked in a light spirit.

"I'm great, mom, is dad there?" she asked again.

"Is there something wrong?" her mom asked as her demeanor turned into a worried tone.

"No, but I have something to tell you and dad...it's wonderful news," Joanie said proudly.

"He's outside cutting the grass, hold on and I'll get him," said Mrs. Compton.

Mrs. Compton hurriedly put down the phone, walked quickly to the door and beckoned for Mr. Compton to come inside. A couple of minutes passed as she tried to get his attention over his movement back and forth and the lawn mower noise. Finally he saw her.

"What is it, Anna?" he asked with a concerned look.

"Joanie's on the telephone. She has something she wants to tell both of us." Anna shouted as Sam stopped the mowing and hurried into the house.

They both picked of the phone, Anna in the living room and Sam in the kitchen.

"Daddy?" Joanie said shyly.

"Yes, baby girl, what is it, are you alright?" Sam said nefariously.

"Why yes daddy, I am better than I have ever been before in my life! I just got married today to the most wonderful boy," she said in a rather quiet way.

"You what?" both her parents said at the same time, as her mother slid down taking a seat on the nearby chair.

"Joanie, who is this boy?" asked Sam trying to keep his composure.

James Surrant, II from the Surrants of Baltimore," she responded proudly.

"Honey, how could you go and do this without so much as a discussion with us? We thought that we could trust you, honey," Sam said tenderly.

"Well, daddy, you can trust me - you know that. It's just that I'm in love that's all," whined Joanie. She knew that she could always win her way when she whined, especially with her dad.

"Well, it's all said and done now, isn't it? When will we meet this special young man?" asked Anna.

"Our plans are to come to St. Louis in a couple of weeks on our way to Baltimore, so that I can be properly introduced to Jim's mother, his sisters and the rest of his family," replied Joanie.

"Well, honey, we love you and look forward to seeing you then," Anna answered.

Sam and Anna hung up the phones in shock. They couldn't believe it. Sam was not prepared for this, not at all and neither was Joanie's mother. Anna walked slowly from the living room to the kitchen. She hugged Sam, trying to console him.

"Well dear, at least she isn't hurt. I guess it could be worse. I just hope that this boy doesn't end up hurting our sweet innocent little girl."

Jim and Joanie arrived at the airport in St. Louis two Saturdays later. Sam and Anna were there early. The flight was due in at ten forty five am. It was just past ten and the excitement they felt was so much that it was uneasy for them. They wanted to see their little girl again, who had obviously became a woman since the last time their last encounter with her.

Finally the time was upon them. Both Sam and Anna had been at the airport for over an hour. They rested in the gate area where Joanie's plane was to come in. They stood up as the announcement was made that the plane had landed, watching person after person disembark.

"There she is, Sam," Anna blurted out, "there's my little girl!"

Joanie's smile said it all! She ran, first to her mother and then her father. Then the three of them hugged long and hard momentarily forgetting about Jim. Jim had never seen this much love and was becoming angry at being left out. He was so used to being the center of all of the action and this was not good at all for his ego. Just as he settled in at the sight of Joanie and her parents, they turned to him with Sam reaching out to shake Jim's hand and Anna following up with the same ritual. They walked together to the baggage claim area Sam on one side of Joanie, Anna on the other side with Jim tagging along in the back of them. Sam went to get the car, while the others waited for the bags. By the time Sam got back curbside, Jim had all of the bags and the party was waiting to be picked up. They arrived at the small but neat and conservative house of the Compton's and began to get settled in. It was to be a short but important visit. At dinner most of how the marriage came to be was unveiled. Jim was tolerable to Sam but was an obvious social misfit and the fact that his family had money was partly the blame for his temperament, Sam thought. But, as long as he was decent to Joanie, that would be the true test.

The visit came and went very quickly. Before they knew it they were on their way back to St. Louis's airport and on their way to Baltimore to meet with the Surrants and the rest of that crew. Sam and Anna were scheduled to be in the Washington, DC area for a three day conference having to do with Sam's war buddies, in five days and would swing by Baltimore before leaving the area. Joanie made her mom and dad promise to stop in to meet her new in-laws.

When Joanie and Jim arrived in the Baltimore Washington Airport, they were greeted by the Surrant's driver, Ben Dunbar. He was a tall slender Black man who must have been in his sixties from his appearance. He was obviously familiar with Jim as he greeted him as master Surrant. Jim appeared to dismiss any of this as a normal course of action and slid into the open door, leading to the back seat of which the driver held for them. Joanie was taken aback by Jim getting in first but chalked it up to his excitement of being back in his home area. Jim pointed out areas of interest as they rode to the Surrant estate.

The compound was surrounded by a big wrought iron gate which was centered by the letter 'S', and opened at the touch of a contraption located on the driver side panel of the Lincoln Town Car. The ride down the long driveway, which was adorned by well-manicured greenery lead to the big house. As they began to slow down the vehicle near the front door of the mansion, two ladies in uniform appeared through the door just before an older very proper white woman came out. She stood in the middle between the two maids watching as the car came to a complete stop. Ben hopped out almost running to get the door on the side of the car where Jim was seated. Joanie slid out of the car after Jim who was all but at the foot of the steps leading to the house. He and his mother embraced in an odd way. Jim kissed her first on one cheek then on the other and that was it. There was barely any touching. Joanie stood near the car as Ben retrieved the luggage. Mrs. Surrant's attention was drawn from her son quickly. She was interested in what Jim had brought home.

"Come here, child," said Mrs. Surrant, "let me take a look at you," she said in a way that would be difficult to describe.

The physical review of Joanie as she walked closer to Mrs. Surrant yielded an uncomfortable feeling for this new bride. It was as if she had to pass inspection of Jim's high society mother.

"Would this discomfort ever be over?" Joanie thought as she shifted from one foot to the other.

"Come," said Mrs. Surrant as she held out her hand for Joanie to come inside. Mrs. Surrant, the two maids, Jim, Joanie and Ben one by one entered the house. Joanie had never been in such a beautiful substantial home. As they walked toward the staircase, Mrs. Surrant turned to the left. The maids kept going forward and Ben proceeded directly up the luxuriant staircase. Jim followed his mother, grabbing Joanie's hand and urging her in the same direction. They entered what appeared to Joanie to be an extensive study. It was filled with oil paintings of mostly older men. There was one painting that was autographed by the painter...it appeared to be a Renoir.

Joanie thought, 'These people are really, really rich..' She had no idea what she was marrying into.

As they were seated, a battery of personal questions were hailed to Joanie by Mrs. Surrant. All Joanie could do was to take them one at a time and answer them as honestly as possible.

"What does your father do for a living?"

"Where are your people from?"

"And your mother?"

Joanie was very uncomfortable and Jim was doing nothing to assist her in the process. He never warned her that it would be this way. After over twenty minutes which seemed like hours, one of the maids brought in some lemonade and three silver serving bowls with snacks. Mrs. Surrant beckoned for the maid whispering something to her. Just as quickly as the maid appeared in the room she disappeared. Several minutes later, Joanie was dismissed by Mrs. Surrant to her room being lead by the other maid who she was told was standing just outside the study door. Jim stayed in the study with his mother. Joanie was glad that it was over for now. Two days passed and more of the same for

Joanie. Her parents would arrive into Baltimore later that afternoon. She knew that she would feel comfortable with them there. On Sunday afternoon, the Compton's arrived.

After a few hours at the Surrant's, the blue blood attitudes of the elder Surrant's was too much for Sam and Anna Compton to stomach. But, for the sake of their little girl, they stayed. As the day rolled by, Sam developed a nervous stomach about Jim's disposition, but decided that he needed to leave it alone for the time being. The Surrant's felt that Jim had married beneath himself, but were not outwardly disrespectful of Joanie.

In the early sixties Jim Jr. was born of wealthy parents, the Surrant's, in the Baltimore Maryland area. He attended Brentmore High School where he was first noticed by the football coach to have athletic abilities. Over the years he was not particularly smart, but was able to be pushed through school because of his father's business successes in the area. The fact that Jim Jr., a gifted athlete, made the junior football team and eventually the quarterback for the varsity High School Team while only being a sophomore was incredible. He was as good as they came at that position; as a matter of fact, the best in the area. So, his teachers let him get away with more than any of the other boys. All of the exceptional treatment over the years created a monster of a kid, and, a very explosive adult.

PART III

The next morning was Saturday as Jim and his family slept in. Waking at their leisure, they lazily came to the dining area for their Saturday morning ritual. But Joanie, the reigning President of the Vintage Society as well as many other charitable organizations in their upscale area, had some of her many duties to perform later today. The children, Jim the Third and Marge, attended private school and were carted off and back by the schools transportation fleet. They had their homework to finish, on Saturday before their normal Saturday afternoon activities.

"Good morning, dear," Joanie said to Jim as he came into the kitchen for his morning coffee.

"What's so good about it?" Jim said in a gruff tone.

"Why, whatever is your problem this morning dear?" asked Joanie being totally used to his other-than-pleasant disposition.

"We had our weekly conference call with that Black Bitch yesterday and my usual run-in with her occurred. She is not strong enough to be leading our pack, always asking why we are behind and this and that," he said grumbling.

"I know that I should have gotten her damned job. They only gave it to her because she's black. It's reverse discrimination, if you ask me!" he spewed.

He was still very tired because he couldn't sleep much last night. He tossed and turned for most of the night. While he was ranting and raving about it all, Joanie tried to interject some positive points about his job but Jim, as usual had the floor and for all intents and purposes planned to continue complaining.

"We have money left from my trust fund, but it is running out fast with the way we're spending it, and I have to keep this damn job! Otherwise, I'd quit," he shouted.

Finally there was a pause and Joanie jumped right in. "Honey, I understand how you feel. Maybe you'll get the job from Toney once they figure out that she is not strong enough for the job," she responded in a sympathetic way.

"Things have a way of working themselves out, wouldn't you agree honey?"

They spoke about the challenges through breakfast, and then they were all off in their different directions as they typically did every Saturday.

The rest of the weekend was the same as always.

On the following Monday morning Jim arrived at the office at five forty five am. He wanted to get there early enough to make sure that there was no tell tale signs of what had transpired on Friday night. He and Holley had never gotten carried away in the office like that before. He thought about it and concluded that it must have been the pressure of the events of Friday that drove him to such an act in the office. He knew that if he didn't physically clean things up and clean them up good, this could be the virtual end of everything for him. The company had strong policies about sexually deviant acts in the office, and this was a classic example of what should never happen.

When he arrived, Holley was already there. She appeared to have had the same thoughts on her mind. They could barely look each other in the eyes. What made this so different from the other times they had sex? It was difficult to explain, he thought. Each of them went about the business of cleaning up the evidence and posturing themselves in their roles before any of the other members of the staff arrived that morning. The day proceeded on without incident. At the conclusion of the day, both Jim and Holley left at their usual times headed for their individual evenings as if there were nothing abnormal about them.

A week later, Jim was scheduled to fly into Chicago for the preliminary work that was being done for the Upper Management retreat, which was scheduled annually by the president of the company. He wanted to go to Chicago to get a feel for what was happening so that he could be beyond prepared. It was their time to review the first six months and plan for the remaining six months. Chambers and the rest of the team would be in attendance. Jim was self assured and very calm in the fact that he and Holley had uncovered over three hundred thousand dollars. The fact that there was a measly quarter of a million still out there was of no real concern to him. Jim had used very little of the money himself. He had finally started to wake up to the fact that he had played around in high school and in college and all of that stuff that his teachers had tried to tell him was coming true as he moved along in his career. He figured, however, that when time permitted he and Holley would find the other missing funds and would be able to account for them. The remainder of the week they went about their business as usual. On Tuesday, Holley took time out to pull more records and a little at a time did the research that was necessary. Jim, on the other hand, went about his routine which included reaching out to all of his store managers. He also touched base each day with his remote office managers, bringing himself up to speed with the latest information. He wanted to be as up to date as possible when he got to Chicago.

The office chatter was at an all time high about Jim and Holley. The tongues wagged as the heads were immediately drawn together like magnets whenever either Jim or Holley walked by. They both seemed oblivious to their surroundings. They had way too much at stake about Jim's responsibilities to even be aware of what was going on. Holley took a personal position about all of this and was driven to research every nook and cranny of the reports to see what she could find. She was determined to cover Jim's butt. June Thomas, secretary to the Director of Business Development, was located directly across from Holley's administrative area. She often filled in for Holley, as she did the afternoon last week when Jim needed Holley to work with him on the special project. Now because the office gossip was so pervasive, Jocelyn was the ringleader they had more dirt to discuss. She had really assisted in starting the rumors, because she was in position to observe the interactions relating to Jim and Holley's relationship. Jocelyn kept her eyes and ears open for anything that she could use to perpetuate the gossip. She wanted to get each and every tidbit that she could muster, mainly because she had no real life of her own. All she had was the job and her nosey friends that she worked with. So for now, she was the queen bee due to her work station location; and any news that she could overhear or that she could see, she brought back to the group.

Holley was successful in locating one more small error, but nothing that would be of any real significance. On Wednesday morning, Jim and Holley stole twenty minutes out of his tight schedule to make one more stab and recovering missing revenues. They were unsuccessful. Jim left on Thursday morning to visit his Northern California stores. He took a junket to San Francisco and was met at the airport by the regional manager responsible for Northern California. He was back in his office on Friday night to wrap up the week. He and Holley bid each other good night and left for their respective lives and, to enjoy the weekend.

Jim and Joanie had their usual routines planned for this Saturday, but because the weather was so delightful, they decided to spend the weekend with the kids at the beach. It seemed as if every family in the area had the same thoughts because the beach was crowded. Despite this they enjoyed each other anyway.

The next morning, he thought to himself as the flight took off from the Los Angeles airport, what would he ever do without Holley? She was way too important to him. He hoped that he hadn't put himself in a situation where it could come back to be a problem for him, but for now he had to do what he had to do. Jim shuffled papers and boned up on all the last minute details as he reclined in his First Class seat on flight 849 headed for Chicago. He took an extremely early flight that morning due to West Coast/Midwest time differences. This was necessary because he was compelled to get in early in order to assess the temperature in the Headquarters Office before things got started in two weeks at the opening reception.

Jim was the only out-of-town executive to arrive two weeks early. He made himself visible to all of the head honchos. It was right up his alley to kiss-up, and everyone knew it. Jim walked right past the receptionist, Blair, who got up from her desk to go after him. She had no idea who on earth he was. As she followed him through the double doors leading to Charles Corbin's Presidential office area, she noticed that this strange gentleman was being received by many of the top officials in the outer office area.

"Jim, welcome back to Chicago," said Charlie Benton one of the technical developers as he extended his hand to Jim.

"John, how is it going? You got any good scoop on Headquarters and this big meeting later this month?" Jim continued.

"Same old same old," responded Benton. "A lot of work and high expectations, but that's why they pay us the big bucks, right?" he asked.

"Everyone's buzzing about the big pow-wow in two weeks. The rumor is that some heads are going to roll. This is the second year in a row that revenues are down in all areas. They say it's time to clean some of you big boys' clocks. So, we understand the pressure is on. I wouldn't want to be in your shoes," Benton said.

Just as they rambled on, other employees heard the chatter and came out of their offices to join the conversation. A few minutes later, Mr. Corbin passed through the area. The men scattered like a bunch of scared rabbits, all except Jim. He took this opportunity to kiss up.

"Mr. Corbin, it's super to be back in Chicago," as he extended his hand to his big boss.

"I don't seem to get up this way nearly enough," he cheesed.

"Well, Jim, you're looking prosperous. I hope that this week of mini meetings before the big shindig later in the month proves to be beneficial to us all," said Corbin, as he accepted Jim's hand to shake.

Mr. Corbin continued on his way, leaving Jim standing right there in the middle of the floor alone. Jim stood there looking kind of ridiculous. He decided to go get checked into his hotel and make some phone calls back to his remote locations and his office. He had to see of Holly had come in early to get started again on the challenges at hand.

Jim took a taxi back to the Park Hyatt on Michigan. The doorman welcomed him and took his luggage inside to the bellman. Jim slinked over to the front desk and got checked into a one-bedroom suite. His digs had a view of the city as well as a slight view of Lake Michigan. He was satisfied. Once his bags were delivered, he tipped the bellman and got on with his tasks.

He dialed his office and waited for an answer...

"Good morning, Jim Surrant's office, may I help you," Holley offered.

"Holley, it's me, Jim. How are things going? What were you able to find out? Are we any closer to our number," he rambled.

"Wait, wait, Jim, one question at a time. I've only been here for forty-five minutes. You basically know as much as I do at this point. My plans are to take apart some of the other documents today and sieve through them one by one, but you as I am sure, you already know as much as I do at this point. Things have not changed since you took off for Chicago this morning.

"I know, I know. But, you know I'm nervous. I have to find those missing funds or Chambers will be on my ass during the big meeting. I can't have that...I just can't."

"Calm down, Jim. We'll find the money but its gonna take some time. By the way...when are you coming back home?" she quizzed.

"I'll only be here tonight and a part of tomorrow morning. I have to get more information on what's what here. Someone knows something and I have to see what I can find out. I want to meet with Chambers too while I'm here. She may give something away with a look or a gesture, or she may slipup and tell me something.

"I'll call you back later, Holley. If you happen to find out anything, call me at 312.555.1234, room 861."

"Okay," Holley said as she hung up the phone.

Jim continued his calling campaign by calling over half of his remote offices to check with the managers. One by one he got updates on the latest figures and staffing alignments etc. The state of his remote offices had to be reported on at the big meeting, and he was determined to be sharp. For each of the remote managers he dictated that they fax complete reports to Holley at his office by Wednesday, by twelve noon this week.

Jim finished all that he could do in his suite and headed back to headquarters to nose around. When he got there he decided to stop off on the forty-fifth floor. He wanted to see how Chambers' operation was running.

The receptionist greeted him, "Good afternoon, sir. May I help you?"

"Toney Chambers in?"

"No, sir, she's not available. Did you have an appointment?"

"No! I do not!" he shouted.

"Would you care to make one, sir? She is in a strategic planning meeting and cannot be disturbed. May I tell her who stopped by, sir?"

"No! I'll call on her at another time."

Jim left in a huff. He mumbled, "...she thinks she is really something...she can't be disturbed...she's in a strategic planning session. That fucking job should have been mine. I am going to make sure she gets what she deserves."

Jim took the elevator to the top floor to see what he could find out. After talking with several of the good 'ole boys...he went back to his hotel to relax. Later in the evening he went down to the fine dining restaurant, for dinner and drinks. Afterwards, he called it a night.

THREE

The restaurant was small and cozy. They met there regularly, and by this time, the owner and the staff recognized them both and knew them by name. Periodically, they would meet at other's places in the immediate area, but tonight they had made plans to be in a familiar place. Toney had had a tumultuous day and the most significant thing to her was to see him and relax. The demands of the day had taken their toll on her and she had to take time out for herself. What better way to do that than to see Grant? He was the most important person in her life at this point, and she needed him desperately. Someone to talk to, someone who would understand was all she needed. It would be as it had been from the moment they met; she could take the world that she had on her shoulders and basically give all of it to him. She knew that she could depend on him to help her sort it all out.

Toney paid the taxi and jumped out at the curb. She, in a very ladylike manner, tiptoed across the sidewalk to the doorway of the restaurant. It was barely dust, with the streets of downtown Chicago crowded with passersby moving aggressively to reach their destinations too. The rush hour traffic was heavy as usual in downtown Chicago at that time of day. Her mind and complete thoughts rested only on entering the restaurant and leaving the cares of the day, including all the accounts of the day, the people, and the cars behind.

As she stepped inside she was greeted by the matrede who was of Italian decent.

"Good evening, Ms. Chambers, welcome back to Vidi's. How have you been?" He asked.

"Good evening, Alfredo," she responded.

"I've been better, but I'm okay tonight, I guess."

She paused and took a deep breath as she allowed her eyes to become accustomed to the lighting in the room.

"Is Grant here yet?" she asked.

A second later, she took a quick look around and finally focused on her friend seated at a corner table having a cocktail.

All in the same instant, Alfredo said, "Mr. Palarme has already been seated."

They started together walking toward the table. Grant saw them and stood to receive Toney. When they arrived at the table, Alfredo pulled out a chair for Toney as Grant reached for her, kissing her softly on the cheek. As she was removing her trench coat, Grant gave her assistance, and then she took her seat. She had a weary look about her. Instantaneously, Grant became even more entangled in her disposition and said, "Honey, I had no idea that this was bothering you this much."

"Today has been too deep for me. I never realized that it could get to this point. Jim Surrant openly defied me while I was conducting my conference call today. He has always been a thorn in my side but he is becoming more and more difficult. He is working to undermine my authority and it is becoming contagious. If the other Assistant Vice Presidents start to feel that they can conduct themselves in the same disrespectful way; I could lose total control of my troops and I will be on my way out. I don't want to become unprofessional and go toe to toe with him because that would bring me down to his level. I'm in between a rock and a hard place at this point," she said as she slumped down in her chair.

"And besides that, revenues in four of my nine areas are down, and ultimately I am responsible for all of it. Somehow I think that some of these people are not trying their best in order to make me look weak as a leader," she said in an almost defeated tone.

"Well, honey, after the meeting in a couple of weeks when they all come to Chicago to get their chance to explain their actions, we leave for a much needed vacation. In the meantime, we'll devise a strategy for a short-term fix. There are other things that we can do to ensure you stay in control of the matters at hand for the duration. We'll discuss some of these things during our vacation, but for now, I want you to relax and enjoy your evening with me, okay?" He said tenderly, with a touch of determination.

She looked into his eyes and slid her hand over to his as she gently smiled and began to ease her spirit. He had such a calming effect on her. From the time they met almost two years ago, he had championed her causes. They were in love with each other and leaned on one another from that period on, as it related to their respective lives and positions.

Grant Palarme was a graduate of Princeton University. He was the product of a family mixed with Negro and Italian blood and stood six foot three. His keen features and beautiful hazel eyes made him the object of desire for most of the females around him. He was an extremely handsome and seriously soulful person with honest hardworking intentions, giving all of the things around him the very best he had. He had been this way since he was a young boy. His days in elementary, junior high and high school brought teasing and a host of juvenile pranks from his white and black male counterparts. It was almost as if he didn't or couldn't have any allegiance to either side. His skin was very fair, almost olive, leaning more toward the Italian side of his family tree with the mixture of Italian and Negro decent. His hair was jet black, straight and shiny giving him almost a Latino flare. So, starting out of the gate after his early school years, he had his personal challenges in all areas of his life, including college and the workplace. Grant found that standing his ground in serious indiscretions was paramount to his well being and to what he was really about. On the other hand, he knew that picking his battles in the other cases, which made up each and every day of his life, was where he had made his reputation count when it needed to.

In college all the girls of all races and backgrounds went for him. Why not? He had it going on! He was the best looking boy they had ever seen, and he was quite a gentle person a well. The white boys were furious with him, because during those days for white girls to be chasing any boys other than white boys was a serious no no, and the black boys were jealous of him too; so he had big challenges ever since he could remember. He went from one thing to another trying to be accepted.

After a while, he just gave up and ignored most of the antics of others. He was simply tired of trying to fit in. He made up his mind that any friendship that was to be made would have to be based on what was inside of a human being. He knew that eventually he would migrate to someone worthy of his friendship; and if not, well, that would just have to be the way it was. After over four years in college he was noticeably a loner. In his fifth year, at the beginning of his first graduate term, he met one young man who became his friend. Brandon was about five feet eleven with a light brown complexion and possessed the inner strength and pride that was a draw to Grant. Brandon had been transferred from the University of Los Angeles for his graduate studies. One evening when Grant stopped off for a pizza at Dumizzo's after class, he literally bumped into Brandon.

"Oooff, I'm sorry man," Grant said. "I should have been watching where I was going."

"Hey, no problem, no harm done! It was probably a combination of your fault and mine," Brandon responded, "I'm Brandon Cummings", as he put his hand out to shake with Grant.

"It's great to meet you," Grant said.

They both ordered and as they stood there waiting for their orders, Grant started a conversation with Brandon. There was something about Brandon's spirit that was easy going.

"Are you from around here?" Grant asked.

"No, not really. I graduated from the University of Los Angeles last quarter and really just arrived in Boston a few weeks ago to do some graduate work. I'm in the law field and understood that this was the place to study post graduate courses, if one wanted to get picked up by one of the big boys in either New York or Chicago," Brandon said proudly and with a big dose of self-confidence.

"This is definitely one of the prime places, if one wants to go beyond a four year school and start fast out of school and into your career. Good luck to you," said Grant.

"Thanks!" said Brandon.

Other people were pushing up to the same area where they were standing and one by one placing their orders.

After a lull in the conversation, "Do you live around here? Grant asked.

"Yes, I live just a few blocks down the street. I have a little place off campus. No more dorm life for me, it cramps my style. Where do you live?" Brandon reciprocated.

"Just a few blocks away, too." Maybe we can get together sometime to play ball or double date or something," Grant said with a subtle enthusiasm.

Once they received their orders, they exchanged phone numbers and went their separate ways.

A few days later, Brandon called Grant to invite him to a Celtics game, and Grant gladly accepted. From that moment on they became fast friends. They hung out when time permitted, and during some of the time they spent together they really shared a great deal of information about one another. They found out that they had a lot of things in common. Each of them had come from families who had a closeness that gave them strength and direction. They were each taught what it was to be real men. And, they recognized these qualities in each other, which is one of the reasons they became such fast friends. Being bright and handsome and full of self- confidence, they had each experienced the jealous rage of other young men in their own right and had determined within themselves that they were on a mission and wouldn't allow anything to stop their progress in life. So, for the most part, each of them was a loner until they became friends.

Grant had been an attorney for over the past five years. He had worked diligently in his law firm and made every moment and case count. He was a corporate attorney practicing contract law and was determined to make partner in his firm. Day by day and week after week, he was at the office early and worked late. He wanted to make sure he covered all his bases. Grant's thoughts were of moving up the ladder after thoroughly proving himself. As the months passed by the firm expanded, taking on more corporations as clients. Many of the clients on the firm's list were the who's who of the fortune five hundred companies. The need for more staff became evident, and through interview after interview, more of the recruits from the college ranks were hired. The new hires were brought around to all of the employees and introduced. They were each given their tasks, a desk and a telephone and then let go to operate. Over an eighteen-month period, Grant witnessed special hand-holding and coddling of two recruits in particular. There were no less than eleven new hires in a relatively short time frame, and all but one was white, and that one was oriental. Grant knew that he had better keep his eyes open and stay alert. Without a word he continued to do his job while observing all that transpired around him. On 'D' day, less than two years later, the announcement came that the two white guys who had had special handling were promoted to junior partner. How could either of them have advanced to the same level as Grant? This situation really reeked. Grant had paid so many dues over the years to get to the level that he had. He was confused and guarded. He knew where this was headed and had to remain alert and highly professional through this process or he might be detrimental to himself. His soulful nature had to be maintained at all costs. Just as he had experienced earlier in his life, he was being looked over again. The twins as Grant referred to them, Nicholas Sampson and Terrance Conners, were still wet behind the ears. Nick was a tad bit shorter than Terry, hence his nickname 'the shorter twins.' He was the one that seemed to be more cunning. Did his hard work really matter to the people who were making these decisions? How could any of this be fair? He was going to make the next move, but it had to be systematic and have meaning beyond what was expected. It could be mistaken for what would amount to a temper tantrum, which would be of little or no use in this situation. He simply had to think this through carefully before he acted...but, he also knew he couldn't wait too long. Grant constantly kept the wise words of wisdom that his Negro mother had instilled in his heart, which kept him from going crazy. She shared with him many erudite things while he was a small boy. The ritual was repeated numerous times as he sat in her lap in a rocking chair on their front porch, in a suburb of White Plains, New York. She always told him, while she was preparing him for his life, "Nothing in life is fair...just do the best you can and make sure to earn respect of others by the actions that you demonstrate." These words were the life and breath that he lived by and with each breath he took so many times during the course of each and every day. From the soul of his mother as she mentored and nurtured each of them, they had the insulation needed to survive. Mrs. Palarme introduced him to God and made sure that he and his sister Elizabeth were well grounded. This fulfilled his personal drive and commitment to himself. His mother wanted to make sure that they had the strength they needed to survive and live a long and happy life, confident in who and what they were. So needless to say, Grant knew a few things about what Toney was experiencing. They had a lot in common, which is why their relationship had slowly flourished over the past twenty-three months. They shared what little free time they had together. Both of their jobs had demands on them with heavy travel schedules and long hours in the office when they were in town.

Grant's firm handled most of the legal issues relating to contract law. Toney's boss, John Sutton, had hired the firm of **Hamilton, Litton and Shuester Law Firm** to represent them on any contract issues that were in dispute with any organization that purchased equipment from any of their computer stores or major orders from the Prophecy Computer Warehouses. The heads of both entities were fraternity brothers from college and shared the wealth of their successes with one another, as was often the case in Corporate America.

"Toney, I have planned for a fabulous vacation for us," Grant said with love and affection. "We have only three more weeks and we will be off to Jamaica for an entire week. So, relax this evening and take a sip of your chilled glass of Kendall Jackson and enjoy the evening."

A few minutes later, their waiter came to the table.

"My name is Ansor, I'll be your waiter tonight," he said in a very upscale way.

"Are you ready to order, ma'am?"

As Toney placed her order, Grant sat just gazing at her with admiration and a great deal of love.

Ansor turned to Grant, "And you sir?"

Grant rumbled off his order to hurry the waiter from the table so that he could get back into just the two of them.

After five or six sips of the wine and the soothing conversation from her guy, Toney was finally relaxing. The thought of Jim Surrant and the others faded away with each word from Grant. They talked what seemed like a few minutes more and their food was there being served. It always seemed like time stood still when they were together. They ate and talked about everything under the sun. Grant really had a way of helping Toney to calm down and get back into what was important for her. About three hours later, Grant paid the bill and ushered Toney to a taxi. He rode with her to her office to get her car. She drove him back to his car and finally he trailed her home. When they got there, he parked his car at the front door watching her as she entered the garage and waited for her to come to the lobby. He walked her to the door. They kissed goodnight. He walked away feeling very much in love. She opened the door to her condominium, then turned to him to say, "I love you. Good night."

"Good night my love," he said smiling and almost skipping back to the elevator.

Toney went in, hung her coat on the coat rack just inside the door, then took a long look at her surroundings. Her apartment was a reflection of the woman. There was an oversized white sofa covered in a rich fabric and two oversized white chairs that corresponded perfectly with the decor and were placed strategically around a very big glass table mounted on an ivory elephant. There were other one-of-a-kind items placed throughout her apartment by the interior decorator she had hired to make her home a show place. She had really arrived. Toney had had many opportunities to entertain at her home and it had to be representative of her image and her position. She walked into her dressing room and began to disrobe one item of clothing after the next. She carefully hung up each garment, pitching her soiled undergarments into the dirty clothes hamper just inside her walk-in closet. She pulled out one of her mid-weighted bathrobes and slid into it. She walked into her bathroom and started her bubble bath. As the tub was filling up with steamy hot water, she lit several candles. Toney walked out of the bathroom, over to the window of her bedroom and looked out onto the skyline of Chicago. What a fabulous city, she thought. She stood there and began to daydream again about her life and where she was now. She walked slowly into the bar area and poured another glass of wine and flipped on her CD player, which featured easy listening jazz. A few minutes later she was completely deluged in the steamy water and thoroughly relaxed.

As she lay there as limber as wet toast, she began to daydream again. All of the trials of the day had begun to seep from her mind. First, the wonderful dinner with Grant in their familiar place, then, the long talk with her confidant. Now taking a long leisurely bath in her hot tub with a series of thoughts, she drifted into another state. As she relaxed in the mellow glow of the candlelight, she took another sip of wine. Her mental state was always eased by drifting back to Lexington when they didn't have very much. But, as most Negro families, they had a closeness which was only rivaled by the relationships they formed with the higher power. When she left Lexington she was sure that her life would be difficult, but never dreamed how much so. All through her days at Howard, she shyly made her way each day. Learning and growing into a plain flower. Her expectation of being away from home, her mom and dad and the only real friend she had ever known was hard. She had no real close friends at college, she just faded in and out with whoever was near at the time.

Vanessa came over to the Washington, D. C. area a couple of times in the four years that Toney made the D. C. area her home. Vanessa was working at the Piggly Wiggly in downtown Lexington and saved her money for a couple of short visits to D. C. Her visits were way too short; she always had to get back because of her job. Toney and Vanessa didn't do a lot when Vanessa came to town. They mostly took long walks and a couple of times went to the malt shop on campus using that time to catch up on everything at home. Together they watched all of the activities on campus. Vanessa had never had the opportunity to become part of this type of environment so she soaked up as much of it as she could while she had the chance. Amazingly enough and as quickly as Toney had met Vanessa's bus when she arrived, she was now waving at her as the bus pulled away headed back to Lexington. Toney endured the good-byes and thanked God for the chance to see her only friend once again.

At the end of each school year, Toney went back home and enjoyed her old life, realizing that she would be moving out of Lexington for good after graduation. Each time she went home, her mom and dad noticed more and more the big changes in her. Their little girl was growing up and becoming more and more sophisticated and self-confident. They often worried though, if she would ever have the strength she needed to make out in the world, because as a child, even though she was so intelligent, her personality was not one of strength and agility. Perhaps the world would help her to learn all that it would require. They would always let her know that they would be there for her if she needed them. It seemed that just as quick as she blew back into Lexington, it was time to go back to school. When she returned to campus it was the same old ritual. Life in the dorm was finally becoming more fun. She was becoming to some extent a part of the in-crowd. In between classes and studying, she watched as some of pretty girls who were being chased by the boys. She never thought that any one would ever notice her, so she just enjoyed being part of the background **...**

After almost an hour in the hot tub, the water was getting chilly. Toney snapped out of her dream state and slid up and out of the tub and towel blotted herself. She applied the usual lotions, potions and creams before putting on a pair of soft pajamas that she pulled from her lingerie drawer and jumped into her rice bed. A couple of minutes later she had drifted off to sleep.

FOUR

Grant was one of two people on the street that early. He left his place about three-forty-five. At four in the morning he was driving down Ohio Avenue headed to the office. His thoughts were of Toney, as they were often, and the evening that they had spent together. He carried an internal smile, which came into plain view each time he thought of her. He loved her so much and felt blessed to have a woman like her in his life. Before his thoughts of Toney left his mind, Grant arrived at the office. He entered the office, which was so still. As he sat down he noticed an abundance of paperwork that wasn't there when he left the night before.

He smirked mumbling, " That Millicent. She must have worked a little late last night to have gotten through so much of this."

He jumped right into his work. His concentration was phenomenal as nearly the next three and a half-hours slipped by. He stopped for a moment thinking about getting another cup of coffee from the fresh pot that he had made earlier. He looked up in shock that it was just before eight. A second or so later he heard Millicent, his assistant, milling around outside his office.

"Grant…Good morning. I'm here, but I'm running across the street to get a bagel and coffee. You want anything?" she asked in her forceful manner.

"Not a thing. I've already made a fresh pot of coffee and had two cups already. I'm good to go, but thanks. Maybe you can get some of the pot that I made."

"No thanks…I want that flavored stuff from Starbucks. I'll be right back," she reported.

"Okay," Grant responded as he went right back to work.

The next time Grant looked up, it was almost ten.

He stood and stretched realizing that he needed to take a break. Brandon crossed his mind.

"Maybe I'll give him a quick call," Grant said out loud.

"Good morning, Brandon. How's it going?" Grant coached much like a big brother would have.

"Hey man. I've been meaning to call you for over a solid week if not more," Brandon said in a sleepy voice.

"How's every thing on your end?"

"SOS, DD, you know? But, actually I can't complain. Shit…it wouldn't do any good anyway. Besides who would care?" Grant followed up with a chuckle in his voice.

"I hadn't heard from you so I was really compelled to give you a quick call to see what was what. Besides, I've been in the office for hours and needed to take a break," Grant said taking a deep breath and reclining in his chair.

"I've been back in Los Angeles for over eighteen months. I really don't think I'm going to stay here. I really wanted to be picked up by some of the big boys in New York or Chicago but, Wagman, Wayne and Smith here in Los Angeles drafted me as you know. I could have taken a couple more courses in Boston while I worked that piece of a job, but I would've been bordering on becoming a professional student. So, here I am. It's been down right disgusting. The things that a man has to put up with in this firm are ridiculous. But, I'm handling it, you know," Brandon rambled.

"The back biting and trying to always get one up on each other and from some of your own people. That's crazy. Black folks will never get it together."

"What's that all about? You mean some black folks are working against you?" Grant queried.

"I'm coming to Chicago in a few weeks. We'll talk more about it then. I've got to get the hell outta here. Anyway, how's Toney? How are you two getting along? Any wedding bells in the near future?" Brandon abruptly changed the subject.

"She's fine. Going through it at work like the rest of us but she's fine. I'll tell you more too when we see each other. Exactly when are you coming?"

"In two or three weeks. I'll call you to give you the specifics. I'm glad you called, man. Tell our girl I send my love. I'll talk to you soon," Brandon said beginning to move around to start his day.

Brandon Cummings was one of five children born and raised in Compton, just outside the Los Angeles, California area. His father, Warren Cummings, was the groundskeeper for the estate of Elizabeth Montgomery the actress. His job was to keep the huge Montgomery estate pruned and worthy of the mansion that it surrounded. He was paid a decent salary, but the fact that there were six members of his family depending on his income, had the family stretching at times. So, Brandon's mother, Hanna, worked to supplement Warren Cummings' income, as a PBX operator at Beverly Hills Hotel. Together the

Cummings' were able to live a little more than a meager life and could put pennies away periodically for each of their children's future. Their home was a little three-bed room house, where Bradley, Brandon and their sisters Briget and Brandy, who were younger all lived, with their parents. Theirs was a normal house, where the neighborhood was located just on the outskirts of all of the drive-by shootings and other unlawful activities took place. Mr. and Mrs. Cummings did all they could to keep their children isolated from the immoral fiber that had taken over the area not too far from the confines of their home. They constantly talked to and were available for their children as much as humanly possible. They wanted the kids to become responsible adults and knew that a good foundation had to be laid down in order for that to happen.

About two years before Brandon left for college, his oldest brother Bradley had been seduced by the streets. He had gone around and around with the bloods, one of the most unscrupulous gangs in the country, trying to keep it all from his parents. The mere fact that this partially polished young man could become embodied with the likes of the people in charge of this awful gathering of people was more than the family could bear. As he thought about it, he remembered from the age of eight to about sixteen, he looked up to Bradley. He was a very cool big brother. Over the years, Brandon tagged along with Brad and his cronies trying to be a big part of Bradley's life. That's all Brandon wanted at first was to be all that Bradley thought he should be. It was difficult being the younger brother. As with most kids, he idolized Bradley because he was his older brother.

"Kid, keep your nose clean and you'll make it," shared Bradley one day when they were hanging out on the front stoop of their house. It was a hazy summer afternoon in 1989 and Brandon was sixteen.

"You don't have a girlfriend yet?" teased Bradley. "Look at the cheeks on that one," as two young girls about fifteen or so walked past them.

"Nope, no one special," Brandon squared back. "Besides, I have my studies to keep me busy right now. That's what's important to me now."

"You can wait on those damned books," pushed Bradley. "You haven't had any pussy yet, have you?"

"No man, you know that. I'm too young for that now. Maybe soon though," Brandon replied. "There is this one girl in Biology though...she's got a real juicy ass."

Brandon was labeled as a bookworm in class, so he didn't have many male friends. Many of the people he had run into in his classes thought he was too quiet and sweet. He was much like the teacher's pet because he was so smart. Bradley had gotten rumor that this was the case and refused to have a younger brother who could be a possible panty-waist. He toughened up Brandon at every opportunity. Brandon whined about it to Bradley and to their parents.

"Stop it Brad, stop it!"

"Stop what punk?" taunted Bradley.

"I won't have no punk kid as my brother," wolfed Bradley.

As they sat there on the stoop that day bouncing insults back and forth, a couple of Bradley's roughneck cronies happened by. They began to tease Brandon puckering up their lips and throwing kissing sounds to him. Bradley broke it up by threatening the boys.

"Get the fuck away from here mother fuckers. Leave my kid brother alone!"

"He's a punk and you know it. Sweet, Sweet," they all bellowed as they ran away.

Shaking his head, Bradley had a heart to heart with Brandon, "You see why you have to change the way you do things? You can't give people the wrong impression. You got to stand up and be a man. Pop some ass and that'll get 'em off you, Bran," Bradley said with brut force as he shoved him back on the shoulder.

Bradley got up and wandered off toward Crenshaw. Brandon sat there thinking things through. He just didn't have the feelings of normal boys his age. He liked learning new things, which is why school was so great for him. He refused to allow what people thought, be the determining factor in the way he would conduct his life. He had to fulfill himself. He knew he wasn't gay. He didn't like boys or girls. So, what was so wrong with that? His mind was on different things and he didn't see anything wrong with it either. He stood up and went back into the house to study. Brandon wanted to make sure he was prepared to get into a good college. That was all that was important to him at this moment.

His parents were doing all they could, and he wanted to do his part. Perhaps a partial scholarship and then things would work out. He studied for a while. He heard his dad come in. It was dinnertime. Every one was there except Bradley. It had become common practice now that they didn't wait dinner for Bradley anymore. He was there sometime and sometime he wasn't.

Later that night, Bradley came back. He was stoned. He tiptoed into the house and disappeared into his and Brandon's room. Brandon was asleep, but was awakened by Bradley stumbling and knocking against his twin bed.

"Wakeup, panty waist…wake up," slurred Bradley.

Startled, Brandon woke with a curiosity that was profoundly perplexing. He adjusted to a position on his bed hoisting himself up on his elbows, "Is this what it means to be a man," asked Brandon to himself as he peered at the clock on the desk? It was after two in the morning.

"What?" asked Brad, "what?"

"You're twenty three years old with no job, no direction. I refuse to be just alive. I have to apply myself, while there is still time for me. They can call me whatever they want to, but I am determined to keep my focus, my direction," Brandon said with measurement.

He got up and helped Bradley take off his clothes and helped him into bed. Their mom and dad had gone to bed hours ago. Brandon was glad that they didn't see Bradley in this condition. It would hurt their hearts deeply. Where was his older brother headed? As Brandon got back into his bed, he prayed for Brad. He hoped that things wauld turn around for him. He appeared to be fighting ghosts. "He just doesn't get it. He just doesn't get it," as he drifted back into the deep sleep that just a moment ago he had been shaken from.

The next day was Saturday. It was a misty morning but the rain was not enough to deter them from the chores that had to be done outside. All of the family was up bright and early except for Bradley. They began their chores early. About nine they prepared to have a big breakfast, as was the norm for Saturdays. Briget and Brandy helped Mrs. Cummings in the kitchen. They had the entire house smelling good with biscuits from scratch, bacon, sausage, the works. Before they sat down, Mrs. Cummings went in to get Bradley. He was still in another world. She shook him several times finally making contact.

"Let me sleep," he spewed with the smell of old stale alcohol leaping from his body.

"Bradley Cummings, you get up this very moment...you are awful. You get up right now," his mother demanded. Bradley lay in the same spot until he heard the sound of Mr. Cummings' solemn voice.

"Boy, did you hear your mother, get up?"

The mere sound of his father's voice shook him to his seat without so much as a touch. He was awakened completely. Was this part of Bradley's inner problem? Was it that he felt he couldn't measure-up?

From a young boy probably because he was the first born, as he saw it, many unreasonable demands had been placed on him. Or, so he thought. He had a hangover to end all hangovers. The morning would drag by for Bradley ....

Grant hung up thinking about what Brandon had said. It was unfortunate that hard work and dedication simply were not enough in Corporate America. Wasn't the objective to just get the job done? And why was there always someone in every situation trying to block someone else?

"Well, the way my mama taught me was that when you do wrong you must pay. And ultimately you pay dearly," Grant said as he turned his attention back to the tasks in front of him.

"Grant, I'm back," Millicent said as she burst through the door.

"Let's see the damage you've done this morning," she said moving over to his out box.

"Damn. What time did you get in...or have you had yourself here all fricking night?"

Grant looked up at Millicent, momentarily smiled and shook his head, immediately turning his attention back to his work.

FIVE

The sun came up over the horizon creating what was to be a glorious day. The weather was crisp that morning with powder blue skies and assurance from each of the weather reporters on the major television channels that it was going to be a perfect day. They guaranteed everyone who listened that today would be a day to remember for weeks to come. Toney listened while she got her last bit of sleep dozing in and out. She woke up early that morning with a queasy stomach just thinking about all that lay ahead for her. She knew she had what it took to manage her responsibilities, but she also knew that it would not be easy to handle Jim Surrant. She lay there in the same spot for a while. It seemed like she was there for more than an hour. Her normal morning routine was to jump out of bed and prepare to recharge her body with the pep that she would need for the day not knowing what she would have to do or be before ten a m. She was normally prepared for whatever the day would bring. Each morning she had to get her juices flowing, so her routine took her from the bed to the bathroom, then she brushed her teeth and immediately to the floor for her stretching warm-up exercises. Then as her routine called for she got onto each of the pieces of exercise equipment in her exercise room. One by one she would spend the allotted amount of time recharging her self. From the stair master, the free weights and the treadmill she normally worked at it hard. But, this morning was way too difficult for her. Was she allowing Jim Surrant to dictate her disposition? This was just what he wanted. At that very moment she dragged herself up and onto her feet. It would take all that she had this morning, but she'd really push herself and push herself hard if she had to. Once she got started, it became easier for her. She started to feel a lot better as she worked out. Finally, forty minutes later, she walked back through her bedroom, peeling off her workout clothes and by the time she was in her bath room she was completely naked and headed for the shower. As she passed the closet, she tossed in her workout clothes, grabbed a towel and wash cloth and stepped in. The water was a little on the hot side, but that's how she liked it. Fifteen minutes later she stepped out of the shower and began to towel dry herself off. She started thinking about everything that lay ahead in the next fourteen days.

Her mind's eye said to her 'One solid week of work before all of the top brass would be in town for their big meeting. I have to be prepared...I just have too. I will do whatever it takes to be prepared. So, I'm in for some long days and into some long nights this week.'

She took a quick walk over to the walk-in closet to select her look for the day and then to her dresser to lay out her personals, which was certain to match what she was wearing.

Toney felt wonderful after her workout. She was happy that she had forced herself to do it. Once she put on her personals, she slipped into a bathrobe and walked hurriedly to the kitchen where she made her morning coffee and had a quick bite to eat. A couple of minutes later she returned to the bedroom to finish preparing for work. Carefully applying her makeup, squirting on a touch of perfume and finally sliding into a sharp lavender two-piece St. John knit, she was putting herself together. She accented her ensemble with a pair of chocolate brown pumps with matching hand bag and a chocolate brown swing knee length coat to top it all off. As she walked very lady like to the doorway, she turned to glance at her accomplishments of all the creature comforts that she had been able to attain for herself, noticing the clock on the kitchen wall. It was six forty seven a m. This was typically the time that Helen arrived. It clicked in her head that Helen, her housekeeper, would be over today to pick up a sweater that she left last week, so Toney wrote a short note reminding her that she and Grant would be in Jamaica when it was time for her place to be cleaned again. Toney didn't want Helen to worry about her while she was out of the country.

On the elevator headed for her car, Toney became angry. Jim Surrant was the only fly in her ointment! She knew he was bound and determined to rattle her cage whenever he could. You would think she knew that and would ignore his comments much like one would avoid the plague. But, while she tried ever so hard, she always seemed to walk right into it. It was as if she fell into his spell and reacted to his unfortunate and intentional off-the-wall commentary.

The talk that she and Grant had had last night gave her a new way to look at her situation. She decided that she would follow Grant's suggestions with some ideas of her own thrown in too.

While she was driving toward the office, she pondered the meeting that was to take place within the next few weeks. Would Surrant show his true colors right there in front of all of the big guys? Would he be on his best behavior? She was sure that he would try to have his best foot forward. She wondered if he had uncovered the shortfall in his revenue? What had really happened to all that money? How would the other Assistant Vice Presidents, who participated in the weekly conference calls position themselves in this situation? There were still challenges in three of their areas as well, but nothing like Surrant's area. More than a half million dollars down is quite a bit!

Toney was at the final red light just north of her office building. She flashed a quick sinister smile as she thought, "I'll be ready for him, and he'll never know what hit him!"

At that moment, she pulled into her marked parking spot and jumped out of the car. She walked toward the doorway heading for the elevator almost skipping, she was so light hearted. As she entered the first floor of the building she waived at the security guards and pushed the button for the elevator. In a couple of seconds, she would be on her way to the forty-fifth floor.

As the doors opened she heard a female voice saying "hold the elevator please"...it was Cameron Beeage, the Director of Special Events & Logistics for Lowes Hardware Group, the largest Hardware manufacturers worldwide, whose offices were headquartered in the same building. Cameron and Toney had met a year before and had lunch together and sometimes drinks periodically. They traded war stories about the constant challenges in their lives, which included their job struggles. Many of the topics that they spoke about each time they met, yielded their separate views, which were uncannily the same most of the time. Cameron was a middle aged white woman who had been on her job for over twenty years and had experienced much of the same discrimination as Toney had, but in much different ways. So, they met often to compare notes. She and Toney had hit it off and had become fairly good friends.

"Good morning Ms. Beeage, how was your weekend?" Toney said almost singing.

"Well, obviously not as good as yours, Ms. Chambers," Cameron said sweetly.

"You'll have to tell me why you're so happy when you get a chance," Cameron continued in an inquisitive way... "it's been a while since I've seen you this happy," she respond in an accepting manner.

Toney whispered to Cameron, as other people were getting on and off the elevator on their ride to the top, "For sure my dear, for sure."

Cameron got off on the thirty-seventh floor and Toney continued on to the forty-fifth floor.

Cameron's job itself satisfied her in all the best ways. She threw herself into it each and every day. She was so good at what she did. In her industry, she was the top of the line in the position she held as the Director, but as in most other lines of work, women white or black were forced to the background in most cases. Cameron knew that there was a Senior Director's job that had been vacated by her former boss three months earlier. She was a "shoe in" for the position. Hell, she thought, she had been doing the job anyway for the last two years. After years of the same abuse, the glass ceiling had pushed her into submission. Year after year she worked herself into a frenzy only to find out that they always brought a white male into the position that had been vacated and would have taken Cameron to the next level. Instead, she had to train the new person, who would eventually be telling her what to do. It just wasn't fair. So, Toney often became her sounding board as Cameron did the same for Toney. Cameron knew that Toney would understand and perhaps could strategize with her on the next step.

When Toney opened her door she noticed that she was the first one there. She turned on all of the lights to the outer office closing the door behind her. Her assistant Sonjia would be in shortly. Toney was convinced that she shouldn't leave the door to the office opened when she was the only person in the office. She knew that was unsafe. She went directly into her office and went to work. A few minutes later, she heard the outer door open and a couple of seconds later, a light tap on her office door.

"Yes?" answered Toney.

"Good morning, Toney," responded Sonjia, "How was your weekend?"

"It was just fine," Toney said. "And yours?"

"Ups and downs, ins and outs. First, one thing, then another," Sonjia said.

"Thank God I have Grant. He is such a leveling force in my life. We relaxed at my place. Saturday morning, we took a walk down by the shoreline and talked about everything. Sunday we went to early church service and stopped by the Ritz Carlton on Michigan for Sunday brunch which gave us another chance to further discuss the challenges at hand. Then, Grant left and went back to his place. One way or another, we are going to work through all of the challenges. What did you and Jimmy do?" she asked.

"Well, nothing as nice as you. Jimmy went fishing with some of his buddies early Saturday morning. He wasn't even expected back until late Sunday. I had to get ready for my family reunion coming up in Cumberland in a couple of months. My sister Rennie and I met to discuss the particulars. We asked several hotels in the area for bids on the reunion last week, so they came in the mail during the week and we met to review them. Afterwards we went to the mall just to look, stopping to have a snack along the way. And later in the evening we went our individual ways. Actually, I was so tired that I decided to turn in early, because the choir at church had a concert yesterday and you know me, I've gotta be in church early on Sundays...so it was indeed a long weekend for me," Sonjia rambled.

"Well, we've got quite a week in front of us...with the big meeting happening right in our back yard soon. We've got to make sure that all of out T's are crossed and our I's are dotted, you know what I mean?" said Toney with a bit of authority and uneasiness.

"The microscopic eyes will be on me to see if I can handle this job. I want to anticipate all of the worst possibilities, so that we'll be prepared for anything. Something tells me that Jim Surrant and the others will also be prepared."

"Toney, I'm here for you in anyway possible...so what shall we do first?" Sonjia asked.

They went on about their way planning and plotting. Sonjia left Toney's office with eleven tasks in her hand. As Sonjia closed the door behind her, all of the other workers had reported to the office. It was already ten after nine. Sonjia got the individuals who had to do with particular tasks, involved.

Toney went about her daily routine. She was on the telephone working through multi-million dollar deals. When Sonjia completed the first four tasks, she lightly knocked on Toney's door interrupting a call to China. Toney covered the mouth-piece of the telephone and said a quick "come in."

Sonjia slipped in almost tipping and moved swiftly to Toney's desk and in-box, laying down the completed work and immediately doing an about face to exit as quickly and quietly as she had entered. Three more high-powered telephone calls and it was nearly at the noon hour.

Toney concluded that she needed to take a walk through her office to visit with the troops. She stopped by Eloise Slant's desk.

"And how are you miss thing?"

"Eloise smiled and said, "Well, miss thing, I'm fine and by the way you look I'd say you are too," she said in an endearing tone.

They both gave a quick chuckle as Toney moved to the next and then the next of the desks lined up in a row until she had spoken with all of the staff one by one, who hadn't already gone to lunch. All of them had come to expect this behavior from Toney, unlike the last person who occupied her position. Jeffrey Baltisom, their former boss, a white gentleman in his mid fifties, was from the old school. He believed that his position was that of the boss and wouldn't lower himself to a relationship with the hired help. During those days, morale was at an all-time low and people were quitting one after the other. Sonjia wasn't the assistant to the Senior VP at that time, she actually held Eloise's position. But, she witnessed all of the power trips of the boss and vowed that she would only be there until she could find something else. After many years of trying to keep it all together, Mr. Baltisom fell on bad health and had to go on disability and finally was forced by his physicians to retire early. The stress and demands of each day were way too much for him to manage. All of the Assistant Vice Presidents under his leadership never made the numbers that were setup for them and Mr. Baltisom's reputation and standing in the company was slowly being wilted.

Toney was the ultimate professional, but she was such a warm and approachable person that each one of her troops felt that they had a special relationship with her and would do any and every thing for her.

Just before Toney returned to her office, she ran into Freddy.

"Hey Ms. C, pretty as a picture as always," he said flashing his wit and a big smile.

"My day is made when I look at you," he fast forwarded.

"Freddy, you are a real character. There is a real compliment in there somewhere, I know. How are you doing?" Toney said turning her complete attention to Freddy.

"I can't complain. I'm just about finished with the morning mail. Only half a day to go. So...things are good. How about you Ms. C? Are you still working way too hard like you normally do?"

"You know how it is...got to keep up. And, having said that, I'd better get back to it. See you later. Okay?"

"Okay...see you this afternoon," Freddy said moving forward with his mail cart.

Toney returned to her office taking up where she had left off. A few minutes later, Sonjia interrupted her to make sure she had some lunch.

"Sonjia, I'll eat later," Toney quipped.

"Well knowing you like I do, you'll end up working through lunch. And you know how important it is that you keep up your strength. So please take a couple of minutes out to eat, okay? Sonjia probed.

"I'll take a couple of minutes now. Thank you for caring," she said sweetly.

"Toney got up from her desk and walked out of the office to the elevator. She pressed the button for the second floor. She was headed to the Deli or one of the other shops on the second floor to get a sandwich and a coke. As she rode down to the restaurant, she thought about all of the things that lay ahead. The elevator stopped and started again off and on. Many of the people gave Toney a quick hello and they were off and on their way back to their offices in the building. When Toney arrived to the second floor she went into the restaurant. She had no special plans for what she wanted, she thought she'd see what looked good. She gazed around the area before checking to see what she wanted. She noticed Cameron seated way back in the corner off to her self.

After Toney worked her way through the line, selecting her meal of corn beef on rye and lemonade, she walked back into the area where Cameron was seated.

"Are you sitting way back here because you want to be alone or can I join you?" asked Toney.

"You are the only one that I would allow around me at this moment," snapped Cameron.

"What on earth is wrong?" Toney asked.

"Remember I told you last week that the Senior Directors' job came open and that I had interviewed for it, right?" Cameron said almost in a teary voice.

"Yes," Toney said in a consoling way.

"You also told me that there was no one else who had as much experience or time in on the job as you and that you were sure that you'd get the position. Have they made a decision already?" Toney asked.

"You will never believe it; they went outside and they hired another white male. This guy doesn't have near the credentials that I do. He's a little more than half my age. After all that I have done for this company, they would do me this way. My family needs this money and I've worked hard for this."

Cameron broke down and cried. Toney consoled her as much as she could, telling her that the job must have not been for her.

"Cameron, please try to put all of this in God's hands. Let him fight your battles for you. We are mere mortals and can't make anyone do anything. All we can do is the very best that we can and pray for the rest," pleaded Toney.

After several minutes of talking, Toney seemed to have calmed Cameron down a bit.

"I do all that I can. I stay late, come in early and I'm at their beck and call and all for what? It's almost as if no matter what I do, I just don't stand a chance," she said as if all the life had been snatched out of her.

"I just have to get my composure back before I go back in the office. Those guys are expecting that I break down, just like they think all women do, so I can't allow them to see me like this. And, what will I tell Peter? He knows all about this and was expecting that I would get the job too. I don't want him to end up doing something stupid," she said.

"Well, let's take the rest of the afternoon to think about what you should tell Peter. We want to break it to him in a way that he doesn't react too badly. At four thirty, I'll call you and we can meet somewhere in the building to put our heads together, okay?"

They finished off their lunch and walked closely to the second floor bathroom together. After Cameron fixed her face and Toney used the toilet, they both walked to the elevator together while Toney continued to console Cameron.

As the elevator arrived at the thirty-seventh floor, Toney said, "Now, you go back in there and be the old Cameron that we both know you can be and don't let those guys beat you at this game. All right?"

"Alright, Cameron said as she started off the elevator. Toney, what would I do if I didn't have you?"

"We're not going to even think about that because you do have me and I have you too," Toney said with a bright smile.

As Toney rode back to the forty-fifth floor, she thought about it. "What on earth is the problem in Corporate America? All the trials and tribulations that these jobs put people through are just not necessary." Toney walked back through her office almost in a trance. In the background the phones were ringing and her troops were hurrying themselves to complete the other assignments handed out by Sonjia earlier this morning. She took her seat behind her mammoth desk and sunk down in her plush deerskin chair. As she rested there, she began to daydream again about all that it took for her to get to where she was....

PART II

During the college years Toney finally began to gain a measure of self-confidence. She was a senior at Howard and was heading her class in grades and respect. The professors were crazy about Toney because of her self-disciplined nature and her eagerness to learn. She was definitely back to her old self. The other students, just as in high school, were drawn to her because she could and would help any of them understand the subject matter and worked with them upon request. She was doing very, very well. It was nearly Christmas time and she wanted to finish everything in time to meet the holiday break schedule so she had to hurry around to finish everything up before she left. She couldn't wait to see her mom and dad and Vanessa again. Many of her classmates had much different plans and were off to the big apple for the Dick Clark New Years Eve Party and she wanted to go too. But, she decided that she'd go to Lexington for Christmas, and the day before

New Year's Eve she could take the bus to New York and hook up with her classmates. After all, she'd never done anything like that before, and she knew that it'd be fun.

Exams were difficult, but as usual when Toney applied herself she came out on top. Several of the girls gathered after mid year exams to plan their trip. They were all to meet at the malt shop later the evening of the last of the mid terms. When Toney arrived there, most of the plans had already been made. She slid into the booth with the others and chimed in.

"Toney, all you have to do is show up...we've done everything else," instructed Alma.

"Great," said Toney, "What's the plan?"

"There'll be eleven of us. We got Sarah to agree to put up her mom's credit card for the room and while she's in the hotel checking in, we'll wait outside. Once she's checked in, she'll come out and give us the room number and the key and one by one we'll sneak in and drop off our big purses with our things in them," reported Betty. She had mostly devised the plan all by herself.

Sarah's parents were the only ones who were well off enough and had credit cards. Most of us were strictly cash and carry for the most part. The hotel was the Mayflower Hotel. We'd simply sleep wherever we could, as if any of us were going to sleep anyway. They synchronized their watches and set the time that they were to meet, then they each headed their separate ways for Christmas.

The next morning, Toney was on Greyhound on her way back to Lexington. On her ride there she thought about the four years that she had spent in the Washington, D. C. area. She had had an opportunity to visit the museums, toured the White House and Capitol Hill. She had worked in the Pentagon as an intern, and some of the things that she saw there were amazing and in many ways like the movies. She participated in a host of activities that had assisted her in rounding off her young adult life. She felt that she was prepared for anything now. She had only six months to go before she would be out in Corporate America starting her career. She couldn't wait. She was ready and just knew in her soul that she would do well.

Her bus pulled into the bus station in Lexington at twelve-forty-two p.m. Her mom and dad were there as usual to pick her up. They were so loyal and faithful to her. She wanted to, more than any thing else, make them proud of her. She disembarked the bus to their open arms and her dad's smiling, beaming face.

"Honey, you look terrific," said her dad.

"Thanks, Dad, you and mom look great too! I'm so happy to be back home. It's been a tough semester. But, thank God, it all worked out," Toney said as she moved to her mom.

"Mom? Mom are you alright?"

She shook her head while saying, "I'm fine Toney. I guess I'm just so emotional seeing you so grownup. It's difficult to let my little girl go," Dorothy said to her while wiping the tears from her cheeks.

"Mom, I'll always be your little girl," said Toney tenderly, "and you'll always be my mom. I promise to come home as often as possible and, whenever I end up...you can come see me all the time, okay?"

Just at that very moment Dorothy got a hold of herself and took a deep breath seemingly exhaling the sadness and inhaling the fact that her baby was home and almost instantly she appeared to have gained her composure back.

"What shall we do first," shrieked Dorothy in a voice and disposition that was now at the other end of the spectrum?

"Whatever you and Dad would like to do," responded Toney, not sure what to make of her Mom's mood swing.

"Let's stop off in downtown Lexington first so I can get the last of the bulbs for the tree at the variety store. That way you can run in to Piggly Wiggly and see Vanessa for a few minutes."

"Great, I haven't spoken to Vanessa in a few weeks...Is she okay?" inquired Toney.

"We haven't seen much of her lately either. So tell her we said hello and we'll meet you back at the car in about twenty minutes," said Bill.

Vanessa was bending over a big box of vegetables when Toney first walked in. She would know Vanessa from the back, the side, or anyway. After all she was the only true friend that Toney had ever had.

Toney tipped up to Vanessa and leaned over to her whispering, "Whatcha doing," which was their childhood phrase.

Vanessa turned to Toney in total shock to see her again, as they hugged each other tightly. Toney hadn't observed the condition that Vanessa was in. As they continued to hug Toney noticed the feel of Vanessa breast pressed against hers. She thought, "I know that Vanessa has always been very shapely, but I can't remember her having so much in that area." As they began to release the bear hugs that they had on one another, Toney got an eyeful. She was pregnant! And she didn't look too healthy either.

"Honey, are you alright?" Toney said with love and concern.

"I'm fine, Tone...I'm just a bit run down with work and everything...things will be alright, Vanessa reported. When did you get here? How long will you be staying this time? When can we sit down and chat? I have so much to tell you."

"Slow down, Vanessa...I just got in. Mom and Dad are at the variety store and I just popped in here to surprise you. What are you doing tonight?" asked Toney.

"Well, my friend, who has this responsibility, (as she pointed to her stomach) and I are supposed to meet tonight to talk about our plans. But, what about tomorrow morning?"

"Sounds good, let's plan on it," said Toney. "But are you sure you're alright?"

"Oh...everything's fine. Stop worrying, worry whort. I'm fine."

They hugged again.

"Well, if you say so. I'll see you in the morning then."

"Okay," Vanessa said standing there watching Toney as she disappeared through the doorway of the store.

Toney walked out of the Piggly Wiggly confused. Vanessa didn't look right. It wasn't the pregnancy so much as there was something very different about her. She had a far away look in her eyes and that concerned Toney a great deal. She walked into the variety store where her mom and dad were at the checkout counter just about ready to leave.

"Did you see Vanessa," asked Dorothy?

"Yes ma'am. We'll see each other in the morning to spend some time." Toney abruptly changed the subject. "Did you find what you needed, mom?"

"Oh, we got everything," said Bill flashing a big smile to his little girl. They all walked bunched up together to the car and started on their short journey home. Toney sat in the back seat pondering Vanessa. There was surely something going on there. She hoped she could help.

As they drove back to the farmhouse she looked at the area where she grew-up remembering most of it and observing the other parts that had changed since she had left. It was great to be back at home and more specifically to be in her old bedroom again. She felt safe and protected from the wilds of the world. She had had some exposure to what life had in store for her, but it was only the tip of the ice-burg. The next thing she knew, her mom was calling her for dinner.

Toney, dinner's ready."

"I'll be right down, mom," Toney yelled.

She found herself jumping up at once remembering when she was a kid and the fact that her father chastised her for taking her time when her mother called her. From that time on, she came as soon as she was called. It was just like yesterday to her. The table was set only this time she didn't have to set it. It was almost like she was a celebrity in her own house. She would do better tomorrow and help her mother set the table, she thought. As they sat down to eat, it was an old-fashioned country meal. Fried chicken, macaroni & cheese, corn on the cob, fried green tomatoes, coleslaw and a mixture of onions, tomatoes and peppers to go along with the mustard and turnip greens and home made cornbread. Boy, how Toney missed the good ole days. But, a girl of her age had to watch how much of this good food she could eat. She wanted to watch her figure for the future and that was for sure. After dinner, they sat by the fireplace chatting about this and that until it was bedtime. Toney went in to take a bath and put on her pajamas and came back to kiss her parent's goodnight. She knew that she was a very lucky girl. She went back into her room and fell on her knees to once again thank God for all she had.

First thing the next morning she was on the phone to Vanessa. She wanted to satisfy her curiosity about the situation. She knew that there had to be a story behind the look in Vanessa's eyes, and she had to get to the bottom of it.

"I'm walking over there. See you in a few minutes," Toney chirped.

"Okay," Vanessa managed to get out. She didn't sound too good at all.

When Toney arrived, they went directly to Vanessa's bedroom. Vanessa got back in bed and Toney sat at the foot of the bed, "Girl, what have you been up to…oops, I can see what you've been up to but who's the lucky guy and when are you two getting married?" Toney teased in order to lighten the moment.

"I'm not getting married," Vanessa said with a measure of shame.

"Hell, Toney, I'm not even sure who the father of the baby is," she reluctantly said.

"Vanessa, you never said a word about this to me. What happened? Did they take advantage of you? What happened?" Toney said in a perplexed manner somewhat afraid of the answer.

"I don't really know," Vanessa snapped somewhat out of control.

"I just started feeling like I couldn't get enough sex. One man after the other. Guys that we went to school with, guys that I didn't even know that well. I was out of control. That wasn't the only part of me that really changed. My mom says that I'm hard to get along with now too.

I'm afraid, Toney. I can't understand it and I'm scared," she said starting to cry.
Toney moved closer to Vanessa to comfort her, "Have you been to a doctor?"
"Yes, but they can't find anything. It's just me…I'm turning into a monster."
"Now, that's ridiculous. No way is my best friend a monster. You just have to work it out with the doctors. Hang in there and everything will be alright."
For the next hour and a half they chatted as Vanessa's disposition calmed down to a purr.

Two days later, Toney left Lexington on Greyhound. She was headed for excitement to experience her first New Years eve in New York with her college cronies. Her life was destined never to be the same again …

PART III

Why can't we just come to work, do our jobs and get promoted based on merit? Why must all of the politics and the games be played?

Why are the moves that upper management makes always so devious? Toney thought, 'I wish there was something that I could do to help Cameron.'

Buzz,

"Yes, Sonjia. What is it?"

"Mr. Parlarme is on line one."

"Alright. I wonder why he didn't call on my private line?" Toney asked.

"He said it was busy," Sonjia said.

"Well, I wasn't on it. Would you have that checked out for me, please?"

"Sure." Sonjia assisted.

"Thanks. I'll take the call now." Toney replied.

"Hi, Grant. Whatcha doing?" she purred as she changed her entire disposition.

"Hi, baby. It's been all work for me today. I got in around four and it's been non-stop. "How's your day?" he asked.

"It's been good. Very productive. I hardly thought about Surrant at all. I know you are wondering if I remembered what you told me over the weekend. Well, I do and he's been put on the back burner for now and that's for sure."

"Oh, I spoke to Brandon this morning. He sends his love to "our girl" as he puts it. He's coming to town in a few weeks so we'll have to have him out on the town with us," Grant said with a huge smile.

"Sounds good. Is he alright?" Toney asked.

"Sure, he's good. He's just having some challenges at his job like the rest of us. But, what's new?"

"Well, honey, I need to wrap up the day and get out of here. I'll call you later."

"Okay, baby. I love you, Tone."

"I love you too, honey, bye."

Toney sat there for a few more minutes then she buzzed Sonjia.

"Can I see you for a moment please?"

"Sure Toney…I'll be right there."

Toney and Sonjia got together to review the day and to plan for the next. The next thing Toney knew, she was on the elevator headed for her car. The day had been long enough.

SIX

Fair or not, the war is upon each of us everyday when we get dressed and head out for whatever we have chosen to do. Toney knew that the question for her at least was, if she was prepared for it or not. Many years had passed from the moment she left Lexington. Her naïve persona back in those days was totally different than the woman that she had turned into over the years. She knew that she could give thanks to God for getting her through the precarious positions that she had been drawn to. But, today she wouldn't be thinking about any of that because she and Grant were off to Ocho Rios, Jamaica. She could put her cares behind her for a few days and recharge. This was her time to unplug and really get into the mode to relax.

Grant was picking her up in thirty minutes. She quickly checked the list that she had made.

"All items are accounted for," she said in a wee voice as if assuring herself. She piled all of the bags one by one near the front door. A few minutes later, Grant was ringing the doorbell. She scurried to the door to see her fellow.

"Hi, honey," he said as she threw open the door. He came in flashing a warm smile giving her a quick kiss on the cheek.

"Hi, Grant," Toney responded displaying a girlish grin.

"You all set to go?" he asked.

Just as the last of the words left his lips, he saw all of the bags, "What in the world… are you moving to Jamaica?"

Toney smiled as she said softly, "A girl has to look good for her man, right?"

Grant thought about her comments and he couldn't say a word. He simply made a swift response while smiling at the thought of how she looked.

"Okay, okay, I'll be right back. I have to start loading all this into the car."

About ten minutes and several trips later, they were off to O'Hare. The drive was very congested as it always was headed out 295. The small talk kept them company during the ride. They teased back and forth about skinny dipping at one of the nude beaches. Grant became very guarded, "Oh no…I'll never let any one else see my stuff…never because it's all mine," grabbing her left knee.

Thirty-five minutes later Grant hopped out of the car to unload the bags in order to have them checked in at the curb. Once that was done, they drove around to find a parking spot, which took another thirty minutes. They caught the shuttle back to the terminal and walked hand in hand to the gate where their flight was scheduled to start the boarding process in twenty minutes. It seemed as if Grant had scheduled everything to the letter.

"Honey, I want a cup of coffee, can I get you anything?" asked Toney.

"Let me walk with you," …the snack counter was just across from the gate.

"Ma'am would you keep an eye out for our things? We're just stepping right there," Grant pointed to the snack counter.

"Okay," as the gray-hared lady peeked out over her novel that she was obviously engrossed in.

"But, don't be gone for too long," she directed.

Grant placed their order and seconds later they were back with the gray-hared lady who didn't even look up as they returned.

"Thanks, Ma'am," Grant obliged anyway.

The lady said without raising her head…"Umhuh."

As they sat there enjoying their treat, Grant began to outline what they were to accomplish during the week. Not only was the coming trip designated to unplug, recharge and relax, but to prepare Toney for the battle ahead. The boarding process began. They were flying first class so they boarded early. Once on board the flight they got settled in and they began the chat outlining the steps that she would take to combat Surrant. The boarding process continued, while they continued their conversation. Since Surrant was the ringleader of her current problems, stopping him was clearly the most important point for her to remedy to ensure her peace of mind.

"May I get you something to drink?" the flight attendant asked.

"I'll take a glass of orange juice," responded Toney.

"The same for me," added Grant.

The flight attendant shuffled off to retrieve their orders.

People were still filing onto the airplane. The line was backed up out into the jet way. One by one the passengers boarded. A couple with two small children boarded. The kids were as restless as they could be. Toney day dreamed of the day that she and Grant would have some little ones of their own. The couple and their kids moved pass Toney continuing down the isle into the coach area. Toney's attention was focused on the kids as she turned to watch them move toward their seats.

"Tone." Grant said to get her attention back to him.

"Tell me the last few of the things that Surrant did to disrespect you," Grant asked while taking notes.

"He out and out said that I was way off base in my assessment on our position referring to his suggestion to take some of the top sales people from our competitors. He shouted out during the last conference call that I wasn't paying attention. Actually I had gone into a semi daydreaming state, but I heard everything that they were saying. And finally Surrant settled down once I rebounded to cut him off at the pass. Why do you need that information?" Toney asked trying to get on the same page as Grant.

"I need to know how this guy thinks, that's the only way that we can beat him at his own game," he reported.

"How's his work ethic? Is he good at what he does? What about his background? Where is he from? His family…who are they? What do his employees think of him? That kind of stuff will allow us to get next to him and began to see from his eyes."

They continued to talk about Surrant. Toney began to realize that she knew much more about him than she originally thought. As the flight took off, Grant got more and more information from Toney. She was developing information as they chatted that completely flowed like a river. Grant collected the facts as he systematically devised the plan.

One that he would disclose to Toney on their way back to Chicago, when he was certain to have worked out all of the details to his satisfaction. He was sure that he'd have it all together by then.

They talked and talked. The flight took three hours. The captain made the announcement that they would be landing in Montego Bay in a few short minutes. Toney had filled out the information cards that the flight attendants had passed out during the flight. Grant and Toney smiled at each other as they held hands upon arriving at the airport in Montego Bay. Their holiday was just about to begin and they were pleased with themselves because they had used the flight time wisely uncovering mounds of information about Surrant and the situation at hand. The plane landed smoothly. Grant gathered their belongings as they waited for their turn to walk with the others down the aisle to ten days of fun. They walked down the steps of the plane onto the tarmac. The weather was beautiful! They had left behind light rain with heavy overcast skies and about fifty-five degrees, which was typical for Chicago in May. Unlike most of the airports in the States, here they descended the steps of the plane onto the tarmac and hand in hand, they went into the terminal to go through customs. There were a couple lines for natives and several more for visitors. The choices were simple. If one was bringing something into the country to declare, one area was for them, and if the visitors had nothing to declare another section was for them. Of course, Grant and Toney had only their personal belongings, so their line was the longest

longest because they were clearly only there on holiday. Sonjia had arranged for transportation for them. She always thought ahead. Toney smiled at Sonjia's gesture. The driver was standing just outside the baggage claim area, which was away from the lines and all of the red tape it took to formally be received on the island. He was holding a sign with the name **TONEY CHAMBERS** in big bold letters. Toney thought about Sonjia as she smiled at the mere fact that Sonjia always thought ahead and made sure she was always taken care of. What a very thoughtful person she was. Grant had collected their luggage, once they were through the lines and had them piled one on the other. He struggled to get the heavy load over to the driver and with the driver's help, they proceeded through the outside doorway. A few minutes later, they were all inside the limousine and on their way to a full week of total relaxation and refuge. They took the scenic route on their hour and a half ride to Ocho Rios. They arrived at the Jamaica Grande, checked in and quickly unpacked. They wanted to get out into the area and investigate the hotel in order to map out the week. Grant had decided that he simply wanted to be a spud on the beach but Toney had an idea that she wanted to take in the activities being offered. So they agreed to compromise. Grant wanted Toney to relax and whatever would ensure that, he would go along with.

Grant spoke with the concierge and made a reservation at Evita's. It was a very popular spot in the hills that was frequented by many island visitors and celebrities. He thought this would be a great way to start on the first night.

"Honey, I'm finished with my shower...now it's your turn," Toney whispered.

She pulled a chair up to the dresser from the side table next to the patio. She carefully put on her makeup and sprayed herself with a touch of her favorite cologne. Then she swept her hair up on top of her head, slipped into her black free flowing sleeveless dress and her black patent sandals. When Grant popped out of the shower and reentered the bedroom, he flashed a quick smile of approval.

"Ah, baby, you look so good," he said while standing there in the raw, towel drying himself off.

"Thanks, baby, you look good too," as her eyes scanned every inch of his well-formed physique.

He was a gorgeous man, and she felt fortuitous to have him as hers.

"I'll be all set in a second or two," he murmured.

Grant lightly sprayed on deodorant then a scant amount of cologne and finally slipped into a pair of gray linen slacks with a black alligator belt, a white silk shirt and black alligator sandals. He looked good enough to eat, she thought. They left the room hand in hand as they often traveled. When they arrived in the lobby, there was native music filling the air. It was a festive atmosphere. It wouldn't take too much for them to get in the spirit of this area. Several of the locals approached them offering to take them to their destination for a small fee. Grant selected the individual who seemed to have the most finesse. His name was Silver. He appeared to be honest. Silver drove them to the restaurant, asking Grant to take a look at his watch in order to let him know when to come back for them. They agreed on two hours and Grant and Toney got out and headed for the restaurant.

"Thanks, Silver," Grant said as he looked back.

"We'll see you at nine thirty...alright?"

"Okay, I'll be back mon," responded Silver.

Grant and Toney walked into the restaurant that was aesthetically pleasing to the eyes. The ambiance was awesome. It had a causal flare with an upscale décor. There were little candles on each table along with very nice china and real silver topped by pink napkins. The room had a real mahogany bar off to the right and a baby grand piano on the left side. A gentleman was seated at the piano playing a combination of elevator music with a twist of island flare. It was very odd but also very beautiful. Along side the man playing the piano was a native who assisted with a guitar who also sang in his native tongue. What a strange combination but they seemed to pull it off. The restaurant was nestled in the hills, which over looked the town below. The view was incredible. As dusk fell, the sun was going down and this had to be the most perfect place on the entire island. As usual, Grant had outdone himself.

They were seated at a table for two on the edge of the restaurant, where they had the perfect view of the area.

"Grant, this is beautiful. How did you find out about this place?" she asked.

"I've got my little secrets," he said in a boyish way with an air of bragging.

"Well honey, you have more than outdone yourself...it's really nice," she leaned over kissed him on the cheek and said in a whisper.

The waiter came to the table to introduce himself, "Good evening mon," he declared. "I'm Almon. I'll be your server. Can I get you a beverage or any TING to start?" he asked in the Jamaican dialect.

"Yes," Grant responded. "We'll have two Jamaican rum punches and water with lemon on the side, please."

"Okay," Almon said as he disappeared through the double swinging doors and was back in an instant.

"Here you are mon. I'll return in a few moments to take your dinner order," as the Jamaican dialect was becoming more familiar to both of them.

Grant said in a teasing manner to Toney, "Da you want anyTING else prettee lady?" mocking the dialect.

Toney quickly said, "SHHHH, before you embarrass him."

They continued their conversation but kept it down to a whisper.

The restaurant was becoming crowded. It was obviously a major attraction in town and Toney and Grant had arrived at a great time to get the perfect location. As they examined the menu Toney saw a few things that she wanted to taste.

"Honey, I want to order several things. We could share them in order to have a good sampling of many items...what do you think?"

"What items are you speaking of," Grant said with one eyebrow cocked up as to question her intent.

Toney had been in many situations since they had been dating where her food selection track record was poor. She typically ordered badly and ended up either sending her food back for other dishes or eating off of Grant's plate. She made her suggestions and he added a couple of items. When Almon returned they placed their dinner orders and settled in with the Jamaican drinks, which hadn't been touched at that point.

After twenty-five minutes of small talk, they were being served. When dinner was finished, they paid the bill and walked out into the night to wait for Silver. They sat down at the entrance on one of the little benches there in a garden type area, which was off to the side of the front door. Several patrons of the restaurant were also seated out there waiting on a table to become available so that they could dine. Fifteen minutes later, Silver drove up flashing a bright smile. They rejoined him in the small van that he was driving. "How was dinner mon?" Silver asked.

"It was marvelous. What a great place for visitors to your beautiful island," Toney shared.

Grant chimed in, "How about driving us around the area? We'd like to get a feel for the territory. We have several more days here."

" Sure, mon," Silver said. "I'd be happy to do it mon."

They drove around for about forty-five minutes, while Silver explained to them what they were seeing. It was a very insightful tour, especially one that was given by a local, which turned out to be the best kind. They returned back to the hotel about ten fifteen. It was much too early to turn in for the night so Grant made a suggestion that they walk out on the beach for a while. Toney was thrilled at the suggestion and the stroll ensued. About twenty minutes of walking on the shoreline they heard island music coming from a little hut right on the beach. There were several cars and multi passenger vans parked around the little building. They walked toward the building and decided to investigate. Timidly, Grant opened the door as an island gentleman welcomed them in.

"Come on in, mon, I'm Bobby Poe, the owner," the man instructed.

"Join us for some fun on the beach," he said as he motioned for them to step further.

Grant scanned the room locating a barstool next to the bar on the very end, stepping aside for Toney to take a seat. Grant stood to the left of Toney watching the activities. They ordered two more Jamaican rum punches. The music was filling the air. They watched the individuals on the floor who had obviously been there for a while. They were jiggling an island type dance and having a great time. A few minutes later their drinks arrived. After several sips, they too were laughing and dancing just like the natives and the others in the club. Grant was pleased and very happy to see Toney let her hair down.

PART II

Jim Surrant asked Holley to place a call to Toney's office to get some updated information on the big meeting. He wanted to see where things stood. He thought that speaking with her would allow him to take the pulse of the situation. It was paramount that he find out as much as he could from her.

"Jim, I have Toney Chambers' office on line three," Holley reported.

"Her assistant Sonjia is holding."

"TONEY CHAMBERS!" demanded Surrant.

"May I say who's calling sir?" asked Sonjia.

"It's against company policy to be screened!" he directed.

"Sir, I'm sorry you feel that way, but I can't give out any information about Ms. Chambers until I know with whom I'm speaking," she continued.

"Well, if you insist," he said sarcastically.

"This is Jim Surrant, Assistant Vice President of the Western Region, is she there?" he further demanded.

"No, Mr. Surrant, she is out of the office this week, on vacation. Is there something I can do to assist you?" she asked very professionally.

"Vacation? With all that's going on she takes vacation now?" he spewed.

"Where is she? It's very important that I find her and find her right now!" he shouted.

"Mr. Surrant, would it be alright if I gave you a call right back?" Sonjia quizzed.

"I'll have to research the exact details of her hotel, etceteras," she continued. "Ms. Chambers made her own plans this time, so I'm not quite sure where she is."

"Yes, I suppose that'll be okay, but I warn you, I'll be expecting a call back in five minutes, understand?" he clattered.

"Now what's your name again?" he asked with a tone of authority and follow-up.

"Sonjia sir, I'm Ms. Chambers assistant," she said proudly.

"Alright then, I'll be expecting your call back. Remember it's urgent and five minutes. Do you understand?" he said piercingly.

"Yes sir," Sonjia exclaimed as she heard the other end of the telephone slam in her ear.

"What an asshole and a rude son-of–a-bitch," she mumbled to herself.

"No wonder Toney is always so distraught whenever she encounters this ignoramus," she continued.

Sonjia's mind fiercely turned to the situation at hand. All she knew at this time was that she had to think and think hard how to handle this situation. The last thing she wanted to do was to interrupt Toney's much needed vacation with the likes of him. Sonjia picked up the phone to call the Marriott hotel in Montego Bay. She made reservations in Toney's name, giving Toney's American Express card number for the guarantee. She asked the reservation agent how much time she had to call back without being charged, if there was a need to cancel. The person on the other end of the phone said they could allow for a six p.m. cancellation, if need be with no penalty. It was only three p.m. Chicago time, so she knew that would work. As quickly as she hung up the phone with the Marriott she picked it up again to call the Jamaica Grande in Ocho Rios to alert Toney of the situation. Neither Toney or Grant answered.

She left a voice mail message for Toney, "If you get in after I've gone home, please call me at home. My number is 847.555.8988, just in case you don't have the number with you. I must talk to you about Surrant. He's insisting that I give him a number where he can reach you. He says it's urgent! I've bought some time with a temporary setup which I'll explain when I talk to you, but please hurry and call…he'll figure it all out if too much time passes."

Sonjia waited for a couple of seconds, picked up the phone again to return Surrant's call, which was exactly four and a half minutes later.

"Jim Surrant's office, this is Holley, may I help you?" answered Holley in the perkiest of voices.

Sonjia thought in the back of her mind, 'she's way too upbeat for her…those California types are boarding on sickening'….

"Good afternoon, Holley, is Mr. Surrant available please?" responded Sonjia.

"Yes, may I tell him who's calling," Holley inquired with a voice oozing with sex, 'Did she think she was having sex?' Sonjia thought.

"Sonjia, Toney Chamber's assistant," she reported professionally.

"I'm returning his call."

"Of course, just a moment please," as Holley appeared to gain some professionalism in her voice. Sonjia thought it was also obvious that Surrant had let Holley know that this call was coming.

He picked up the phone a couple of mini seconds later quipping, "SURRANT! Do you have the information that I need?"

"Mr. Surrant, I researched Ms. Chambers calendar. She was determined to make these arrangements for her vacation on her own and one to remember, so she refused to allow me to set the plans up for her. Now, there were many pages of scribbled notes regarding her final plans, but they are difficult to decipher. The most legible notes indicate that she might be at the Marriott in Montego Bay, Jamaica, but I'm not sure. When she left, she told me that she'd check in with me each day. So, the number for the Marriott is 809.555.4400. If this works out for you please let me know. If not, I'll give you a call tomorrow, once she has checked in with me, okay?" she reported in detail.

"That's down right stupid! Someone so allegedly on top of her game and no one knows where the hell she is...how ridiculous!" he bantered. "Believe me, I'll be back on the phone with you first thing in the morning!" he fired at Sonjia.

"Perfect," Sonjia thought, "I've bought some time!"

Sonjia watched the clock. She hoped and prayed that Toney would call her back as soon as she picked up the message.

Surrant placed a call to the Montego Bay Marriott.

"Good afternoon, Montego Bay Marriott," the operator answered.

"Toney Chambers, please...she is a guest," Surrant said rigidly, as he sat at his desk leaning back in his lush chair strongly tapping his Monte Blanc pen repeatedly on his desk mat.

"I'll check for you sir, one moment please," the operator offered.

After a second or so, the operator came back to the line, "thank you for waiting sir, she has a reservation but hasn't arrived yet. May I take a message?" asked the operator.

"No ma'am, I'll call her back," Surrant responded.

He hung up the phone, pushed back in his chair and began to plot. "Hmmm."

As quickly as he leaned back a light bulb appeared to shine in his mind. He picked up the telephone and punched in another number quickly.

"Donner and Gamble," a phone clerk answered.

"Guy Gamble," demanded Surrant.

"Just a moment please."

Toney and Grant were having a great time. They danced for hours virtually becoming temporary natives. They were both so amazed at how much they were enjoying themselves so completely. Grant was happy to see his woman let her hair down. She deserved to have a good time, after all that had happened lately. He was pleased seeing her so happy. And, especially since he knew that this was only the tip of the iceberg for Toney as far as Grant was concerned. After all they still had nine whole days of fun in the sun to go. The time really flew by that evening. By the time that they got back to the hotel it was almost midnight. Grant opened the door, stepped aside to allow Toney in the room first. She floated, in her lady like manner collapsing on the foot of the bed.

"What a completely stunning day," she coo'd.

"I could totally get used to this, couldn't you honey?" she asked.

"It wouldn't be difficult at all," he answered while assisting her by taking off her shoes.

He set her shoes together close to the wall away from the bed. As he turned to walk back over to her, he noticed the red message light illuminated on the telephone, indicating that there was a message.

"We have a message," Grant whispered.

Toney sat straight up, "Wonder what that's all about? Only our parents and our secretaries know where we are. Neither of them would call unless there was some sort of an emergency."

Grant picked up the phone to retrieve the messages.

"Honey, it's your office. Sonjia needs for you to call her as soon as possible. I know it must be very important, if she asked that you call her no matter what time it was when you got in. She even left her home number, just in case you didn't have it with you."

With the last of Grant's words, Toney appeared to sober up. She leapt from her lounged position on the bed, scooting to the telephone in what seemed to be one motion. Grant had written down the phone number that Sonjia left and had gotten a dial tone and proceeded to dial the number. As the phone began to ring, Toney held her breath...what could it be? Sonjia would never interrupt her vacation unless it was of great importance.

It was the middle of the night in Chicago. Sonjia picked up the blaring phone with the wimpiest of voices... "Hello?"

"Sonjia, it's Grant, we just got your message, sorry to wake you. What's going on?"

"Surrant called! He was incensed that Toney left town with things in the air about the big meeting. He had some questions that he needed to ask her so that he'd be prepared for the meeting. When he found out that she was on vacation, he blew-up. He demanded that I tell him where Toney could be reached. I wouldn't give him any information. In fact, I sent him in another direction. I called the Marriott in Montego Bay to make a reservation there to throw him off track until I could talk with you. He seemed fine with the information that I gave him, but I told him that Toney would be checking in with me everyday and that I would get back to him."

"Sonjia…take a breath. We're on the case now, so take a breath," Grant said in a soothing manner.

"Now, one thing at a time…why did you make a reservation at the Marriott in Montego Bay?"

Sonjia began to explain her rationalization. By the time that she and Grant concluded the conversation Grant had a complete understanding of the story and Sonjia knew exactly what she was to do next.

Grant said, "Sonjia, you really thought fast on your feet. No wonder Toney loves you so much. Get back to sleep and we will call you at the office in the morning."

When they hung up, a plan of action had taken place.

Grant explained everything to Toney and together they devised a next step.

They freshened up and met in the bedroom of the mini suite that they had checked into earlier. After they popped a bottle of the most expensive champagne available, they toasted the first day of their trip, they engaged in a long sultry kiss, which ultimately led to their making hot and steamy love and finally they drifted off to sleep entangled in each other's arms.

SEVEN

Relax and release. The essence of this vacation superceded their expectations. This time together was so needed for both of them. To be able to get away from the hustle and bustle of Corporate America which renders each of us helpless to our individual plights each day was just the prescription needed. Day in and day out most of us work so hard through long and endless days with little thought to much else, our lives belonging to what we do for a living and not to ourselves. We build the special moments of our lives around the little personal time that we take to seek mental asylum. How sad. Much of the adult population of the world pushes onward five to six days a week, running as fast as we can to make someone else rich, taking very insignificant amounts every two weeks for ourselves and our families. But, what choice do we have? It's clearly the way the system is set up. And, in the shadows of making big companies bigger, we get less and less and are asked for more and more from these entities. In the bounty, we get a piece of what amounts to a loaf of bread, if we're lucky as the reward. How profound! What does it all mean?

Toney's very first act that morning was to give Sonjia a call at the office to make sure that they were on the same page about everything, chiefly regarding Surrant. Not as though Toney had to answer to him. She just wanted to make sure that while she was away he wouldn't screw up anything for her. Sonjia and Toney spoke for the first time since she and Grant left Chicago.

"Good morning, my dear," said Toney softly. "I understand that Surrant is at it again."

Sonjia shrugged, "Yes ma'am. He was his normal rude and ridiculous self yesterday. But, I threw him off your trail."

"Thanks for taking care of him yesterday but, never you mind Sonjia. I'll place a call to him this morning. This call will shut him down until we return. Since there's a three hour time difference between here and California, I've still got time for a leisurely breakfast and I'll have him on the phone in a couple of hours."

"Is there anything else you need?"

"Only one thing, please call me back once you've spoken with him. I'd like to know the last phase of this situation just in case he calls me again, okay?"

"No problem, will do. You went above and beyond the call…you are absolutely the best. Thanks for everything!"

Grant had walked out onto the balcony, while Toney was on the phone, to look out at the cool aqua blue water of the Caribbean and to concentrate on the morning waves. There was something so tranquil about big bodies of water to him. Why couldn't it stay that way for him and his intended? She was such a special girl and he loved her so much. One day they would be man and wife. He felt lucky to have found her. They leaned on each other to have an outlet from what each of them had chosen to do for their life's work. His job was no better, but at least the fact that he was a man, assisted him in the outcome of most of the situations he encountered.

"Honey, you ready for breakfast?" purred Toney.

"Absolutely, I'm famished after those drinks and that hot love you gave me last night," he said flashing his handsome toothy smile.

He walked back into the room sweeping her up into his arms and laying a long wet kiss on her. She blushed saying to him, "That's what got us in trouble last night, remember?"

"I don't call it trouble," both of them chuckled and walked toward the door to head out for breakfast.

Always hand in hand they left the room going down to the main dining room for breakfast. They went through the buffet selecting the mangos and other precious fruits from the island and many regular breakfast items that they were accustomed to in the States. They took a seat near the pool, which over looked the ocean under some shade trees. While they ate they watched the other visitors both in the restaurant and the ones headed toward the water. Everyone was moving about as if they had a sense of purpose or direction. Grant thought ahead to the special day planned for Toney. An hour or so later they were finished with breakfast.

Toney had to get back to the room right after breakfast to make the dreaded phone call to Surrant. They headed back and upon entering the room Grant returned back to the balcony to lounge while she made contact.

PART II

Guy Gamble arrived in Montego Bay. By the time he cleared customs it was late. He checked into the Marriott around 1 a.m. He had to catch the nine p.m. flight out of Los Angeles. His orders were to locate his prey and rough them up. He was being paid handsomely for the job. Typically, the jobs ranged from broken legs to murder, whatever the pocket could afford. It would be a bit more difficult outside the continental USA. When he arrived at the hotel, he took a look around the area to set up his plan. What allies or dimly lit areas could he approach his victims, take care of them, and leave them lying there for hours undetected. He located an area that could do in this situation and moved swiftly away from the area back to the hotel to get a little shuteye.

The next morning at five a.m., Gamble got dressed in a pair of off white pants, a straw hat and a colorful island print silk shirt and walked to the front desk. He asked about the early scheduled front desk clerk, "Would you please give me the room number of my sister Toney Chambers? I'm in town to surprise her."

"Sir, I am not allowed to do that due to the policy of the hotel. If you like, you may ring the room and ask the guest for the room number," she said as a professional.

"Well, that would spoil the surprised, wouldn't it?" he said stomping away from the desk.

Gamble hung around the lobby for a while and decided to give little Miss Toney a ring on the phone. According to the description that Surrant had provided, he hadn't seen anyone who remotely looked like her. Guy picked up a house phone.

"Marriott operator, may I help you?

"Yes, operator, would you please ring Toney Chambers?"

"One moment please sir."

"Sir, thank you for waiting. Ms. Chambers was a no show for last night. Perhaps she will arrive today. May I take a message for her?"

"No."

He became quiet as he thought things through.

"Sir, can I help you further?" she inquired.

"Uh, no ma'am. Thanks."

"What in the hell? A wild goose chase? Gamble rushed back to his room. He paced and paced, from one end of the small but efficient room to the other. The time difference was holding him back. Surely to God by this time Surrant was on his way to the office or he'd try to reach him at home. Maybe his pretty little wife has some input" he said to himself as he rung his hands in impatience.

"The son-of–a-bitch. Making me waste my time. He'll pay extra for this."

Gamble picked up a local newspaper and swung it under his arm as he retreated to the lobby and the hotel restaurant to grab a bite to eat while he waited.

"How did this mix-up happen? Surrant is loosing his touch," he mumbled.

Gamble gobbled down two cups of black coffee and some bacon and eggs. He paid his check and returned to his room, immediately getting on the telephone to get in touch with Surrant.

Holley had arrived at the office early as usual and was surprised that Jim's private line had begun to ring so early.

"Jim Surrant's office, this is Holley, may I help you?" she subscribed?

"Yeah, is Surrant in?" grunted Gamble.

"No sir, this is his assistant, is there something that I can help you with?" she asked.

"No, not a thing…when do you expect him?" he further distanced himself.

"He should be arriving at anytime now. May I take a message?"

"No, I already told you that. I'll call back!" he grumbled.

He hung up the phone. Holley stood there in a bit of a trance not sure what to make of the call. She had been involved in ninety-eight percent of Surrant's dealings, but never had she spoken with this guy. What was this all about? And, so early in the morning. What was Surrant up to?

For now she decided to put it on the back burner and move on to her day. But, as clever as she was, she'd keep her eyes and ears wide open.

When Surrant arrived in the office she never said a word. Instead, she approached him with the normal one-on-one attention and moved right into the business at hand. Twenty-minutes after Surrant had arrived, his line rang again. Jim jumped on it before Holley could get to the telephone. She was making a fresh pot of coffee in the break room. She only heard one ring and he answered the phone, then Surrant got up from his desk to close the door. How strange that was. There were only the two of them there at this hour…what was he trying to hide? Holley ran to the door to try and hear the conversation. She heard him say, "Damn that bitch! Stay put. I'll call you right back!"

He slammed down the phone and before he could rise to his feet, another ring. He jerked up the receiver, "Surrant!"

"Surrant, I understand that you've been looking for me, is that right?" Toney said with a bit of impatience in her tone.

"Oh, hi Toney. (He never called her by her first name…never) I was trying to reach you yesterday. Thanks for calling me back. I was caught off guard by your vacation with the big meeting coming up so soon. I just wanted to run some numbers with you to make sure we are on the same page. That was the reason why I was calling. But, if you'd rather wait until you're back, I could understand that," he said with a hint of shrewdness.

Toney knew right away that he was up to something. "No, Surrant, as a matter of fact, we can review the numbers right now if you like. I brought some work with me in order to make sure I was prepared when I returned."

They spent the next few minutes going over the same numbers that they reviewed on the last conference call. His numbers were still off, but he was making strides to clean them up before he headed back to Chicago.

"Will that be all?" Toney inquired guardedly.

"Yes, I suppose so. By the way, where did you disappear to? I hope it was to one of your favorite spots."

She said, "no, not really. I wanted to visit Jamaica. So, Grant and I are in Ocho Rios." She said before she really gave it any thought.

Surrant said, "Well, have a great time and I'll see you in Chicago. By the way, thanks for taking this time with me."

"Oh, no problem at all. I hope it helped. Goodbye."

When she got off the phone she turned to Grant to get his feedback on what he thought that was all about. He was incensed that she told him where they were.

"Honey, why did you do that?" he asked bewilderedly.

"Do what?" she asked innocently.

"Tell him exactly where we were. He didn't have to know that. I thought that was what you were trying to avoid?

"Well, actually, I told him that we were in Ocho Rios and not where we were specifically. If he were to try finding us, he'd have to look at all the hotels in the area and by the time he did, we'd be back in Chicago. Besides, what would he do with that information anyway? He put his finger on me and I think that's the end of it for now," she explained.

"I hope you're right," Grant said with reluctance.

PART III

At about ten thirty that morning, Grant and Toney woke from sleeping-in that morning. They got up, showered and threw on some cutoffs and tee shirts to go down for coffee. Grant had already explained to Toney that he had planned for brunch, so the traditional breakfast would have to wait until the next day. After coffee, they walked to the area where there was table tennis as well as other sporting games. They played a couple of games. Grant allowed Toney to win or so he said. About noon, they left the game area and went back to their room to change into their active beachwear. A few minutes later they were back in the lobby to meet with Silver again. He had been hired to meet them at twelve thirty to take them to the docks where Grant had setup a special afternoon for his lady. As they rode along Silver once again pointed out significant areas along the route. Fifteen minutes later they arrived at the marina. Grant thanked and paid Silver reminding him that he was not sure of the exact time that they would return, so they would have to get a taxi for transport back to the hotel. A private Yacht was hired to take them sailing. Toney blushed and being the gentleman that he was, Grant held out his hand for her to assist her with boarding the craft. It was a gorgeous day, perfect for sailing. The Yacht was supplied with fresh island fruit, pastries, coffee and mimosas. He had thought of everything. Just short of an hour later they were docking at a small private island, where Grant had arranged for two island musicians to be in place playing the Jamaican type music...one was a vocalist who played the steel drums and the other was a guitarist. Also waiting for them on the island was a chef from the hotel, whom Grant had also hired just for the day. He had arrived before daylight to set up. The chef had a barbecue type grill fired up and ready to go. The smell of the treats that were being prepared was phenomenal. Grilled shrimp and lobster were on the menu as the main course for their late lunch. When Toney realized that this was all for her benefit, tears came to her eyes. She had never been as happy as she was that very moment. Grant poured him and Toney mimosas. They sat on the sand looking out at the main island and the tiny people moving about. They chatted about everything under the sun. The chef approached them almost an hour later to let them know that their specially prepared meal was ready. Grant stood reaching out his hand to help Toney to her feet. Her chair was pulled out for her as she was seated in front of a gourmet meal. If life were to be any better than this, she didn't know if she could bare it. The meal was stupendous.

"Grant, this is excellent. Thank you for such a lovely afternoon. I wish I had thought of it because I want to do something nice for you too."

"You do?" Grant said smiling.

"Well, yes I would," Toney said seriously.

"Okay then," Grant said as he stood from his seat and kneeled at her side.

"Then marry me, please marry me," he asked as he pulled a ring box out of his pocket and opened it.

Shocked, pleased and knocked entirely off her feet she, burst into tears, "Oh, Grant! Yes! Yes my love, I'll marry you!"

Grant took the two carat ring out of the box, nervously putting the massive ring on her finger.

PART IV

Surrant gave Gamble a call back immediately.

"Marriott Montego Bay," and before she could get the rest of her spill out, the caller on the other end of the phone shouted....

"**Guy Gamble room 821,**" he said as an order to her and obviously feeling pretty good about himself.

Shocked to hear someone screaming a demand on the line, the operator said, "Just a moment sir, I'll ring."

The party answered...

"This is Gamble," in a manner as if he had staked a claim.

"Gamble, the black bitch called me as soon as you hung up. How stupid is she? She as much as told me where she was. Her fucking secretary gave me the wrong information earlier, but I'll take care of her later. We're on the right track now. She's in Ocho Rios."

"Yeah? Where in Ocho Rios?"

"She didn't say, but there aren't too many ritzy resorts in Ocho Rios. And, I know her. She wouldn't stay just anywhere. She's a St. John wearing bitch, so you know she's got to keep up the image. Get checked into the Jamaica Grande Ocho Rios and call around to the top three joints there. She'll be registered at one of them I'd be willing to bet. They will be registered in either her name or that half-breed boyfriend of hers name. His name is Grant Palarme. P A L A R M E. Call me back when you get there to give me an update."

"Keep your shirt on, Surrant. I'll give you a call," he said as he hung up.

Gamble threw the few things that he'd brought with him into his suitcase and was out of there in a flash. He was on the first bus headed to Ocho Rios. It was a long bumpy ride and one that he didn't particularly like taking because in his line of work, he had to be able to make a fast departure, which wasn't possible being so far from an airport. But, Surrant was in trouble and he had been good to Gamble over the years, so he would definitely do this for Surrant. Gamble was Surrant's go-to man when things got tough. He was a college schoolmate who was also one of the football team members at Clemson. They hung around together after classes and football games being disgusting jocks, getting drunk, picking fights with other guys and groping girls. He was thrown out of school for doing drugs and holding up a gas station to help pay his tuition. He hadn't faired too well after that, but was fortunate to run into another schoolmate a few years after college and together they started their Private Investigation business, Donner & Gamble. Gamble added his own personal twist to this otherwise legitimate business. He had done a few outside jobs that Donner wasn't aware of which could ultimately cost the team their license. But, Gamble left each outing whistle clean and far, far from scrutiny of the law. He had, on one occasion, actually killed two people for money. So, this job that he was doing for Surrant was a breeze as he saw it.

The bus had been going for over an hour and a half. While he rode he devised his plan. He wanted to get this over with as soon as he could. In and out was his plan. He was deep into meditation when he heard one of the passengers blurt out…

"Did you see that? There is a completely naked person…Did you see that?" Conversation ensured, as they all started to get a glimpse of the person that they saw. As they rode along the conversation got loud and then a few minutes later died out completely. Finally, they pulled up the slope of the Jamaica Grande. The bellmen were there to retrieve the luggage. Gamble stood there waiting for his luggage. He would not let anyone take his bag. He wanted to keep it close by.

"I have a reservation…Fox, Tim Fox.

"Just a moment sir," responded the desk clerk. He presented a credit card, and a driver's license.

"Would you like to buy the plan for meals sir? That will be thirty five dollars per person per day," the clerk asked.

"No, I'll take the regular package," said Gamble.

"Alright sir. Please sign the two areas on the card which are circled and we'll be all set.

"Thanks, sir. Here are your keys. You are in the north tower and the elevators for the north tower are that way. Enjoy your stay."

With that Gamble picked up his bag and went to go get settled.

When he was unpacked, he picked up the phone to see if his target was at the same hotel.

"Toney Chambers room please," Gamble said subtlety.

"One moment sir. Thank you for waiting…I'll ring.

As the phone began to ring, Gamble covered the receiver, Hot damn, I've hit pay dirt!"

"Sir there's no answer, may I take a message?"

"Uh, no ma'am. I'll try again later. Thanks."

Smiling, Gamble took a shower and got dressed for the evening. He wanted to go out to see what he could see. Surrant had already described her, so he wanted to see if he saw anyone fitting Toney's description.

Toney and Grant sat on the beach of their private island watching the sun go down. It had been a tremendous day. All of Toney's cares were so far away. She wanted to pinch herself to see if she was dreaming. This was only their second day of vacation and what a very special two days it had been. As they boarded the yacht Grant held his hand out for her to assure her safety coming on board. They stood on the deck near the front of the craft enjoying the breeze as it hit their faces while blowing through their hair as they sailed along. The main island that had appeared to become smaller and smaller as they rode out into the blue water earlier was now becoming larger as they approached it again.

Most of the locals, as well as the vacationers on the island, had gotten cleaned up from their day at the beach, sailing, horse back riding or touring and were now dressed for dinner. Grant and his new fiancée, were just concluding their day and waltzed through the maze of people to get to their accommodations. Grant opened the door to their hotel suite, stepped aside allowing Toney to enter first. She did but once she was inside she turned to him and crooked her little finger at him taunting and teasing him to go with her…a second later they were in each other's arms sharing a sultry kiss. One by one they got showered and dressed for another evening out. An hour later they left the room and blended in with everyone else.

Silver had told Grant about another island hot spot, which was three blocks from the hotel. They decided to walk there. Grant felt that even though the downtown Ocho Rios area was questionable, three blocks would be all right after dark. He and Toney strolled to the spot that they had been directed to. Many of the other hotel guests had the same plans and were also headed in the same direction. Dinner was nice, but at this point Evita's took the prize. Grant and Toney decided to go back to the hotel to enjoy the party there. At the hotel, the breakfast area had been turned into an island paradise. Many of the servers were adorned with island garb which added a certain flare to the ambiance. Lanterns lit the way to the area and were place in large numbers all throughout to ensure the festive atmosphere. There were island musicians with their dread locks and steel drums and other instruments enthralled in the music, which enticed dancing, which signified a vacationer's Shangri-la. But, all that really mattered to Grant and Toney was that they were together. Anyone could see that they were in love. They drank, danced and enjoyed the remnants of the evening, and at one o'clock they turned in for the night.

The next few days it was more of the same. On the sixth day they decided to spend most of the day at the beach. They had done everything except the beach and going into the city to shop for souvenirs. That morning when they woke, they lay in bed talking about this and that. At ten thirty their phone rang.

"Hello?"

Dead silence on the other end of the phone.

"Hello?" Grant said once more.

The other end of the phone was still open but there was no conversation so Grant hung up.

"It's probably some kids or something. I'm going to jump up and take a shower. You want to grab some breakfast downstairs honey or room service?"

"Room service? No my love. We're in the islands. Who wants to stay cooped up in the room with room service. Besides, I want to show off my new ring, you know," Toney said holding her hand out for Grant to take a look.

"It looks perfect on the hand of the most beautiful girl in the world, too."

A few minutes after Grant was in the shower, the phone rang again.

"Hello?"

"Black bitch. You'd better watch out," click.

Toney stood there frozen. Her entire demeanor changed.

Grant came out of the shower whistling. When he saw Toney's face his mood shifted.

"What's the matter honey? What happened? Are you alright?"

"The phone rang again after you went into the bathroom. When I answered it a man's voice on the other end of the phone said, "Black bitch. You'd better watch out. It startled me that's all."

"I'm calling the hotel manager. I want to see if they can trace these calls," Grant said infuriated.

"No honey. We will not allow anyone to interfere with our vacation. Besides it's a phone call that's all. And, besides we only have a couple of days left here so let's get started. It'll only take me a minute and I'll be ready. We're only putting on our swim wear, right?"

"That's right baby...it's the beach today."

Grant sat there wondering if these calls meant anything. He heard the shower running and while Toney was in the shower he investigated the chances of a trace.

"Hello, we've been getting harassing calls this morning. Is there a call trace system in place?"

"Sir," the manager said, "there is nothing that we can do. We haven't ever had this problem before. Maybe it's someone calling at random, playing a prank. I'll let our security department know about this and they will be in touch with you. I apologize for any inconvenience."

Grant hung up. He sat there thinking to himself that he needed to keep his eyes open.

"There's something that's not right about this," he said out loud.

"Who are you talking to, honey?" Toney hollered from the bathroom.

"Oh, no one, baby....I'm just talking to myself. You almost ready?"

Toney stepped out of the bathroom in her bathing suit.

"Yep...I'm ready," she said reaching for her cover up.

"Wow, look at you. I'm not sure I want anyone else to see all of my stuff," Grant said getting up from the chair and walking coolly over to Toney.

"You are a beautiful woman," he said tenderly.

"I'm going to protect you always no matter what."

Toney smiled.

"You ready?" he asked again as he walked to the door and held it open for his lady.

They got down stairs to the breakfast area and had a light breakfast. While they were eating Gamble appeared in the breakfast area too. He took a seat a couple of tables over from them and ate and read the newspaper while keeping an eye out for Grant and Toney's movement. After breakfast they went on the beach. They chose a couple of lounge chairs near one of two trees on the beach area. They put sun screen on each other and lay there enjoying the sun and the view. After an hour or so, Grant felt playful. He wanted Toney to join him in the water.

"Come on baby. Come on," he coached.

"Maybe later..you go ahead though," she said continuing to lounge.

Grant jumped in. Two minutes later he was way out in the water. Toney rose to her elbows to see where he had gotten to. When she realized how far out he was she became afraid for him. She sat up and started to beckon for him. He hadn't noticed her but had begun to swim back anyway.

Later that evening, just as they had done in each previous night, they went out to dinner and decided to turn in early.

The next morning was the day before they were to leave the island. They decided to go in to town to shop. After breakfast, they struck out for the shopping area. One store after the other they pulled out their Visa cards to purchase special items for members of their staff's and others. Grant bought his mom and sisters a gift, and Toney had something for her mom and dad and Vanessa's baby. By the time they headed for the last of the stores, they wanted to grab a sandwich. They stood at the corner waiting for the light to change while they were researching the area to see what was close. Just before the light changed Grant and Toney both were pushed hard in their backs which hurdled them in to the oncoming traffic. They were both hit by a car which was trying to miss the changing light. Pandemonium ensued. Other visitors, islanders and all came to the aid of Grant and Toney as they lay there in the street bleeding with their packages lying all around them. The driver of the car got out and also tried to help. They were both conscious.

"Are you okay?" one man asked. The ambulance is coming…someone has already called."

"What happened?" Grant asked.

"Who pushed us?"

"Pushed you? Someone pushed you? We didn't see it. We heard the car's brakes screech, which is when we turned to see what was going on. Wow, someone pushed them," the man said out loud starting to look around for any one looking suspicious.

Someone shouted that they saw a man running away from the scene.

"Toney. Toney, honey, are you alright?" Grant asked turning to his lady.

Toney was lying there very still. She was breathing shallowly.

"Oh my God Toney, are you are right?" Grant shouted raising her head to cradle her in his arms.

She began to come to, "What happened? Grant what happened to us?" she asked looking up at all of the sea of faces that stood there looking at them, "What happened?"

"I don't know baby…someone pushed us and we ended up being hit by a car. How are you?"

"I'm not exactly sure. Hopefully they can get us to the hospital or something."

Seconds later a siren was heard in the distance. A few moments more they were on their way, packages and all to the hospital. Three hours went by while they sat there bleeding and hurting when finally they were called and examined by a doctor. They both checked out. They would be fine. No broken bones or fractures and especially no head injuries. What a way to end an otherwise fabulous vacation. But, they both knew it was time to go. As they rode back to the hotel, Grant pondered the thought about the phone calls earlier. Did they have anything to do with the accident? Or, was it an accident? He didn't want to jump to any hasty conclusions, but in his heart he felt that something was up. The next morning they packed and headed for the airport in Montego Bay.

EIGHT

A bump in the night startled her from her sleep. It was a good thing that she took the Excedrin PM when they got in last night. She was still jittery from the flight and the thoughts of the accident. It was a really great vacation other than the accident. She felt like they had been gone for an eternity. All that had happened. What was it all about? Who was that man and why had they been singled out of all the people on the island? The special way that Grant had set everything up was so loving. Every moment was special except for the accident. What had Toney so revved up was the fact that she and Grant had devised a plan that was foolproof. Surrant had better be on his toes from this point on she thought as she got up to investigate the noise. She tipped toed through the condominium. There was nothing there, nothing at all. Was it all in her mind? Her thoughts shifted to the day ahead as she got back in bed for a few more minutes. It was only four a.m. and the effects of the sleep aid were still hanging on. She drifted off again and at five a m the clock alarm sounded. She jumped to her feet realizing that she had to get going. She wanted to be in early because she just knew she had a lot to do. Her routine was waiting for her. She worked out, took a shower, prepared her coffee, and got dressed as she normally did. She moved forward continuing with her routine, breaking it only when she looked for her makeup which was still in her cosmetic bag, so she started to finish unpacking. As she looked through her luggage she retrieved some of the smaller gifts that they had bought. They had brought back so many souvenirs. She had a trinket for just about everyone in the office. She wanted to make sure to take the gifts the first morning back since the week would be so full of the big meeting and the fallout from it...whatever that might be.

At the break of dawn, she was on the elevator headed for her car. She felt pretty good considering. The drive was fast considering there was very little traffic. A few minutes later she turned in to the garage of her building. She waved at the security guard and pulled into her parking space. Two large shopping bags, her brief case and her laptop was a bit much for her to struggle with, but she managed. On the way to the forty fifth-floor she thought about everything that had happened over the last few years. She had come a long way, but the more ground she covered the more she had to deal with. The next moment she thought about the condition of the office. She knew that there would be a huge pile of work waiting for her in the office.

She stuck her key into the door and walked into the virtually dark, quiet office. How peaceful she thought. In a couple of hours it would be buzzing with chatter, phones ringing and people moving about. Everyday in their operation was nonstop. As she crossed the outer office floor she recalled the first time that she walked into this place. She was shaky at best; knowing that this is what she had worked for during all the proceeding years from the days when she was over worked and drastically underpaid. During those days she often wondered if things would ever get any better for her. Would she ever get her just do? She opened the door to her office and quickly put down her load, turning on the light in the same motion. She was still so sore all over. Her eyes moved swiftly to her desk area.

"Hummmm" she grunted.

"Sonjia had obviously worked overtime to have me this organized," she mumbled to herself.

Her stack was measurable, but nothing nearly like her thoughts. She carefully took a seat behind her massive desk and began to plunge away at her work. About forty-five minutes into it, she heard someone in the outer office.

"Hello?"..."Hello?" Toney hadn't heard him initially. Marvin saw the lights on in the outer office and the door open and stepped inside to investigate.

"Is there anyone in here?" the guard asked with a very puzzled, perplexed tone.

"I'm here," Toney responded strongly with a hint of concern. "What seems to be the problem?" she continued as she raised up swiftly with an obvious sense of purpose from her desk forgetting about her fragile condition?

The guard was just about at the entrance of Toney's office when Toney got to the doorway. They met at Sonjia's desk.

"I wasn't sure there was anyone in here," the guard said. "The door to the outer office was standing open with no lights on in the outer offices and the appearance of impropriety.

"Oh, hi Marvin. It's only me. Did I leave the door open?"

"I guess you did, Miss Chambers. You've got to be more safety minded. This is a public building and anyone could wander in here. It's just not safe for a woman alone," he cautioned.

"Of course you're right, Marvin. I had several packages in my hands when I arrived. I guess the only thing that I was thinking of was to get the heavy load out of my arms. I promise to be careful," Toney chimed.

"Well…okay, Miss Chambers. If you promise to watch it, I'll let you get back to work. I'll lock you in here. You've still got about an hour before the regular gang arrives. I'll see you later," he said as a granddad would have.

With the last of his words he walked cautiously to the other side of the outer offices and closed the door behind him.

'What a nice man,' Toney thought as she went out into the outer offices and turned on all of the lights, the copier and started a pot of fresh coffee. By the time she got back to her desk, she sat back in her comfortable chair and sipped her freshly made cup of java. She reflected on the last few weeks. Time really does fly by, she thought to herself. It seemed like it was just yesterday that I was just sitting here planning our vacation and since Grant and I were in Jamaica, she thought. Things were getting way too complicated. Who was that crazy guy anyway? I wonder was that an accident or was it intentional? Who would want to hurt either of us? Toney sat at her desk trying to focus on her work. Not only was she daydreaming about other things in her earlier days, but now she felt continual danger since their near demise over the weekend as well. She had to make a concerted effort and push herself to focus now. Sonjia was the first to arrive. The rest of the gang began to arrive and one by one the office filled with the employees who reported to Toney. Toney and Sonjia shared a brief hug as Sonjia welcomed her back into the office. 'Sonjia...you have no idea how much Grant and I thank you for thinking so fast on your feet during that situation with Surrant."

"That's no problem...none at all. You're right. He really is a piece of work. I don't understand how you deal with him so often," she reported.

They met briefly and reviewed the week.

Toney handed Sonjia a pile of work and Sonjia scooted out to her desk to begin her tasks.

The buzz of the intercom shook her back into the present.

Buzz...buzz

"Yes Sonjia, what is it?" as she forced herself back to then business at hand.

"The rough run of the second blush of the information you needed to look at is just about complete. Do you want me to bring it in now or did I interrupt something?" Sonjia asked.

"It's okay. I can look at it now. The meeting is tomorrow and we need to be prepared. Bring it in," Toney said.

A couple of seconds later Sonjia tapped on the door and in the same motion came through the door with the report.

"How do we look?" Toney asked pointedly? Anyone could tell that Toney was under some sort of strain.

"We're almost there, I think," Sonjia said.

"All we need is a once over and clarification here," as she pointed to page 7, the second paragraph and the two charts on pages 101 and 116.

"Everything else looks real good."

Complete silence fell on the room as Toney reviewed Sonjia's areas of concern. A couple of minutes later Toney took her pen and made some adjustments.

"It's nearly ten now. Try to have these changes to me by eleven. I'd like to take them with me downstairs, while I can grab a bite to eat and review everything. I want to make sure that everything is all done by two. I have to leave early today, and since the review with Charles and me starts at seven in the morning…and, then the next day I go on first… I have to be ready."

"Okay, I'll get right on it," responded Sonjia

Toney went back to the paperwork stack that she had to work through before lunch.

Sonjia went back to her desk and began her tasks. When she sat down, Amber was staring at her so much so that Sonjia felt her eyes seemingly looking straight through her.

"What is it Amber?" asked Sonjia.

"Why are you staring at me like that?

"We've noticed that there is something going on with Toney. What is it? She was spaced out when we saw her this morning. You can tell me," Amber said.

"She has the big meeting coming up. Everyone is stressed. If you think Toney is out of it...you should see the people upstairs," Sonjia explained.

Actually that wasn't the real deal, but she had to protect Toney. She knew that Toney had a lot on her plate. If it weren't for Grant she would be in over her head. The job...where funds are missing in four to five areas, jealousy, insubordination with Surrant and the others, the accident in Jamaica, Vanessa's problems...what else could she bare? Thank God her parents were doing fair. Toney was such a gentle giving spirit. The years had made her a bit tougher, but not nearly tough enough. If she hadn't been born smart and developed a natural ability for business, she would have never made it in Corporate America, Sonjia thought. At ten minutes to noon the intercom buzzed....

"I know you didn't want to be disturbed, Ms. Chambers, but its Mr. Parlarme," announced Sonji'.

"Thanks, Sonjia...this is a welcomed interruption believe me. You seem to know me so well.

"Hello handsome, purred Toney...how's your day?"

"All better now, just to hear your sweet, sweet voice. How are things going and how are you feeling?"

"Really, really busy but still a little sore from the accident. The finishing touches to redefine my primary objectives for tomorrow are coming along nicely. Sonjia is such a help. We should be ready by two to two thirty today. I think I'm still on target for leaving early. Since we were out all last week, I got a few errands to run. What about you…how's it going? How are you feeling?"

"Basically the same old same old. I'm a little sore too, but that's all. I've got my own challenges here too, but I'm coping. The two wiz kids are really feeling their oats today. I found out that they have been through my case load trying to get the boss to turnover some of my best money makers to them. It never stops. But, if I'm any kind of man at all, I can handle it. As a matter of fact, I rather like the mental gymnastics. One thing about it, we've been conditioned to deal with it. Unlike those who've had everything handed to them…you know what I mean?"

"Honey, you're so upbeat. Thanks for always finding the right words to say. They really keep me going. I love you."

"Tone…I love you too…I'll talk with you later this evening,, okay?" said Grant as if someone walked into his office.

Toney returned to the stack of work that she had. She was knocking it down one item at a time. At twelve-fifteen Toney took a break. She had been going non-stop since she arrived before six this morning. She stood at her desk and stretched. She decided to go downstairs to grab a quick bite. On the way out, she stopped by Sonjia's desk to get the latest updates in order to mull over them at lunch. Sonjia looked up sort of surprised that Toney had taken a break on her own. She never did that. Sonjia thought about it and she was certain that she was always talking Toney into walking away from time to time. This was very good, she thought.

"Sonjia, Give me whatever you've finished at this point. I'll read over it while I'm downstairs. And, by the time I get back you should be finished with the rest right? Then, you can go to lunch while I review whatever remains...how does that sound?"

"That sounds good...because, I'm almost finished," she replied.

Sonjia handed Toney a stack of documents.

"Thanks...I'll be back in thirty to forty-five minutes. Take any messages, okay?" Toney said as she walked away. All eyes were on Toney. She was still in a semi fog and everyone could tell it. Before she knew it Toney was on the elevator headed to the cafeteria. She wanted to take a seat in the rear out of the site of any would be intruders. She wasn't even in the mood to say hello to anyone. She had to stay focused. There was way too much to lose and she had to be at the top of her game from the first moment to the very last word. The elevator stopped on the thirty-seventh floor. As the doors opened Toney saw two men waiting to board the elevator and what appeared to be a woman standing in back of them. When the two men boarded, the woman became visible. It was

Cameron and it was clear to Toney at that instant that she was obviously just barely existing. She looked drained.

"Hi Cameron. How are you?" Toney said, as she seemed to leave the personal fog that she was in, in order to reach out to this nice lady who was obviously hurting.

"Oh, hi Toney," she barely got the words out.

"I didn't see you. I guess I was a bit out of it," Cameron said in a depressed demeanor.

Before Toney could say a word Cameron continued…

"Things have been a bit challenging since I saw you last. The big guys have slipped another one in on me and I just feel like my back is against the wall. What do I have to do to be treated fairly?" she said with her eyes filling up with huge crocodile tears.

"I mind my own business, I work hard, I do the best job not withstanding any of the other employees and they have told me so on more that one occasion. Why do they treat people like this?" she said as she broke completely broke down.

The other passengers on the elevator began to feel uncomfortable. They started squirming and became restless. It was evident as they began turning around taking quick glances at this sad woman and finally looking at one another with questions in their eyes. With the exception of the soft moan of Cameron's weeping, silence fell over the elevator car. The elevator doors opened up to the second floor, where everyone got off and headed to their destinations.

Toney had reached out for Cameron during the ride down and was holding her with tenderness.

"Why don't we get a table in the back like we did before and talk this through?" she asked as they walked arm in arm toward the restaurant.

"That's fine," Cameron replied in a tearful somewhat muffled voice. "But, I don't see what it will help in the end. I'm getting the short end of the stick either way you look at it. And after it's all said and done there's not a damned thing that I can do about it anyway."

Cameron walked over to the buffet line, pulled a tray and started walking through the line. She walked as if there was a ton of lead in her shoes. Depression was her complete being and it showed.

Toney went to the only area available where a table had just been vacated in the center of the rear of the room. She put her stack of papers on the table to claim it for them and went to join Cameron in the line. Toney pointed out to Cameron the area of the table that she had claimed for them and motioned to her that she would join her in a second. By the time Toney got through the line and eventually to Cameron, her mind was completely engrossed in Cameron's troubles and completely off of her tasks at hand. Toney took a seat and immediately began to console Cameron in the best way that she knew how.

"Things will get better...you've just got to hang in there," she said tenderly.

"Did something else happen since we last spoke?" Toney asked.

"Hell yes! Those sons of bitches brought a barbie-doll-looking girl into our department who was formally a lead administrative person. They gave her a Senior Meeting planners job. She has no experience in meeting planner and has no accountabilities as they relate to the job itself. They are paying her very close to what I'm making with promises to promote her to my same job title and money in six months. What could they be thinking about? This bitch has to be fucking one or more of them or maybe something even more graphic. I just don't know how much more I can take. I'm being pushed to the limit. And, the low down part about it is they want me to train and share my knowledge with her. They must be out of their fucking minds," Cameron said in a much louder voice.

At this point she didn't care who heard her. Her mood changed within a split second. She moved swiftly from a depressed state to one of pointed agitation. She was salivating.

"Cameron, calm down. Calm down, sweetheart. Don't allow these guys to get you this upset. You're not doing yourself any good at all," Toney said with authority and understanding. It was not as if she hadn't been in similar situations as well.

"The state that you're in you can't be thinking rationally. The way to get back at them is to be the best that you can be. Do the best job of any employee that they have ever had. Start looking for another job somewhere where you will be appreciated. The fact that you have allowed yourself to gravitate to this state is an indication that some strategy is needed. We have to talk more about this, but I have to review my paperwork and get back. There is a big meeting tomorrow that I simply have to be prepared for. It'll take me the next two hours to get through the final preparations. The two days of meetings should be done by Wednesday night. Can we get together on Thursday? You know I'll help you in any way that I can."

Toney's soothing conversation and sincere words seemed to quiet Cameron's despair somewhat.

"Toney, for the time that we've known one another you have always been a good friend. I want you to know that I really do appreciate you in every way. You are a very special person," Cameron quipped.

"I'm a real mess right now, but I promised to pull myself together and think things through," Cameron continued.

"That's good. I know it's unsettling, but this can be handled. Now, where did you put my stack of work," Toney said looking around the area where they were seated.

"What work," Cameron asked?

"The work that I put down to mark our spot," she said in a panic.

"I never saw any paperwork. The table was bare when I sat down here. The only reason that I sat down here was because the table was the only one available."

"Are you sure?" Toney asked beginning to lose some control. Some of those documents were confidential. They lay out some projects that would be for special eyes only.

She jumped up asking those nearby if they had seen her work.

"Have you seen the papers that I laid here," she asked the first two men feverishly.

Startled each of the individuals that she approached rared back shaking their heads saying or indicating no.

"I had some papers lying on the table here, have you seen the papers?" she shuffled further and further.

"Have you? Have you?" as she moved from table to table quizzing people, she got nowhere.

Finally one lady spoke up saying, "there was a man walking away from that table a minute or so after you laid your papers down."

"What man? What did he look like? Which way did he go? Please, it's really important," Toney pleaded!

The lady responded," I didn't really pay that much attention."

Cameron was still dealing with her situation mentally, but she had begun to pull herself together enough to try assisting and consoling Toney.

"Honey, don't you have additional copies upstairs? Maybe one of the people from your office recognized what the papers were and didn't see you and picked them up for you. Let's think the best thoughts," Cameron tried to persuade her.

"Maybe you're right…I'll rush right upstairs to check it out. I'll see you later," she rumbled.

Toney walked fast to the trashcan, dumped her trash and in one motion shoved toward the elevator. Her dainty steps turned into clunky wide steps and a couple of seconds later she was impatiently pacing while waiting for one of the cars to take her back to her office.

PART II

Grant had had enough too. He worked through his backlog of items keeping an ear out for the action in the office. He hadn't been back long enough to find out what all he missed. It was a ritual for him to come back from a business trip or vacation and have staff movements or people fired or even hired while he was out. His office door was half open giving the passerby's the illusion that he was fast at work and oblivious to the chatter that was going on. Little snatches of conversations floated through the air along with telephones ringing and the natural sounds of an office environment. There was not much that he could make out. His secretary Millicent Fuller was a gossipmonger who participated vigorously in the stories that were hot in the office. She was quite at the moment enthralled in her work. She was an attractive, real dark skinned heavyset woman with long dyed red hair about five feet two, who dressed well and had superb secretarial skills. She had long one-inch sculptured nails painted red and wore heavy makeup. He had determined a few weeks after he arrived at the firm to let her be the conduit for him in obtaining valuable information about the office. Besides, this was her character and who was he to try and stop nature? He had chosen the right course with Millicent. She had over the years given Grant some valuable information and on a couple of occasions the information that she provided him saved his neck. Sarah Gaunther the Senior Partner's secretary and Millicent were good friends. Sarah's long blonde hair was highlighted with gray. She was in her late forties and not easy to get to know. Millicent initially was the last person that Sarah wanted to get to know but because of the administrative revolving door, the two of them had outlasted all the others. They migrated to each other several years earlier and had been tight since then. They frequently went to lunch together and shared moments of information sessions at least a dozen times everyday.

"Hi, Grant, welcome back! How was vacation?" Sarah asked as she walked down the corridor past Millicent noticing that Grant's door was ajar.

"Oh, hello Sarah. Our vacation was exceptional this time. My lady and I had a wonderful and much needed break. What did I miss while we were away?" Grant inquired.

"It was the same old thing if you ask me with the exception of the mail room incident, but you'll have to ask one of the other attorneys about it.

I'm too embarrassed to talk to a man about it," Sarah said turning red in the face.

Millicent chimed in, "Well I'm not, Grant. Beverly Gardner, the fucking troublemaker was caught in the mailroom screwing on top of the box table. She and Harold, yes married Harold, were bumping and grinding all over the room. They said that it smelled awful in there and that she was butt naked. He had her legs hoisted in the air bumping her up against the equipment. We heard that the noise they were making was what got them busted. I could understand more if it was nine or ten at night and everyone was gone, but it was about six o'clock. Why, half of the staff was still here, how stupid. How loose can a woman be?" Millicent said almost in a whisper.

"She deserves whatever she gets. Besides, she's a hellion. Nobody's protected around here with her around, so it's better if they kick her ass out of here in any event," she continued.

Sarah was mortified as she stood there with Millicent going on and on. She couldn't believe that Millicent was going on like she was. She loved Millicent, but she had tried continually over the two years that she had known her to smooth off some of her rough edges. She felt that Millicent had come a long way from where she was, but knew she still had miles to go.

"Millie...that's enough. Give the girl a break," Sarah persuaded.

"A break? Has she given anybody else a break? That bitch deserves whatever she gets," shrieked Millicent.

Several people looked up in the immediate area when they heard her, as her voice got a little louder.

"Millicent would you step in my office please?" Grant said as he thought to himself... 'Why did I even ask that question?

Millicent got up and sauntered in to Grant's office, "Yes?"

Millicent turned to Sarah saying, "Girl, I'll see you later."

Sarah nodded her head to Millicent and continued down the corridor to her area.

"Mill...you've got to control yourself. This is still a business and I know how worked up you can get, but you've got to control it, okay?"

"I'm sorry, Grant. Beverly has started something with all of us and now we've got her. Everybody pays in the end."

"I believe that too, but you have to keep it down, okay?" he cautioned.

Before Millicent could answer, Grant hit her with a question that would get the information that he was really after, "While I have you here, have the boys been behaving? Any updates on them?

"Three days last week they were both in the board room with the old man. We all saw them through the smoked glass window. The powwows lasted at least three hours each time. No one has a clue what it was all about, because the doors were closed. It looked like serious stuff though. They went through mounds and mounds of papers. The old man asked me for the Kendricks and the Lavery files. One thing may or may not have had anything to do with the other but ain't it funny, they didn't need the files while you were here? And, when the meeting broke on

Friday, the shorter twin, as the girls and I call him, was smiling and whistling for the rest of the day. Believe me there is something up," reported Millicent.

"That's good to know Mill. I knew that I could count on you," Grant told her.

"Now get yourself outta here and get back to work. And, keep yourself calm, okay?"

"Okay Grant, I'll keep my eyes and ears open. And I'll get as much out of Sarah as I can. You know she sees and hears a lot!"

Millicent loved this king of shit. She was really into it, as she got up and quickly walked back to her desk. The office was at its regular level with people hovered near the coffee maker full of chatter about their weekends, bad jokes and other things. Grant and Millicent's area was directly across the corridor for that space which gave them a bird's eye view of all of the office action except what transpired within the four walls of the individual offices. As Grant had witnessed in the past, all the closed-door conversations had their way of making it to public knowledge. One of the participants or the other would eventually run their mouths to the wrong person and the whole office would be gossiping about it. Grant had gotten caught up in that once in his career vowing to keep his mouth shut from that point on.

At noon, Nicholas Samson stopped by, tapped on Grant's door, pushing it further open.

"Hi Grant! Welcome back. Want to get some lunch?"

"Sure, Nick. Give me fifteen minutes and I'll stop by and pick you up. That'll give me time to put this to bed before we go," Grant said with a straight face.

It was time to play poker. Sleeping with the enemy was his favorite game. Although Stanley, the old man, was fair…he was naïve to a certain degree and could be persuaded if the right mix of information were put together. Grant had to find out the plan. Nick had been sent to go to lunch with him to get some pertinent information from him. But, Grant had other thoughts. It was time to separate the men from the boys. Grant was next in line for a partnership and the shorter twins wanted to bump him out so that one if not both of them would have his spot.

NINE

Terror was in her heart and written all over her face! Some of the information was confidential. Some of the information was brand-new and cutting edge, which could be rendered priceless. She had spent hours on end for months working on over half of the items in the stack. If the information had gotten into the wrong hands, she would be devastated. And, if the information had been stolen by someone who was out to get her, now couldn't be a better time for them to make her look bad. But, right now she couldn't be sure of anything. And, if the information had been stolen for the sole purpose of giving it to one of their competitors, it would be very damaging. At least her presentation was first at the meeting. Nothing could stop that, she thought. She would give one hell of a presentation and then the new trend setting standards would be trademarked and she would be safe. She would put the plans in action before anyone else could and have the rights to the trend setting ideas and this madness would be over.

"What on earth is going on?" Toney mumbled to herself. "There wasn't another computer-related organization in the building that she knew of. Maybe it was a visitor to the building? Maybe Cameron was right. It could have been one of my guys. Maybe even someone for the top floor. At least if it was someone for the boss's office I can get the information back. I'll get a slap on the wrist, but I can handle that, she thought.

All sort of things ran through her mind as she paced. It was lunchtime and everyone was moving about. Most of the traffic was headed out of the building. All of the elevators were homing at the top of the building. A few more minutes and she'd find out what was what. The elevator took forever to get there. Seemed as if she paced with her heavy legs and feet for an hour. Everything was moving in slow motion to her. It was in fact only a few minutes, but it seemed like a very long time. The ride on the elevator to the forty-fifth floor was like a slow boat to China it appeared.

When she arrived to her floor, Toney barely waited for the elevator doors to fully open and she was out. She raced down the corridor and threw herself through the doors of her outer offices. The noise of Toney hurling herself against the door to force it open startled her employees that were in the immediate area. Her staff noticed her spaced out look immediately and her body language demonstrated that her normal persona was missing and replaced by the takeover of a total lack of self-discipline. She was hell bent on getting to the bottom of the mishap in the cafeteria which had successfully erased all of her regular daintiness, professionalism and other characteristics which were always in tact but now were virtually none existent at that moment.

"Sonjia, would you come into my office, please? I need you desperately," she said as she rushed past Sonjia's desk. She shoved into her big solid oak door, as they entered her office. Toney stepped aside and allowed Sonjia to walk in first.

"What's going on Toney? You're frightening me. You look like you've seen a ghost," Sonjia said very concerned.

"I was merely going to the cafeteria to get something to eat," Toney stammered!

"I ran into Cameron. She was so upset," she continued.

"I tried to console her, which totally took my mind off of the tasks that I had to take care of. I laid down my paperwork to mark the spot where we wanted to sit-down. By the time that I got my food and joined Cameron...my paperwork had disappeared. Just disappeared. Can you believe that? It's crazy. I don't know what to do."

"Toney, whatever you need. I'll do whatever I can for you," Sonjia pledged.

Silence fell over the office for a couple of seconds. You could almost hear Toney's mind working trying to resolve this mess.

"Sonjia, I want you to challenge everyone in the office to see if one of them picked up the paperwork. Maybe they noticed that it was mine and got it for me thinking I had left it there by mistake. Will you check into it for me? If I do it myself right now, I'd be a dead giveaway," she said shakily?

"I could conceivably be in big trouble," she continued as she fell back into her chair in despair.

"Sure, Toney. Relax. I'll take care of it. Some of the employees are at lunch, but everyone will be back inside thirty minutes. In the meantime, I'll reprint what I gave you. You can review it and we'll move forward so you'll be prepared for tomorrow, okay?" Sonjia said in a soothing voice.

"The last month has been uncanny. It's first one thing then another. I'm loosing control altogether. I'm falling apart. I've never been this weak...never," Toney whispered.

Sonjia moved over to Toney and put her hand on her shoulder saying, "It'll be alright, you'll see."

Sonjia quietly walked out and closed the door.

Toney sat back and looked up at the ceiling. She wanted to try and calm her nerves.

She chanted to herself… "it'll be alright…it'll be alright," as she closed her eyes to gain control.

A moment later she had started to daydream again about another of the rough times that she had in her earlier years. She had been through hell a few times and each of them was really at the hands of someone else. Those were the only times as she recalled that she completely lost control. She was so young. She had grown to be a very good-looking young lady with scores of self-confidence now, she reminisced. She was five feet-five, very pretty with a voluptuous body and now so much further along than when she left Lexington. She had actually become quite a woman. College had really been good for her physical self as well as intellectually. It was time for her to set out on her own and make a way for herself in this world. She was a spiritual being who with the love and strength of God had made it from the farm to college to Corporate America. Fresh out of school, she had taken a typing test and passed for it for a secretarial job at Xerox. That was the only entry-level job available and she thought it prudent to at least get her foot in the door. She had set her sites on and hoped to be hired at either Xerox or IBM. Her degree was in a new field in the college's curriculum, computer science. All she needed was to that first push to join one of a major fortune 500 companies and she knew she could do the rest. She wanted to take the job that would offer the most money. The benefits at that time were not the issue for her. She wanted to be able to afford all the things that she hadn't had before, so money was the consequential issue. Three days later, she was called to take the test for IBM and passed as well. She weighed each offer and accepted the IBM position. How lucky could she be? She had been hired out of college at IBM. She remembered how excited she was. She couldn't sleep the night before she started. She wanted to make a good impression on her immediate boss who had nothing to do with actually hiring her. The screening route for IBM was strictly through Human Resources. At first, Joyce was pleasant. She was thoroughly surprised that Tony was Negro. Joyce had had very little if any interaction with Negroes. But, Toney's credentials spoke volumes for her intellect and her accomplishments in school. Joyce initially displayed an obvious caution about Toney. It made Toney feel uncomfortable and unwelcome, but she chalked it up to the fact that they were just meeting one another. As had happened in the past, Toney was sure that she could win Joyce over. Joyce on the other hand had determined that she would watch Toney closely as she confirmed her fears about Toney and see where that took her. As the days turned into weeks, Toney did all that she could. She came in early, stayed late. That's why she could relate so much with Cameron and what she was going through. She went over and above constantly. So, the first ninety days in Corporate America was working out even though she and one other person in the building were the only two Blacks there. For the first time in her life, she was making two hundred and thirty six dollars and fifty-two cents every two weeks. She had landed an awesome job. Six weeks into the job, she befriended Sally, Thomas and Ralph, who were all programmers. They liked Toney almost instantly and had begun to invite her to lunch often and eventually to their favorite bar, which was only a few blocks from the office. Toney felt like this was her ticket. As days went by she felt more and more like she was at home. She really hit it off with some of her other co-workers too...everyone, but her boss. Joyce didn't like the fact that Toney was fitting in so quickly. The fact that Toney was black was a turnoff to Joyce. She walked around closely observing. Toney's naivete had her where she hadn't expected anything was wrong. One day toward the end of her third month there, near the end of the day, her phone rang from an inside extension.

"Toney Chambers, may I help you?"

"Toney, this is Joyce, would you please come down to my office?"

"Yes Joyce. I'll be right there."

Toney immediately raised up from her desk, walked briskly across the twelfth floor and took the elevator down to the tenth floor. Toney's area was located on the twelfth floor next to the systems programmers of which she gave administrative support. She approached Joyce's office door and gave a light tap on the window indicating that she had arrived. Joyce beckoned for Toney to step inside.

"Hi, Joyce," she said light heartedly. "What can I do for you?" Toney inquired.

"It has come to my attention that you are turning in documents with multiple errors. I've been keeping copies of all of the work with the errors. I've asked everyone who you provide administrative support to, to copy all the work that you do for them and give it to me before they ask you to clean it up. And, I've also been informed that you still don't know how to use the magnetic typewriters after almost ninety days on the job. What is your problem? You are taking too long to get up to speed and to do the job that you are being paid to do and there is the matter of all of the errors. Your hundred and twenty-day evaluation is coming up soon. If things don't get any better, you'll be written up and the next thing will be termination," Joyce said sarcastically.

"I'll clean everything up. I can type over eighty words a minute. I was the best in my class in college, but the magnetic typewriters are something that is so new, it's taking me some time to get used to them. Perhaps you can give me some assistance and I can learn faster." Toney asked.

"You've had your training. Why should you get more training than anyone else? No special favors. IBM is an industry leader and you're lucky to have a job with such a prestigious organization. Stay late, come in early, you're on your own," she smirked.

"I'm sorry you feel that way. Who's idea was this? Don't you like me? Why won't you help me? You know I work hard and that I have the credentials. Why are you doing this?" Toney asked in a quandary. Joyce said sarcastically, "You're one of many and no more special than any of the others of your kind. You're on your own. We'll talk again in a few days.

Joyce put her head down and started to work on the papers in front of her totally ignoring Toney. Toney sat there for a few seconds longer and decided that this meeting was over when she got up and walked out of Joyce's office in shock. And to think that she thought everything was going so well.

The next few weeks were awful. Joyce was lurking over her shoulder at every turn. She watched Toney to make sure she wasn't late coming back from lunch that day. She was standing at the door when Toney arrived in the morning and when she left in the evening. This went on for almost a month. Toney was becoming a nervous wreck. A week later, Joyce got word that she was being transferred to New York. But before she left, Joyce made sure to get Toney out. During Joyce's last week, she called Toney back into her office.

"Well Toney, you didn't make it, sweetheart. The best that I can do for you is to get you to agree to a mutual separation so you can find suitable employment elsewhere. Here's your pink slip," she said as she handed the paper to Toney.

Toney went crazy. She saw red. She was first in shock and then lashed out. She stood up and literally crawled over the desk after Joyce. Joyce was in shock. She hadn't expected this from such a young kid. Toney ended up in the chair on top of Joyce as the two of them toppled over falling to the floor. Toney began to punch Joyce in the face while Joyce shielded herself from the feverish licks. A few seconds later they picked themselves up, both off balance as Toney grabbed Joyce in the collar. She lifted her up with strength that was as much a surprise to Toney herself, as it was to Joyce.

Toney said, "If I ever lay eyes on you again, I'll kill you, bitch. You are evil and one day you will get yours."

Joyce's eyes bugged out of her head. She was both afraid and shocked. Toney released the lock that she had on Joyce and turned and walked away. She didn't know what to think or what to do next. She packed her few belongings and walked out of the building on her own. As she got to the very front door of the building, security approached her walking her to the street while telling her that she was never allowed back on their property again.

The feeling that she had at that time was much like the feeling she was experiencing at this very moment. What would she do now? Who had the papers?

Tap, tap, tap on her door sounded.

"Who is it?"

"Toney… it's me," Sonjia said.

"Come in…did you find out anything," Toney asked frantically?

"Nothing. No one knows anything, "Sonjia said bewilderedly.

"I've discretely asked everyone. No one knows anything about it. The staff is asking questions. What should I tell them?"

"Nothing. Tell them that I misplaced some work. That's all they need to know. I'll take it from there. Sonjia here's what I've already looked at with corrections. Give me a copy of everything that I had when I left for lunch along with these changes. I'll review all of it while I'm at home. I'll still be all right. The reception kicks off at six thirty tomorrow evening. And, the opening remarks on Wednesday morning. I'll be ready," Toney said sounding stronger.

"That's the Toney that I know and love. I'll be right back with another copy," Sonjia said backing out of the door.

As soon as the door to Toney's office was closed, Toney started packing up. Sonjia sat down at her desk and started printing the complete corrected presentation.

June asked her, "what's going on with Toney. Is she losing it?"

"June, you've got your nerve asking me something like that. If I told Toney what you said you'd be out of here. I'd back away if I were you," Sonjia said sharply.

With a looked of being slapped across the face, June went back to her work immediately because she knew that Sonjia meant business.

A few minutes later Sonjia went back into Toney's office. Toney had finished packing up everything except the packet that Sonjia had for her, then she was ready to leave.

"I've had enough for today. Thanks so much precious for your support. I don't know what I'd do without you. Seems like I'm saying that continually lately, right?"

"That's what I'm here for. Either we win together or we lose together. Try and get some rest. It's been a hell of a day for you. We'll try it again tomorrow."

Toney nodded yes and with her body slumping as to admit defeat, she drugged herself out of the office to the elevator.

Toney boarded the elevator. She thought about the events of the day and couldn't do anything but laugh out loud and shake her head. Things were really weird. Her mind immediately shifted to Surrant. She wondered if he had anything to do with any of this. She wouldn't put it past him. But, how? He was in Southern California and she was in Chicago. The hair on the back of her neck stood up. Would he dare go this far? She had better start being cautious. While she walked to the parking lot, she was careful of her surroundings. The situation with Marvin this morning and the door being left open could have ended up a disaster. As she started her car she had the feeling that Surrant really did have something to do with this. Her thoughts shifted to the accident in Jamaica. Was he behind that too? She picked up her cell phone to place a call to Grant. She wanted to apprise him of the mishap and her thoughts about Surrant.

"Mr.. Parlarme's office, this is Millicent may I help you?"

"Hi Mill, how are you? Is he there? " Toney asked innocently.

"Miss Chambers, how are you?" she responded cheerfully? Grant went to lunch with one of the twins. Can you believe it… the twin came to Grant and asked him to lunch? What is that all about? This just keeps getting better and better, don't you think?"

"Why? Did something happen this morning or while we were gone," Toney asked as she settled in to her car seat?

"Three big meetings with the old man and the twins. The shorter twin came to me to ask for two of Grant's files. He said the old man wanted them so I couldn't question it. We all watched through the smoked glass window of the board- room. Like I told Grant, I can't swear what it was all about, but it looked like they were up to no good."

"Really? Grant and I are both having our challenges. Mill, please ask him to give me a call when he gets back. I'm on my way home, so have him call me in the car or at home, okay?"

"OK Toney…take care."

Toney hung up the phone. It was amazing to her that people were always operating in such an underhanded ways. Who could anyone really trust?

Toney got out of her car remembering that the gifts the she and Grant brought back from Jamaica were still in a heap on the sofa in her office. She had forgotten to pass them out with all that she had to do. She grabbed all of the stuff that she had brought home and headed to her condominium. She opened the door, walked in with the thought on her mind that she needed to call Sonjia to ask her to pass out the gifts. She had everyone's names on each one. She put the key in the door turned it and gently opened it stepping in while leaning over to pick up her brief case. As she turned around she was started by Helen her housekeeper. She had stopped ' by to pick up her sweater, which had been there for over three weeks. She had forgotten it so many times.

"Hi Helen! You frightened me! I wasn't expecting you. You were just here on Friday, right? Everything looks so nice and fresh," Toney rambled.

"Toney dear. What's troubling you? You startled me too…I wasn't expecting you to even be at home at this time of day. I'm packing to go to Alaska to visit Anthony and his family for two weeks and even though it's rather warm in Chicago now its only in the mid sixties in Anchorage. So, I really needed this sweater. So what's happening? Why are you looking so worried? Tell me about it," Helen asked.

"There's so much going on, I can't even think of where to begin."

"How about the beginning? That's always a good place to start don't you think?

"Okay," Toney said. "But, first I have to make a phone call, change clothes and I'll tell you all about it."

Toney went into her bedroom throwing her load on her bed. She sat on the side of the bed to call Sonjia.

"Sonjia, Dear…I left all those gifts that Grant and I bought for the staff in Jamaica on the sofa in my office. Would you please pass them out? I wanted to do it while I was there but today turned in to such a nightmare."

PART II

Grant and Terry, one of the shorter twins took a taxi to the Jamaican Kitchen on South Michigan. Grant wanted just one more taste of Jamaica and then he'd put it away for the rest of the year. He and Toney had enjoyed so many things about their vacation and Grant wasn't ready to quite let it all go yet. Terry was game for anything that Grant recommended. He was after something and Grant was going to take him for a ride, while he was trying to get whatever it was that he was after. They arrived at the Jamaica Kitchen around twelve fifteen. There was a line out the door, which as far as they could see they lined up eleven people back. This would give them a real good chance to chat.

"How did things go last week? Was it busy in the office?" Grant said casually.

"No more than usual," Terry suggested.

"I understand that we have a few more clients that came on board last week. Have they been screened to see which of us will pick them up?" Grant asked to imply that he gave the thought that it could have been either of them.

"We all have such a heavy load already," Terry coached.

"It would be difficult for either of the Junior partners to take on any more, don't you agree Grant," Terry conived?

"Actually, I have a good handle on my accounts. Its always a little hectic after being out for a weeks' vacation, you know? But, if you're organized and have a good secretary one can keep up," Grant persuaded. They were next to be seated. They were shown to a nice little table by a young girl who walked them there swiftly and with purpose. The patrons could all see that she had been taught to deal with the rush of the lunch crowd. She stopped abruptly at the table slated for them and slapped down the menus, which she had cradled under her arm. She turned to walk back to her other tasks as quickly as she had walked them there. The table was right at the window overlooking the lunch time activity at the corner of South Michigan and Madison where the street changed from North Michigan.

The shorter twin said, "Grant, excuse me man. Ma'am, where is the men's room?"

"It's right over there," as she pointed in the direction that Terry was to take.

Grant took his seat and a look around to see all of the people in the restaurant. The activity outside made Grant think of Toney and where she was now. He hoped that she had made it through the morning with flying colors. She had a rough time coming up in business and he would definitely be there for her no matter what it was. A few minutes later Terry was back.

"This is a pretty nice place Grant. I wonder why I had no idea it was even here," Terry mentioned as he took his seat?

"I'm not sure. It's not as if this is a place that's hidden for God's sake. It's a real popular restaurant and the food is awesome," Grant recited as if he were coaching Terry.

"Tell me," Grant said, "what is really happening with the new folks that were hired last week? What is the thought process? I hadn't had a chance to talk with the old man since I got back. Where is he thinking of putting them? There hardly enough room for all of the folks now?"

"The area where Birch, Manley, Stein, and Barnes sit is being redone. They are going to take all of those offices out and make them cubicles. That way that area can accommodate another eight to ten people easy," Terry explained.

"When was all of that decided," Grant said trying to maintain his objectivity. After all he was the Senior attorney and Terry and Nick were still just wet behind the ears. He couldn't believe that all the plans of the firm were being discussed with them and all of this while he was away on vacation.

"Oh, it was decided last week. The old man was asking for suggestions while Nick and I we're meeting with him. We took the plans of the office and played around with them and that's what we came up with. The cubicles will actually start right by your office," Terry revealed.

"No shit, Grant responded.

"Why do you say that," Terry asked?

"Well, that is the oddest spot in the office. If we moved to cubes, that will put the cubes right in the center of the office. The noise factor alone will be staggering for the people there. If we move to cubes, it should be either at one end of the office or the other…not in the center," Grant wildly explained.

Grant's mind was running a mile a minute. These guys want the cubicles in the center near me to distract me. These son of a bitches. They are too much.

"So, what else is happening," Grant cleverly changed the subject.

"Nothing much. I'm interested in finding out if the account base is even for those of us who have been there for a while. How many strong cases do you have? I think I have too many," Terry exclaimed?

For people who have been there for a while. The shorter twins have only been there nine months. What the hell does he mean?

"Well guy, I don't think I have enough," Grant responded.

"But, how many do you actually have," Terry pushed?

"Why do you need to know that," Grant cautioned?

"Just conversation, that's all. The fact that we don't have access to each other's case loads makes me wonder. I was just asking, that's all," Terry said as he backed off.

The waitress walked up to the table asking for their order. The moment she walked away the conversation resumed.

"How many cases do you have," Grant volleyed.

"Eight. Eight and they are working me to death. But, they are little shitty cases. Not much meat to them, you know? You've been there for over five years, so I bet you have at least twice that many as I do. You've got some big cases don't you? One's that could really make or break a career, right?"

"You could say that, I guess. But, I've put an awful lot of work in on these cases and in many instances the work that I've put in helped to make them the big cases that they are. It's called paying your dues," Grant sarcastically said.

"There are no short cuts Terry. There is no shortcut to success. Hard work is the only way. You either pay now or you pay later. Personally, I would rather pay while I have it. And, if anyone…I mean anyone tries to take my cases, I won't be a very gracious person, so don't try and get any cute ideas."

"Who me. Never. I was just asking as Terry started to back down a bit. The waitress brought them their food and disappeared back into the kitchen. Grant and Terry ate in virtual silence talking periodically about nothing. They finished their lunch and headed back to the office. For the remainder of the afternoon Terry and Nick were busy at it in between each of their offices. They were working hard to strategize their defense.

TEN

Her eyes opened at four thirty-three in the morning. Lately, she hadn't needed her alarm clock. There was so much going on. Helen had proven to be of the most instrumental in help to her. Toney knew that God had always taken special care of her and she was grateful. She was more than blessed to have developed a solid relationship with her creator very early in her life. Many days since then, when the chips were down, there would always be something or someone there to give her guidance. Someone or something was always there to let her know what her next step or move should be. She prayed to God that today's events were led by Him. That her presentation would be flawless. That she would be able to make strides that would set high standards in her industry to benefit mankind. She was that kind of human being. She always wanted to do the very best that she could, not only for herself, but for everyone involved. Who had the papers? Would they show themselves today? She just knew in her spirit that Surrant was somehow involved.

A couple of seconds after she opened her eyes, she jumped out of bed to begin her daily routine. She was in for a very long day. The reception started at six, but she had an early meeting with Corbin to run through what she was to present. Everyone would be arriving one by one throughout the day. She knew that she had to get into the office early to cross all her T's and dot all of her I's. Her morning routine ended about forty-five minutes after she woke up; then she was off to the garage in her building. In the back of her mind she knew that she had to be cautious. There were just too many things that had happened, too many strange things. She tipped toed off the elevator at One North Lakeshore through the doorway leading to the garage. She peeped and peered from side to side, moving out toward her car only after she was sure that she was alone, ensuring her safety. She couldn't believe that she was becoming paranoid. She reached her car and nervously retrieved her keys from her handbag, quickly opening the door and sliding in. Once she was safely in, she locked every door, she started her car, and drove out onto the street. The strain was way too much for her. She had to do something about this. She couldn't see herself living her life afraid of her shadow. Situations in her life had toughened her up substantially, but this was way too much for her.

After a fifteen-minute drive, she arrived at the garage of her office building. There were several cars there early. She had thought that she would be the only one with thoughts of getting there early to be ahead of the game. She got out of her car and headed for her office. She waved at Marvin, the third shift security guard, and continued toward the elevator.

Marvin yelled... "Ms. Chambers, just so you'll know, I noticed that your office was open again, during my early morning walk around the building. I checked it out and didn't see anything unusual; so I locked it and continued on. What's going on?" he asked.

"I left early yesterday and would have to ask Sonjia, my assistant. Thanks for being so alert. I'll have to check it out after the meeting" Toney rushed on.

"Okay, Marvin scuffed...but, be careful, alright? There's something uneasy to me about all of this. We haven't had anything like this in this building over the past seventeen years; so this is making me uneasy…things happening with no explanation at all. Just be careful, is all he said walking away while pushing his hat back on his head and scratching his right temple area.

"Okay, Marvin. I'll be careful, I promise."

The elevator came and Toney stepped, on armed with her reports that she scoured over last night after speaking with Helen. She arrived to the forty-fifth floor and scooted to her office door, opened it, and went in. She remembered that the last time she entered into her office this early, she left the doors open and caused Marvin adjeda. She wanted to make sure she did it right this time, especially being heavy minded. She walked through the outer office area and pushed through to her office. She flipped on the light, instantly noticing that her office had been turned upside down.

"What the hell?" she thought becoming visibly swept over with fear.

"What's going on here? Marvin said he looked and everything was fine and that there was nothing going on here," she said out loud.

She dropped everything instantly, called Marvin and began pacing the floor. In what seemed mere seconds Marvin was there with two other security officers.

"Ms. Chambers, I knew it in my bones that there was something going on and that this was just the beginning…I just knew it. Who's after you? How long has this been happening? I'm calling the cops. They'll get to the bottom of this," Marvin said in a protective tone.

"How much more can I take?" Toney thought as she flopped down in her chair.

She sat there with her head buried in her hands wandering what was going on. About ten minutes later, two uniformed police officers entered the office. They took a thorough look around at everything. They asked a million questions; then at about eight o'clock they left. The whole morning was shot. This was way too deep for her.

Sonjia arrived about thirty-five or forty minutes later. Four other employees also came in about the same time. Sonjia and the others had been kept outside near Sonjia's desk for several minutes being questioned by two additional officers. She was so worried about Toney not knowing exactly what had happened. She tried on three occasions to talk the officers guarding the door into allowing her to enter. She was denied on each occasion. Eventually, after about forty minutes, she was allowed to enter Toney's office. Sonjia ran to Toney and they hugged tightly.

"What happened? I was so worried that something had happened to you. Why are the police here?" she asked while taking a look around.

"Someone broke in here, literally tearing up the place. It was strange. Marvin told me he had been up here just a couple of hours before and he didn't see a thing except that the door was unlocked. Then, when I arrived, the office had been ransacked. So far, I can't tell if anything is missing. I have to settle down and take inventory. What happened yesterday when I left? Who was the last one out? Was the door locked?" Toney asked one question after another.

"I was the last one out," Sonjia said. "I'm always the last one out when you aren't here. And, I personally locked up. Are you alright?"

"I'm fine, I guess. There's so much going on. I can't think of anything right now, but the meeting. Thank God that I still have most of today to finish getting myself together. The only thing that I have to face right now is Corbin and the opening reception. I can handle that. Actually that gives me a little less than 24 hours before my debut. We can pull this off, Sonjia, I just know we can. I've made several changes to the presentation and even added a few things working overtime last night, I even surprised myself when I was done. Let's clean things up and get rolling. Okay?"

"You bet we can, Toney! I'm all yours...let's get started," Sonjia agreed.

They went to work. Their focus and drive was fluid. Toney called Corbin's office to put her pre work with Corbin off until late in the afternoon. By one-thirty they were done with everything. Pie charts, graphs, written materials. Fifty pages, including details of everything. Everyone in the room would be included. She wanted it to be an interactive presentation. That way she could permanently get their buy in. Her changes were significant. It was a collection of pertinent information that would set the industry on its ear from updated numbers to customer service initiatives and follow-up on individual customer care.

Toney felt good about it all. She had hit some snags over the past few weeks, but that would all be behind her now.

Mr. Corbin got word of the mishap from this morning. He and Marvin came into Toney's area to give her his support.

"Is she in?" Mr. Corbin asked Sonjia as he continued walking past her and opened Toney's door in the very same motion with Marvin, in tow.

"Toney? Are you all right? What happened here this morning? I just got the word. Was there a security-incident report filed?"

"Yes Charles, I'm fine."

Toney shook her head and motioned for Charles and Marvin to take a seat.

"I'm fine. We took care of everything. No one knows what this is all about. But, we put it aside for now and went back to work. We're all fine and I hope that it wasn't anything that we have to even think about again."

"We'll get to the bottom of this, believe you me," he said.

"I only have a couple of minutes; so, just as long as everyone is okay. And, about the review of your presentation... I trust your work. I always have. Let's skip that and I'll be surprised along with everyone else. So now, I'll get back to work," Charles said getting up and moving out.

"Marvin, I expect that you and your people will work with the police to get to the bottom of this. Keep me in the loop. We can't just have any and everyone walking in here anytime they want to," Corbin said as he walked out with Marvin right behind him.

Toney shook all of this off. She really didn't have a choice. But, in the back of her mind she knew that she was being stalked and she couldn't help but to believe that Surrant was behind it all somehow.

Toney, with Sonjia's assistance, moved at a fast pace trying to regain some appearance of order. They picked things up putting them in their proper place. There was glass on the floor where several of the expensive vases and picture frames from the artwork on the wall had been smashed.

"Who would do such a terrible thing Toney? "Sonjia asked while continuing her tasks. "Whoever it is, is sick," she continued.

"You have got to be the most understanding and the easiest person to work with. Who would do such a thing?" she asked as she started to cry."

"I just don't get it!"

Toney stopped what she was doing and went over to Sonjia to console her. She led Sonjia to the sofa where she brushed off the residue from the break in and they sat down. Toney said, wiping Sonjia's tears away, "honey you have to remember that there are some real sick people out there. Marvin and his people will work with the police and somehow they'll find out what's going on. Until then we have to be very careful. I'm counting on you as I always do to keep your eyes open and watch your back. Everyone knows how fond I am of you, so if they're after me I'll be worried about you too. Make sure to always be with someone when you're coming or going. Make sure to keep the doors locked to the office while you're here alone or if you're the last one here at night double check whether you've locked up and call one of the security people to walk you to the train station. I'm praying that this will be over sooner than later, but we don't know that so we both have to be careful. Okay?"

The tone of Toney's voice seemed to soothe Sonjia's fears. They both got up and straightened a few more things out and got back to the business at hand.

It was one o'clock before Toney realized it. She picked up the phone to place a seven million-dollar phone call to Japan. It was a trip that she had put off taking for four weeks because she knew she had to take a vacation before the big meeting. Her nerves were on edge and her entire career hung on the success of the mid-year meeting. Japan was still at least three weeks away. She had persuaded her Assistant Vice President in Japan to hold off the customer until the first of August. If she could get Mr. Yamaguchi settled down until then, she would have the time to win him over again during seven full days that she would carve out for a trip the orient. She recalled how long it took for her to win him over in the beginning. Mr. Yamaguchi didn't welcome the opportunity to work with women. It was known world wide that most of the Asian culture didn't readily accept women in business roles, as business participants and especially as business leaders handling million dollar deals. After over a dozen meetings over the years with Mr. Yamaguchi, Toney had proven herself worthy in his eyes based on her display of knowledge and business savvy. But, the call today would let her know when she needed to be there.

"Good afternoon Prophecy Computers Tokyo, Donna son speaking, May I help you?"

"Comnich guba, Donna son, Is Mr. Bukura available?" she asked in her broken Japanese.

"Oh, Ms. Chambers son. Good afternoon...he is out, but back soon. Should I have him call you back?"

"Yes, if it's within the next two hours. After that we will all be in the midst of the mid-year review and I will not be available for the next two days. Do you know where he is? Can you get to him soon and have him get back with me?"

"I will do my best. He had two appointments but, I'll try to catch up with him and have him get back with you within that timeframe."

"Thanks, Donaa son. Have a good afternoon."

"You too, Ms. Chambers son."

Toney hung up the phone and went right to the next item on her list. A few seconds later her private line rang.

"This is Toney."

"Hey good looking, what's up?"

It was Grant wishing her luck for tonight.

"We won't get a chance to see each other with all that we have going on, but I wanted you to throw me a couple of kisses over the phone."

Her thoughts shifted completely to Grant. She intentionally kept the events from this morning from Grant. She saw no reason to alarm him about it. After all, what could he do about it anyway, but worry about her?

They coo'd and giggled and talked sweet talk, which was interrupted by Sonjia.

"Excuse me, Toney, but your call from Japan is on line one."

"Thanks, Sonjia. I'll take it now."

She continued for a few seconds with Grant.

"Grant, I'll call you tonight. It's my call from Japan. I should be home by nine," Toney said.

"Okay, good looking. Let's talk then. I have to tell you about the shorter twin. My lunch with him today was strange and too deep for me," Grant said with a chuckle in his voice.

"Okay, baby, I can't wait to hear about it," she responded softly, gave Grant a kiss and clicked onto the other line.

Toney swiftly shifted gears. In a strong authoritative voice she answered her other line,

"Toney Chambers."

"Ms. Chambers son. Bukura here. I suspect that you want a status report on Mr. Yamaguchi son," he continued without seemingly taking a breath.

"He has been spoken to several times and we have agreed to postpone our updates until August 10. He's out of the country until August 2. I suspect that it will take him a few days to get caught up when he gets back, so we're right on target with early August. Did you get my report? My statistics are all in line. My revenue is right on target, so I should be all set. Sorry I couldn't be there this week."

"No you're not. You guys dream of ways to miss this meeting. Frankly, I can't blame you. When I worked in your spot a few years ago, I felt the same way. But, be that as it may...thanks for the update. You've done a great job with Yamaguchi. Just a great job! I'll get back with you next week with specifics on our plans for my trip. Thanks again, Bukura." Toney said breathing a sigh of relief.

PART II

Toney had a few minutes to relax before the reception. Her favorite thing was to go down to get a latte from Starbucks and a pretzel from Auntie's Pretzels. She decided that she'd do that, especially in light of the fact that she had nothing to eat since yesterday. She got up from her comfortable chair and breezed by Sonjia.

"I'll be right back. I'm going downstairs for a latte and a pretzel. It's only three o'clock, and with no lunch, I'm getting a little hungry. "

"Okay, Toney. I'll be right here."

Toney left the office feeling pretty good about everything regarding the meeting. There was a cloud still hanging over her about all of the mystery. Who wanted to see her hurt? Why? Her relationship with Surrant was a little strained, but she would never have thought that he would go to these measures. If it were Surrant, he'd eventually show his hand and have to pay for what was happening. If it wasn't Surrant, she just couldn't imagine who it could be.

When she got down to the Starbucks coffee station on the restaurant level, she noticed it was very quiet in the area. She and another lady were the only two people ordering coffee at this time of day. Starbucks reminded her of the day that she had first gotten hired at Prophecy Computers so many years ago. She paid for her order, stopped by the pretzel hut and found herself on her way back to her office. She tiptoed past Sonjia, who was busy at work, and went back into her office, got seated back in her big overstuffed chair and began to enjoy her treat. After she was done she rared back to relax. This would keep her satisfied until the reception, which was in a couple of hours. She sat there thinking about the presentation the next morning. She was compelled to get up again and go to the Boardroom to get a feel for the proceedings in the morning.

"Sonjia, I'm going upstairs. I'll be back in a while. Just take any messages for me," she said as she walked at a moderate pace as she exited the offices.

She took the elevator to the fiftieth floor. She gave Chae, the main office receptionist, a quick hello as she brushed by headed in the direction of the Boardroom, which was just about five steps from Corbin's office. Toney opened the Boardroom door after waving at Terry and whispering..."I'll be in here for a few minutes."

Terry smiled and nodded her head okay, turning back to her tasks.

The room was sterile and cold with no life, but tomorrow would be another story. The huge mahogany table with the subtle black leather chairs, which surrounded the table, spoke volumes. The room was adorned with expensive paintings of the past Presidents and Board Chairs since the days when the company was young and just coming into its own. The audio-visual equipment, which was a huge component of the effectiveness of the room, was the envy of the industry. As expected, only the best for the headquarters location. If her office and the remote offices had as much as they did, surely the headquarters office would have the very best. Toney took the seat at the opposite end of the table from the President's chair. She was one step from that spot and shuttered at the thought of the possibilities. But, why not? She had gotten this far. Her handling of the opening session tomorrow would determine her strength and ability to lead the entire organization into the new millennium. Corbin would be around another three years max, and then who?

Toney swirled around in the chair to get the full effects of the power of the room. It was impressive and she was very thankful to God for allowing her the position that she had. It was by His grace that she had come this far. She felt compelled to pray for all that she had been given. She prayed for tomorrow and the perfection that only God could grant her. She asked for his words not hers to take over her work. She fell on complete silence for the next few minutes then stood and walked out refreshed and renewed.

When she returned to her office Sonjia handed her two messages that had come in for her. Toney went into to her office to return the calls and finally had a few minutes for herself before the reception. She reclined in her chair, and before she knew it she was back daydreaming about the first time she walked into Prophecy in . . .

When Toney walked into the Prophecy Computers remote office in Washington, DC that morning looking for a job after such a heartbreaking week, she was impressed. The receptionist welcomed her immediately.

"Good Morning, ma'am, how can I be of assistance to you this morning?" she asked very professionally.

"Good morning," Toney replied.

"I'm here to answer an ad in the newspaper. Can you please tell me whom I should speak with?"

"Certainly. Please take a seat. Someone will be with you in a moment."

Toney turned around to see where the seats were and which she wanted to take in order to be in a good position to view the entire operation or at least as much of it as she could see. The environment was professional, comfortable and appeared to be progressive. She saw six other African Americans moving about in the office. She had high hopes that this would work out for her. She would put her best foot forward and try with all she had to make this work. Five or six minutes later a very well dressed lady came out.

"Ms. Chambers?"

"Yes, I'm Toney Chambers."

"Good morning, Ms. Chambers. Please come with me".

"Sure," Toney said bouncing to her feet and following as she had been asked to do.

The lady took her to a conference room and motioned for her to take a seat as she closed the door behind them.

"My name is Brenda Sullivan. I'm the Director of this remote location for Prophecy. Thank you for coming in today. We are always looking for new people with an interest in the computer business", she said while pouring herself a cup of coffee.

"Would you care for a cup?"

"Yes. I take cream and sugar please."

Ms. Sullivan prepared the coffee and gave it to Toney as she took a seat.

"What can we do for you today? I understand that you saw our ad in the newspaper?"

"Yes I did," Toney said while reaching into her bag to retrieve another copy her resume and her school transcripts.

"My thoughts are to get on board with a growing company and grow with it," Toney continued. "I've enjoyed school, and my professors have all told me that I've done well. I hope that I get a chance to prove myself in your company."

Ms. Sullivan looked up from her review of the paperwork, peering over her glasses. She said, "I see."

She went right back to her careful review of Toney's story and a few more seconds later said, "Give me a minute. I'll be right back," as she walked out of the room with Toney's paperwork in her hands.

Toney took another sip of her room temperature coffee after which she began to bite her nails. That was an act that she had never remembered doing before. She chalked it up to nervousness.

Five minutes passed. Then ten. What was going on? Just as her next thought was forming, the door opened. Ms. Sullivan and another lady entered the room.

"Ms. Chambers, this is Ms. Roman. She is the Assistant Director of the office and supervises the programming area. I would like for the two of you to talk about your interest in our company. Once you have done that, we'll chat again, okay?"

"That's fine, Ms. Sullivan, thank you. Good morning, Ms. Roman."

"Good morning, Ms. Chambers. Your records are very interesting. We are extremely interested in you. I have several questions and if all goes well we can move to the next step. How does that sound?"

"That sounds great," Toney responded with enthusiasm.

Toney and Ms. Roman stayed in the conference room for the next hour talking about this and that. When Toney emerged from the conference room, she had a strong inkling that she had been hired....

She just as suddenly came out of her daydream again.

It had been another strange day, but she had made it through. She had one more thing today, the reception. She'd see Surrant and do some detective work on her own about the weird activities of the past few weeks. She could help herself so much if she could just get a reading on Surrant. Tonight she'd see what he was made of.

PART III

Feeling some relief, Toney rose from her chair and went into her restroom at the back of her office. She freshened up and left the office for the day. It was time to shine. She was due at the opening reception of the mid-year meeting. She didn't want to be the first one there but couldn't be the last either. When she arrived, the area was more than half full. It seemed that most of the muckity-mucks had gotten there early to do their biannual kiss ups. Toney loved it because it reminded her of the earlier days when she was in their shoes and how so many of them tried to discourage her. She gracefully moved around to each of the small pockets of people saying hello and flaunting her stuff. She was incredible and really knew how to work the room. Finally she ran into Surrant.

"Well, Ms. Chambers, you're still standing huh?"

"Oh for sure Surrant. And, I hope you'll be still standing too after it's all said and done."

She continued on laughing and talking with some of the others, thinking what a strange thing that was for him to say. Surely, he's not that stupid. He wouldn't put someone on me to harm me and openly brag about it, or would he?

An hour later, Corbin stepped up to the microphone to welcome everyone. He spoke about the objective of the gathering and what he hoped it would yield. He gave an overview of the status of the company of which he said he'd go over in more detail the next day. He thanked everyone for coming and bid everyone a good night. A huge round of applause ensued, led by Surrant, which was obvious to everyone. He was at it again…kissing up. Most of them stayed for several more minutes talking in small pockets then little by little they excused themselves to retreat to their accommodations for the evening.

Toney walked out with some of the others. She said goodnight and got into her car and drove off. When she got home she took off her clothes, took a quick shower, then climbed into bed shortly afterwards. She gave Grant a quick call to tell him that she was bushed and that she'd talk to him after the meeting tomorrow about the shorter twin and their lunch. Grant was tired too, so he agreed and they called it a night.

ELEVEN

One by one beginning at six forty-five in the morning they arrived in the reception area and were directed to the pre-function belt of the Boardroom. The area where they assembled was indicative of a flourishing company in Corporate America. From the imported marble floors partially covered with richly textured plush oriental rugs, adorned with the finest of office furniture and embellishments, to the rich dark woods that made up the doors and moldings, this was opulence at its finest. The rich Boardroom was set with thirty black leather overstuffed chairs set around the table. For this meeting there were extra chairs setup around the perimeter of the room to accommodate the additional attendees and other interested parties. A small side table was included near the end of the Board Table adjacent to the end of the table where Mr. Corbin would be seated. The tiny table was for Mr. Corbin's Executive Assistant, Terry Mabrey. She was always seated near Mr. Corbin for big meetings taking notes and making sure that everyone had whatever they needed and so on. There were only three females, two white and one African American, in attendance. The rest were Caucasian males. Some old, but most of them were relatively young appearing to be in the early to mid thirties. These were all of the head honchos of the company, starting with Charles Corbin the President and CEO, the fifteen member Board of Directors, Toney, and all of her Assistant Vice Presidents and their Managers. It was time to roll up their sleeves and determine where they stood financially, where they were headed, and what they needed to do to stay ahead of the game. Who would fall out and who would stay? What would the new direction of the company be? Would it stay on the course that they were on now, or would it chart a new course?

The agenda had been set. Each presenter had thirty minutes with the exception of Toney, who led the way. She would take the first half of the morning giving a preview of the company in the early days and where they were headed, and all the following presentations to be completed by each of her Assistant Vice Presidents. Toney was on first, and her presentation encompassed an overview of the entire two days. Q&A periods were limited to fifteen minutes for each presentation. There were a total of ten scheduled presentations.

"Good morning, ladies and gentlemen," Toney started, demonstrating poise and confidence.

"Today, we embark upon what Charles and I hope to be the proof we need to elevate Prophecy Computers, Inc. to its next prosperous phase. We are a force to be reckoned with in the Information Software and Hardware Industry," she said as she stepped to the side taking a small sip of water.

"Today and tomorrow will be spent reviewing our current status and the initiatives that we will put in place to elevate our company to the next level. I expect that each of the presenters will review the success of his overall responsibilities. And, in addition each will provide an overview of location status, its current revenue standing against the forecasted revenue, how each of them stacks up to the action plans that have been laid out to each, and action plans and strategies for the future growth. Yes, we will review an abundance of information in a very short period of time. So, take copious notes, and if there are questions, please hold them until the end of each presentation."

Toney moved to the overhead projector, turning it on. Her first order of business was to address the statistics of the company on a glossy, which overviewed Prophecy in the very beginning.

"I think it is important that we refresh our memories of where we have come from and where we are now. This is necessary in order to appreciate where we are headed. In this view, Prophecy was in its infant stages, where we began in this humble two-bedroom house in Queens, New York. In those days Mylon and Frank Samuels, our founders, had a vision. Fresh out of MIT they wanted to find a better way to communicate. With the onset of the technology age just on the horizon, they each had a dream on how they saw themselves contributing. We have come from that humble environment, in less than twenty years, to a billion-dollar company with more success on the horizon if we select the right people, train them under Prophecy's standard way of doing business, and incorporate the issues relating to the customer first. If we do these things there is no way that we can lose," Toney started as she got a round of resilient applause.

She continued chart after chart and graph after graph, systematically unveiling her magic. It was a power-packed presentation. Three hours into her work, participants were busy at work taking notes, nodding their heads in agreement and listening intently to each and every word. Toney paused periodically for questions, comments or thoughts.

Several people added their input, as each person seemed to really become involved in the meeting, which is exactly what Toney was after. There were some brilliant people in that room and she knew it. People who had made immense contributions over the years and had the company's success clearly at the heart of their work. This meeting had become all that she had hoped or dreamed it would be. She was at the top of her game.

It had always been the philosophy of the founders of the company to hire the right people, pay them well, educate them on the business and leave them alone to do the job that they were getting paid to do. That philosophy had led them to the success that they enjoyed over the years and would continue under the helm of Charles Corbin and his successor.

Twelve noon Toney had concluded her detailed work by giving a recap of her talk in a capsulized format. She was simply outstanding. It was time for lunch. Toney was psyched.

TWELVE

Somewhere in time when she was younger she dreamed constantly of success. These thoughts had been with her for what seemed like forever, and it mirrored this very moment. She hoped and dreamed that she would be the victor of a moment such as this. The big meeting so far was all that she had hoped it would be. Her presentation was huge. She had pulled it off! Toney had the entire cast of characters spellbound, and point after point they were riveted. She had prayed just before she walked into the Boardroom that day, and her prayers paid off. It was three p.m. She had taken up the entire morning and still had a couple of hours to go before it was over. At noon they broke for lunch. After they partook in a group meal she had a moment to take a break, which was long enough to call Grant to bring him up to speed. She darted off to her office to take a breath and steal a moment for herself. As she entered her office and breezed past the receptionist, her staff hadn't expected her but once they saw her they gave her a standing ovation. They had all heard about the presentation from the old man's secretary. She had gotten her update from the snatches of conversation she picked up from the morning break. She shared the information with a few people and they shared it with a few more, and before she knew it all of the employees at the headquarters were buzzing about it. Word had spread like wildfire.

"Thank you, thank you all. But, remember…we're a team and I couldn't have done any of this without each and every one of you".

She continued through the office, quickly reflecting again on the first time she'd walked in this area and just as quickly as she thought about it, the thought left her head. This was her moment of truth, and God had protected her again.

Toney hastily picked up the phone to call Grant. They spoke for a fleeting second and she was off again.

It was the Toney Chambers and Company show. Toney had prepared to lead the way with a detailed overview of her plans for each of the remote locations, which was the foundation of all revenue sources for the company. But, as she thought about it...that's why they were paying her the big bucks. Basically, the laurels of the company lay heavily on Toney, and her team. Her presentation had led the way and her Assistant Vice Presidents presentations were to follow one by one and had to be in sync. The group was on their fourth presentation and obviously running just a bit behind, which was normal.

"The graph you are looking at gives you the figures from 1997. Take a look at the summer months. Sales are traditionally down due to many of the decision-makers being on vacation or taking long weekends, etc producing less time for the work on their desks. The trend is for sales to pickup in September of each year. Look at the fall and winter months of 1996. They are in line with the fall and winter of 1997. We can look for more of the same for the fall of 1998. Because the economy is doing so well and consumers are in a purchasing mode, we should strike while the time is right. Our sales force should be out in record numbers right after Labor Day following up on the calls that were made in the spring. That's the way to make an impact on the bottom line," Toney interjected in the middle of the talk.

Corbin said, 'It sounds to me like you know what you're talking about Chambers. It's already after six. We'll continue the second half tomorrow morning."

The group moved to a light reception gathering into small groups to discuss certain points of interest developed during the long day of the meeting. An hour later, they were having a planned dinner, and around eight, they one by one left for the evening.

When Toney got home she called Grant to say goodnight.

"Hello," Grant said sounding a bit out of it himself.

"Hi baby. How's my guy?" Toney purred.

"Tired. I'm real tired, baby. What about you? How is the meeting going? Got to be a lot, right?"

"You can say that again. Most of these guys only do what they have to. It's embarrassing. So, naturally, I have to pick up the slack or again, it will look like I'm not leading my troops. It'll be over soon though. Real soon. What's happening with you?" Toney changed the subject.

"Let's wait until your meeting is over to talk about me. The twins are still at it, but I'm hanging in there. It gets trying sometimes but I'm fine. I love you, booby," Grant said sweetly.

"I love you to, honey. I'll try and give you a quick call in between the events of tomorrow, okay?" Toney said turning over to be in position to hang up the phone with Grants response.

"Alright, baby. Sleep tight," Grant said as they both hung up and turned off their lights.

Before Toney knew it her clock was going off again. It was time to get up and get at it. She went through her morning ritual and was off to start her day. She arrived at the office about an hour and fifteen minutes before the start of the day to get a few things off her desk. She managed to do that even before Sonjia arrived then she made it upstairs in time for coffee.

The meeting was moving into its second day. One after the other the participants stood and presented their plans for the remainder of the year and an overview for the coming year. The company's standards had been upheld in each presentation. They had set many company records, and new standards were being set.

Jim Surrant's presentation was eighth and was missing a few links. Toney had taken copious notes with plans to add them to her point-by-point critiques of each individual. She thought to herself as she sat there listening... "We've been over this too many times for him not to have it together." His presentation lasted for an hour and ten minutes, and then they were on to the next one and then the next, taking time out for questions and answers of each.

PART II

Toney went back to her office again to check her messages, return some phone calls and relax for a few minutes. She rushed in trying not to think about the marathon meeting that they had all experienced. She had been the hit of the show as Charles had suspected she would be, but all of it had her feeling drained. On second thought she decided she'd just sit quietly for a few minutes and then get to those messages.

She picked up the phone to buzz Sonjia, "Sonjia, please hold my calls for a while. I'm just going to kick my shoes off and relax before I get started again."

"Okay, no problem," Sonjia declared.

Toney did just that. She kicked her shoes off and rared back in her comfortable chair. Before she knew it she could only hear the phones ringing, but at this point the ringing was becoming more and more distant as she drifted further and further away...she was daydreaming again....

When she walked out of IBM she hadn't realized what had happened. She was in shock. Real shock. It took a couple of days to sort out the actions as they happened, that sent her into this tailspin. She was out of a job and in effect on the street again. School was no longer a shield for her. This was for real. She hadn't saved any money at all, she hadn't had time to…she had been working for only just under three months. Her shabby off campus apartment rent would be due in a little more than a week and a half. That would be Three Hundred-Seventy Five Dollars, which was due each month, and the rest went for utilities, clothing, and food. Plus she wanted in a few months to start saving for an old beat up car. Something to get around in would be sufficient but this was not the time…that was a few months off. The part time job at the campus fountain shop and the monies that her parents scraped together to help her had dried up when she landed the job at IBM. The two Hundred Thirty six-dollars and fifty-two cents really looked good now.

On the morning of the fourth day of being fired from IBM, she got up, showered, dressed and hit the pavement. The morning was crisp. She walked the three blocks to the bus stop in order to get to the train station of the METRO and waited with the others. She stood at the back away from the others just watching and listening to the different pockets of conversations. She hadn't been in the train station at this time of day, so this was a completely different crowd than the one she rode with at six in the morning when she was on her way to IBM. From their conversations many of these people were job hunting too. She shook along on the bus. As she rode, her thoughts were to stay in the computer field because that was the field she knew would satisfy her soul. Seventeen minutes later she was at the train station. She disembarked the bus and with quickness in her step made her way to the platform and waited attentively for the train to arrive. A couple of minutes later the train was pulling into the station. They all boarded and took seats.

Toney had taken the newspaper ads with her. She had three potential jobs circled. Her plans were to take her resume and school records, which she had put into ten separate packages for her potential new employers. She arrives at the first company, which was Xerox. She thought about the first time that she walked through the doors. She was all set to take the typing test or whatever she had to do to be considered. She took the test then and passed with flying colors. Greed sent her to IBM over Xerox, and now she was back with her tail seemingly tucked between her legs. She simply had to try it again. She would be mighty lucky if they still had jobs available.

"Good morning, I'm here to fill out an application for a position," she said professionally to the young lady behind the cage-like area. "I've brought my resume if you like. It has my college records attached as weli."

The young lady offered no conversation. She merely shoved the application to Toney and pointed her to the area where she was to fill out the paperwork and move to the next window.

Toney stopped before following the young lady's gestures to ask, "Once I fill out the application, what do I do then? I've been here before but I need to know if the procedures are the same."

"Absolutely the same, so if you've been here before then you got it down, right?" the girl said with no real feelings.

Perplexed, Toney moved to the area where the others were standing and began the painstaking task of filling out the long and detailed application. She thought back to the last time that she was here before. There had been a very nice white hared lady at that window. She was gentle and very self assured and helpful. Toney thought as she went through the process that the lady must have retired.

Several minutes later Toney found herself standing in the next line to further along the process. Thirty-five minutes passed and she was finally the next person to speak with an interviewer.

"Toney Chambers," the middle aged woman said softly.

Toney bounced to her feet full of hope and promise. She said a short prayer and stepped quickly after the lady who lead her through a hallway which looked much like a maze, to a little interviewing room. The lady who led stepped aside, invited Toney in and closed the door behind them. They both took a seat. The lady read through the application and read over Toney's resume and her school transcripts.

"I see here you applied with us several months ago." Before Toney could answer, the lady continued. "And, we offered you a job, which you turned down," the lady said with raised eyebrows.

Feeling that the truth will out, Toney told her the story, "Yes. That's correct. But, I was also offered a position with one of your competitors at the same time, which was paying more money. I thought at the time that money was the number one decision making factor that I should consider. I have had a change of heart since that time, which is why I'm back here," she added.

"Well, I understand. What happened there? Why are you back here?"

Again Toney couldn't find an opening to get her response in before the lady went forward. "And anyway, your timing is off. We don't have any positions open at this time. We'll keep your application on file and give you a call. This company is difficult to get into. You really should have taken the offer that was given to you. It might be a while now," the lady said quickly, not even looking at Toney.

"Is there an opportunity in the near future?" Toney asked as upbeat as she could muster without showing her disappointment, grateful to finally get a word in.

"We'll let you know. You never can tell," she said as she stood suggesting that Toney stand and allow herself to be dismissed.

"Well, thank you for your time. I hope to hear back from you soon. Should I call back in a few days?" Toney asked?

"No, ma'am, absolutely not. We'll call you," the lady interrupted.

The lady was leading Toney back out to the waiting area which they reached shortly, afterwards turning quickly turning to say, "Thank you for coming."

"Ms. Amsterdam? Ms. Amsterdam?"

"Here," another young lady said as she stood and moved toward the interviewer.

Toney stood there in a quandary. She had never been whirled through a process like this so fast. Her head was spinning.

Toney timidly left and walked a couple of blocks feeling lost before she got herself together. She passed by Starbucks coffee shop that was just down the block. She wanted to take a moment to get herself together and plot her next stop.

After ordering a latte, she took a seat in the window area. She sipped her drink while watching the people walk by. A half-hour later she was energized and ready to continue her trek. She was restored to mental status before she started again by saying a quick prayer. Then she was off to her next stop, feeling a bit more self-confident.

Toney had circled four other computer-related companies that advertised that they were hiring. None of the companies was of the same caliber of the IBM's or the Xerox's of the world, but she had had a chance with both of them and had blown it. She had to get what she could. Her first stop was at Abhrams Personal Computer Parts. She felt as if she was intruding on the receptionist. She had a huge piece of gum in her mouth, and while chewing it she moved it in and out of her mouth. It was disgusting. What kind of company is this? And to have this person out front was scary. A minute later, the receptionist was blowing bubbles in between her cooing and giggling while she continued her conversation. Toney stood there waiting to be acknowledged, but the girl kept on talking to the person on the other end of the line. Toney took a seat and politely waited. The way that the petite blonde girl spoke, she was on a personal call. Exactly four minutes later, she hung up in one movement, looking up at Toney in the next motion asking, “May I help you ma’am”?

“Yes. I’m here to apply for the position that is advertised.”

“Alright. I’ll let Mr. Drawn know you’re here.”

She got up and swished off to the door behind her. A second or two later she was back to lead Toney through that same door. As they walked back into the guts of the operation of this business, Toney was surprised at the activity that was hidden in the rear of the receptionist area. They reached an office where a white hared older man stood as they approached the doorway of his office.

“Good morning, ma’am, I’m Harold Drawn, please have a seat.”

“Thank you, sir. My name is Toney Chambers, ” Toney said politely as she started feeling a little better about this company and her chances of being selected to work here.

The receptionist excused herself as the white hared man return to his seat asking Toney, “ What can I do for you this morning?”

“I noticed that you have an ad in the paper regarding a position that you have available. I would like to talk to you about the position,”she said handing the man a packet containing her resume and college transcripts. The interviewer reviewed her paperwork for well over a minute and gently laid it aside. “Your records are very impressive. As much as we could use an obviously highly intelligent person such as yourself, I would be deceiving and misleading you if I told you that we still had any positions available. We just hired a young lady two days ago who I hope will work out for us. I'll keep your information on file and call you if anything opens up." Mr. Drawn stood and walked around his desk offering his hand to shake Toney's.

"I certainly wish you luck in you search," he said.

Toney stood and accepted the old guy's hand, shook it saying, "Thank you for your time."

Mr. Drawn walked with Toney to show her the way out. Somehow as Toney found herself on her way to her third possibility, she was very encouraged because of the receptive nature of Mr. Drawn.

At eleven thirty she walked through the front door of Prophecy Computers. She was immediately impressed with the feeling which took her over when she opened the door. It was listed as an up-and-coming company in the New York Stock Exchange, so she was hopeful that this could be her chance....

"Buzz, buzz."

"Toney," Sonjia called.

Toney shook herself back to reality, returning from the reclined position that she found herself in.

"Yes, Sonjia. What is it?"

"They're calling for you. They're about to go back into session."

"Okay...thanks. I'm on my way," Toney responded as she stood, quickly maneuvering her way around her desk and through the door. She pushed past Sonjia and through the office like a blur. Thirty seconds later she was on the fiftieth floor where she rejoined the rest of the executives.

The lunch hour came and went as they rounded five o'clock and yet another reception and dinner together. There was some fine work done and presented, and then there were many things that needed to be tweaked. All in all it wasn't bad with the exception of Surrant. As they stood having an after dinner cocktail, they congratulated each other on the work presented.

Even Jim Surrant complimented her on her work. What a shocker that was. Some of the information that Toney presented covered some of the voids in Jim's presentation for which he was thankful.

THIRTEEN

Corbin took center stage. He was glowing. His talk referenced all of the material in a capsulated version that had been presented. The way he saw it, his company was on the cutting edge and he wanted to let his troops know that he appreciated all of the loyalty and hard work.

"Our mission is to become the industry leader. We can only do that by providing superior products and superior customer service. We have to maintain our status by continuing to exceed the expectation of our customer base. If we do that, we will keep the customers that we have and gain new customers because of our reputation. When I think of where we came from over fifteen years ago, we have done an outstanding job. We've hired and developed the right people with little exception. These individuals have worked tirelessly to build the company that we enjoy today. Looking back at the very beginning, we started with only two remote offices in Washington, D.C. and New York and eleven people. These people had a vision and the strength and fortitude to see their vision through. It was a rough start and one that we won't soon forget. But, looking ahead there are some great possibilities on the horizon and with leaders such as Toney Chambers, we can't miss. Toney, would you please come up here?"

Very surprised, Toney stood and walked briskly over to Corbin.

"This woman has been a rock for this company," Corbin said as he extended his hand to Toney. She has worked with reckless abandon to further the position of Prophecy worldwide. Because of her, we have secured three of the largest accounts possible in Japan and not to mention the domestic account base that we enjoy. I remember the first time I met Toney. She was barely out of college, but had enough confidence in her abilities to be three people. We took a chance on her, based solely on her academic information and what a find she turned out to be. She is not only a mentor and role model for many of our employees, she is one of the only openly approachable leaders that we have. That takes skill. To keep it all straight and moving forward, where her priorities remain intact is the definition of the individual. On behalf of the entire company, we thank you for just being you, and the fine job that you do," Corbin concluded.

He handed Toney a beautiful crystal statuette of a Phoenix with Toney's name engraved on the gold plate along with the date and Prophecy Computers. Toney was speechless. Everyone stood with a roar of applause. What a moment for her. What a moment indeed. If she had any doubt that she had arrived, this moment erased all doubt. Toney received the beautiful statuette and stepped to the podium as Corbin stepped aside.

"No one could have ever convinced me that a moment such as this was in my future. The things I do each day are acts from my heart. I have lived that way from the very first day that I walked into Prophecy. I felt welcomed and needed, which allowed me to be the best that I could be. I can't tell you that there has not been some trying moments, but all the storms have been weathered because of many of the people in this room. This award is for all of us. Yes . . . all of us. Thank you, Charles. Thank you very much. I will leave you with one thought, "Our tomorrow is being carved with the actions that we take today, and greatly depend on the initiatives that we make for ourselves, and Prophecy. Good luck to you all."

With the end of her speech, Corbin brought the meeting to a rapid close. They had been together for two and a half days, and that was enough. It was time to get back to work.

"Corbin left immediately. The rest of them stood around for several minutes shaking hands and one-by-one as they had arrived, they left headed back to their individual destinations. Toney spoke with each of her Assistant Vice Presidents reminding them of the impending conference call the following Tuesday.

Toney still couldn't shake the feeling that someone was after her. Who stole the papers and why? Her mind was free now that the meeting was over. She thought about it many times since all the madness started. She wanted to include Grant in her plans, but she didn't want him hovering over her and she knew that he would if he knew about all of this. She had definitely decided to hire a private investigator to seek the truth. She wouldn't try to live her life shrouded in all this mystery. If it was Surrant, she wanted to know. If it was someone else, she wanted to know that, too.

FOURTEEN

The taxi ride to O'Hare the next morning was humdrum. Jim didn't quite know what he was feeling. He was glad to be getting out of Chicago. Somehow he couldn't shake Diane. She had been awesome.

"Two trips to Chicago in a little less than three weeks and nothing to really show for it, except for Diane," he thought.

"The only thing I'm sure of is that I'm not sure of anything anymore," he said out loud in an almost defeated way.

He knew that after all that the big meeting had brought out, the early flight back to Southern California was going to be an anticlimactic one. He hadn't slept well for the last two nights, and his six-thirty a.m. flight wasn't early enough for him to get the hell out of Chicago. Jim had not faired as well as he had expected, especially because he had always been the fair hared boy in the past. He had in most cases had things go his way, but now it appeared that it was time to face the music. Jim knew that there were many people in the company that could make him fall if they put their minds to it. He knew that he had better watch his back. His demeanor was low key as he thought about the things that might be coming. He had never felt so low in his life. He got out of the taxi, retrieved his bag and walked in a slumped manner slowly to the gate area. He was about twenty-five minutes early. When he arrived in the gate area he took a seat and waited, fumbling through some of the prepared papers that Holley had provided him for the meeting. Some of the material that he presented was excellent, but he was missing the boat in too many areas to mention, especially when the spreadsheets and graphs referring to the revenue were presented. Questions started coming from everywhere. Question that he couldn't answer. His style was to point the finger elsewhere. Maybe his assistant or maybe one of the regional managers. But, all in all, he knew that it was his ultimate responsibility to be prepared and to keep those people on target.

He sat there reading through some of the notes from the meeting trying to make some sense of where he had screwed up and his next move. All he could think about was the fact that he had been found out. The fact that he was tall, handsome, and blonde didn't carry the weight that it used to. His challenge was to prove to the group at large that he and his team were on target, which he couldn't do because of the target issues that most of the other Vice Presidents had responded to and the main issues, the missing funds. About fifteen minutes after he arrived at the gate area, it started to fill up with other passengers. Soon the airline started the boarding process. Jim was booked in first class, so he and the other suits were called to board first. Five or six minutes later he was seated and rummaging through his brief case. He pulled out some of the documents that he needed to study. He wanted to make the time on the flight count. He had to find the money. A few minutes later he stared off into space. The other passengers continued the boarding process. He sat there for a few more minutes plainly staring into space and in his own world. He hadn't spoken to a soul…as a matter of fact ten to fifteen minutes had passed and he didn't recognize the fact that there were any other people around him. He was definitely in his own world.

"Sir, would you care for something to drink?" the flight attendant asked.

"A martini," Jim said in a reserved voice as if his mind were totally somewhere else.

The flight attendant looked at him in a perplexed way thinking that it was only just after seven in the morning and someone is ordering a martini.

"Sir, that was a martini?"

"Yes!" Jim snapped.

"Alright, sir. How would you like that?" she coached.

"A double vodka martini, shaken not stirred," he directed.

"I'll be right back, sir..." she said walking away shaking her head and mumbling to herself... "An alcoholic James Bond, I guess...there's got to be a better way."

She disappeared into the refreshment area. A few minutes later she was back in front of him, handing him his martini, and eventually she moved on. Jim settled in taking a couple of large sips of the concoction. He wasn't aware that he had quickly consumed over half of it before he had had any food. He reviewed the paperwork that he had set aside for a few more minutes until the effects of the drink had rendered him motionless. Several minutes later he had dosed off to sleep. The gentleman seated next to him wasn't happy to have this seemingly troubled man seated next to him, especially realizing that the flight was relatively long.

The flight took the customary three and a half hours. The co captain announced that they had been cleared to land. The lead flight attendant made an announcement on the P. A. system preparing the passengers with the connecting gate information. This shook Jim from his slumber. He woke in a startled state. He had created a nightmare for the gentleman seated next to him. His papers had fallen to the floor, some under his seat; some crumbled in his seat. He had made a mess. Drunk, snoring and dribbling all at the same time was what he woke up to. The front of his shirt was wet with the dribble, and as many people as he was visible to were fixated on him as he came to. He was embarrassed about it, but couldn't understand how he could have dozed off like he did, especially in light of the one drink. He also was shocked at the amount of time that had passed and simply couldn't believe that he was already in California.

Jim stood as soon as the seat belt light went off. He wanted to be one of the first people off of the plane and he was. When he got into the gate area, he saw Joanie standing there waiting for him. She always tried to be at the airport to meet him when he was out of town on business. It was a ritual for her. She was still so in love with him.

"Honey, it's six-forty-five in the morning. You didn't have to be here this early to meet me. Holley had a car scheduled to pick me up," he said sweetly as he threw his arms around Joanie.

He was happy that she was there. She had been the only constant thing in his life for years. He really needed her now. He kissed her on the cheek. Jim sunk down into her arms. He needed to feel her love. It was the very first time out of all of the years that they had been together that he felt this way.

"I missed you, dear. I always miss you when you've gone. Besides when I pick you up I get to see you sooner. If your company car picks you up, I'll have to wait at least two more hours before you get home," she said softly, releasing the hold she had on him. You've obviously been drinking. Why so early? You've been through it, huh? You can go into the office later. Okay?" she rolled off her tongue one word after the other.

"You're so good to me, honey. I don't really deserve you, you know that? he said in a lovable way."

"Well you might be right but, I'm stuck with you, right?" she giggled.

They reached the baggage claim area and stood at the carousel where the luggage from the flight was to come up. A few seconds later Jim picked up his garment bag and they waltzed out into the morning headed for their car.

Joanie slid in on the passenger side of the 450SL while Jim popped the trunk sliding in his luggage and slamming it shut. He took a look up at the blue sky as he walked along the side of the car thanking God to be back at home and with his beautiful wife. His thoughts wandered to the clandestine meetings with Holley over the time that they had known each other, and a feeling of guilt rushed into his conscience. He had always been a dog of a man, and he couldn't understand why he was suddenly developing a conscience. Maybe he was finally growing up.

The drive to Manhattan Beach was moving along relatively fast. The traffic in the Los Angeles area hadn't gotten too bad at this hour of the day. There was always a lot of traffic, but it wasn't bumper to bumper this early. Jim and Joanie chitchatted about this and that while they rode. "How are the kids? What's the story with them?" Jim asked in an effort to lift his spirits.

"Oh, they're both doing this and that. They need to be with you more. You're always so busy."

They pulled into the driveway about seven forty five. Jim opened the trunk to get his bag and followed Joanie into the house through the kitchen door. Amy, the housekeeper, was at the kitchen sink washing dishes. She was there Monday through Friday, rain or shine.

"Mr. S, you been gone again," she teased. You are always gone somewhere. How long are you here for this time? Welcome back," she continued.

"Can I get you some coffee?" she asked.

"Hey, you. I came back for you...only for you," he teased back. "I could really use some of your coffee."

Jim took a seat at the kitchen table. Amy poured him a cup of coffee and brought it to him.

"What about you, Mrs.? Can I pour you a cup?" asked Amy.

"Not right now," Joanie said.

"I'll get some in a bit."

"Okay. Suit yourself," Amy responded.

Jim just sat there with his elbows on the table and head hanging.

"Mr. S, what's eating you?" said Amy.

"Looks like you're carrying a load. You better unload or it could put you in a bad way."

"I'll be alright. I just gotta work at this a little at a time. I'll be alright."

"Okay, if you say so. But, you can always give your burdens to the Lord and he'll handle 'em, you know," directed Amy as she walked through the kitchen headed to the bedrooms. She wanted to get started in another area of the house in order to give Mr. S, a moment which she recognized he desperately needed.

Jim finished his coffee twenty minutes later, took a deep breath and stood to go take a shower and to lie down for a moment before getting dressed for work.

At twelve o'clock, Jim had had some rest and a chance to sober up completely. He thought about the challenges that he was facing. He reluctantly rose to his feet and began to get dressed for the office. He was feeling sorry for himself, which was doing him absolutely no good at all. When he was dressed he took a couple more deep breaths, then charged ahead. He knew that Joanie was out in the garden at this time of day. He walked directly there to tell her that he was leaving. He stood at the door with a partial smile on his face watching her as she snipped and pruned each flower with such love. He really loved and admired her so much. Three or four seconds later he opened the door leaning out to let her know that he was leaving.

"Honey, I'm gone. If you need me I'll be at the office...probably 'til late," he said with tenderness.

Joanie stood from her kneeling position, "Were you able to get a little rest?"

"Yes I was...a little bit. That drink that I had on the flight really knocked me on my ass. I guess it was because I hadn't eaten. That's the last time that I'll do that," he pledged.

The drive down the Freeway was uneventful. Traffic at anytime of day in the Los Angeles area was tight, but at least his delay of going to the office was a smart move. He anticipated no more than a thirty-five minute ride over the normal hour and ten minutes that it normally took him from home. He thought as he rode that he could get all of his problems worked out if he could get Chambers' help. But, why should she help him? he thought.

It was his fault that the situation had gotten to this point. The higher you go the more help you have around you, and the more accountable you become for everything, it appeared.

Jim pulled into his marked parking space. He acknowledged the security guard, got out and walked without a sense of purpose across the garage toward his office.

Two of his employees were parking their car as they were returning from lunch. Surrant greeted them offering his hand to each one after the other.

"Melanie, Martha, how's your day going? You getting a lot of work done today," Jim teased?

"Mr. Surrant, we know you, and if we don't get the work done you'll make us pay," Martha chirped.

Melanie gestured that she felt the same way.

Melanie continued as they walked along, "And, if you're not here, Holley steps in and takes over. She may even be a little more difficult when you're not in. So, you bet your sweet bippy that we've gotten plenty of work done." Surrant thought as he opened the door for the ladies that he had been a complete asshole, so many times to all of his troops. They had hung in there with him giving their remote office all they had everyday, and this was the very first time that he's even given his actions any thought. The operation wasn't a small one. He had five sales managers, their administrative assistants, four programmers, two trainees, three maintenance fulfillment contractors and an attorney on staff to review all corporate contracts as the sales people brought them in. Holley managed the entire operation, and he managed Holley.

Jim's arrival at the office was a welcome sight for Holley. She had been doing both his job as well as hers. She had often told Jim the difficulties that she faced whenever he was out but, Surrant could care less. He thought he had given Holley a break hiring her with her background. He only did it for very selfish reasons, because she typed over ninety words a minute and that she looked so good.

"Jim, it's about time you got here," Holley said as she followed him into his office. "There's a lot happening. The main thing is that I found more of the missing funds, but there's still a huge amount still out there. What have you decided on that?"

"I've got no plans. Besides, I left that in your hands. The meeting in Chicago gave me even more challenges. I was put on the spot three times. Chambers will be calling me to follow-up on the pertinent issues because I was proven to be the weak link in her chain. I'm concerned, but let's go over the urgent matters that I have here and then we'll talk about specifics, okay?" Jim said, taking a deep breath while managing to flash a shallow smile.

Holley smiled back and gave him support by saying, "There's nothing that we can't accomplish together, you know what I mean? These three thank you for your business letters should also go out today."

"Back an envelope to mail them to Kenders. He has to sign them before they go out. It's not due until the twenty-eighth. Wrap this trinket for me. My aunt's birthday is in eleven days." I still have enough time to get her a gift. I can't take a chance on my mother getting on my case, if auntie doesn't get her gift and get it on time. "

Surrant and Holley walked through the rest of the urgent items and also worked through many of the other items as well. They were actually knocking out his waiting stack of work relatively fast. Before Jim realized it, it was four thirty.

"Holley, I've had enough today. I'm still trying to get over the Chicago trip. I'll see you on Monday okay?"

"You're going home? I can't believe that. What's wrong with you? There's so much that we still have to do to be ready for next week...to be ready for Toney Chambers and the questions that you just told me she'd be asking and you're going home already? That's not like you, Jim. What's wrong?" Holley questioned.

"I just don't have it today, you know? I just don't have it. I may come in tomorrow but today, I've had enough. There are still things that you can get done. That's why I pay you the big bucks, but I'm out of here," Jim said as he finished packing up his things and moved toward the door. Holley stood there for a moment speechless. What was the deal with Surrant? What had the trip to Chicago done to him? Had it been that devastating?

Holley walked back to her desk noticing that there were only a couple of people still hard at work. Most of the employees had taken the opportunity to leave right at five to start their weekend. Most Fridays she could count on Jim asking her to stay for a while in order for them to work through some emergency or another. But tonight she was there alone, and it felt very strange. She was so used to him and his predictability. Something was happening with him. This was a completely different side of him. She was used to being in control, but that was not the case today. She finished a few more tasks and decided to call it a day as well.

Jim got into his car admitting to himself that he was feeling boxed in. Holley was able to find some of the missing funds but he had to get the other items in line that would be of use to him. He could only hope that Holley was as successful early next week. But right now he had to get back to his safe haven...to Joanie and the kids. While he rode he thought of a million things. Could he bounce back totally? Could he still be the main candidate for Chambers' position? He had to come up with some sort of plan. But right now he was just too tired. And Gamble. What had he been able to really accomplish? He was supposed to make sure that Chambers was taken care of so that he could slide right into her spot. The thought of Gamble not handling his end of their bargain pissed Jim off. Surrant picked up his cell phone to call Gamble again. After eight rings, Surrant gave up for the moment. He'd get back in the saddle on Monday.

FIFTEEN

Toney stretched and gaped as she sat on the side of her four poster rice bed with her legs dangling. She woke to soft music coming from her alarm clock. She remembered the first early day at Prophecy, when she got out of bed at four thirty in the morning in order to be the first one in the office. It was four thirty a.m. again over fifteen years later. The night came and went so fast. But, it was finally Friday. It had been more than an eventful week! Toney had proven to herself that she was even stronger than she thought she was. It was all over but the shouting. She was drained, because she had to put so much into the week. The fact that she had gotten through the big meeting with flying colors and all of the strange events so well was amazing to her. Realizing that the big meeting was over actually gave her energy. She was looking forward to the weekend...she pledged not to bring any work home with her this weekend. It would be one of relaxation and the chores that had gone undone over the past weeks. She would also fill part of the time with other items that she had to get done. She went through her regular morning routine and arrived at the office before six. As normal for her, she began to work the minute she hit her office. Her focus had to be on wrapping up last week's activities, planning her Japan trip and setting up the conference call for Tuesday.

Sonjia tapped on Toney's door as soon as she arrived.

"Good morning, Toney. I know you've just finished with the meeting and that you're probably wiped out, but I need to talk to you about Freddy. He's gotten into it with three people this week. I've tried to talk to him, but he isn't hearing me. Now, he's an excellent employee under normal circumstances, but there is something going on with him. You know that we're all used to him laughing, teasing and joking with us, but he's actually gotten mean. Real mean. Can you talk to him for me?" Sonjia asked appearing a little upset.

"Hi, Sonjia. Sure I'll talk to him. Let Fred know that I want to see him the minute he arrives. Is there anything else that I need to know about?" Toney asked as a measure of catching up on what had happened over the last two plus days.

"Nothing of any significance," Sonjia uttered.

"Although, Cameron called to see when the meeting would conclude. She said she really needed to talk to you. But, she said it could wait," she continued.

"Okay. I'll give her a call in a while."

Sonjia left returning to her desk. Toney went back to work. At eight thirty on the nose Freddy arrived. Sonjia had been watching the main door while she went about her work to ensure she got to him when he came in. Finally, he came through the door seemingly dragging a bit.

She got up and walked toward him, "Good morning, Freddy. Toney wants to see you first thing. She's waiting for you now," Toney instructed.

"Hey, Sonjia. What's this about? She never wants to see me one-on-one. What's going on?" he said defensively.

"Well, she does now and if I were you, I'd hightail it in there pronto. You know Toney, she does not like to be kept waiting," Sonjia said with a little parody.

Freddy immediately turned around heading for Toney's office, still talking to Sonjia. "Am I in trouble or is she giving me a raise?"
Sonjia gestured with her shoulders in the air and her hands palm up indicating that she didn't know. After a couple of light taps on the door Toney responded, "Come in."

"You wanted to see me Ms. C?"

"I most certainly did, young man. Please take a seat," as she motioned toward the chairs just in front of her desk.

"Tell me about it," she said.

"Tell you about what?" he asked.

"Alright Freddy. We won't play this hide and seek game this morning okay? What's going on with you? You're tense, irritable and very short-tempered lately. There must be something going on. I want to help but I need to know what it is before I can do that. You can tell me that it's none of my business, but as long as your work doesn't suffer I'll accept that. I'd really like to help if I could though."
Freddy was at the brink of tears and tried to hold back. He was silent for a moment. Finally, he whispered as if he were trying to fight back the tears, "It's personal. It's embarrassing. If I find that you can help, I'll let you know, okay? I really do appreciate you, Ms. C. You're very special to care."

"We have to be here for each other. That's the way it works," Toney said as a measure of support. "Come and see me anytime."
She stood up to walk Freddy to the door.

"Please let me know if there is something that I can do. Okay?" she expressed as she stood by the chair waiting for him to rise.

"I will, Ms. C. Thanks," he said as he stood to make his way to the door with Toney.

He walked through the door and as he got just past Sonjia's desk, he turned to Toney to say thanks again, but she had already closed the door. Toney stood with her back to the door for a moment, thinking about their conversation, then walked back to her desk.

She sat there wondering what Fred was so upset about. She knew that he was a homosexual with a checkered past, but he was a good worker and a decent person, so she always felt that it was his business. She lived by the motto, 'live and let live.'

A few minutes later she picked up the phone to call Cameron.

"Good morning, Electrical Paging Association, may I help you?" the receptionist answered.

"Good morning, Ms. Beeage, please."

"She isn't in yet. May I take a message?"

"Yes, please ask her to call Toney Chambers. She has my number."

"Certainly ma'am."

Toney hung up and went right back to the next thing on her list of to do's.

It was already nine thirty. Toney pulled the folder with all of the information regarding her Japanese customers. She reviewed the entire file from cover to cover. She wanted to bone up on all of the information before she placed the call to Bukura. Marvin Bukura had transferred to Japan over three years earlier and had gotten to know the lay of the land well. His name could now open many doors and be easily mistaken for one that was Japanese. He was about five foot five with dark hair, and if he had had any oriental features at all, one would easily mistake him for Japanese. She counted on him to keep the three big Japanese customers that they had loyal to Prophecy and to help land deals with the four big customers that Prophecy wanted. Her trip to Japan was to wine and dine Mr. Yamaguchi, the largest of these customers, because they were trying to land his account. His account was worth seven hundred million over ten years. She couldn't afford to miss this. This account would surely put her in the driver's seat for her next opportunity, when the Board of Directors narrowed their choices for Corbin's replacement. Rumors said it would be Toney, but she had never dealt seriously with rumors. After she completed the file, she put it aside to try and get in touch with Bukura. She picked up the phone to buzz Sonjia.

"Yes Toney, what can I do for you?" Sonjia inquired.

"Sonjia, try to get Bukura on the phone for me and I need you to call the AT&T operator to setup the conference call for Tuesday. Do you have those notes from the meeting transcribed yet? I need to take them home with me and review them over the weekend."

"Alright, I'll try to reach Bukura for you. The AT&T conference call has already been setup for nine a.m. on Tuesday. The notes from the big meeting are just about done. Terry, Mr. Corbin's assistant, is transcribing the first half and I'm doing the second half. So, we should have them completed by three. Would that work for you?"

"Sure. That'll be fine. Would you see if Cameron's in yet? It'd be great if I could get with her before the end of the day."

"Sure, no problem. I'll do that right away."

"Thanks," Toney said as she hung up the phone.

Toney took this opportunity to go through her mail for the morning. She came across a postcard from Helen, which coerced a smile. She was apparently enjoying her visit to Alaska with her son and his family. She then allowed her body to collapse in her chair. The week had been rough. She reflected on the past ninety days as a whole. There was much too much happening. The missing papers were the strangest of all the mysteries. The situation in Jamaica could have been a prank by some of the islanders, but the papers, who could want them? With the near mishap and the complexities of her job, she had to take the edge off of the way she was feeling. These incidents had no place in her life, so she thought about it at length. She didn't have time for this stuff and had to find a way to remove it from her life.

Toney's next move was to select an investigator. She knew nothing about this business, but for the sake of privacy regarding the situation, she'd have to select one on her own with no input from anyone. She picked up the yellow pages and turned to the area marked Investigations. She was surprised that there were so many listed. She decided that she would go about this systematically. She started at the beginning and worked her way through. Her first call was to All About the Truth Agency.

"All About the Truth. This is Valerie, may I help you?"

"Good afternoon, Valerie. May I speak with your lead investigator?"

"Our lead investigator? Ma'am do you have a name," the voice on the other end of the phone said with a slight bit of impatience as if she were busy."

"No. This is new for me. Is the owner available?"

"There are actually four people who own the company. Which one would you like?"

"I'll tell you what, I need to speak with the person who has solved the most mysteries recently. Can you tell me who on your staff has done that?"

"I can do that. That would be Fin Babbitt. He is the busiest one on the staff. I'm not sure that he can take your case, ma'am, because he is just that busy. He's out right now, but I can take a message if you like."

"When do you expect him? I'd prefer to call him back. I have to be careful how this is handled, so until I can talk with him, I can't leave a message."

Reticence filled the air for a second. "He'll be back before five," she said.

"Okay. It's already one thirty. I'll call back at five. Thanks," Toney said feeling somewhat relieved.

Toney jumped up from her desk with a burst of energy, to run down to get some yogurt. She was meeting Grant at six for dinner so yogurt would be just the thing to tide her over until then.

She breezed by Sonjia's desk as she usually did when she darted out of her office to run an errand.

"I'll be right back," Toney rushed.

"Okay, Toney. Bukura's out. His assistant will call me back when he comes in. She said he's expected about four, Chicago time."

"That's perfect," Toney said continuing toward the main door. "I'll be right back. I'm going for yogurt. Care for anything?"

"No, ma'am. I had a full lunch as you should consider doing once in awhile," Sonjia said shaking her finger at Toney.

Toney left and a few minutes later she was back. She ran into Freddy who looked her up and down saying, "Um um um...if only I were a man!"

Toney smiled telling Freddy, "You'd better behave, young man. Remember the rules, no sexual harassment!"

Toney kept moving and in an instant she was right back in front of Sonjia.

"Any messages?"

"Not a one," Sonjia said as she handed Toney the completed transcripts from the meeting. "While you were gone, Terry called from on high to let me know that she was done with her half of the transcripts. I ran up to get a copy of hers along with the disk. I took her a copy of mine with my disk too, so we're done. I'll check her part, as I'm sure she'll do as well."

"Great...thanks," Toney recited as she whisked herself through the door of her office.

Toney took her seat, finished her yogurt and started to review the paperwork. A few minutes later she needed a break. Her eyes were getting tired, so she leaned back to relax for a minute.

The next thing she knew, she was daydreaming again **....**

The first year at Prophecy was mind boggling for her. She was learning so much from Ms. Roman.

"Toney, Jane, Beverly and Bill here are your tasks for today. Give Jamie and Tiffany their tasks once you've figured out how they can assist you. Try to figure out each of the tasks on your own. This will teach you more than you'll know. Only come to me with questions that you can't figure out on your own," she said everyday.

She was right. By the time they worked through each of the problems on their own, there were very few that she actually needed to give them instructions on.

Ms. Roman worked them hard, but she taught them a lot. A year and two months into the job Ms. Roman was promoted to the New York office. Toney was in shock and couldn't believe it. She and Ms. Roman had become so attached. This was great news for Ms. Roman, but what about their relationship? She had really mentored them to the point that

they couldn't figure out where they would be without her. They all wondered whom they'd get for a boss. For two weeks straight there were three different individuals in and out of the office.
Paul Conners, Senior Programmer, ran the office while the search was on. They all thought that he should have been promoted to the Director. But, the big guys saw it differently.

A month after Ms. Roman had left, they all received a fax from the front runner of the three potential Directors. The fax was basic with the same questions for each of them. It posed questions about their work habits and even went into their personal lives. He asked questions like how long in the industry? What each person's last evaluation results were like? What each of us did on our days off? This was very much out of the ordinary according to the people on staff. This guy wanted to know with whom he would be dealing. He was very different. Three weeks after the questionnaires were completed and faxed back to him, he came in for the employees, Paul and other senior managers to interview him, before he was hired. There was something extremely strange about this guy, but She couldn't put her finger on it. Two weeks later, Dick Negri was hired as the new Director of programming. She had a feeling that she needed to keep her eyes on this guy because he was too happy go lucky. He wasn't a bad looking guy, about five foot eight with a tall slender build. He had started to lose his hair and for a white guy in his late thirties that was unusual. He had a loud laugh, which went all through them and was activated at the slightest little thing. He was extremely hard to read, so one never quite knew what was what. But, one thing was for sure, he really knew his stuff. There wasn't much information out there about Dick personally, so they all had to take things one step at a time with him until he slipped up and showed his true colors. And, they all felt that he would slip up eventually if there was anything about him that hadn't yet surfaced. One minute he was happy go lucky and the next he was unapproachable. Day in and day out they worked and watched keeping mostly to themselves at first. After the first ninety days or so they were all confused and felt that the best thing for them to do was their jobs and everything else would take care of itself.

They moved along into the first six months of Dick at the helm. He was really smart with a paucity of fresh creative new ideas. It was obvious that anyone, who wanted to, could learn a great deal from him.

One day before seven in the morning Toney found herself alone in the office. She had decided to get in early to get some paperwork done before the interruptions of the day held her hostage from the number of tasks that she would be able to accomplish. She stopped by security to get an office key to open the door for herself. She slid through the door quickly locking it behind her. She flipped on the lights and stepped to her cubicle, unloading the big bag that she carried, which had all of the necessities that she needed for the day. She took her seat turning on the overhead light and got to work. Not ten minutes later, she heard someone else entering the office. Toney stood up peering over her cube to see who it was. It was Dick. She hadn't gotten too deeply involved at that point.

"Good morning, Dick, you startled me," Toney said in a delicate voice.

"Good morning, Toney." He said somewhat surprised to see her there as well."

"What are you doing in so early?"

"I haven't been in early before, I usually stay later in the evenings to get my projects and regular work done on a timely basis. I just thought I'd come in early this morning to get a jump on the day," she said proudly.

He shook his head in acceptance as he continued through the outer office area, entering his office and turning on the lights. "I see," he said speaking to her from over his shoulder.

Over an hour passed and no conversation of any kind took place. At seven forty, the troops started to arrive, and little by little the chatter and the business of the day began. Dick's office became the early spot for his favorites Paul and Bill, together.

The momentum of the players on staff rose to an all time high. The assistant programmers, the programmers, the secretaries and even Dick, Paul and Bill were turning out product. They were headed toward the team of the year for the company. They were all churning along so smoothly that day, when they learned that the lead programmer had accepted a Supervisors position with the competition several blocks away. When Paul turned in his resignation, he was escorted out of the office immediately. It was necessary to ensure that the integrity of Prophecy's top secrets and new products that were in the works were maintained and not carried out with him. One by one the word got out about Paul and the fact that there was a vacancy.

Later that afternoon the chatter began, "I wonder who'll get Paul's job?" Tiffany Mathis said out loud looking at Toney.

Toney was next in line for the job and everyone knew it.

"Toney, are you gonna throw your hat in the ring? You'll be the first African American to hold that position with Prophecy," Jamie Landers mentioned.

"Yeah, girl, take that damned job. That'll give the rest of us hope, you know," Tiffany pushed.

"Besides, company policy says it has to be you. You've gotten top marks on producing top level programs since you walked through the door. I've heard them talking about you and how smart you are. The programs that you've developed have made the company a ton of cash and that should be all they look at, right?" Jamie continued.

"That's what they should do, but when have you known them to do what they should do?" Toney said in a sarcastic way which surprised even herself.

"I know that's right. But, that all depends on how you handle things," Jamie continued.

"What harm would it do if you let them know that you know?"

"Besides, they expect that you'll sit still for whatever they decide to do. You've got to become more assertive. They'll never get rid of you...you're too valuable to them, you know," Tiffany quipped.

"You may have a point, but I've been with the company less than three years," Toney said.

"So what?" Tiffany said.

"Yeah, so what? And, the fact that you've turned out so much new product in such a short time is what can put you over the edge too."

"Well, I'll think about it over the weekend," Toney remarked with her forehead bunched up.

They all went back to work keeping an eye out for anything they could hear....

Toney shook herself back to the moment. It was five to five. She had to get the call in to Fin Babbitt. She really needed him. She had to get to the bottom of the mysteries. She placed the call again.

"All about the Truth, this is Valerie, may I help you?"

"Hi Valerie, is Mr. Babbitt available?"

"Is this the lady that called earlier this afternoon?" Valerie quizzed.

"Yes it is," Toney answered. "Is he in?"

"I told him that a lady called and that you'd call again around five. He's expecting you. He said the fact that you didn't leave your number was intriguing to him, so hold on , okay?"

"Okay," Toney said with a partial smile on her face. She found this whole thing astonishing. Just as that thought swept through her mind she heard a voice on the phone.

"This is Babbitt," the voice growled.

"Mr. Babbitt, uh, I have a problem. I hope you can help me," Toney fumbled.

Total silence took over.

Babbitt said impatiently, "And?"

"Well, I'd like to come to your office and sit down with you to tell you all about it. Is that how it works?"

"You can begin by telling me your name. My schedule is very busy…not much time to sit down and talk. I have to decide first if I want the case. Who is this anyway," he forced?

"My name is Toney Chambers. I'm Vice President of Prophecy Computers on Lakeshore Drive. There have been some strange things happening to both my boyfriend and me. I've got to get to the bottom of it," she explained.

Silence once again fell over the phone. Babbitt's mind was working overtime. This was big. The Vice President at Prophecy? This could mean big bucks for him.

He cleared his throat, "Be here at ten o'clock on Monday. I can get more information then. The address is," he started.

"Toney interrupted, "I have the address. I'll see you Monday at ten."

They hung up the phone. A feeling of calm swept over her. She was making a move on her own to clear up this problem. Toney wondered about Babbitt's abrasive manner, but for as much as she knew all Private Investigator's were like that.

She prepared to leave for the day, and within two to three minutes she was breezing through the office wishing everyone a great weekend.

SIXTEEN

Grant yawned as he asked Millicent the first question of the morning. He hadn't slept very soundly and was still struggling to wakeup. He had been at the office for over an hour and a half and was trying to focus on one of the two big cases that he had to develop, when he realized that she had arrived. There were several precedents that he was researching in order to develop a sound position on both cases within the next thirty days. She had just put her purse into her bottom left desk drawer and taken her seat.

"Good morning, Miss Mill. Do you have the Fountroy file?" Grant grunted from the half-closed door of his office.

"I thought it was in my file cabinet," he continued.

"Hi, Grant. I don't have it. As a matter of fact I haven't seen it. When was the last time you had it?" Millicent chirped.

"I really don't recall. Seems like I had it just before Toney and I left for Jamaica. It's one of the accounts that could put me over the top," as anticipation creeped into his demeanor.

Millicent got up from her desk marched to Grant's office, closed the door, and took a seat.

Startled, Grant turned toward the area where Millicent had plopped down.

"What is it Mill?" Grant asked.

"I remember. I told you that one of the shorter twins came to me asking for one of your files? Well, if memory serves that was the file. I thought you got it back?"

"No. I don't remember having it for a while." Grant said looking puzzled.

"Those bastards are up to something, Grant. You had better watch them. Something's not right, believe it," she said as only she could.

"I'll take care of it," Grant cautioned.

He got up and walked down to Nick's office. Leaning in partially into his doorway, Grant tapped on the door.

"Hey, man, you got a second?"

"Sure. What do you need?"

"Actually, I need my Fountroy file. I can't seem to find it. Mill thought you might have it."

"She thought I might have it?" he said very defensively as if he had been attacked.

"Why would I have it? I most certainly do not have it," he said in a wounded posture.

"Okay, if you say so. But, why would Mill think you had it? Several people in the office have reported that you'd been in my office a few times while I was out. Were you rambling in my office while I was on vacation?"

Nick lost it.

"Why would you ask me a question like that?" he questioned loudly.

The shorter twin's scheme was becoming unmasked beginning with this particular interaction. Grant saw through Nick's antics based on his actions about this incident. He began to review each of the questions that Nick had asked while they were at lunch yesterday. It was as if he was cross-examining Grant. What did Nick really want and what was he really after? No way was Montrose, Chairman of the Board going to let these young guys, who didn't even know who they were themselves, get a promotion to partner. Neither of them was what the firm needed as official partners. Nick couldn't look Grant in the eyes while the exchange came to a conclusion for the moment. Grant stood there shaking his head and now becoming very suspicious about what the twins may be capable of doing. In reality though, he knew that whatever they had planned had to be heavy. The fact that he had watched the way they operated, from their very first day, gave him a strange feeling. Anything to get ahead. No one was safe. Grant felt that no amount of suspicions could even begin to describe what the shorter twins were capable of. He was poised for the game and continued to arm himself to combat them when the time was right.

Grant began taking mental notes on both Nick and Terry from the one-on-one encounter with Nick and the lunch with Terry. They were much too young to have a real grasp on the type of cleverness it would take to win at the game that they were setting up. Grant had been poised for just such circumstances. He hadn't thought much about it in his earlier years, when he was being conditioned and becoming so thick-skinned. And, to think, this was all because of the way he looked. This society is sick, he thought. That's what we have all become. The value of one's self worth in others eyes is predicated upon the way he or she looked. What a testament to the future of society, Grant thought as he stood there, watching his colleague squirm trying to figure out a lie to tell. He was desperate and wanted Grant off of his case, probably so he could sneak the file back into Grant's office and pretend that nothing had happened. Grant continued to think as he tuned Nick's lies out of his head. He thought that times were hard then, but his determination became more and more keen as he pushed through the days when he was the outcast for no apparent reason and how he had always tried just to be accepted just for himself. Envy and jealousy can tear people apart, and to think that the way that a person looks or doesn't look can do that much to someone else. He stood there thinking of how amazing all of this was to him.

"Nick, I'll look again but I'm sure it's not in my office. By the way, what was it you needed when you were in my office?" Grant asked calmly.

"Uh, umm, I was looking for a black marker. I was putting together some flip charts for the old man and only had color markers, so I had checked with everyone else. Mill wasn't there, so I took the liberty of going into your office and looking in your desk. I hope that was alright?" he said trying to rebound.

"Sure. That's fine. What is mine is yours. Right?" Grant said walking away.

By the time that Grant got back into his office area, Millicent was on the phone.

"Here he is now, Toney," Millicent said putting the call on hold.

"Grant, Toney's on the phone."

"Thanks, Mill," Grant responded as he passed her desk.

"Well, what in the hell happened?" she asked impatiently.

"Shhh Mill. I've told you, you've got to watch your mouth. We're in the office…and, you might offend someone. Besides, I'll tell you later," he followed up while reaching for his phone.

"Okay. Okay," she said getting back to work.

"This is Grant," he followed through.

"Hi, pudding. What cha doing?" Toney teased.

"Hi, baby. Just this moment, I got back from having an unreal confrontation with Nick. It was unbelievable. That son of a bitch! He just insulted my intelligence. Damn. Can you believe it?"

"Honey, I never hear you talk like this. Calm down and tell me what happened."

"There's some real underhanded shit going on here Toney and I'm going to get to the bottom of it. But, I've got to be careful. They've got a plan and I don't. They're a lot further along in their plan and they are executing it too, but I'll get it together. Here's what happened," Grant said as he started to tell Toney all about it.

After about four minutes of an update, Toney had the complete picture.

"Just like Surrant, the twins can be dealt with. It just takes some strategy sessions. Let's talk tonight honey," she said.

"That's fine," Grant said.

"Have a great day and don't let anyone spoil it for you," Toney whispered in a condensing tone.

They hung up the phone. He sat there for a moment mulling over what had just transpired and decided to get back to work. He had gone as far as he could with the research of the Merriday case when he decided to put it aside for the time being. He turned to the massive stack of work that he faced, diligently worked through each item in his IN BOX systematically as he always did. All that could be heard was the distant ringing of telephones, chatter several times over, the clicking of Mill and some of the other secretaries nails hitting against the keys of each of their keyboards. A couple of hours later, he took a short break to get another cup of coffee to finish off the morning. While walking from his office he took a quick glance around his area of the outer office noticing that everyone appeared to be in their own little world, working on their own little tasks. He walked into the copy room, which housed the coffeepot and the water cooler. The first thing that he noticed was that the back door to the back entrance of their suite of offices was propped open, which he found very odd. There was an unmarked truck backed up to the door with two men dressed in what appeared to be moving uniforms. They were loading onto the truck some of the office furniture from the corridor adjacent Grant's particular corridor.

"What the hell?" Grant thought.

He decided to challenge them. If they were legit, there would be nothing lost. If not, he could help to avoid an awful robbery.

"May I help you, sir?"

"No," one of the men said abruptly.

"We're doing just fine," while he continued to take the articles that he was holding to the truck.

"May I see your papers, please?" Grant asked.

"Hell, no," the smaller man said as he hauled back his fist and struck Grant in the jaw, causing his coffee cup to go in one direction and Grant to be knocked off guard.

"What the...? Grant said as he got his balance back. "Mill." "Mill." "Call the police!"

Mill heard Grant's panicked voice, getting up to see what was happening. By the time that Millicent got to the copy room both the moving men had boarded the truck and started the engine.

"Mill, you've got to call the police. The license on the truck was TTYM 439, Ohio plates," Grant said standing there holding his face.

"Are you alright?" she asked.

"Don't worry about me, call the cops," he said in a rough and demanding tone.

Everyone who worked near the copy room area had heard the bruit about and had started to gather around. Both the shorter twins came running.

"What the hell's going on here, Grant? Are you okay?" asked Terry, the taller twin.

"Sure. I'm fine," Grant said.

There were at least twenty people now gathered at the doorway of the copy room.

"Everyone, please get back to work. Things are fine. Please, just get back to work," Grant demanded.

He kneeled down to begin picking up the pieces of glass that had scattered all over the little area, even into the furthest corners of the small area. Mr. Montrose heard about the robbery and made his way to the area.

"What happened here, Grant?"

"I walked in here to refresh my coffee. I noticed that the back door had been propped open and that a truck was backed up to the door. Thinking how odd that was, I became suspicious. There were two men dressed in what appeared to be moving company uniforms. They were working from that corridor," he said pointing to the northern corridor.

"I challenged them and all hell broke out. I got slugged unexpectedly and they took off. Mill is calling the police," Grant concluded.

With that said, two carloads of Chicago's finest arrived on the scene.

"Good morning, who called this in?" Sergeant Billings asked.

"I did, officer. I called at the direction of Grant Parlarme," Mill said pointing to Grant.

Sergeant Billings walked over to Grant, "What happened here, sir?"

Grant gave the officers the story starting at the beginning being sure not to leave the smallest detail out.

Sergeant Billings conferred with the other officers. After their short conference concluded, they all went about their individual assignments. They combed the complete area of the break-in. They checked the lock on the door, dusted for fingerprints and so forth. While all of the preliminary work took place, Grant went back to his office to pull himself together. It was lunchtime. Most of the office workers took their lunch breaks with only one topic on their minds. For the rest of the morning that's all one heard. But, Grant had some suspicions of his own. After all of the years that he had been at this firm, nothing slightly resembling this had taken place. There were just too many coincidences in the past few weeks. "There is something wrong…very wrong here," he thought.

PART II

Toney slept in for the first time in months. She wanted to take some time to examine the whole shebang. She needed to look at every single thing that had happened. Every single angle. She wanted to make sure that she would be one step in front of whoever it was that was after her. Her body clock had jolted her just before five a. m. A few minutes later, as a matter of routine, her alarm clock sounded. She turned over to disengage the clock then settled in again for a few more winks. As she lay there, she realized it was Saturday. The meeting with Babbitt consumed her mind. She wanted to be ready for Babbitt on Monday. She tried to doze again but finally gave up after an hour or so, jumped out of bed, and skipped to her bathroom to wash her face and brush her teeth. She ran through the office area, sweeping up a pad and pencil and headed for the coffee-pot. She slapped the pad and pencil down on the counter, putting on a pot of coffee. A second or so later she sat down on one of the bar stools and started recapping the strange events one by one with all of the circumstances pertinent to each. She took a break a few minutes later, poured a cup of coffee and resumed her task. In less than an hour she finished her preliminary stab at compiling the information. It was time for her to run to the nail and hair salon. Her appointments were at ten and eleven. An hour and a half later she was back ready to start preparing for Grant.

She poured another cup of coffee and continued her morning routine. An hour and twenty minutes later, she was interrupted by the phone.

"Hello." she replied.

"Hi beautiful. I'm about five blocks from your place. Are you ready?" Grant swooned.

"Just about. No need for you to come up. By the time you get here, I'll be at the front door."

"That sounds like a real winner. I can't wait to see you," he whispered.

"Me too, honey. Where are we going?" Toney asked as her heart started to flutter.

"It's a surprise. We haven't been to this place for over a year. I'll see you in a minute."

Toney finished the last of the things she had to do, picked up a sweater and headed for the lobby of the building. She looked flawless in her white silk slacks, a leopard print cammy with a matching silk sweater, patent leather mules and hand bag. She had covered herself with both their favorite perfumes, Dolce Gabanna. It was a rich full-bodied fragrance usually worn by very discerning women. Grant was waiting in his 450 SL convertible. He had the top back and his shades on and was wearing a huge smile as she pushed through the door. He immediately got out of the car to participate in a foot race with the doorman to seek the victory of who would open the door for this beauty.

"Hi, honey you look ravishing." Grant shared the feeling that Toney was everything he had ever wanted.

"Thanks for the compliments, pooky. You are always so sweet. What would I ever do without you?" she said sweetly, looking at him in a deeply adoring way.

"You never have to consider that because I will always be with you. Always my love."

"Let's take a walk down by the shoreline, and maybe we can grab a bite to eat at the Seafood Haven in Navy Pier," Grant encouraged her.

"That 's great. We haven't been there in a while."

He parked the car and rushed around to Toney's side to assist her from the car.

They walked through Navy Pier, window shopping and ended up at Seafood Haven. It was crowded but to the two of them, they were the last two people in the world; so they really didn't even consider the wait as an imposition. Forty-five minutes later, they were seated. Grant had engineered a window seat with a view of the water.

The hostess said as she showed them to their table, "I apologize for such a long wait. These window tables are at a premium, especially on such a beautiful clear day. What can I get for you to drink?"

"Never mind the wait. It was okay. I'll have a Diet Pepsi with a wedge of lemon," Toney said, taking a look around at her surroundings.

"And, I'll have a coke to start," Grant said picking up the menu.

"Baby, what looks good to you?" he asked.

"Let me see," she responded, picking up the menu and giving it a once over.

"Well, we're in one of Chicago's best seafood spots, so I think I'll have my favorite, soft shell crab. What about you?" "King Crab and lots of them," Grant said with a twinkle in his eyes.

Their waiter was back within five minutes with their drinks and immediately took their food requests and shuffled off again into the kitchen area. They sat there discussing this and that when Surrant's name came into the conversation.

"Have you been working our plan?"

"You know that I have. I make him accountable for each and every thing that he is supposed to do. I have stopped covering for him in any area just as we discussed in Jamaica. He's starting to unravel. He couldn't get any help from me at the meeting. I interjected during his presentation only when it served my own personal agenda, and he walked away looking really shaky. I am paying special attention to him each week on the conference calls, jotting down any and all comments that he makes, right or wrong. I have begun to keep a folder on him regarding his indiscretions and otherwise. Believe me, baby, I am all over him and he doesn't have a clue. He will ultimately be his own undoing.

"That's great. As we decided, the only way to beat them is to let them beat themselves. We can never come off seeming like we are out to get anyone because we will look like the villains. Right?"

"You are so right. How did you get so smart?"

"Thanks for saying so, honey, but by and large most people who have a negative agenda ultimately screw themselves. After all, that is the rule of the Bible, and the Bible is the best manual on how to live that any of us could have. I pay very close attention to scripture."

"I love you so much, Grant. So very much," Toney said reaching for his hand across the table.

The server brought their food as they got comfortable to enjoy the meal. Over an hour passed. They sat there content from an enjoyable afternoon waiting to get their check. Grant paid the bill and they left the restaurant. They took a stroll on the pier and two hours later called it a day, because they both had work to do. He initiated a long wet kiss goodbye, dropped Toney off, reminding her that he'd pick her up at eight for church. She got out of the car turned to Grant blew him a kiss and a smile and daintily walked into the building headed to her condominium. She went into her place, changed clothes and immediately jumped right back in to her list for Babbitt. She finished the list and began to research Tokyo for her oriental trip that was coming up. She finally sat down to rest for a few minutes before planning her schedule for next week, which was to begin with her visit to Babbitt.

On Sunday morning, she lay in bed confident that she was prepared for what lay ahead for her. Before she even put her feet on the floor, she thanked God for allowing her to be a part of the living again that morning. She emotionally arranged her prayers for the service that she and Grant would attend later in the morning. After her first cup of coffee she began the task of getting dressed. It somehow was not the joyful routine that she had experienced on most mornings. Something in her spirit was off. She didn't know what. Maybe it had to do with the fact that it was necessary to hire a Private Investigator. But she had to do what she had to do. She knew that she just couldn't tell Grant. He'd be divided between what was on his plate and her, so she had to shield him…at least for now. Toney felt the need to talk to her mom and dad, so she gave them a quick call to check in. They spoke for over fifteen minutes allowing her to wrap up that call and jump into the shower so that she'd be ready when Grant got there. They attended church and once the service was over Grant announced that he had made special plans for them at a surprise restaurant for brunch.

Fifteen minutes after leaving church they were holding hands while they cruised along chatting about everything under the sun as they did often when they were together, shortly they arrived at the spot where Grant had made plans.

"Grant, I had all but forgotten about Noonans. This is incredible. You brought me here when we first met. As a matter of fact this was the location of our second date. How on earth did you remember?" Toney said pleasantly surprised and pleased.

"You bring out the best in me, you know. It's hard to keep pleasing a woman who in her own right has so much on the ball. So, it's fun for me to try."

The early afternoon was fantastic. They reminisced and chuckled and thoroughly enjoyed one another. Several hours later they were once again on their way home to enjoy the afternoon. Toney insisted that Grant come up to her place for a while.

"You really don't have to ask me twice. I have a ton of work waiting for me at my place, but I can certainly spare a few hours for my best girl," he said playfully.

Later in the afternoon after Grant had gone home, jazz filled the air, she poured a glass of wine and prepared for the week ahead. She took a break after putting together the ensembles that she would adorn herself with each day. The wine made her kind of light headed, so she decided to lie across her bed for a few minutes.

Toney woke with the blaring sound of her phone. It was Grant.

"Hi baby. I just wanted to call to say good night," Grant said strongly.

"Honey, I'm glad you called. I laid across the bed for a moment and had drifted off to sleep. I need to get up and properly prepare for bed. You're always saving me from myself," she said with a smile in her voice.

"Honey, have a peaceful night," he said as he slightly chuckled and they hung up.

SEVENTEEN

Toney tossed and turned most of the night, even though she and Grant had enjoyed the majority of the weekend together. She managed to fall into a really deep sleep sometime just before three. She remembered looking at the clock several times. As usual, her body clock woke her at five, but lying there motionless for so long while she thought things through enabled her to drift off to sleep again. When she woke, it was eight fifteen. Somehow her psyche was troubled and working overtime, probably because of the appointment with Babbitt and the strange circumstances over the past few weeks that had forced her to hire a Private Investigator. And, in accepting this fact, she realized that there could really be trouble for her. This acknowledgment made her look at this predicament as a threat to her personal safety. This shouted to her that there was possibly something seriously wrong in her life. All of this was now confirmed, which frightened her terribly. The sheer thought of a meeting with a Private Investigator had her subconsciously shaken. She woke up with a nervous stomach. Could this be the first day toward the freedom from her stalker? She had to take action after all because she knew there must be someone out there with an ax to grind and she had to get to the bottom of it before someone really got hurt. The day for her to meet with Babbitt was upon her; now he could surely find out what the madness was all about. The first thing that she had to do was to check with her office, to make sure things were going smoothly. Once that was done, she finished getting dressed. She found herself standing in the middle of the floor wondering what she was to do next. She couldn't remember so she moved on. Her nerves were trying to take over. Realizing that she hadn't eaten since two o'clock the day before, she tried to eat a bowl of cereal. A half bowl was all she could manage. Then she poured a cup of coffee into a to-go cup, making sure the top was on securely. She picked up her notes shoved them into her briefcase, and within ten minutes she was out the door.

Toney's elevator ride to the garage gave her a moment to think. She wasn't losing it. She had been standing there in the middle of the floor trying to remember what it was she was after. She was after her notes. She started talking to herself… "Stay calm…stay calm. This will be over soon." It was nine fifteen in the morning. She hadn't been in her building during the week, at this time of day in months. There was an eerie silence in the building. Not much happening at all. When the elevator opened to the garage, she noticed a total of six cars left there. Normally when she left in the morning the garage was full to capacity. She walked across the parking deck and halfway there, one of the cars in the garage started its engine. She was alarmed at the thought of a couple of movies that she and Grant had seen, where this scene led to the car in the garage running down the victim. Who was it starting the car? She couldn't tell if the car belonged there or not. She hadn't paid attention to which cars were which before. The dark colored car with smoked glass windows backed out of the parking space turning toward her. She ran to find shelter behind the closest pillar in the garage turning her head as she ran to get a good look at what was happening. The car sped in her direction headed for the exit, barely missing her as she reached the pillar. Was that someone after her? How did they get into her secured garage? Was all of this in her mind? Was she going crazy?

Toney's heart was racing so fast, it was as if it was just about to jump out of her chest. "Calm down, calm down," she said to herself over and over again.

"I know I have to talk to Babbitt now. Someone has got to pay for this," she said out loud becoming very angry.

"I don't fuck with anyone and all of this is going on. I hope that it is Surrant, so I can get him off my case once and for all," she said with force.

She got into her car slammed down her briefcase, put the key into the ignition, started the car then put it in gear and drove off to meet with Babbitt.

Before she knew it she was driving like a bat out of hell down Michigan Avenue, peering out of her rearview mirrors, wondering if she was being tailed. When she realized what she was doing, she took hold of herself.

"Calm down, calm down," she said slowly.

"Calm down," she said again as her spirit took over all account of the morning which seemed to give her a bit of peace about it all.

"I've got to maintain a cool head," she coached herself.

She made a sharp left onto LaSalle Street and began looking for the address.

"Let's see...442, 468 ah...there it is.... 484. She drove around the block in the immediate area in search of a parking lot which was close by. After parking, she walked up to the attendant in the little booth to get a ticket.

"I'll only be a half hour," she whispered.

The attendant said nothing pointing to the sign, which listed the prices. His attitude was as if Toney was little more than an interruption.

Toney looked at the sign, nodded her head indicating that she understood, holding her hand out for her ticket.

"Thanks," she whispered again.

The attendant still saying nothing, handed her the ticket and went right back to doing whatever he was doing when she walked up. Toney walked with a sense of purpose to her destination. When she reached 484, she took a deep breath before walking in. She had high hopes that Babbitt could resolve these mysteries. He just had to. She walked over to the marquis looking for the suite number for All About the Truth, Suite # 501.

On the elevator, she took two more deep breaths, which gave her the momentum that she needed to face what was ahead.

When she opened the door to the offices, she was very surprised. She hadn't expected such a professional environment.

"Good morning, ma'am, may I help you?" the receptionist said.

Somehow her voice hadn't given the impression that it was Valerie the same person that answered the phone when she called on Friday.

"Yes. I have a ten o'clock with Fin Babbitt. Is he available?" Toney asked airing a false sense of security.

"Yes, he's in. Please take a seat. I'll let him know that you've arrived," she assured Toney.

Toney took a seat. She nervously picked up one of the magazines in front of her and flipped through the pages trying to conceal the state that she was in. Fleeting thoughts flashed through her mind unmasking the reason she was there and a surge of strength overcame her. She had to be strong. "Something like this can throw anyone. Yes, anyone at all," she thought. A few minutes later, a tall thin man appeared through the outer office door, holding it open with one foot and extending himself over the threshold with the other foot. He looked tired and acted pushed for time. He appeared to be a foreigner who had beautiful big dark dreamy eyes, jet-black hair a slightly large nose and an olive light complexion.

His aura was taunting and mysterious. Toney instantly felt like she was doing the right thing.

"Ms. Chambers?"

"Yes. I'm Toney Chambers," Toney said as she rose to her feet. "Mr. Babbitt, I presume?"

"Yes, but please call me Fin. Please," he said extending his hand. "Alright Fin. But, only if you'll call me Toney," she negotiated.

"You got a deal," he agreed.

"Please follow me. It appears that we've got some information to exchange," he continued as he walked down the short corridor to his office with Toney in tow.

He pushed the partially opened door to force a complete entry area, walked in turning around to welcome Toney. He motioned for her to take a seat in one of the two chairs positioned in front of his desk. As Toney slid into the closest chair, Fin closed the door behind her.

"Now, what can I do for you Toney?" he asked taking the seat behind his desk.

Toney started from the beginning. While she was talking she took inventory of his office. There was absolutely no resemblance to her office. Even though his office was professional, there had not been a great deal of money spent on these offices. Yes, they were very professional, but no opulence at all. She realized how fortunate she was to work in the environment that had been setup for her. He had a standard desk made of what looked to be blonde wood, which matched all of the doors in the offices. The desk was accented by a black leather chair that had formed the shape of his or someone's body over time. She also noticed as she walked in that the chair was lunged back free from the assistance of anyone forcing it back as if it had been programmed to do so after years of someone being in that position.

"Well, Fin. I have had so many things happening over the past few months. At first there were just little things that I chalked up to life. Strange little things like putting my purse in one spot in my office, going to the rest room and finding it in another spot when I returned, which I thought I had just made a mistake. Most of the employees, especially my assistant, had already gone for the day. Eventually, the little things turned into larger things, which is why I'm here. More recently, I've been frightened. I've never been a complete push over, but the events recently have had me on edge. Take the trip that Grant and I took to Jamaica. We were out walking around just getting a flavor of the island, when someone just walked up to us and pushed us in the back out into the oncoming traffic. Grant and I ended up in the hospital. We discussed it afterwards and thought maybe it was some truth or dare that the island kids were playing which turned sour. Then as recently as this morning, as I was coming out of the building, a car sped toward me trying to run me down. There's not much tangible evidence. I don't get it. Why is someone after me?" Toney uttered as she started to cry.

"Calm down, Toney. That's why you're here. We can get to the bottom of it together," Fin said gently.

"I've got a battery of questions for you," he said shifting in his seat.

"Does that mean you'll take the case?" she said with a ray of hope.

"Yes. I'll take the case on one condition," Fin said.

"What's that?" she asked with a hopeful look on her face.

"If you promise to calm down and stay calm. These things are nerve-racking, but there is usually a very simple explanation for them. It's usually someone who's jealous or envious trying to get one up on the subject or just plain trying to drive them crazy in order to get them out of the way. Either way, we'll find them. They usually do something to single themselves out, and that's when I'll be there to point the finger at them. That's what I do," Fin said with a huge air of confidence as he flashed his smile.

"Now, I'll need a list of all the mysteries. I'll need a list of the individuals who you feel would try and invoke harm on you. I'll have to know the people who are the closest to you. We'll have to have many, many conversations while the investigations are underway. By the way, who is Grant?" he asked.

"Grant is my fiancée. Why do you ask?" she said with her expression turning to puzzlement.

"You mentioned that you and he were together in Jamaica. That's normally where I start. You see, many times these things are traced back to someone who has constant access to the intended victim. After we eliminate the people closest to the subject, then we cast a wider net. Does that make sense?" he asked.

"I guess so. But, Grant would never hurt me. Never," Toney stated emphatically!

"You're probably right, but until the process of elimination begins, no one is ruled out," Fin said with authority.

They continued to talk for another twenty minutes. Toney handed him her list of what had transpired over the last two months. Fin read through Toney's list after they concluded their conversation, "Toney, you have some very good information here. It's more than I normally have to begin with. I'll get started in a couple of days and get back with you. I charge seventy-five dollars an hour, plus expenses. Can you handle that?" he asked with concern.

"Yes, I can. That'll be no problem. The only thing is, I don't want Grant to know right now. I just don't want him to worry about me, you know?"

"I won't tell if you don't," Fin assured her.

She stood to leave after shaking his hand.

Fin walked Toney to the door of his office and down the same corridor that they had followed over an hour earlier. They passed the receptionist area where a different lady was manning the phones.

"Good morning, All About the Truth, may I help you," the lady said answering the telephone.

"Yes sir, he's on another line, will you hold?"

Toney recognized the voice. It was Valerie.

"Hi, Valerie. I'm the voice on the other end of the phone from Friday. Thank you so much for the help you gave me," Toney said appreciatively.

"No thanks necessary Miss…???," Valerie responded?

"Toney Chambers…I'm Toney Chambers," Toney said to her extending her hand.

Valerie stood to extend her hand as well. They shook quickly as the telephone rang again cutting the handshake short, forcing Valerie to get back to her job after saying, "Good luck to you."

Toney and Babbitt walked to the door.

As Toney walked through the door she turned to Babbitt, "Thanks for everything. I hope you can help me. I really do."

"You promised me back there that you'd calm down. And, that you'd leave things to me. That's why I took your case. So, what's it going to be?" he said sternly.

"You're right," she said taking a deep breath. "You're right and I did promise. I'll calm down and leave things with you. I'll talk to you in a few days," she said as she turned and walked away.

PART II

Grant had been at the office since seven. His structured morning necessitated a break. Toney flashed across his mind.

"I haven't spoken to my lady today," he said out loud as he swirled around in his chair to pick up the phone to dial her number.

"Toney Chambers' office, this is Sonjia."

"Hi, Sonjia. Where is she?"

"Hi Mr. Parlarme. She's not due in till eleven."

"Eleven? What do you mean? She didn't tell me that she had anything going on. Do you know where she is?" Grant asked with concern.

"No. Not really. She told me on Friday before she left that she'd be in around eleven this morning. That's a first for her unless she's on the road, you know. But, I'm sure she's alright or she would have told one of us...don't you think?" Sonjia said as if she was trying to convince herself.

"Yeah…I guess. But, there's been so much going on everywhere. I like to know where she is so I can make sure she's safe."

"Well, if she's not here by noon, I'll call to let you know. Okay? Let's not create a problem if there isn't one," Sonjia said.

"You're right, but I have to be on my job about her."

They hung up. But, Sonjia was beginning to get worried too. There was too much going on. And, if Grant was concerned that was a problem. He has always been her rock.

Just as Sonjia hung up the phone, it rang again.

"Toney Chambers please."

"She isn't in. May I take a message?"

"Yes. I'm Sergeant Billings, Chicago Police. When do you expect her?" he asked.

Sonjia's heart began to race.

"What's happened?" Sonjia asked in a panic.

"When can she be reached?" Sergeant Billings asked.

"She should be in shortly. Would you care to leave a message?"

"Yes. Please ask her to call Sergeant Billings at 312.555.8101, ext. 61. Please. It's important." he pushed.

"Certainly," Sonjia said in a fog. "I'll let her know."

Sonjia sat there with a worried expression on her face. What has happened now? It couldn't have happened to Toney or they wouldn't be calling here for her. But, why are the police calling for her? And, where is she? It's already eleven fifteen, she thought.

June got up from her desk and came over to Sonjia, "Is everything alright? Is Toney alright?"

"June, if I've told you once I've told you a thousand times, stay out of Toney's business. If she ever finds out that you're gossiping about her business, you're going to lose your job. Stay out of it," Sonjia said sharply.

"I'm not gossiping. Toney is a nice lady. I'm just concerned. Many of us are concerned," she said stepping closer.

"Stay out of it, June. That's the last time I'll warn you," Sonjia cautioned.

"Well, if you won't share any information about Toney...what about Freddy? Where is he? It's nearly noon and no one has heard from him. That's not like Freddy. He's been acting strange for the past month. I hope he's okay, too," June said sounding almost like she meant it.

"You know...you're right. Talk to the others. See if he's called in and maybe we didn't intercept the call. That could be, you know."

"Okay," June said.

"She seems to get a kick out of being in charge of something. Anything at all," Sonjia said as June scuffled off.

Two minutes later, June was back, "No one has heard a thing, Sonjia. Maybe I should call his house to see if he's there."

"No need. I'll handle it. Go back to work. And, thanks for asking around," Sonjia said trying to take control of the office.

Sonjia looked up Freddy's number in the company directory. She dialed and waited as the phone rang nine times. No answer and no machine. Maybe he was on his way.

Toney walked in as Sonjia was hanging up the phone.

"Toney, are you alright? We were worried," Sonjia said as she followed Toney into her office.

"I'm fine. Why were you worried? I told you that I'd be in late."

"I'm sure you know why. You're a creature of habit, and when a habit is changed, normally something's wrong...that's why. Mr. Parlarme called."

"What did you tell him?"

"Just that you said you'd be in around eleven," Sonjia responded as if asking for approval.

"What did he say?" Toney snapped before she realized it.

"Just that he was concerned and that you hadn't mentioned anything out of the ordinary when you and he were together over the weekend."

Toney sat there for a moment and in an instant went into action.

"Okay, Sonjia. That'll be all," she said as she picked up the phone and began dialing.

"Hi, Mill, is Grant in?"

"Hi, Toney. He sure is. Just a moment."

With that Sonjia walked out and closed the door. Sonjia was perplexed. There was something wrong. It was odd because this was the first time that Toney had shut Sonjia completely out.

"Tone? Are you alright?" Grant whispered.

"Sure, honey. I'm just fine," she said trying to sound as if things were normal.

"I didn't know that you had an appointment this morning. Sonjia wasn't sure what it was either, so I was naturally concerned, baby," he continued to whisper.

"Is it anything you want to talk about?" he continued.

"No. Not really. Just an errand," she said being careful not to completely lie.

He'll be glad I took care of things once everything is all said and done, she thought.

"Okay, baby. I just wanted to hear your voice. Call me later if you get a minute."

"I sure will, honey," she said throwing him a kiss before they hung up.

Toney sat there thinking about the morning. She went over all of the details in her mind. It would be a delicious euphoria, if Fin could locate the culprit and put him in jail. She had a burning passion to get her life back to normal. She had to show the courage and the confidence it took to solve the mystery. If Surrant was behind this, she would have his head on a platter.

"Buzz. Toney. I hate to interrupt, but a Sergeant Billings of the Chicago Police phoned. He said it was urgent that you give him a call. The number is 312.555.8108, ext. 61."

"Did he say what it was about?"

"No. I asked but he said he had to speak with you."

"Thanks, Sonjia," Toney said quickly hanging up and just a fast picking up the phone again to dial the Sergeant's number.

"Twelfth precinct, Officer Harris."

"Good afternoon, officer, is Sergeant Billing there, please?"

"Just a moment ma'am."

A few seconds passed while Toney paced behind her desk.

"Billings," the Sergeant answered in an official voice.

"Sergeant Billings, this is Toney Chambers. You called me earlier this morning?"

"Yes, ma'am," he said trying to tone down the sharpness of his voice.

"There's been a murder"... he said pausing.

"The victim had your name as a contact reference in his wallet. It was Fred Talbert. Did you know him?" the Sergeant asked.

Toney fell back to her desktop. Her body became limp.

"Freddy murdered?" she shrieked.

"That can't be. He was at work on Friday kind of upset. We spoke about his mood over the past few weeks, which was very unlike him. He said he'd be fine. What happened?" Toney said unable to hide her panic.

"His body was found in a small park in South Chicago. It appeared as if he was beaten to death. From all we could find after searching his person and his apartment, he had no next of kin. He had your name and number as a reference in case of emergency."

Silence fell over the phone while Toney gathered her thoughts and got a mental picture of Freddy sitting in her office on Friday.

"Ms. Chambers, are you there?"

"Yes. Yes officer. I'm here. What would you like for me to do?" Toney asked as she flopped down in her chair in despair.

They spoke for a few more minutes. When Toney hung up she felt wiped out. "Could anything else possibly happen?" she thought. She had to tell the staff. That would be difficult. She had to wait until the end of the day to do it. When Toney got herself together, she called Human Resources to let them know of the tragedy. Then she called Corbin's office and left him a message that he should call her right away. She knew that he was on a trip to New York and expected that he called his office frequently. She picked up the phone to buzz Sonjia.

"Yes, Toney," she responded.

With a weak voice she said, "Sonjia, will you step in here please?" Sonjia hung up the phone and rushed to Toney's side.

"What is it Toney? What is it?"

"Please have a seat, Sonjia," Toney said with sadness.

"It's Freddy. He's been murdered," Toney said as tears streamed down her face.

"Murdered? That's impossible! He was just at work on Friday and it seemed like he was getting back to the old Freddy. Especially after you spoke with him. The rest of the day he was the same old Freddy. What happened?" Sonjia shrieked.

"He was beaten to death according to the police."

"Is that what the police wanted with you this morning?"

"Yes it was. It seems as if Freddy had my name and number as an emergency contact."

"This is awful…just awful," Sonjia spewed becoming visibly shaken.

"Yes, it is," Toney said raising from her chair.

She walked around her desk to sit beside Sonjia.

"We have to gather the staff to let them know," she said putting her arms around Sonjia.

"It'll be tough getting through this, but together, we'll manage. Besides you and I have to maintain a brave front for the rest of the staff, you know?" Toney concluded.

They sat there consoling one another while Sonjia cried for a couple of minutes recalling the humor that Freddy brought to many otherwise bleak stressful days over the years.

"Toney," Sonjia broke away saying, "you mean to tell me he has no family?"

"That's what the police said," Toney recalled while walking away and beginning to pace. You never would have thought that. He was so outgoing and so open. It was as if he had everything and didn't have a care in the world. All of that reversed for him in the last few weeks. I wonder what changed? I wonder where his parents are? Did he have any brothers or sisters? It's times like this that we realize, while we spend so much time with the people we work with, we actually know so little about any of them," Toney said almost in a trance.

"What will we do first?" Sonjia said with her face displaying an array of emotions one after the other.

"Well, Sergeant Billings asked if someone from the office could come in to identify the body. I put in a call to Human Resources to see what company procedures are. No one has called back at this point. I need for you to follow up on that. Then I'll see what's next, okay?"

"Alright Toney. I'll handle that but, if it's all right with you, I'd like to sit here for a few more minutes to get my feet back under me? This is just too unreal," Sonjia said taking her seat again.

"Honey take all the time you have to. Regretfully, we really don't have to be in any hurry now. Poor Freddy's dead, so we can't help him. All we can do is to make sure he gets a proper burial and keep good thoughts of his humor," Toney reported.

Toney finally realized that over forty minutes had gone by when she noticed the phone on her desk was all lit up indicating several calls were on hold.

"Who's at your desk fielding calls?" she asked.

"Oh my God! I got up from my desk when I heard the strain in your voice and didn't think about coverage," Sonjia said springing to her feet. Sonjia opened the door and June had taken a seat at Sonjia's desk. She was stretched out with all the calls. June heard the door open and showed a sign of relief when she saw Sonjia.

"Just a moment sir, her assistant has just returned. She'll be right with you," June said as she put the caller on hold.

"Why didn't you tell me that you needed me to cover for you? I tried to answer your phones from my desk but many of the callers needed information from your desk. I had to make the shift. What's going on? Are you alright?"

"That's a matter of opinion but let me take this call and make a few more and I'll let you know what's happening," Sonjia said as she took her seat to take care of the caller who was holding.

"Sir thank you for waiting. What was it that you needed?"

Sonjia did as she normally would and took expert care of the customer. When she finished, she called human resources.

"Mary, is Jonathan in? There's a very important situation that I need to see him about."

"Yes, Sonjia, he's here. We also got a call from Toney. Is everything alright?"

"No, not really. I'll come up to see you. Just tell Jonathan that I'm on the way. Thanks."

"June. Please take over my desk. I'll be right back. If Toney asks where I am, just let her know that I went to Human Resources and that I'll be right back," she said walking away at a fast pace.

A few minutes later, Sonjia was back.

"June just let me talk to Toney again for a few minutes," she said holding up her index finger and walking past June who didn't have a chance to say a word before Sonjia was opening Toney's door and closing it behind her.

"Toney, I spoke with Jonathan. He's going down to the coroner's office to identify the body. They are also looking into any insurance that the company has on Freddy. The only thing left is to alert the staff. Do you want to do that now?"

"No. I've thought about it and we should really wait until the end of the day. That way, we'll get a full days work out of them. Lord knows you and I have left a lot of our work on the table today, but it couldn't be helped."

"Okay. What time should we call them together," Sonjia asked?

"Four o'clock. That'll catch the early outs. We don't want anyone going home and learning about this on their own," Toney directed.

"Have you been able to catch up with Charles?" Sonjia asked Toney.

"No, I left a message in his office, but never got a call back. Call Terry for me. Find out exactly where Charles is. Maybe we can catch up with him ourselves. See if he has his cell phone with him. Maybe that's what we need to do is call him on his cell phone."

"I'm on it," Sonjia said as left.

Toney leaned back in her seat. A feeling of hopelessness came over her as she thought about everything, What is going on, God? There is so much negativity going on around me. I don't believe that any of this is a coincidence either.

EIGHTEEN

Surrant tried in vein to catch up with Guy Gamble. It was going on three weeks since they had actually spoken. Since then they had been playing a fierce game of telephone tag. Surrant was champing at the bit to see what if anything Gamble had been successful at doing to knock Toney off her high horse. Had he been successful at scaring Toney enough that he would drive her crazy...to make her appear unstable? Just do subtle things, one at a time, was the direction that Surrant had given. Gamble and Surrant had collaborated on the particulars. Mental anguish was their aim to promote an appearance that Toney would be unable to lead the pack. Surrant was swept away with the thought of Toney's job. The prestige...the power, he had to have it no matter what. He was only tenacious when he was indulging in wickedness. What kind of person was he? No respect for anyone, so he couldn't have any for himself. Everyone, who knew him, knew that, so anyone was fair game.

He knew that he had to be in early on Tuesday because of the next conference call. He wanted to hook up with Gamble to get an update before then. Jim wanted to know what to look for, if anything, in her voice during the call. He wanted to feed onto the successes of Gamble. After all, that's why he had been paying Gamble so much money. He wanted his money's worth. Four hours into his day, he took a break.

"Buzz"

"Yes, Mr. Surrant?" Vivian answered.

"Who's this?" Surrant wrenched

"This is Vivian, sir. Is there something that I can do for you?"

"You can start by telling me where Holley is!" Surrant shouted.

"Sir, she went to lunch. She has me filling in for her until she returns. She told me that she also had an errand to run."

"Something, she said, that she couldn't take care of after work. Is there something that I can do for you, sir?"

"Try to get Gamble on the line again. His number should be on Holley's Rolodex. I need him badly, right away."

"Alright, Mr. Surrant. I'll let you know what happens," she chirped.

Jim slammed down the phone. He began to thumb through his in-box. More and more work was piling up. He couldn't get through it fast enough. While he worked, Toney continued to stand around in the shadows of his thoughts. She was looking for something, anything to get him on, and he couldn't allow that. "Call her; call her," his mind told him over and over again. After a few seconds of his mind games, he picked up the phone to dial her number.

"Toney Chambers' office, this is Sonjia, may I help you?" Toney's assistant answered.

"Is she in?" Surrant grunted.

"Yes she is, sir. She's on another line at the moment. Is there anything I can assist you with?" Sonjia coaxed.

She knew that Toney was in no frame of mind to deal with Surrant, and she was sure that this was Surrant.

"No. I need to speak with her. Tell her that Jim Surrant called and that I'll try again later. I'm too damned busy to be holding for anyone," he said in a frustrated tone and hung up.

Sonjia hung up while shaking her head saying out loud, "This guy is weird. He's trouble if I've ever seen trouble."

"Buzz."

"Yes, sir. This is Vivian, what is it? Have you reached Gamble?" Surrant demanded.

"No. Not yet. Your wife is on line two. I'm holding on line one for Mr.Gamble. They're not sure if he's in," Vivian reported.

Without so much as a word he clicked off the intercom with Vivian and joined Joanie on line two.

"Hi, Joanie. What can I do for you?" Surrant barked.

"Well, dear, I see you're having a bad day. A little grumpy are we?" Joanie said in her normal sweet disposition.

"I apologize, honey. Things are as they always are here. Pressure and more pressure. Is everything alright?" he asked.

"Sure, everything's fine. I just wanted to take a moment out from the gardening to give you a call. What do you want for dinner?" she asked sweetly.

"Whatever. You know me...I'm not choosy. How did the kids do in school today?"

"I guess they're doing fine. It's only twelve fifteen. They're not home yet. Soon though. What time will you be home tonight?" Joanie further chirped.

"Not sure right now. I'll call you," he said cutting the conversation short.

" Okay, honey. I'll talk with you soon then," Joanie concluded hanging up the phone.

Five more minutes passed by and no report from Vivian.

"Buzz."

"Yes, Mr. Surrant. What can I do for you?"

Jim went ballistic.

"What the hell do you mean what can you do for me? I asked you to get Gamble on the damn phone for me. No response. None at all. You are incredibly incompetent. Can you follow instructions?"

Vivian sat there taking the insults, speechless. "How does Holley put up with this shit?" she thought while he was hurling his insults.

When Surrant was finished, Vivian calmly said, " Mr. Surrant, I'm still on hold for Mr. Gamble. No one has responded yet. I'm still on hold. So, if I can get back to that line…I'll let you know the outcome," Vivian said with mild sarcasm.

"Alright," Surrant grumbled slamming down the phone and feeling like a fool.

A few seconds later the intercom buzzed again.

"Surrant."

"Mr. Surrant, Mr. Gamble has gone for the day. His secretary said that she tried to catch him but he pulled off obviously unable to hear her attempts to get his attention. She also attempted to reach him on his cell phone, but that line has been continually busy. Once she gets in touch with him, she will let him know that you need to speak with him," Vivian said.

"That's fine. Let me know when he calls back," Surrant ordered and slammed down his receiver.

Vivian sat back in Holley's chair pondering the moment. "What an asshole Surrant is," she thought. A moment later she shook it off as the phone rang and she went back to work.

"Prophecy Computers, Mr. Surrant's office, may I help you?

"I have a repair problem...Our system is........"

Vivain sat there fielding the calls that came in for the next forty minutes. The last call she took was Gamble calling back.

"Surrant. Is Surrant in? Gamble here," the caller announced.

"Just a moment sir."

"Buzz."

"Yes, what is it?" Surrant barked.

"Mr.. Gamble on line one, sir," reported Vivian.

Without a word, Surrant clicked off the intercom and onto line one.

"Gamble, I told you almost a month ago to stay in touch with me. What the hell is happening with Chambers? I need constant updates. I'm paying you a whole lot of damned money and I want results," Surrant pushed.

"Keep your shirt on, Surrant. This shit takes time if it's to be done right. We've been successful in our four outings. You said no physical stuff, so I've had to lay off. Playing these cat and mouse games are not my cup of tea, so I've had to be real creative. The last time I saw her she was really wigging out. I think there's some other shit happening to this chick. She's about to blow and I haven't giving her the run of the house treatment yet. She's weaker than you think. Keep you shirt on," Gamble cautioned.

"Here's what I've got in mind for her in the next two months, provided I can find out what her schedule is….."

While Surrant was on the phone, Holley returned.

"Hi Viv," Holley said cheerfully.

Vivian stood immediately after Holley's hello, offering Holley her seat.

"You can have this guy. He's pitiful. He's so miserable inside. He's mean, disrespectful and all that. The next time you need to leave, please ask someone else to sit in for you. I was two minutes from cursing his ass out and walking away," Vivian said as she walked away shaking her head.

"Buzz."

"Jim, I'm back," Holley said cheerfully.

"Where did you go? Why didn't you tell me you were leaving?" Surrant said jealously.

"Why Jim dear, I didn't know you cared," Holley teased.

"Don't play games with me, Holley. I'm in no mood for it. It's already after two. The follow up conference call is tomorrow. Have you had time to finish the research on the money? You know what I went through last week in Chicago. And, you know that Chambers is going to harp on the subject tomorrow. I have to have a faxed copy of the update on her desk before nine in the morning or I'm dead meat. If we have to stay all night, I need an update. Where do we stand now?" he asked.

"I've been working on this night and day and there is nowhere else to look. We're down a quarter of a million dollars, and there is no more, anywhere," Holley said.

"That's impossible! How can that be? Get the accountant for our region on the phone. I didn't want to bring anyone else into this, but I don't have a choice now. Tell him he'll have to balance the books. I have to know about each and every detail. Tell him he needs to go back as far as the last audit and start from there. I have to have an answer tonight. Before he leaves. I don't care how long it takes. We've got to find that money."

"Oookaaay, Jim, but its already after two," Holley reminded him.

"I don't give a damn, Holley. He's supposed to be keeping up with the fucking money anyway. That's not what you or I get paid for. If there were questions about the cash, he should have brought it to my attention long before now. It's my fault for not paying attention, but it's his fault for not catching this shit!"

Irritated, Jim slammed down the phone. Holley sat there for a moment to think things through. She jotted down a couple of notes then decided to call Forbes in accounting.

"Forbes here," he answered noting that it was a call from inside the office.

"Forbes, this is Holley. Jim wants you to run a report on the funds since the last audit. He needs to see what the numbers were relating to the revenue coming in for sales, the expenses and the bottom line. We're down a quarter of a million, and he has to have a report on Chambers desk before the nine a.m. conference call in the morning."

"How long has he known that he had to have this? This'll take a couple of days minimally. No way will I have it before five when I leave. Besides, I've got three other tasks on my desk that have to be completed today," Forbes said.

Holley listened attentively then, "Forbes, you don't understand. This is not a request. It's mandatory. Mr. Surrant needs this by nine a.m. Chicago time tomorrow for the weekly conference call. You really don't have a choice."

"Holley, I've been with this company for nine years, and I've never been treated this way. He has no respect for my personal time. I work hard from seven to five and obviously that's not enough. I must say, I'm very disappointed. I'll start on this right away. I guess the customers that I've made promises to will have to wait. It'll take me about twenty minutes or so to smooth things over with them and I'll get on this right away. What is it that I'm looking for exactly?" Forbes asked defeated.

Holley said in a supportive manner, "We're looking for a quarter of a million dollars. I've been over this at least a half dozen times. We started out a half million down. I found a quarter of a million, but I just don't see any more."

"Okay. How long will you be here?" Forbes asked Holley.

"I'd much rather report my findings to you instead of him," he continued.

"I'll be here. So, if you find anything out, let me know, okay? I will in turn let Surrant know."

Once the conversation was over, Forbes stacked all of his former priorities in three neat little piles. He called the waiting customers offering them flimsy excuses, then went into the computer to pull up all the latest entries from January 1. He felt that the best thing to do was to start at the very beginning, the day after the most recent audit. If he started now he could be out by eight or nine, maybe. His printer was running nonstop with report after report. He had put the year together with one report after another. He initially felt that this would make it easier than having to review rows of numbers with no totals for hundreds of rows. It turned out as he began the painstaking task of finding a needle in a haystack that this may save him an enormous amount of time.

"Buzz."

"Yes, Jim?" Holley answered.

"See if you can get Chambers on the phone for me again. That idiot that you had sitting in for you was useless. She never got back to me on anything that I asked her to do. She was trying to get Chambers on the line and served no useful purpose to me. I know you can get her for me," Surrant rambled.

"I'll see what I can do, Jim," Holley cajoled.

"Toney Chambers' office, this is Sonjia may I help you?"

"Hi, Sonjia, it's Holley. How are you?"

"I'm fine, I guess. We've got a lot happening here, so I'm not sure from one time to the next exactly how I'm doing," Sonjia said.

Holley was sitting at her desk making hand motions and her eyes rolling back in her head indicating, 'yeah, yeah, yeah...let's get through this.'

"I'm sure you'll make it through," Holley said softly in a tone to disguise her real feelings.

"Is Toney available? Jim needs to ask her a few questions before the call tomorrow."

"Sure, she's here...I'm not sure she can talk at the moment though. She's juggling a thousand balls right now. Do you have any idea what Surrant...uh, I mean Jim needs?"

"He didn't say. He just asked me to see if I could get her on the phone. Can you please ask her if she could take a quick call from Jim?"

"Sure, please hold," Sonjia said placing the call on hold and giving Toney a buzz.

"Buzz."

"Sonjia, what is it?" Toney answered in a snappy tone much unlike her normal demeanor.

"Surrant's secretary is on the line. He's called a couple of times today but, with everything that's happening I thought I'd keep him at bay."

"You might as well put him through. He'll just keep calling until he gets me anyway, so I might as well get it over with."

"This is Toney, Jim. What can I do for you?"

"Toney, it's Holley. I'll get Jim for you right away," Holley rushed.

"Buzz."

"Yes, did you get her for me?"

"Yes I did. She's on line one," Holley said in a tone expressing the fact that she knew how to work it.

Jim picked up the line, "I would think you'd make yourself available to us especially after that long meeting last week. Surely to God you must know that we needed to review some of the items from the meeting especially in light of the call tomorrow," Jim scorned.

"Good afternoon, Surrant. I'm doing fine, and you?" Toney said taking a deep breath and trying not to let Surrant's bad disposition make an already intolerable day become even worse.

"What can I do for you today?" Toney asked taking control of the conversation and leveling the mood of the call.

She was so good at this. She thought that Jim was not worth the scum on her shoes, so why allow him to rule at any point?

"What are the points of clarification for the call in the morning?" Jim asked in a gruff way.

"I left Chicago with several items that I had to work on."

Toney interrupted, "Have you found the answers that you needed for those items yet?"

"Yes, for most of them, and the final item is being worked on now. When I talk to you in the morning I'll be on line for sure. But, I need to know what the call agenda items are. I refuse to be caught off guard anymore," Surrant warned.

"Alright," Toney said.

"If you're caught up, basically that's all you have to have. The agenda items are basic at best. The call will review quickly the recap of the meeting. Since I'll be out of the country next week, my focus will be on my trip.

"Oh. Where are you headed?" Surrant inquired interrupting the flow of Toney response.

"I'm meeting with Bukura in Japan. Why?" Toney responded before she took time to think about letting Surrant in on her plans. She thought about letting the cat out of the bag as Surrant continued on with his conversation. Surely he wouldn't dare be all the way over there in the Orient, if he were the culprit who was after her. But, she thought about that too...it would be easy for him to find out where she was through anyone at the corporate office, so she might as well act as if she didn't care if he knew. She couldn't hide the fact that she would be in Japan from Surrant even if she wanted to. "If I keep his plate full here in the states, he wouldn't have time to travel to the orient," she thought.

"So, Surrant, there are several items that I'll need from you to complete while I'm away. I'll call you back after the group call tomorrow to give you your instructions. Until then, I believe you have everything you need?" she asked.

"I suppose," Surrant grunted.

"Alright then. We'll speak again in the morning. Have a great evening," Toney said politely with a grin in her voice.

Surrant never knew what hit him. He had, however, been successful in getting her travel plans and a tad bit of information on the call, but he had to make damned sure he had his numbers in line or he knew that would be the beginning of the end for him.

"Buzz."

"Yes, Jim. How did the call go?" Holley asked.

"It went fine. Have you checked with Forbes? How's he coming along?"

"I haven't checked with him. I thought I'd give him some time to work it out. Why interrupt him now? If he had anything to report he'd be on the phone to me. I won't interrupt him right now."

"Alright," Surrant groaned.

"Let me know as soon as you hear anything."

"Okay," Holley said hanging up the phone while congratulating herself again on how she was able to manage Surrant. She was the only one who could put out his flame. She managed him even better than Joanie. She had worked hard to get to this point and wanted to eventually make this work for her future.

PART II

It was five minutes until four and time for Toney to collect the troops.

Charles had just gotten back with Toney. They had a lengthy talk about the situation with Freddy and agreed on the method that Toney had selected to handle it. Jonathan, the Human Resource Director, had also returned from identifying the body. It was Freddy. How sad. She got up from her desk, walking out to Sonjia's area.

"Sonjia, It's time," Toney instructed as she walked back into her office to receive the members of her staff.

Sonjia went to each person individually to quietly instruct that they were to go into Toneys's office immediately. One by one and two by two they filed into the office. Each of them had questions written all over their faces as to what this was all about. Once they were all there, Toney began.

"I know that you all wonder why I've asked you to join me. I also know that many of you have noticed that there has been something in the air today much out of the norm. I have some very sad news to report to you. Freddy Talbert is dead," Toney said as calmly as she could muster. Terror took over the faces of many of the staff members. June reached for the closest person to her. Jamie allowed June to lean on her because she found June's body necessary for her to retain her as well.

"The police found his body yesterday, I wanted to tell you as a group so that we could all help each other through this period of mourning.

"What happened to him?" one member of the staff questioned.

"We're not entirely sure at this point. The police are investigating."

"We've known for several weeks that there was something going on. Freddy just hadn't been himself. We've all tried to help, but he kept pulling away from us. I know this is a trying time for all of us," Toney said as comfort.

"If any of you need to see a counselor, Human Resources has setup daily visits until you have worked through your challenges with this tragedy. The only thing that I ask is that you alert Sonjia when you will be away from your areas, so we can provide coverage. Does anyone need to stay to get themselves together before leaving?"

There were no comments from anyone. They were all in shock.

"Thanks for coming, and please let me know if any of you need me," Toney said as she dismissed them.

They all walked out in small clumps. Their heads were together discussing Freddy. Toney knew there would be no more work done for the rest of the day. That is why she waited until this hour to get them together.

Toney closed her door and tried to put the bad news behind her getting ready for the conference call the next morning and trying to reach Bukura's office to make sure that she was on target for her trip. She kept seeing visions of Freddy with his big bright smile, switching as he walked through the office making his wise cracks at Toney whenever she managed to surface. Would her office ever be the same?

NINETEEN

It was a rough night for Toney. She thought about her employees and how they handled the news of Freddy's untimely death. She knew that there would be a strain on everyone for the next few days, if not longer. She also knew that many of her employees would have rough nights, because she hadn't slept well either. She thought about the expression on Freddy's face over and over again, the last time she saw him. She kept seeing that expression on his face during their final conversation. She recalled him telling her that things would be all right for him. That made her think about all of the challenges that she had had over the past couple of months. She wondered if they were at all connected. But, how could Freddy's death be connected with her trials? She threw the thought out of her head as she went through her morning routine. She cleaned her face and looked closely in the mirror, just before applying her makeup. The fact that she hadn't been sleeping well was beginning to show on her face. She had to find some solace somehow. Her mind shifted to Fin as she began to apply her makeup. What was he up to? And, how much had he uncovered in the day and a half that he had her case? She moved to her dressing room, got dressed and was out of the condo within twenty-five minutes. It was six fifty-five when she pulled into her parking space. She had become very aware of her surroundings. She wouldn't allow certain things to surprise her or to creep up on her again. She had to maintain her wit, but refused to be held hostage to whoever it was stalking her. She hadn't had to be so careful before, but she could manage it if she were pushed. And, she was being pushed. Toney got out of the car and walked over to the elevator door keeping an eye out for any unwanted intruders. She arrived at the lobby level of the building and waved at Marvin and another guard seated in their area having a cup of coffee. Marvin waved saying, "Good morning, Ms. Chambers. I'm so sorry to hear about Freddy."

"Thanks Marvin. It's certainly a tragedy. He was so young and full of life. I hope they find out who did it," Toney said sadly nearing the elevator bank.

When Toney arrived in her office she locked the door behind her. She was through being careless. No matter how busy she was she would take all the necessary precautions. Especially until the culprit was caught and perhaps by then it would become a way of life for her. She thought of how society had evolved into an environment where no one is safe. She had a mound of work to get through today since there was not much at all accomplished yesterday with the appointment with Fin and Freddy's death. Then there was Freddy's funeral on Thursday. Toney got down to business. She plowed through three hours of work in just over an hour. She heard someone in the outer office stirring about. She got up to investigate. She was indeed different now because before she would have let the person stirring come to her, but no more.

She parted her office slightly. She saw a shadow moving over to the left of her.

"Who's there?" she shouted.

"It's me, Toney. It's June."

"You're mighty early, June. Sonjia is normally the one who gets in early. Are you alright?"

"I'm okay, Toney. I couldn't sleep, thinking about Freddy. I thought I'd just get on up and come on in. Maybe keeping myself busy, I can make it through this time."

Toney came out and took a seat at Sonjia's desk just across from June.

"You know, we'll all probably have to lean on one another. Freddy would have wanted it that way, don't you think?" Toney asked June.

"You may be right, Toney. One step at a time. Has a date been set for the funeral?" June asked.

"Yes. It has. It'll be Thursday. I have to get back to work now, but if you need me, let me know," Toney said getting up from Sonjia's desk and moving back into her office. She forced herself to get back to work right away. "June was correct about one thing, keeping busy was paramount. Yes...keeping busy and watching your back," Toney mumbled to herself, jumping back into her work head first.

Fifteen minutes later, a light rap on the door, followed by Sonjia leaning in to say hello.

"How are you fairing, Toney?" Sonjia asked.

"I'm holding on Sonjia. How about you?"

"It's been a strange night. I told my husband about it. He said he'd run into Freddy a couple of times and that he was with some questionable characters, two very polished white boys, but felt that Freddy knew what he was doing," she said hunching her shoulders.

"Well, you never know," Toney said.

Sonjia turned to leave, "Let me get to work. I'm so far behind after yesterday. Oh, by the way," she said turning back to Toney, " we want you to come to our family reunion. It'll be early next month in Cumberland Park. We decided to have it later in the year when it was cooler. It'll be on a weekend, so most everyone can make it. I'll tell you all about it after you get back from Tokyo."

"That sounds like fun. We'll talk about it," Toney said.

"Buzz."

"It's Tuesday, Sonjia. Just a reminder...the conference call."

"I'm on it," Sonjia said.

The Tuesday morning call went as planned. It took an hour and ten minutes to review all of the information on the agenda. Each participant was careful to cross every "T" and dot each "I" because Mr. Corbin's office had to be made aware of updates regarding the shortfalls brought to light from the big meeting. Toney hung up feeling that she had put together the information from her troops that was necessary to indicate that she was at the top of her game. She picked up the phone for the call back to Surrant. She had to put his situation to bed for once and for all.

"Surrant. I told you yesterday, I'd call you back to talk one on one. Do you have the items that we need to discuss?"

"Yes," he said unwittingly.

For the next twenty minutes, they reviewed everything. When the call was done, they were both feeling a little better about each other.

The thing Toney dreaded the most was finding a replacement for Freddy. But, she didn't have a choice. She had a business to run and needed a person to deal with the mail. She and Jonathan in Human Resources had conferred two times during the day, deciding on the way to proceed.

Toney took a breather from the morning. Her thoughts of Freddy's death made her stop and think about everything. She started to put all the components of her life in perspective. She worked all the time, taking very little time out for what was really important in her life, except for Grant, and even they didn't see each other enough. What about her parents? She hadn't been home in several months. The best that she could do was a phone call once a week. That was not nearly enough. It was never like this before. What about Vanessa? How had she been doing in the months since Toney was at there? The last time she was able to have a meaningful conversation with Vanessa was seven or eight weeks ago, and that exchange was cut short by an office interruption.

"I've got to change some of this. There has to be a way where I can do a good job and have a life too. There has to be a way," Toney said out loud while getting comfortable in her chair.

"Once this mess is behind me, I'll make a concerted effort to get my life back on track."

She sat there with her eyes closed. "All I need is a moment and then back to work."

Before she knew it she was back at the early days of Prophecy....

"Dick, I want to formally apply for Paul's job. I have the tenure. I've done a good job. I've made the company a ton of money since I came on board. And now, I have the experience," Toney said before Dick could get a word in.

"The big boys have other ideas. They already have their eyes on one of the hot shots out of New York. That individual has more experience at another company. So, I don't know," Dick hedged.

"I plan to talk with the big boys then. This is my chance and I think I should have it," Toney fired back.

"I wouldn't do that if I were you, Toney. They want all actions for raises, promotions and staff issues to go through the proper chain of command. So, I wouldn't do that if I were you," he said repeating himself.

"Okay, well…I've gone through my immediate supervisor. I want this opportunity. When will you give me an update?" Toney cornered.

"I'll see what I can do. I wouldn't count on it though," Dick cautioned.

"Why not?" Toney asked respectfully.

"If this company is what they claim it is, I should count on it. Ms. Roman told me that if I worked hard and made the company money, my future would look bright," Toney recited.

"I'm looking for big things from Prophecy. I hope I wasn't wrong about this company," Toney said as she stood to leave Dick's office.

Dick said nothing. He sat there looking at her in the oddest way. He didn't now what to think. Toney had from the time he had observed her been a withdrawn nerdish type person. One that he could count on when the chips were down. One that knew her place and one that he knew would not push or cause trouble. This was a different side of Toney that he was seeing for the very first time.

When Toney joined the other members of the staff in her area, they crowded around her cubicle to get the scoop.

"What happened?" Jamie inquired.

"Did he try to push you away like we thought he would?" she continued.

"He sure did," Toney responded as she appeared to gain more and more self-confidence.

"You girls were right on the mark. The only difference was, the excuse that he used was that the big boys have their eyes on a hot shot from New York. He came up with that one really fast. I wonder why he doesn't want me in the job. Is it because I'm a woman or because I'm black?" Toney said sadly.

"Maybe both," Tiffany said.

"It's amazing how many excuses the system will come up with not to give us our just due. I can't believe it. You've come in here and have been successful at blowing the roof off the business and he's hedging to promote you. He doesn't want to see your black face in the office next to his. I bet it's him and no one else," Jamie said angrily.

"Yeah. And, if I were you, I'd push back. He's not expecting that any of us will push back. Or, that they can tell us anything they want to and we're stupid enough to buy it. It's a damned shame," Tiffany said looking in Dick's direction.

"That motherfucker is just like the rest of them. Remember how he and Paul were always together? That was his boy, but you don't quite fit the bill. You don't have 'the look.' Well too damn bad. Kick ass, girl. Kick ass! Don't let them get away with it. It's a damn shame that hard work and success is not enough for the system," Tiffany said as she walked away shaking her head.

As the next week passed Toney thought it best to keep to herself, maintaining a low-key disposition and attitude and to just keep on top of her work. Dick spoke with her sparingly, about only work related issues. At the end of the week, just after lunch she started thinking. She wasn't going to go back to her dingy apartment and have this situation on her mind for the entire weekend. This thing had her very much up in the air. The fact that he had not given her an answer either way was ridiculous. She looked at the big clock on the wall toward the back of the big area where all of the cubicles were located. It was twenty after two. She'd give him until three thirty. It was Friday and he was known to leave early to get lost in a bar…any bar. She couldn't let this happened this specific Friday. She had too much at stake. She monitored the clock. At five to four, she went into confront Dick again. He had been in so many closed-door meetings with staffers from other departments, so she waited her turn. When Dick was free, she stepped into his office.

"I need to speak with you for a moment," Toney said as she took a seat before Dick could take offense.

"Well, have a seat won't you?" he said sarcastically.

Toney ignored his comments and moved forward with the purpose of her visit, "Dick, I want to get an update from you. It appears that you've been evading my issue all week, and to be honest, I thought you needed the time to get your thoughts together about how you wanted to approach the situation. But, as we moved through the week, it became more and more evident that you have no answers for me. Have you even talked to the big boys yet?" Toney said directly.

"Yes, I have spoken with them. They were against it all the way. I asked them to allow me to make my staff moves as I saw fit. They said they'd think about it. Leave it to me okay?" he said sounding almost sincere. "These things take time."

"Okay, but when will you know?"

"Soon. Very soon." ....

Toney was shaken from her daydream by the sound of crying in the outer office. She stood abruptly to make her way to the door. It had to be one of the employees.

"Sonjia, what's going on out here?" Toney said as she interrupted Sonjia hugging Imogene.

"Imogene just came back to work. She took two days off to get some tests done. She hadn't heard about Freddy," Sonjia said still hugging and consoling her.

Toney joined in putting her hand on Imogene's shoulder, "We're all shaken about this, Imogene. It's terrible. Would you like some time to be alone? You can use my office or we can have one of the counselors in Human Resources speak with you about it?"

"No Toney. I'll be all right. I guess the shock of it threw me, that's all. I heard three people in a little huddle, near the front of the office talking about it and...I don't know. Have the police found out anything?"

"Nothing. The police told me that they'd let me know, but so far nothing."

"Ladies, please let me know if there is anything that I can do. I've got to get back to work, okay?" Toney said as she walked back into her office and closed the door.

There was so much going on around her. How she was managing to keep her wits about her was a testament to her personal determination that the negative side of life would not destroy her, only make her stronger. She sat there for a moment reviewing all that was going on when her mind wandered to Cameron.

"I hadn't had a chance to talk with Cameron. I wonder how is she doing?"

She picked up the phone to give her a call. They hadn't really spoken in detail in several weeks.

"Good afternoon, Cameron Beeage please."

"She's on another line. Will you hold?"

"Yes, I will."

Just over a minute went by.

'Cameron Beeage, may I help you?" the lady said not sounding at all like Cameron.

"Cameron, is that you?" Toney asked.

"It's me or what's left of me," Cameron said strangely.

"It's Toney. How are you girl?" Toney asked in an upbeat manner.

"I'm here. That's about it," Cameron said almost in a fog.

"Well, what's going on?" Toney continued.

"Toney, you don't have enough time for me to get into it, especially not this afternoon," Cameron said despondently.

"It's so late in the day and all," Cameron said.

"You never know. After all, what are friends for? Want to grab a cup of coffee? We can meet on the second floor for a few minutes," Toney said continuing her upbeat manner.

"No. Not today. I have a deadline that I have to meet. I still have to do all the work while others get the glory," Cameron said as if she had little or no humility left.

"Well, maybe tomorrow then?" Toney asked.

"Yeah. Tomorrow," Cameron agreed.

"Okay, tomorrow then."

"Okay. Bye"

What was going on with Cameron? Toney thought as she sat there stunned. She didn't sound right. Her job was taking over the whole woman. She'd have to get with Cameron in the morning. She didn't sound too good. Not at all.

As Toney wrapped up her day she thanked God for all that she did have and prayed. She got up to leave for the day when her parents flashed across her mind.

"I'd better call mom and dad before I leave here."

She put her brief case on the sofa closest to the door and went back to her desk to place the call. The phone rang four times. That was strange for her folks. Never more than three rings was what she remembered.

"Hello?" her mom answered.

"Mom, how are you and dad doing?" Toney said as she finally got an answer on the other end of the phone.

"Hi, honey, what a surprise! We're doing fine. Just fine, although your dad seems to have the last of a bug. He's been down for three days but getting much better though. How are you? Is everything all right? You seldom call during the week like this. Is everything all right?" her mom said displaying a measure of concern.

"Oh, mom, I'm fine. I've just got a lot happening around me...the staff, some friends that kind of stuff. I just needed to hear your voice. That's all."

"I'm looking forward to coming home for the holidays. That's a couple of months away. You guys got anything special planned?"

"Not yet. But, we can if you want to. Let's talk about it on Saturday when you call," Dorothy said.

"I won't be calling Saturday. I have a trip to Tokyo coming up. I leave on Friday night. I come back a week from Friday. So, we can talk when I get back. Let me speak with dad for a minute."

"Okay, baby. Just a minute," Dorothy said as Toney heard her mom call Bill..."Bill its Toney, honey. Can you pick up the phone in there?"

"Hello, Toney. How are you darling?" her dad asked sounding kind of weak. "How's my girl?"

"Dad, you don't sound well. Mom said you had the flu. Do you feel better? Have you been to Doctor Willey? What does he say? Should I come home?"

"Hold it, honey. Don't go off on the deep end here. I'm doing much, much better. Jed came to see me here at the house. He told me that I had caught a virus. I'll be fine in a week or so...just like new. How are you? Are you okay?"

"Thank God for Doctor Willey. He's still making house calls. What an anomaly! You'd never hear of such a thing in the big city. I was just telling mama that I'm coming home during the holidays. Maybe we can create some old times with the three of us being in the house again."

"That sounds like fun, baby. I'll talk to you after the Tokyo trip. You take care of yourself and be very, very careful. We love you."

"Okay dad...I will. I love you both too."

Toney hung up the phone, picked up her brief case and left for the day.

PART II

Charles returned from New York the next morning. He and Toney had a lengthy meeting scheduled for nine o'clock. There had been a host of things that had developed since he left. As was usually the case, Toney spent much of the morning on the fiftieth floor. Their weekly meetings were typically thirty minute tops, but today her estimate was that it would be no less than a couple of hours. She couldn't afford the time with everything else that was on her plate, but she couldn't afford not to spend the time either, with all that was happening.

"Sonjia, you know where I'll be. Remember that I'll be there for a while, so hold my calls. If things run into the conference call time, I'll call down to let you know," Toney said as she breezed past the desk.

On the elevator ride to the fiftieth floor a host of things ran through Toney's mind. When would Babbitt call? Has he found out anything? Who was really behind all of this? Poor Freddy, who killed him? Wonder will Surrant ever get it together? The shorter twins...what were they up to? So much to think about...and, as if the job itself wasn't a hand full.

"Good morning, Terry. Is he ready for me?" Toney said in her charismatic, personable manner.

"Yes, Miss Thing!" Terry teased.

"He just buzzed me to ask if you were waiting. He's been on an international call and just got off the telephone. Go right in," she straightened up, giving Toney a wink.

Terry thought the world of Toney. She was proud to see a woman handling business the way that Toney had always done... keeping business, business.

"Good morning, Charles. So nice to see you looking so chipper," she complimented as she took a seat in front of him.

"How was New York?"

"Ahhh, there's nothing on earth like New York, Toney. We took several high level customers to dinner and the theatre and on the last night we treated ourselves to dinner and theatre. Mary and I needed some time to get away...you know?" he said raring back in his succulent chair.

"How's everything going here?" Charles asked.

Toney started filling Charles in, and as it turned out their meeting ran over about thirty minutes pushing her to the last seconds of the scheduled conference call.

Arriving in her office area just in the neck of time she breezed by Sonjia's desk saying," Sonjia, please get me connected to all the folks for the call."

"Okay," Sonjia said calling the AT&T operator giving her the code for the call.

TWENTY

The office was too quiet. So quiet that one could barely hear the normal buzz of the office environment taking care of the company's business. Freddy was being buried today. And from all accounts, observing the mood of the employees, he was being gravely mourned by every member of the staff on the forty-fifth floor. Sonjia, Imogene, June and the others were as somber as they could be, trying to deal with the service that they would each attend later in the day. The uniform of the day was to be black, which spoke volumes about the mindset of the staff when they got dressed this morning. Knowing that the service would be difficult for each of the staff members, Toney knew she had to lead by example, meaning that she had to appear strong even if she wasn't. She was closed up in her office trying to get through the paperwork that had to go out by the end of the week. It was already Thursday. The week had literally shrieked by. Close to nine that morning several of the employees had somehow made their way to each other. They were huddled together in the coffee break area discussing the murder. Fallon Miles was a relatively new employee who, like most people, had never been in an environment where a murder victim had worked. She was hired as part of the typing pool, an entry-level position. She had only slightly gotten to know Freddy, but liked the way he lit up the room whenever he was around. She initiated the conversation.

"It's a shame that someone would murder Freddy. He seemed like a very decent person," Fallon said.

"He was. He had his questionable side like many of us do, but for the most part, I looked forward to seeing him everyday, if nothing but for a laugh," June mouthed.

"Yeah. Me too. He was certainly good for a laugh, but it was more than that. He was good for uplifting any of our spirits. I know many days when I was down, or angry about something or just plain didn't want to be here, he came through, and before he left he had me laughing or so tied up in one of his stories that I forgot all about my problems. It takes a very special person to do that. A very special person," Imogene said sadly.

"Isn't that the truth?" Sonjia chimed in.

"Freddy will be sorely missed. And, I just know the police will find out who murdered him. It was strange seeing his picture on the news and hearing the anchor person talking about someone that I knew...you know? It's like this has hit too close to home. But, if we all help each other and think of the good times, maybe it won't hurt so bad," Sonjia shared.

"Sonjia, what's Toney saying about all of this? Is she as blown way about this as we are?" June asked.

"Naturally she's taken aback about this whole thing. But, you know Toney. She is the most difficult person that I know to read. She carries a lot on the inside. Her loving and accepting nature won't allow her to prejudge a situation or to guess about anything unless she has evidence that the certain thing is the way it appears. But, having said that, I personally know that she is hurt about the matter. After all, the police did call her to let her know that he was found. They didn't call his parents, his sisters or brothers, uncles or aunts, they called Toney. That tells you that she and Freddy, like many of us, had a very special relationship too. So, she has to be hurting as well."

"But remember, Toney is the boss. She has to maintain the appearance of a certain strength for all of us; she can't afford to have us feel that she has a common relationship with us or a weakness. We're not on her level, even though she treats us well. That's just the human side of her," Sonjia continued.

"You're right, Sonjia, but Toney doesn't appear to be as uptight as the rest of us. I wonder if she knew something more about this earlier? Toney's been stretched out a lot lately. You remember a couple of weeks ago, when she was so spaced out? What was that all about? I wonder if that was related to Freddy's untimely demise?" June continued.

"How dare you say such a thing?" Imogene shouted.

"You really have a big problem alluding to that. How would Toney have anything to do with this?" Imogene proclaimed further.

"June, I've told you about saying things like that. Your mouth is eventually going to write a check that you ass is going to have to cash. If Toney ever heard you saying things like that, you'd get fired on the spot. When will you learn?" Sonjia rapped.

A couple of seconds later, Toney buzzed Sonjia. She didn't get an answer. A second or so later, Toney opened the door of her office headed out into the employee open area to see where everyone was. She was surprised that no one was at their desks. She walked along the main aisle of the office searching from side to side, as she walked. Finally, she saw the group huddled together. Approaching them she asked, "What are you guys up to?"

"We were just talking about Freddy and how much he'd be missed," Sonjia defended.

"He will be missed," Toney said in a doleful way.

"We'll get our chances to say goodbye to him this afternoon. I need for all of you to try and get some work done until that time though. We have had to work with these thoughts on our minds all week, which has put us all behind. So, I need all of you to make a concerted effort to help me out, okay?" Toney reminded them skillfully.

A collection of okay's was mumbled as the group disbanded to retreat to their individual areas. After getting a cup of coffee in the outer office area, Toney walked over to Sonjia's desk.

"I need to see you in my office, please."

Sonjia felt that she was about to be reprimanded about something that had only happened once or twice in all of the years that she and Toney had been together. She stood immediately following behind Toney fearing reprimand for being part of the group, especially losing site of her duties, which was typically not her way.

"Yes, Toney. What is it?" Sonjia asked bewilderedly.

"What was that all about? I buzzed you twice with no answer. Why were there so many of you gathered in that area, letting the office fall off to itself? Needless to say, I was surprised that you were right there in the middle of it all. I know this is a troubling time for all of us, but we still have a business to run. The staff is surely sidetracked and I know it's hard for you too, but I have to count on you to maintain some objectivity especially as it relates to the office," Toney continued.

"You're right, Toney. It's just that we've never had anyone who we've known and worked with murdered. Freddy was such a part of all of us that it's...well, it's hard," Sonjia said managing to hold back the tears.

"I know it's hard. I feel it too. You know I do. But, I keep my mind on other things, which helps a lot. That's what I need you to do as well. The staff needs both of us and we have to be there for them, right?"

"You're right," Sonjia agreed.

"Well, here's what I need for you to do. Stay with them. Encourage them to keep their minds and hands busy with work. Let them know that it'll help them in the long run to stay busy and keep their minds occupied while dealing with Freddy's death. It's going to get easier, but only in time. His smile, his laughter, his joking nature will be missed. But, there's nothing that we can do for Freddy now, aside from keeping his memory alive and enjoying the thoughts of the good times."

"You're right," Sonjia said with a pause. "You're right."

There was no use in Sonjia trying to tell Toney that she was leading the conversation with attempts to console the employees and to conclude it, because she was right.

Sonjia got up saying to Toney, "I'd better get busy. One o'clock will be here before you know it."

Toney sat there for a moment pondering her disposition. She felt odd. She couldn't put her finger on just what it was she was feeling. She somewhat shook off the feeling...at least enough to get back to her task list. She had to finalize her stack of work, task by task, now narrowed down to nine or ten items. She also had to fill Freddy's position with a temporary employee for now. That would have to do until she got back and could find the right person for the position. Her spirit had to lead her to be extra careful how she described the person she wanted to Human Resources, because she had all of the other employees to think about. Things were so volatile at this time, because of the way Freddy died. Human Resources began the screening process immediately, making sure that the final candidate had no physical features like Freddy. And, then there were the other criteria to consider. That would be much too much for the staff.

"Buzz."

"Yes, Sonjia?"

"Toney, I have your car all set up for the trip to O'Hare on Friday. The car will pick you up at home at six fifty a.m. Your flight leaves at eight fifteen a.m., so you should be there in plenty of time. Bukura's secretary has set up a car for you in Tokyo, basically, the same as the last time. Do you need me to go to the bank to get you some cash?"

"Thanks, Sonjia. No, I'll take a walk around eleven thirty, before the service to get some cash. That'll give me a chance to get some fresh air and have a moment with Cameron."

"Just a moment, Sonjia, that's my private line. I'll call you right back," she said clicking off of office line one and connecting to her private line.

"Hello?"

"Toney, it's Cameron. You got a minute for me?" Cameron said appearing to be rushed.

"Sure, Cameron. I was going to call you in a few minutes anyway. It looks like great minds think alike, huh?" Toney shared.

"I apologize about yesterday, but I was in a funk. My head was spinning and spinning hard. You won't believe what has happened. I told you that they brought this little cheerleader looking girl to my department, right? She's been all in Summers' face everyday. They asked me to train her, which I did. What choice did I have? Now, they're looking at her to move her to the next level. She's already been brought in at my level with no fucking experience and now the next level? I know she's fucking someone. She's not that bright, nor does she really work that hard. Every night, I'm the only one left here to finish the loose ends. She's out drinking with Summers and that crew. Now, I hear that the promotion that I should have already gotten is going to her. Toney, if they do that, I don't know what I'll do," Cameron said sounding like an insane person.

"Come on, Cameron, don't put the cart before the horse. That's a rumor. Why haven't you gone in to have a one on one with Summers? He appears to be a reasonable man. And, what about the Human Resources department? Can't they help?"

"Hell no. These people do what the hell they want to do. They create jobs for some people and phase out jobs to get rid of some others. It's crazy. I'm appalled at the way they conduct business. It's becoming a free for all and if you don't have 'the look' that they want, or if you don't fuck 'em or kiss their asses, you're out. Or, at least they find a way to stifle you and put you in a menial position, out of the public's eye. It's fucked up. The other day, I came back to the office and I was the first one in. I saw a pair of panties on the floor of Summers office. I couldn't believe my eyes. The panties were extra small. That leaves most of the other females in the office out, because the other women are almost as large as I am. Can you believe that they were fucking in the office? How lewd," Cameron said as if she were a run-away train.

Toney interrupted, "Cameron, you wanna get a bite to eat? Come on...let's take a break."

"Alright, what the fuck...I can't win for loosing anyway. They won't miss me, so what the fuck. I'll meet you downstairs," Cameron said hanging up the phone.

Toney hung up thinking that she'd never heard Cameron curse so much. She was becoming a loose cannon. Or, more like a bomb ready to blow.

"She has to get some help or she's going to blow," Toney said as she got up from her desk to go meet Cameron.

Before she got to the door, she remembered that she also had to go to the bank for cash. She went back to her desk, pulled out her purse, got her wallet and she was on her way.

"Sonjia, I'll be back before it's time to go to the service."

When Toney got downstairs Cameron was no where to be found, so she just hung out by the elevator bank. Ten minutes, fifteen minutes, twenty minutes, no Cameron.

"Where the hell is she?" Toney said as she paced and looked at her watch.

Just as Toney headed for the pay phones to call Cameron's office, she stepped off of the elevator. She looked like hell. "This woman, who was the salt of the earth was experiencing hell on earth and all for a job. How cruel," Toney thought.

"Hi, darling. How are you?" Toney said as she reached for Cameron to give her a big bear hug.

"Hi Toney. It's really nice to see a friendly face."

"Let's get a bite to eat and maybe go out of the building for a few minutes to get some fresh air. What do you say?" Toney said.

"That sounds good. Where do you want to go?" Toney continued.

"Doesn't make me any difference. None at all. I have no real time to be back," Cameron said.

"Well, I do and you probably do too. You don't want to give them reasons to fire you, do you?" Toney asked softly.

"Who the fuck cares at this point? They don't need me. They need the cheerleader," Cameron said smugly.

"Let that bitch handle things. They'll see. They'll see," she said.

"Well, I've got to get back," Toney said trying to change the subject. "Freddy Talbert was found murdered on Sunday and his funeral service is at one. So, I've got to get back, but I certainly have time for you."

"Murdered? Wow. Which one was Freddy?" Cameron asked appearing to take her mind off of her problems.

"He was the thin black gay guy in the office. The one who was always talking loud, cracking jokes and telling little funny stories," Toney explained.

Cameron's mood instantly changed. She was honestly interested in Freddy and what happened to him.

"What happened? You said he was murdered?"

"Yes. That's what the police said. We don't have the particulars right now, but there are several cops working on this case."

"Far out. So, the funeral is today?"

"Yes it is. It's in an hour, so I need to move along. I've got to be back there for my troops, you know," Toney said stepping up the pace of her stroll with Cameron.

"Let's stop here at Giordanno's pizza place. I'd like to have a beer and a slice of pizza," Cameron said.

"Well, okay if you say so. But, how about an O'Doul's instead? You don't want to mix alcohol with the mood you're in. You might pop someone," Toney said smiling.

"An O'Doul's sounds smart," Cameron said managing to force a smile for Toney.

They stepped inside being early enough to get any seat in the house. The waitress addressed them immediately as they placed their orders. They sat there chatting which appeared to loosen Cameron's tension. Forty minutes later they were walking back toward the office building with Cameron in a somewhat better mood.

"Wait for me, Cameron. I have to run into the back for some cash. I'm headed to Tokyo tomorrow and need to be prepared," Toney said flashing a big smile at Cameron.

"No problem, I'll sit right here on this bench and wait."

Toney went in, got in line and took care of her business. Ten minutes later she rejoined Cameron and they strolled back to their building. Toney stooped on a dime when they entered the building. "Cameron, you've got to promise me one thing."

"What's that Toney?" Cameron asked knowing exactly what Toney was going to ask.

"Please take each step slowly and remember that you're in control. Don't let them keep you so up tight. You're a good person and you work hard, so no matter what, they can't take that away from you, right?"

"I know you're right, but that's easier said than done. Those son of a bitches are trying to drive me out after all I've done there for so many years. Summers and I had an impromptu conversation in passing a few weeks ago. He told me that loyalty and stupidity go hand in hand in today's workplace. So, if he can say that to me after the way that I've helped to build the business, there is no telling what they'll do. I'll certainly try to maintain, but I can't promise you anything at this juncture. Actually, I'm at the end of the road about all of this, but I thank you for always being there for me. You've been a good friend and I'll remember you always," Cameron said as she pushed the elevator button. The thought ran through Toney's mind that Cameron was saying goodbye. They hugged, just before the elevator stopped. She got off on thirty-seven. The uneasy feeling that swept over Toney was chilling. She knew somehow that this was definitely not the end of this predicament. She wished that there was something more that she could do. But with the funeral, the trip to Japan, Fin Babbitt, Surrant and the other issues, her plate was running over.

Most of her staff was ready to leave when she returned. She had made arrangements to have the office covered. Fallon had been drafted to stay behind because she knew Freddy less than anyone else in the office. Most of the employees piled into a few cars to make the trek to the church in South Chicago more economical. Sonjia, June and Imogene rode with Toney. They spoke of pleasant times with Freddy, which forced a couple of mild chuckles as they rode along. Finally, after about twenty-five minutes later, they parked down the street from the church, parking on the street about a half a block away. There were a host of different types headed to the church, which yelled to the rooftops how many lives that Freddy had touched. The most notable type was the gays in attendance. Many of the well dressed people were blatant gays so there was more than likely many hidden secrets that went to Freddy's grave with him about many of the faces of the people here. Before Freddy started with Prophecy he worked at IBM, so at the other end of the spectrum were the different, but similar business types in attendance. The service brought together two completely different worlds.

The funeral service was very tastefully carried out. Several individuals spoke interestingly warm words as they stood to eulogize the deceased, painting a picture of someone quite perplexed. Toney couldn't help but to think that she really never really knew Freddy as she listened intently to the stories that were being shared. What really struck Toney as odd was the fact that no one from Prophecy stood to share their thoughts. Maybe it was her job to do that, but she had hoped that the individuals who worked closer with him would be the presenters. When the pastor stood to ask for the last of the presenters, Toney stood to give a short dissertation. It was short and sweet. The talk brought back a flood of memories in an instant reminding her of the valedictory speech that she gave when she graduated. Each speech was to lead people to go forth and better themselves after a milestone in their lives has passed. With the last of her words the pastor rose again to wrap up the service. Tears flowed freely as row after row emptied to walk out after the casket was removed from the sanctuary and loaded into the Hearst. Few of the attendees had opted not to go to the gravesite much as Toney had urged her troops to do. That would be too upsetting. Better to remember Freddy as he was, she coached, keeping the sadness to a manageable minimum. When they got back to the office, there was very little work done. The staff was oblivious to the needs before them. These needs were last in their minds and for good reason. Toney on the other hand got right back to work. She prepared to return her calls after riffling through the messages, putting them in an order of importance. Eighteen messages, which had passed the limit of her expectation in such a short period of time. Eighteen people had to talk with her. Would it forever be this way? Sonjia handled many of the callers in an ordinary day, but because she was hurting too, Toney decided to take up the slack. One by one she knocked them down starting with a message from Babbitt. Had he found out anything? Was her challenge coming to a head? She could only hope that it would be this facile.

"Fin Babbit, please," Toney chirped.

"He's out. May I take a message, please?" the receptionists probed.

"When do you expect him?"

"He just left. Not sure when he'll be back. He didn't say."

As the day wound down Toney sat at her desk putting a lid on her undone tasks. Each of the undone items could surely wait until she returned. Nothing was earth shattering. Her staff had also finished their day and started to head home until there only remained Toney and Sonjia.

They hugged about forty-five minutes later and also left for the day.

PART II

When Toney arrived home she had just enough energy to take a shower and get into bed. She had to rely on another Excedrin PM for tonight. She had so many things running through her head that she knew she wouldn't have a peaceful rest. She took the pill and just lay there looking up at the ceiling. She instantaneously fell into a day dreaming state again, which seemed to relax her a bit ....

On Thursday afternoon practically two months after Paul left, Dick finally walked over to Toney's area and said, "May I see you please?"

"Sure. I'll be right with you," Toney assured him as she raised up from her desk to see what he wanted.

"What can I do for you, Dick?" Toney asked.

"Please be seated. I've got some good news for you," he said with a half-baked grin on his face.

It was plain to Toney that the plastic look on his face was forced. He was clearly about to tell her something that his heart wasn't in.

"Toney, you have been promoted to the lead Programmer. Congratulations," he mustered.

"You will keep your same position in terms of your location, but your raise will begin today and will be reflected on your next pay check.

Your increase will be five thousand dollars annually," he said as if he were about to choke.

"Thank you, Dick," Toney said in a shallow manner, without the benefit of an expression.

"You don't seem to be excited about it. Is there something wrong now?"

"Well yes since you asked. Why am I being forced to stay in the cubicle as your number two person? Why is my increase only five thousand when you and I both know that Paul was making fifteen thousand more than I was when he left? What's going on here?" Toney said as she exhaled and started to feel some signs of firmness.

"You have only been with the company less than five years, and a five thousand dollar raise is excellent at this point."

"That is incorrect. I have been with this company five years, five weeks and eight days to be exact, and I have functioned successfully with contributions in excess of 300% annually and as if I have been here for ten years or more. The programs that I have been successful at developing and the revenue that I have generated have been staggering. So, why is my increase only at five thousand dollars?"

"That's what I've been instructed to give you."

"And, what about Meagan? How much are you bringing her in at?"

"Meagan? How did you know anything about Meagan?"

"Never mind how I know. Why are you keeping me from sitting in the Senior Programmers office? All of the Senior Programmers have sat in that office since this office was built, and now because it is my turn the rules change?"

"If it is any of your business, I am bringing Meagan to our department from Public Relations. She will handle all of the administrative side of the programming tasks for this location. It's really a better deal for you anyway. It'll be less work for you. She needs to be in Paul's old office so that she and I can have eye contact, since she will be working along side me constantly."

"I can handle my job. I don't need for anyone to do my work. And I'm not sure I heard you right. She will be working along side you and not your number two person? That's strange. Well, this is your office to run, but, I am not happy about this. And, the money...I insist that you go back to the drawing board on my raise. My contribution warrants more than five thousand," she said as she stood to make her way to the door without another word.

Toney had never been so angry in her life. She was also very embarrassed. She would be the number two person in the office and rightly so, but she wouldn't get the pay to substantiate it or the recognition with the office to give her the appearance of being the number two person. This was awful. It was just as Tiffany had said. The conditions of her promotion had her in a deep depression. Meagan was slated to start in the Programming area on Monday. She had had little to say to Meagan as the years progressed...typically no more than hello since they had never worked closely together. She really wasn't angry with Meagan. Toney figured that Meagan was doing what she had to do for herself. But, Meagan had to know that there were other people in the department who should have gotten that office over her. She just had to know that, being an intelligent woman.

On Monday morning, Meagan reported to Programming. Something was up. Something big. All of the secretaries and other staffers were in an uproar over the latest episodes. Little pockets of people discussed the ins and outs of the situation and all agreed that it would get to be a lot uglier as the weeks passed by. At the end of the day Dick called Toney on the intercom, "Ms. Chambers, please step into my office."

She walked slowly that way feeling like she was about to throw up. The sight of him made her sick. "Yes, Dick, what is it?"

"Please close the door and have a seat. I have great news for you," he said with a smile. "I have been able to get you five thousand dollars more. So you are at a ten thousand-dollar increase. Does that make you happy?"

"Somewhat...I guess," she said without expression.

"Thank you," she said as she stood to make her way out of his office.

"Well, I hope I can count on you for your contribution to remain high. We will talk again soon."

She walked out with the thought of how sick he made her and with the belief that he'd get his in the end ....

TWENTY ONE

It was already eleven. Where had the evening gone? It was as if she was in a perpetual fog. Toney's thoughts of Freddy lingered into the evening and the night. It made her lonely for her mom and dad. Her spirit was restless because she hadn't seen them in so long. Everything that was going on in her life had her completely occupied, leaving no time for much more than work and the necessities that keep her afloat. She had promised her parents that she would get back to Lexington for the holidays, so, she had to work to that end. No matter what, she had to take a whole week for home. She owed it to herself, her parents and to Vanessa. She packed carefully. She had become an expert at packing due to her frequent trekking for Prophecy. Some of the trips were for the day only, some for a couple of days, and some, like this trip, were for multiple days, so she wanted to be prepared.

It was eleven thirty when she decided to pick up the phone to reach out to her parents.

"Hello mom. I just wanted to reach out to you and dad before I leave for Japan. How's dad coming along?" Toney said sounding worn down.

"Hi baby. You father is much better. He's sleeping right now. I don't want to wake him unless you really need to talk with him. The doctor said that the more rest he gets the sooner he'll be up and around," Dorothy shared.

"Then by all means, let him sleep. I just wanted to hear your voices, before I left. The car will be here real early in the morning to pick me up, and I'll be out of touch for the week. If you need me, call my office. Sonjia will know how to reach me," Toney instructed.

Otherwise, I'll call you guys when I get back, okay?" Toney shared.

"All right baby. Be safe. We love you," Dorothy said just before hanging up.

"Bye mom," Toney whispered.

Toney finished packing, took a shower and put on her pajamas. She finally fell into bed around one thirty and went to sleep quickly.

TWENTY TWO

It was a new day for work, but she was psyched about it because today she could physically get away from all of the bizarre events of late. She'd miss her sweet Grant, but a week would fly by and they'd be together again. She had the honor of representing Prophecy in Tokyo again, and for almost a week she would have her attention focused on something very different. She had traveled to the orient only once, and at that time she didn't have enough savoir fair to really know what to do with the opportunity. Mousy, new at the game and too shy for the opportunity, she followed the leader then, rather than arrive there as the leader.

She woke at four a.m. with the assistance of her alarm clock to make sure that she was ready when the car arrived for her. Sonjia had scheduled the car for six forty-five. Her plane was to depart around eight, so they would arrive at O'Hare in enough time.

At precisely six forty the driver stepped into the lobby of her building, "Good morning, sir. My name is Steven Williams from Cursory Limousine Service. I'm here for Miss Chambers. Would you let her know that her driver has arrived, please?"

"Good morning. I'll give her a call for you. She's going again. She's on the road a lot. Have a seat if you like," the guard responded.

As the guard dialed the unit number, the driver took a seat and picked up one of the magazines neatly place on the coffee table for visitors.

"Hello?" Toney answered.

"Good morning, Ms. Chambers, this is Billy. Steven is here from Cursory. He's waiting for you here in the lobby. Do you need help with your bags?"

"Yes, Billy. I could use a hand. Please send the driver up to assist me. Tell him I am ready to go."

"Okay, I'll send him right up."

Minutes later Toney handed the driver two bags, turned to take a look at her place, clicked off the light, and moved along with the driver to the elevator and then the lobby, more than ready to go. He put her into the back seat of the car and her bags into the trunk. He slid into the front seat of the Town Car, started the engine and put the car in gear to start their short journey.

The driver had on easy listening music while they rode in the light traffic, for Chicago standards anyway. In thirty minutes she was standing at the curb watching while her luggage being unloaded.

"Ms. Chambers, just to verify your airline. You are traveling on All Nippon Air, correct?"

"Yes, Steven, All Nippon."

She tipped Steven and thanked him for being prompt and courteous. She beckoned for a skycap, which swiftly came to her.

"Good morning, ma'am, may I help you?"

"Yes, sir," she said as she handed the skycap her ticket.

"Ms. Chambers…you're traveling to Tokyo today. May I see your identification please?"

"Did you pack your bags yourself?"

"Yes I did," she said while reaching into her bag to retrieve her identification.

"Have your bags been with you since you packed them?"

"Yes, they have," she answered handing him her driver's license.

"Did anyone give you anything to take on board the aircraft?

"No, sir, they did not."

"Thank you, Ms. Chambers," the skycap said handing her her license and her ticket back along with her claim checks.

"Have a great flight," he said smiling at her.

Toney shared a hearty smile with him and gave him a tip and continued on to her gate.

At six fifty five, she was seated in the area just across from her gate. She took out her laptop while she waited to answer and send a few e-mails. She was infamous for making sure that everyone had enough to do, while she was on the road and this trip would be no different. So, she loaded everyone down. She looked up taking a break from her work to notice that the gate crew began the boarding process. And, as it is with most airlines, First Class passengers were called to board first. Toney closed out of her program, picked up her carry on bag, brief case and laptop to make her way to her gate area, through the receiving line and eventually down the jet way to her seat. She briefly thought about her last trip to Jamaica with Grant. It was such a wonderful trip. She forced herself not to think about the accident. She wanted to put all of that behind her. The remaining passengers filed on the flight. The flight attendants were a combination of oriental and Caucasian, which hurried themselves to get the passengers comfortably seated in anticipation of the Captain's announcement of departure. Moments later the Captain gave the conventional talk, and they were on their way. Toney and the others settled in for the marathon flight. Being as driven as she was normally, she pulled out some of the preparatory work for the encounters that led her to the orient. Her heart raced thinking of sealing the deal on the largest account in her career. She had made many significant strides in her career, but they had all been just preparation for this big opportunity. Now she had the chance to bag the big one, and she wasn't about to let it get away from her. In between the work she was doing and the personal thoughts she was having about everything under the sun, the airline offered a meal and a movie once the initial flight rituals were performed. She was interested in watching the movie "Soul Food" because she had heard so much about it but hadn't taken the time to see it with Grant. There were so many of the facets of the movie that hit home with her…the closeness of the family, the big Sunday dinners, the friends and family that gathered around during the holidays.

Three hours of the flight time had passed. Toney became very sleepy, deciding to let nature take its course while she complied closing her eyes for what she thought would be only a few minutes. She slept for over an hour waking to the flight attendants offering more refreshments that she declined. She had to put everything aside while she took this opportunity to go to the rest room. When she returned to her seat, she once again got comfortably seated, placing her belongings strategically around her for easy access. She sat there for a few minutes idle which led her down the path to a daydreaming state again **...**

There had been no announcement about Paul, the lead programmer's replacement. Dick Negri was hemming and hawing about it all. He had been on the phone to Chicago about the hand that he had been dealt and his thoughts about who was to succeed Paul. He knew that Toney Chambers was intelligent, but he also knew that she was not worldly. Maybe he could pull the wool over her eyes and slide someone else into the position that by right she had worked for. He just was not happy with the fact that he'd have a black girl as his second. But, he also knew that Prophecy was political and that if he didn't do the right thing, it could come back to haunt him. The corporate office gave Dick the instructions to promote Toney. That was not what he wanted to hear. With the decision made for him, Dick dragged his feet. Two weeks passed by and more and more talk ensued.

Tiffany asked Toney, "You want to grab some lunch?"

"Sure. What time?"

"Twelve thirty?"

"Okay, I should be finished with this project by then. Stop by to pick me up."

Dick passed by just as Tiffany was about to leave Toney's area, "What are you girls doing…slacking off?"

"Hardly," Tiffany returned with a hint of sarcasm.

"We very rarely have our heads together, like some people with offices do," hinting that with all of the meetings that take place in Dick's office which are obviously about any and everything other than business. "And, besides Mr. Negri, I haven't been a girl in fifteen years, so I'd appreciate it if you wouldn't call me that."

"You're kind of sensitive aren't you honey?" Dick retorted as he continued to his office.

"That silly son of a bitch. Who does he think he is?" Tiffany said in a whisper to Toney.

"Listen, Tiffany, what's the use? I told you that the only thing that I care about is being treated fairly. Pay no attention to his words. I only pick the battles that I can win, you know?" Toney said confidently.

"And, the war of words with a fool is not a battle that I care to enter. If you say nothing, he'll go away, and one day his words will catch up with him, don't you think? Besides he has so many infractions that by the end of a given day, I'd be too tired of fighting, if I took them all on, right? So, forget it unless it's something like him calling you a bad name. Now I'd go to the mat on that one," Toney defended.

"You're right. But he really gets to me. He's something else though," she said walking away.

"I'll see you in a couple of hours. We've got to talk."

Toney went back to work. She finished with her immediate task and moved on to the next. She was so driven. She was also very detailed and could produce in a fluid manner...much more than any of her counterparts. That was why she couldn't understand why Dick hesitated about her and hadn't responded to her at all about the promotion. She had made up in her mind to go in to talk with him by the end of the week if he hadn't gotten back to her.

Tiffany stopped by Toney's area at twelve thirty-three.

"You ready to go?"

"Yeah, I'm at a good stopping point. Where are we going?"

"It doesn't matter. I really don't have that much cash. Payday is still four days away. How about McDonalds?" Tiffany suggested.

"Fine by me. I'm a little strapped too. I remember the days when I made only **Two Hundred and Thirty-six dollars and fifty-two cents every two weeks** and I don't make much more than that now. Girl, with rent, electric, food, transportation, clothes - what few I have - and all of the rest...it's rough," Toney said.

"I know that's right. At least you make more than me. Look at me, forty and still a typist. I wish I had gone to college," Tiffany said with her head hanging down.

"Why didn't you?" Toney asked as if she clearly did not understand.

"No money. My family is from Southeast D.C. The folks in that area for the most part are hurting. When I landed this job seven years ago, I thought I had arrived. But, the raises for line employees are minimal each year, so it's rough," Tiffany said sadly.

They had gotten to McDonalds. The lines were long. It appeared that everyone in the area had the same thoughts or everyone was running a bit short on funds. They finally made their way to the front of the line, ordered their hamburgers and fries. Once they were served, it was so crowded that they had to stand by waiting for a seat. Three or four minutes later they were successful.

"Listen, Toney, I have some news that I wanna share with you, and I had to get out of the office to do it. I wanted to make sure that no one in the office heard me telling you this. Dick has been working on bringing Meagan DuPree to our department from advertising. She has no programming experience, but he wants her in our department. The rumor is that he has been stalling your move until he can make her move happen. Then, he can put her in Paul's old office on some bullshit premise and promote you keeping you where you are. That way he's still spitting in your face with your promotion. We also heard that he'll be promoting you in title only. You'll keep your same responsibilities. Meagan will have all of the technical programming responsibilities with the exception of actually programming. The office and the responsibilities. That's some shit, you know? You really have him over the barrel as far as your promotion, but he can certainly make you look bad with the office shit. I told you...that son of a bitch is something else."

Toney sat there silent for a few minutes trying to digest it all. She looked up from her food while she was still chewing. "It stands to reason with him. Right now I really don't care because all I want is the money. I really need the money. But, can you believe these people? No matter how good you are and how hard you work, you're still not good enough to be promoted on merit with no strings attached. When will they ever learn?" Toney said calmly.

"Thanks for letting me know about this," Toney said weakly.

"You seem to be handling all of this pretty well," Tiffany said marveling at Toney's endurance.

"What choice do I have? He's the boss. I can't make him do anything. But, if I believe the words of the Bible, he'll have to pay for what he's doing, and I plan to leave that up to God."

"Where's Jamie today?" Toney asked to change the subject.

"She called in sick today. That heffa ain't no more sick than you or I. She's just trying to stretch out the weekend."

It was almost an hour later as they walked back to the office. Tiffany and Toney teased each other laughing back and forth as they moved along. When they arrived back in the office Meagan was in Dick's office with the door closed. A feeling of letdown came over Toney as she thought about Joyce at IBM and now Dick. Were they all alike? Was there some scheme afoot with all of the people who had the power to mess with people's lives? All of this even though the lives of the people that they had control over gave them the best of the best? She just simply did not understand **...**

Just as Toney got deep into her daydream she was brought back by the announcement that they were on their approach to Tokyo.

"Ladies and gentlemen, we have been cleared to land in Tokyo. The weather is overcast with a high of seventy-six degrees currently. Please enjoy your stay in Tokyo and thank you for selecting All Nippon. We look forward to being of service to you again in the future. With the conclusion of the announcement, Toney along with the others began to collect their personal belongings to prepare themselves to disembark the craft. Twenty minutes later Toney was walking down the jet way to the gate area in Tokyo. A driver who had been sent to pick her up was standing at the entrance with a sign displaying the name "TONEY CHAMBERS.

"Good morning, I'm Toney Chambers."

"Good morning, Ms. Chambers son. I am Hedio Jung your driver. Welcome to Tokyo," he said with the traditional Japanese bow.

"Well thank you, Hedio, it is wonderful to be here. Will you be taking me to the Hyatt Tokyo?"

"Yes ma'am, Miss Chambers son. Mr. Bukura son will be there to meet with you once we are there," he continued smiling and bowing.

"Alright," Toney said as they moved forward to the baggage claim area. Little conversation ensued until they were out on the curb at the limousine.

"Ms. Chambers, please let me get you seated and I'll put your bags in the trunk," he said smiling and bowing.

"Alright Hedio, that will be fine."

Once Toney was shuttled to the hotel, the driver opened the door for her. She walked into the hotel to a welcoming committee of Prophecy Tokyo employees. The other hotel guests watched in bewilderment wondering who this individual was. Perhaps an American movie star?

"Good morning, everyone. How kind it is for you to greet me upon my arrival. Thank you for all of the very special actions that you have taken. Mr. Bukura, it is great to see you again," she said as she extended her hand for him to shake.

"Ms.. Chambers son, welcome to Tokyo. Your accommodations are ready. Please follow Ms. Moon son. She will be your personal assistant while you are with us. Please call on her for anything you may need," he said as he accepted her hand to shake and motioning for her to move forward into the lobby toward the front desk area. Toney felt really special. Like maybe she had really arrived. And, to think she was worlds away from all of the troubles of late. She was grateful for the pause in the norm. Toney and Ms. Moon son proceeded to the elevators while Bukura and Toney chatted about the plans for the remainder of the day. The plan included dinner with all of the employees of Prophecy. It was scheduled for seven. It was eleven so she had time to take a nap.

"Ms. Moon son, I am fine. I will call you in a few hours and we will make plans then. Right now, I want to take a nap, okay?"

"Yes ma'am, Ms. Chambers son," she said making the tradition bow.

"I will wait for your call."

Toney went into her room allowing the bell man to bring in her bags. She gave him a tip and dismissed him courteously.

"Thanks you so much for your help, sir."

She took the next few minutes to unpack. She carefully organized her things. She took a long hot shower and put on her pajamas sliding into bed, immediately falling off to sleep…it had been a long trip.

PART II

Tokyo was a beautiful city, but at night it was spectacular. When Toney woke it was dusk. She had an hour to prepare herself for the evening. Her driver would be at the front door at seven sharp to pick her up. The Tokyo staff would be awaiting her arrival. This would be a very important dinner meeting. These were the two accounts that Toney was in Tokyo to close for the company, which were based in Tokyo. So, the enthusiasm of the Tokyo office employees would be key in the maintenance process, to create a continual partnership once the accounts had been brought on board. It was imperative that these customers experience follow up on a timely and efficient basis. She was there to make sure the group recognized the importance of these major accounts.

Toney dressed carefully making sure she represented a figure of authority, but also one with an approachable demeanor. She had to complete a balancing act that was her signature with well over ninety-five percent of the people that she encountered. Her makeup was applied to accommodate the occasion. She dressed in a sleek, well-made suit with clean lines. Her accessories were very professional and understated, which was intentional in order to assure that other female members of the dinner party felt under whelmed and so that the men could appreciate her position and intellect.

The car arrived promptly at seven. She was standing there waiting. She was ushered to the car by Ms. Moon and they were on their way. Fifteen minutes and a short tour later, they arrived at the restaurant. It was the most popular Japanese restaurant in Tokyo. Toney entered the restaurant where a section of the eatery had been reserved for Prophecy. The staff stood offering a round of raving applause for Toney. She was surprised and very thankful for their support. She could only hope that the remaining portion of the evening went as well.

"Thank you, thank you very much," she said bowing as the customary sign of the country.

"Thank you very much. Please be seated," Toney said as her chair was being pulled out for her to take a seat.

Once Toney was seated the staff took their seats as well.

"I want to thank you all for taking your personal time to dine with me tonight. We certainly could have met in the office on Monday morning, but I thought that this would be a nicer way to become acquainted. Once we've all ordered, I would like for us to all introduce ourselves. Then, we will sort of let the evening take us to where ever it will. Is that alright with you?"

A collection of yes's verbally and the shake of some of the individual's heads were given and were unanimous.

Small groups of conversations developed as the waiter approached the table and began to take drink orders. Once that was done Toney asked for each persons attention again to give the group an overview of the state of The Company from the corporate perspective.

Ten minutes later the drinks arrived. They each introduced themselves to Toney. Bukura offered a toast to the success of the corporate visit. From his lead each person joined. A few minutes later the waiter was there again to take dinner orders.

At the end of the evening, which had gone nicely, Toney thanked them for coming and wished them a great weekend. She shook each person's hands as they left. Then, she and Bukura stayed behind moving to the bar area for an after dinner drink and conversation regarding the plan for the coming week. About eleven o'clock Toney was on the elevator heading for her suite and to bed for the night. The jet lag was taking over fast.

On Saturday morning Toney was rested and raring to go. She had plans to see the sites with her new found maturity. Things would be totally different than they were so many years ago. She wanted to see the countryside first and had made plans for Hedio to pick her up at nine a m for the first part of her day. He was there on time. She had gotten dressed in a business casual flare toting her camcorder to record the memories that she wanted to take back and was waiting for him when he arrived. She was excited about today. Hedio pointed out some of the landmarks of his beautiful, historic city as they rode out of the city headed for the countryside. These would be sites that she would catch later in the week as her fine-tuned plans unfolded. Heido's first stop was the Japanese rain forest. Toney was amazed. They got out of the car and walked through the first one hundred yards or so to get a real feel for the area. It was beautiful. She had never seen trees so green and with so many various shapes and sizes. Her camcorder was in full use as they moved along. She would have to come back here someday with Grant and their children.

The next item on the agenda was for Hedio to take Toney through some of the villages and hometowns in the countryside. She wanted to see the differences in the neighborhoods, which were so vastly different in the states. As they traveled Toney and Hedio spoke about different things, making their time together nice and very educational. At three o'clock

Toney said, "You know, I'm a little hungry. What would you recommend I have for a snack?"

"How about an oriental patty? It is a combination of Japanese and Chinese oriental favorites prepared in a patty."

"That sound great. Let's do that."

After they ate, they headed back into the city for the day.

"Thank you so much once again. You are the best. I will see you tomorrow. Don't forget I would like to visit a church in the morning," she said as she got out of the car.

"Yes ma'am. I will be here."

When Toney got to her suite, she returned her calls the last one being to Grant. She wanted to be able to hear his voice and talk for an extended amount of time.

She ordered room service and turned in for the day.

On Sunday morning she once again got dressed and headed for the motor lobby of the hotel to meet Hedio. He arrived at nine and took her to the closest thing the Japanese had to offer as a Baptist church. She worshiped and in an hour she was out and on her way to see the sites of the metropolitan area. And again that night she took dinner in the hotel restaurant alone to gain a little solitude before her big week.

On Monday morning she was rehearsed and ready. She was well dressed. She had prepared for this day and prepared well. Her curtain call was only hours away and she was ready. Hedio was there to pick her up and take her to the meeting place, which had been designated as the Prophecy Tokyo Boardroom. She wanted to get there early enough to see the members of the staff in order to say hello and to further the relationship that she had started on Friday night. They were genuinely happy to see her.

At eight o'clock Mr. Yamaguchi and two of his henchmen arrived. They were immediately shown to the Prophecy Boardroom where Toney and Bukura were standing waiting to receive these valuable visitors. An elaborate breakfast had been set up for the meeting. Bukura offered to prepare coffee for the group. One of Mr. Yamaguchi's personal assistants stepped up to the table to prepare a cup of coffee for him and took it to him. Mr. Yamaguchi was the type that wanted to get down to business without a lot of fanfare. Toney had her presentation on Prophecy and the plan all laid out for him. Two hours later Mr. Yamaguchi had seen enough.

"Ms. Chambers son," he said starting to stand in an abrupt manner. I have seen enough. Prophecy is a product that my company can use. Now, the bottom line on the deal is what you can provide me in terms of a package. I will not pay more than market and if my number of units grows, I expect the price will shrink. We can further discuss it on the golf course on Wednesday. We are setup with a tee time of ten am. We will see you then," as he turned and walked away with his henchmen in tow.

Toney's head was swimming. She was in. This was the largest of the two deals. One deal was done.

The nature of the second customer was to discuss business over dinner. It had been setup for Tuesday evening at Harrigan's an Americanized restaurant offering steaks.

PART III

Grant was lonely without Toney. It was already Wednesday and because of the time difference, he hadn't spoken to her as much as he would like to have. He worked constantly to try and make the days full. His plate was full too. He had to keep up with both Terry and Nick. The shorter twins had been extremely busy. Much of the past few weeks they had been seen with their heads together much more than usual. There was something definitely up. Early that morning, Grant walked in around six thirty. The boys were already in and behind closed doors in Nick's office. When Nick saw Grant pass his office through the window leading to the corridor, he abruptly raised from his desk to get Grant's attention.

"Good morning Grant," Nick said clearing his throat and opening his door.

"Good morning Nick," Grant responded immediately stopping and turning in his footsteps. He gradually walked back toward Nick who was leaning, partially out of his office doorway.

"How's it going, Terry?" Grant acknowledged making sure that Nick and Terry both recognized that he had seen the two of them engaged in deep conversation.

"Hey man...How's it going?" Terry shouted in a deep voice.

"No way to really tell, you know. It's still real early. But, it'll be alright," Grant said while continuing..."but, I'm not one to give up quickly, so it is all good. What can I do for you guys?"

"Just a thought," Nick said. "I want to let you know that the Merriday case has been given to me. "Gill thought that you were moving a bit slowly on it. My case load is down and I asked him to let me take a stab at building the case, okay?"

"I'll have a conversation with Gill. I'm not real sure that I'm okay with that," Grant said calmly. "But, this is not a conversation that I should be having with you. Carry on," Grant said as he turned to walk away seething.

The nerve of those underhanded motherfucker's. Montrose and I will have it out about this as soon as he arrives," Grant mumbled to himself as he reached his office and walked in flipping on the light.

Grant sat there numb for over ten minutes. He was so still. His mind was running. Thoughts of a physical confrontation crossed his mind, but that would surely bring him down to the shorter twin's level.

"They have tried and tried to get me off base and they have lost. I refuse to lose. I flatly refuse," he forcefully chanted.

Grant pulled the Merriday file. He set it on the corner of his desk where he could see it as if he needed a reminder that he was to see Montrose at eight. He tried to settle down. It was very difficult.

"Those sons-of-a-bitch come in early to strategize about how they want to get over, but they haven't realized that I am a formidable opponent," Grant said out loud in hopes that they would catch an ear full.

He thought to himself that he was falling into an irate state of mind, which was their plan. Just the sheer thought of that helped him to calm down. He started going through the items in his in-box. He wanted to blanket his mind with work to make sure that the time passed quickly. Again, before he knew it, he heard Mill outside his door.

"Mill? Is that you?"

"It's me Grant…You expecting Halle Barry perhaps?" she said in her comical manner.

"Mill, come in here. I need to see you," he said cutting through her satire.

Millicent stopped in her tracks. She hadn't heard Grant sound so urgent in months.

She walked swiftly to Grant's office, "Honey what's the problem? Grant are you alright?"

"Close the door, Mill. I have to talk with you," he said getting up from his seat and walking over to the door to close it himself. He looked shaken.

"What happened Grant?" Millicent said turning serious.

"Those sons-of-a-bitch are fucking with me. I won't stand for it," Grant said walking back to his desk after closing the door.

"Who? What happened? What's this all about?" Millicent asked with great concern.

"The twins, they are at it again. They have been talking to Montrose about my two big cases. They say that he has given my cases to Nick. I can't believe that. I have put many hours in on those cases and he expects that I am just going to walk away without a fight? That's silly."

"Grant, the first thing that you have to do is calm down. You are smarter than they are. You can outthink them and even outwit them. So, my suggestion is to calm down and think things through...just like you are always telling me to do," Millicent said in a soothing voice.

"Thanks, Mill. You're right. When you get angry, you forego the ability to reason and you can lose your objectivity. I'll step back and think this through. This shit has been going on too long, and I plan to resolve this now. No more. I can't keep working like this, so if I have to leave here, I will," he shared.

"Well, you and I are a package deal, if you go I go too," Mill patronized as she stood to go back to her position.

"Thanks for the ear, Mill. I'm on tract now. Really on track. All I needed was some reasoning and you've given that to me. Thanks," Grant said as he stood while Millicent left the room.

At eight o'clock Grant took the Merriday file and headed for Montrose's office. He had just gotten in and was on the phone. Grant motioned that he needed to speak with him. Montrose motioned for Grant to step into the office and take a seat. A few minutes later Montrose hung up.

"Good morning, Grant. What can I do for you?" Montrose asked.

"I ran into Nick and Terry this morning. Nick mentioned that you wanted me to turn over the Merriday case and maybe the Fontroy case to him. I became incensed. Then I thought about it. That's not the way you work. My thought was to come in and talk it over with you. Now, Gill, you more than anyone know how much sweat I've put into this firm. I am working toward becoming a partner. And, I should be the next one in line. Now you've brought in the new attorneys and that's fine, because we need some young hungry people. But, they're not ready to run things. They don't know enough yet. They're still wet behind the ears. I hear that they are being considered for a partnership. They haven't even paid their dues yet. Aggressive and hungry, yes, but just not ready for a partnership, if you know what I mean?"

"Whoa, Grant. You're getting a little ahead of me. I told Nick that he could see if he could work on the Merriday case with you. I thought he could learn something from you. Now as for a partnership, those two work very hard. They're smart and intuitive. I am interested in them for the future. If they have the moral values that I need and the where-with-all to make a partnership work for them, then good for them. That hasn't been determined at this point. Now you…you've proven yourself over and over again. Good things are in store for you. But, don't let the youth that those two display deter you from what you're doing. One thing has nothing to do with the other," Montrose said.

"Thanks for your time, Gill. I'll see you later," Grant said standing and making his way to the corridor and back to his office.

When Grant returned to his office Millicent was interested in finding out the results of the meeting with Montrose. He explained everything to Mill while they met behind closed doors. Grant's phone rang while Millicent was still sitting with him. It was Brandon.

"Hey buddy. How's it going?" Grant said in his normal manner indicating that he was totally back in control.

"Hey man. I'm following up to let you know when I'm coming to Chicago. I didn't say it before but I'm coming to Chicago for an interview with Landson, Main and Berber. They have a position open for a lead attorney in criminal law that I'm looking at. Even if I don't take it, or if they don't take me, it'll give me a chance to see you and Toney.

My flight gets in Saturday after next. I'll be in for six days. Can you pick me up at one?"

"Sure, Brandon. I'll be there. Toney told me before she left that that's the weekend of her Assistant's family reunion. So you have to go with us to that once we pick you up, okay?"

"Sounds like fun. No problem if they won't think I'm crashing the event," Brandon said with a smile.

PART IV

Toney's dinner was eventful. The conversation was full bodied and the meal was succulent. She was in the throws of selling Prophecy to her customers from Aoiki Electronics. They had fifteen hundred offices globally, which had to be outfitted with computer systems. Burkura had set things up well. After two hours over dinner at Harrigan's Tokyo, after much conversation the hedging customer signed the contract. A meeting of the minds had matched. They had champagne to celebrate the moment, a perfect way to end the evening. Toney returned to her hotel room around nine thirty. She was drained. The week had been eventful, and the excitement of the multimillion-dollar deals that she had closed took her breath away. She would talk with Charles in the morning to catch him up on everything.

She packed her bags with the same care that she had demonstrated when she left Chicago and headed to the orient. She had exceeded her wildest expectations on this trip and couldn't wait to get back so that she could spend some time with her guy.

In the middle of the night she called Chicago to give Corbin the latest. She had instructed Bukura to send Corbin an e-mail outlining the terms of both agreements, but she wanted to hear the excitement in his voice. "Charles, I know you're about to start your day, but here's the scoop." They spoke for five minutes then Toney made her way to finish her chores so that she could be ready to leave for the airport the next morning.

TWENTY THREE

On the plane ride back to Chicago, Toney toppled. She had a full week and was ready to see some familiar faces. She slept for several hours as they continued their trek from the orient. When she woke, the patrons on board the flight were just about finished with the movie that had been offered. She collected herself and shuffled off to the lavatory.

When she returned, she got settled in again and thought about the week. She had accomplished quite a bit and was elated that things had gone so well. It was difficult though because she had to deal with men of a completely different culture, who weren't accustomed to dealing with women in business. Making sure she was culturally correct at all times took a lot out of her, so she was in no mood to work. She just relaxed and decided to take it easy while she could, and before she knew it she was off to her daydreaming state again ...

Toney's first encounter with romance back in those days came on the heels of her first major promotion at Prophecy. She met one of her neighbors on her way to the office. It was at the bus stop the morning of her third day of her new Senior Programmer promotion. At the time, they were the only two people there waiting and began to talk. Things went very smooth. They seemed like naturals together. Once they reached the Metro station, they bid one another farewell with the promise to talk again soon. The very next morning each of them made it their business to be at the bus stop at the same time, with high hope that the other felt the same way.

"I go to work at about the same time every day, what about you?" Daryl mentioned during their talk.

"I just recently started catching the bus at this time. I had different hours before last month. I just got a promotion at work, so my responsibilities changed and so did my hours. So, I'll be here every morning about this time at least for the time being," Toney said proudly.

"That sounds good. I'd like to talk some more," Daryl said.

"I think I'd like that as well," Toney said modestly.

A couple of months into the new relationship, Toney and Daryl started dating. He was fairly good-looking, sort of rugged though. He hadn't had any education beyond high school, but Toney wasn't a snob…all she thought was that he seemed to be nice. Toney and Daryl spent time together each morning on their way to work, and some evenings on the weekends. Daryl was a blue-collar worker at a fiber glass plant located in Maryland. He had been there for eight years. He was in his early thirties, a little older than Toney, but she thought he was nice and wanted to simply enjoy his company. Besides, he was the only man that had paid any attention to her as a woman. About six months into the relationship, when Toney had developed a fondness for Daryl, he started missing her in the mornings and became hard to reach over the weekends. She decided to do some investigating and found out that he was a womanizer and a user. She noticed that whenever they were together, he always asked to borrow money from her. So, needless to say, she made herself scarce to him quickly. She had enough to deal with that was negative. Besides, her job was becoming more and more perplexing. Dick was constantly going off the deep end mainly on Toney. One day he asked to meet with her about a project that he gave her to complete.

"Toney, let's talk about the list of programs that the Addelay Company has submitted to the marketplace. I wanted you to find out how close theirs are to the programs that we have out. Did you get that done?" Dick asked in a tone that was difficult to describe.

"Yes I did, Dick. I found all of the information out that you needed. I gave it to Mandy yesterday. Didn't she give it to you?" Toney reported.

"I saw that shit. That's not what I asked you for at all. I said to you that I needed to know what they had that was different from ours and how it was different," he said with his voice picking up volume.

"No you didn't, Dick. You asked me to find out what products they had out there that were different. And, that's what I did," Toney offered rather meekly, unable to belied that he was going off on her the way he was.

"You're incompetent. You're supposed to be my second and you're not doing the job. I need someone who's going to help me. It's a good thing that Meagan is here…I need you to concentrate on helping me out and not maintaining your position as the star Programmer," he said in a sarcastic loud uproar.

Everyone in the office stopped what they were doing and looked in their direction.

Toney was embarrassed to the hilt. What was wrong with this guy? He seemed to have a multiple personality disorder. What would he do next?

"Dick, I have never been a Senior Programmer before. Besides, you keep asking me to Program and as a matter of fact you gave me a quota for new programs…one that is the same as the others in that area, so I have to keep creating. What on earth would you like for me to do other than to follow your direction? You're the Director, aren't you? I do what I'm asked to do and you asked me to find out what products the competition has on the market and how close theirs are to what we have out there. Well, I did that," Toney said while tears swelled in her eyes. "You can't follow directions, that's why I need Meagan here. That's why she's in the office next to mine. I need someone to help me," he said screaming as he stood up and walked out of his office away from Toney.

Toney was humiliated. She stood up and walked to her desk feeling that all eyes were on her. She could have sunk through the floor. All she wanted was to get away from Dick. He was a loose cannon, but the people at the top seemed to let him do whatever he wanted. When she got to her cubicle, she took her seat immediately closing her eyes to say a quick prayer. She had to remove herself from this moment in order to make it through. A few minutes passed. One by one the other employees went about their business. She, little by little, eased herself back into her work trying to put this episode of Dick Negri behind her. Later in the afternoon, she and Dick passed by one another several times seemingly having no use for one another. She had assisted in formulating a wedge between them but she had to stand up for herself. She had to speak up about this promotion. Her thoughts were that Dick had to promote her or face an EEOC case and the fact that he was forced to do that had him on the offensive. He could make things intolerable for her to force her out. Dick just didn't realize that he was helping Toney to develop character that she didn't even know she had herself. She was becoming more and more determined to stay at any cost. She was becoming more determined that he was not going to win. Just like in school when no one liked her because she was a brainiac, she made it work for herself, and now that she was a full grown woman she was going to make sure that the likes of Dick Negri wouldn't win. She had to make sure of that and that Negri would never run her off. Besides she loved her job and most of the people that she worked with.

"Girl, can you believe that stupid motherfucker? He acts like a damned fool. And, in front of all of the staff. You could take his ass to court and blow him away, if you wanted to," Tiffany spewed.

"Tiff, you're right, but I refuse to be brought down to his level, you know? Dick is a fool and sooner or later he'll lose," Toney said with her head down still suffering from complete embarrassment.

"Yeah, I know, but how much of this can you take? I know you're still hurting from the breakup with Daryl and not to mention this shit here, which is ongoing. If there is anything that I can do for you let me know. I think that the reason that Dick talks to you like he does is that he's trying to shake you loose from this place. Don't let him do it. Don't let him do it, girl. If you do, he'll win and that's what he wants," Tiffany said.

"I know. He won't win. He may knock me down, but he can't keep me down. I'm damned good at what I do and I like my job. He won't win, I assure you," Toney said appearing to gain some of her self-assuredness back.

Dick passed by again snapping, "Tiffany don't you have anything you could be doing? If you don't then I shouldn't be paying you for coffee clutching."

"How do you know that I'm not working Dick? Is it just because I'm talking to Toney? You really don't know, do you?" Tiffany smarted off standing with her hand on her hip and giving Dick attitude with her sister attitude working.

"Girl, I'll talk to you later. I need this damned job, so I guess I'll get back to it. But, that motherfucker is going to get his," she said as she turned to walk back to her cubicle looking in Dick's direction.

"Okay, Tiffany. Don't get yourself into trouble with him on my accord. I can handle my situation," Toney cautioned.

"Girl, growing up where I did, I know how to handle myself. Don't worry about me cause I'm definitely no pantywaist. Think about yourself and how you plan to defuse this son-of-a bitch 'cause he's out to get your ass."

Toney sat there for a few more minutes and felt that she needed to get out and get some air. She needed to think things through. As she walked down Pennsylvania Avenue, she thought about D.C. and what a powerful place it was. She thought about Lexington and her mom and dad and Vanessa too. She knew she had to make this work. She had been given this blessing, and she had to do all that she could to make this work. She had gotten out of the rural area and she wasn't going back a failure.

Almost a year went by. More of the same ensued. Toney was becoming stronger and stronger at combating Dick's animosity. Toney's work became more and more top level as a senior. She was able to keep up her programming posture and maintain the senior responsibilities as well. The mere fact that she caught on so quickly to everything around her was a definite plus for her growth. And, even Dick was unable to stop that. The Vice President at Corporate responsible for all of the regional and remote offices reviewed each location's performance weekly via conference calls and quarterly visits. He noticed that there were excellent results coming in from the D.C. location. He wanted to get to know more about the people who were making these things happen.

It was late spring and time for the office to prepare for the annual visit from all of the top brass. The staff went about their normal routines setting aside time to prepare the office and the material that would be inspected. When that day came they were ready. Dick stood out front to welcome the brass.

"Good morning," he said in a fake deep voice, "Welcome to the D.C. office," as he stood there shaking everyone's hands as they entered.

"Good morning everyone," the Vice President shared. We're delighted to visit with the location of the year. Dick, you and your employees have turned out more valuable product and kept your revenue in tact better than any other location. We have planned for a celebration this evening for you and your staff."

This came as a shock to everyone.

"Give yourselves a hand...you have done an outstanding job and the company gives you thanks."

The applause took over. Was it Dick who had done such a good job even though he was an asshole?

The Vice President continued..."we have brought with us a couple of awards that we would like to give out and so forth. Let us begin the tour and we will see each of you around four o'clock to complete the presentations."

Dick introduced the staff to the visitors. Afterwards, they left to begin the tour. The staff went back to work as normal.

At four o'clock, they all got back together in the conference room. Four individuals were recognized. One by one their names were called and an overview of their contributions acknowledged, plaques presented. The last of the individuals to be recognized had a speech delivered before the name was called. The Vice President listed eight areas that were impacted by this individual.

"The corporate offices wish to thank this individual for her dedication" even though it's my understanding that it has not been easy here for her," he said looking over at Dick, "her vision, hard work, imagination and foresight in the items that she has fostered for Prophecy. Because of this individual we have made over three million additional dollars and produced nineteen innovative programs for Prophecy's growth into the future, which are best sellers out in the marketplace. She has been hailed as a people person with the mindset that this company is looking for in its future leaders. Prophecy Computers thanks Toney Chambers."

The applause was astounding. Each of the staff members rose to their feet. Toney was in shock. To be recognized this way was a monumental feat, which she never dreamed of.

Toney started to the front of the room to accept the plaque. This would be a day that she would remember forever. She'd have to call her mom and dad to let them know about it ...

The flight attendant asked, "Ma'am, would you care for some refreshments?"

"Yes, thank you," Toney said as she reached over to accept the turkey sandwich and salad. She was smiling remembering that accepting that plaque back then was the first time she knew in her heart that she was on her way up.

PART II

Vanessa had made it through three sessions with the doctor that Toney had provided for her. They were testing her for this and that and the other. There were no plausible reasons for what she said she was experiencing that made any sense. What was it? The Doctor ran test after test and seemingly could find nothing that made any medical sense to him. He read books on the symptoms that Vanessa described. Nothing. Doctor Mills decided to consult with other doctors who specialized in difficult disorders. Weeks passed and still nothing. Meantime, Vanessa was becoming more and more difficult to live with...she had developed an intolerable fetish for cleanliness. She fussed for almost no real reason, she talked almost nonstop and she had to have sex no matter what. Her behavior was out of control. They ran more and more tests, still nothing. Two months after the testing started, Doctor Mills and the others hit on some remarkable information. Some new data on the horizon, which had been discovered by a doctor in Switzerland, fit two thirds of the symptoms described by Vanessa. Doctor Mills wanted to learn more about this disease, so he took a trip to the Swiss Alps to consult with Doctor Moderine, the specialist of the new data.

Vanessa gained weight and became pregnant with her second child. She had delivered a bouncing baby boy only two months before.

"Mom, I'm sorry that I'm so much trouble. I wish it were different," Vanessa said to Mrs. Donovan with huge crocodile tears in her eyes.

"I'm causing you and dad and Toney so much trouble and you are the people who matter so much to me in my life. I don't want that baby," she said pointing to the crib five feet away.

"I don't want the one that I have in my belly either. What will I do mom? What will I do?"

"Honey, you don't mean that. You have a beautiful baby. You'll learn to be a good mother. These things happen," her mother said sweetly. "Besides Toney'll be here for the holidays…won't you be glad to see her and to introduced her to the baby?"

Vanessa's face brightened at the mention of Toney's name.

"Is it for sure that she's coming home for Christmas?" she asked with anticipation.

"That's what her mom told me. It'll be good to have her home again for a little while, right?"

PART III

Grant could only think of one time when he was happier than he was at this moment. That was when he and Toney were in Jamaica and she agreed to become his wife. Other than that he was never so happy in his life. He was smiling from ear to ear. He would see her in just a few minutes. He stood at the exit of the jet way waiting for Toney to deplane. They hadn't seen one another in a full week and they had had very little conversation over this period due to the vast time difference. He had to make sure that this only happened on rare occasions. He was in love with her, and couldn't stand to be away from her for this long.

Finally Toney stepped over the threshold. Their eyes locked and instantly they were in each other's arms sharing a long wet seductive kiss. It was apparent to everyone who noticed that the two of them were in love.

"Baby, it's so good to see you. I've missed you terribly. You are under my skin and I love it. How was your trip?" Grant rambled with adoring eyes.

"I'm glad to be home and to be with you, honey. It was a very long and taxing trip, but I managed to get what I went after. God blessed me with success. But, enough about that. How are you, honey? You look a little tired. Are you alright?" Toney asked as they walked down the concourse to the baggage claim area.

"I haven't been sleeping well. It's been a real humdinger working through the situation at the office with the shorter twins. They have been making a real mess of things. Montrose is involved. But, honey let's get you home and unpacked and in my arms before we discuss all that, okay?" Grant said holding her arms leading her to the train.

"That's fine, baby," Toney purred and looking at him as if she could eat him alive.

"I can't wait to get home, get a bath and into bed with you."

They picked up her bags and Grant loaded them into the car. In less than fifteen minutes they were on their way to her place.

"How's your mom?" Toney asked Grant.

"She's fine. I told her that we'd be there for Christmas. Are we still on for a trip to New York together around Christmas?" he asked to gain her commitment.

"Grant, you know I'm supposed to be going to Lexington at Christmas. My dad's been ill and mom needs my help. Plus, Vanessa's been under the weather too, so I can't get out of that."

"But, we had made plans to go to New York. What can I tell mom and the girls?" he said sounding disappointed.

"Let's check to see how much time off we can both manage. If we can take a minimum of ten days then we can do both. Five days in each place...how's that?"

"That's great if we can get that much time off at the same time. We'll talk about it more once we see what's what," he said trying not to show too much disappointment.

They rode along in silence for a while. Grant was thinking that this was the first possible impasse of their relationship, but he couldn't be too hard on her with all that they both had been through. He only hoped that Toney would stop trying to take on the world with all of the other things she had on her plate. One person shouldn't try to handle all that stuff, he thought.

"I spoke with Brandon. He'll be in next Saturday. Maybe we can take him out on the town after we pick him up."

"Next Saturday? That's the weekend of Sonjia's family reunion. Did you forget that we promised her that we'd be there?"

"No ma'am. As a matter of fact, I told Brandon that and that I thought he'd be perfectly welcomed there too. Did I speak out of turn?"

"Oh no honey. Sonjia will be delighted for us to bring a friend. I'll let her know on Monday. I really don't think that it will be a problem at all."

They pulled into the parking garage of Toney's building. Grant rushed to open her door, immediately moving to the trunk to begin unloading her luggage. Toney walked to the elevator and held it open for Grant who was loaded down with three of her heaviest pieces.

"Only two more pieces and we're all set, baby. Then, I can get a real kiss," he said smiling at her.

She stuck the key into the lock to open the door. Grant stepped inside walking straight back to the bedroom, finally unloading the three pieces of luggage. He wanted her to be close to where she would be able to unpack conveniently. He was always thoughtful that way. On his second trip to the garage, he rushed in order to get back to her. His thoughts were only of making love to his lady. Grant grabbed the remaining two pieces of luggage and was walking back to the elevator when he noticed a dark car headed directly toward him. No horn, no nothing. Grant had to think fast. He ran in between two parked cars as the mysterious car sped past him going no less than seventy-five miles an hour.

"What the hell?" Grant said breathing deeply. "What was that all about?"

He stood there nervously thinking of the incident. Seconds later he collected himself and headed toward the elevator cautiously looking around as if to expect another car to run him down. He put the bags down and paced in the elevator until it arrived at Toney's floor. His thoughts were consumed with what had just happened.

"Should I tell Toney about this or would this be just one more thing on her plate?" he thought.

He debated it for as long as the elevator ride took and decided to handle it on his own, but how could someone get into the building with the security system that was there.

It just didn't make any sense to him

When they got back up to her place, Toney drew her bath in the Jacuzzi. She decorated the bathroom in a very romantic way. She had a minimum of twenty candles lit around the bath area and the bed. She started the CD player, setting the mood with soft listening music. She was setting him up. It was obvious to him that she missed him as much as he missed her. Toney was hanging up the clothes that she could, and had put aside the things that had to go to the laundry. She finished up that chore and baited Grant into the bathroom, taking off her robe revealing her nudity, which was all the coaxing, he needed. They whispered to each other taking advantage of the chilled glasses of Kendall Jackson that they both loved. Once they fooled around in the tub, they dried one another off and moved the hot and tempestuous mood to the bed. The love that they made was unsurpassed as they engaged in a marathon love making session. It was beautiful, as they gave themselves to each other completely.

TWENTY FOUR

It was already Monday. Time to get back in the saddle again. Toney had been out of the office for over ten day's altogether. She had to take the entire weekend for both herself and Grant. The job had taken it all from her over this period. Even though she enjoyed her trip to the orient, and the fact that she could get away from all of the madness for a while was a plus she needed to face the music now.

"What has Babbitt found out?" she mumbled as she walked across the garage to her car.

Her thoughts shifted to the near mishap with the unidentified car two weeks before.

"That will undoubtedly be one of the first things that I do when I get into the office. I have got to call him," she said talking to herself.

Twenty minutes later she was in the lobby waving at Marvin again.

"Hi, Marvin. Has everything been quiet here while I was away?" Toney asked keeping her pace moving toward the elevator.

"Hi, Ms. Chambers. Welcome back. We haven't heard a peep from the crooks," Marvin shouted.

"Nothing at all," he continued.

"That's good," Toney said continuing to make her way to the elevator.

"See you later," she said as she rounded the corner into the elevator core.

Sonjia had been hard at work while Toney had been gone and it was obvious. Toney's office had several piles of work. Sonjia had numbered the piles in the order of importance, one through six. She got down to business at once, starting with the stack numbered one first. This stack had all of her important messages included in it.

"Good, Babbitt called twice. Maybe he's on to something."

She diligently tackled the work in front of her. At ten minutes past seven, she stopped to go into the outer office to make coffee. She could really use some caffeine to boost her energy levels. Once she made and poured her cup, she headed back to work through more of her tasks.

At seven forty five she heard a light knock on the door.

"Yes? Who's there?" Toney said feeling that she was safely locked in the office, so it had to be someone who belonged there.

"Yes? Who's there?" Toney said again sounding concerned and rising from her desk. She was starting to feel uncomfortable.

"Oh, its me. It's June. I didn't hear you before. Welcome back Toney. How was your trip?" she asked coming through the door.

"I saw your light on and I noticed that there was fresh coffee made, so I figured you were already in," June continued.

"Hello, June. It's good to be back home. The trip was successful. It's always good when your mission is accomplished. How are things around here? How's the staff doing? Is everyone coping with Freddy's death? I know it's a lot to contend with, but we can make it if we all stick together, you know?" she reminded June.

"Some of us are doing better than some of the others. The news helps to keep us on edge about it though. Every night when I get home there's some blurb about it on the news to keep it fresh in my mind. That's why I came in. While you were away did you talk to the cops?"

"Well…no. I was in Japan. I couldn't take care of any of that, way over there. Why do you ask?" Toney said becoming perplexed with June's question.

"Because they had your name, that's why. There is no other point of reference about all of this. Some of us think that whoever did that to Freddy could be looking at us next. Maybe there is a connection?" June said nervously.

"June!" Toney said sternly, but in a soft way while getting up from her desk and moving closer.

"There is no reason to think that you or anyone here is next. That's unrealistic. Who brought that up anyway?" Toney continued.

"I did. After I thought about it. Your office was broken into. They had your name. Are you somehow mixed up in all of this?" June blurted out as she started to cry.

"June why would you say such a thing? What makes you feel this way?" Toney said reaching out for June to comfort her.

"I don't know. I'm scared that's all," she said as she moved away from Toney. She made it obvious that she didn't want Toney to touch her. Toney took a seat on the sofa near where June was standing. She was in shock that June would say a thing like that to her, and that she back away from her. That she would make such an accusation was insane. Did others think that she was involved in this too? Did they think that she was anything other than a victim? Had she been acting suspicious? When the papers were missing, she had come back to the office and told no one but Sonjia what was going on. When the office was broken into, no one saw that she was upset, except for Sonjia. And, when Freddy was killed, she put on a strong front for the sake of the staff. Should she have been emotional like everyone else? Should she have shared her feeling with her staff?

Sonjia walked up.

"Hi, Toney, welcome back," she said with the brightest of smiles before she noticed the tension in the air.

"What's going on here? Why are you crying June? Toney are you alright?" Sonjia asked all in one breath.

"I've just been knocked off my feet. It seems as though June thinks that I had something to do with Freddy's death. I can't believe that a member of my staff could see me in that light," Toney said looking as if the wind had been knocked from her sails.

"June, I told you that this would get your ass fired. I can't believe that you confronted Toney with this nonsense. Please excuse us," Sonjia said as she stepped inside Toney's office indicating that June should leave.

"Sonjia, you knew that a member of this staff felt this way and you never told me?" Toney said airing disappointment.

"Yes I did, Toney. But, I warned June to keep her mouth shut. She had no basis for her accusations," Sonjia defended.

"Has she made these statements in front of other staff members?" Toney asked taking a long deep breath.

"Yes she has. Do you remember when you came out of your office and we were all standing together near the copy room? That's when she said other things. I told her then that she would be fired if she ever mentioned anything like that again. So, I guess this is it for her," Sonjia said asking for permission to start the paperwork to relieve June.

"No, let me think about this. I don't want to be hasty about this. She may just be afraid."

"That's not the case, Toney. There's more," Sonjia got two words out when the telephone rang.

"Just a moment, Toney, let me get that," Sonjia said racing for the phone.

"Toney Chambers office. This is Sonjia, may I help you?"

"Miss Chambers please," the caller announced.

"May I tell her who's calling sir?" Sonjia screened.

"Yes. It's Babbitt."

"Babbitt?"

Toney instantly jumped up from her seat, hearing Babbitt's name.

"Sonjia that'll be all for now. I'll see you in a bit. I need to take this call."

Toney said taking the receiver from Sonjia's hand and insisting that she close the door on the way out. Once the door was securely closed she began to speak.

"Hello. Fin?" Toney said making sure that he was the caller.

"Yes, Toney. I'm glad you're back. Can you come to see me? I have some updates for you, but I also have a lot of questions."

"Sure. When would you like to meet?" Toney asked anxiously.

"I know you just got back in town, but can we meet this afternoon? Actually, the sooner the better. I'm down to a process of elimination now and need to know which way to go from here. That will all depend on your answers."

"I can see you around two or three. Will you be in then?" Toney asked with anticipation.

"Let's make it five thirty. I should be back by then. The secretaries will be gone then so, just knock on the door and I'll let you in."

"Okay. I'll be there," Toney said hanging up the phone.

The moment Sonjia saw the light on Toney's phone go out she got up form her desk and headed back in to finish her talk with Toney.

"Toney, we have to finish this," Sonjia said walking back into Toney's office without so much as a knock.

"Okay," Toney told Sonjia as she took a seat behind her desk.

"Let's finish it," Toney concurred.

"Look. June has been a pain in the butt for several months starting with Freddy when he was going through his challenges. Then she started in on you. I put any and everyone in their places, if there is something said about you that's not right."

"So, there have been others saying things then?" Toney asked.

"No, not really, but when June started her stuff, the others began to question what was happening. You really have to fire her. She's a bad seed and we need to let her go. She's been warned and there is too much going on around here to let it go any longer," Sonjia said in an excitable manner.

"Calm down, Sonjia. We'll manage this situation, but we have to make sure things are handled in a manner that is becoming the situation. Leave it to me, okay?"

"Okay, Toney. If you say so, but this can't be let go for too long. June is trouble especially if you want to keep moral in the office high and everyone producing."

"Okay. I'll get back to you on that. Now get back to work," Toney said with a bright smile on her face.

Toney worked straight through for the next few hours. She kept a watch out on the clock, because she had an eleven o'clock meeting with Corbin. They were scheduled to get together to discuss the particulars of the two contracts that Toney had closed in Tokyo. These two deals catapulted Prophecy to the next level and levels above all of their competition in the marketplace.

"Buzz."

"Yes Sonjia?"

"You have a call on line one. I'm not sure who it is though. They wouldn't say," Sonjia maintained.

"Okay. I'll take it," Toney said without a second thought.

"Good morning. This is Toney Chambers, may I help you?" she answered as she normally would.

"Hello?"

"Hello?"

The person on the other end of the phone began breathing heavily and finally gruffly said, "Good morning my ass. You're in deep shit and have been a very lucky bitch at this point. I'm going to get you, just you wait," the coward said holding the line and breathing hard some more.

Totally startled, Toney began to shake visibly, "What do you want?"

"I want your ass. You think you are so much, but I want your ass and I won't rest until I get it."

"Don't you dare call here again!" she shrieked.

"I'll get the police involved if you continue," she said without thinking.

Toney slammed down the phone and immediately put her head in her hands.

"This has got to stop. Damn that Surrant. This is driving me crazy. Thank God I hired Babbitt. I can't wait until I meet with him tonight."

Toney got up from her desk and walked out to the outer office. She was once again looking out of control as if there was something very wrong with her. She walked past Sonjia without so much as a word. The next thing that she realized was that she had arrived on the second floor. Much like a zombie she walked through the food line grabbing the first thing that she saw. She paid for her food and walked back to the rear of the room and took a seat. It was only ten thirty eight, so there was virtually no one there so she could take her pick of tables. She sat there aimlessly eating what she had selected, thinking about all that had happened. Who could it be? Why had she been targeted? She knew that she treated most people with dignity and respect. Nothing in her past warranted this. Ten minutes later she found herself back on the elevator headed to her office to pickup the contracts that she had negotiated. She wanted nothing to interrupt the joy and feeling of complete success that she felt once the contracts were signed. Thank God nothing could take that away from her. And, the phone incident would be another item that she'd let Babbitt know about. Whoever this was would be found out and she hoped they would spend many years in a maximum-security system. It would be the least that they deserved.

"Maybe I should tell Grant, but maybe I shouldn't. Is there anything that he could really do about it anyway?" she said to herself as she picked up the folder, which contained the contracts and headed up to the fiftieth floor to meet with Corbin.

As the elevator climbed, Toney thought about June. Did she really believe that she was involved with Freddy's murder? How could she? June had been one of the employees who had been with her the longest. Perhaps June was a risk that she didn't necessary have to deal with. She'd have to see how it all played out. Toney walked into the Executives offices anxious to review her catch with her boss. This multi million dollar deal was monumental and she knew it...that's why the situation concerning June and even the phone call paled in comparison.

"Hi Terry. He is expecting me. Is he available?" Toney said to Corbin's secretary.

"Sure Toney. I'll let him know that you're here," Terry comforted.

"Mr. Corbin, Ms. Chambers is here."

Terry hung up the phone a second later quoting, "He'll see you now. Congratulations on your Tokyo trip. I heard it was extremely successful."

"Thanks Terry. It was a long trip, but thank God I came back with the prize," Toney said as she walked in to talk with Corbin.

"Well…you're the star of the company for sure now and have been for a long time Toney," Corbin said as Toney walked in and closed the door behind her.

"Congratulations! You have bagged the big one. Now, let's see what the terms are," Corbin continued, as he stood to allow her to take the seat in front of him while he held out his hand for her to shake offering his accolades.

"Thanks Charles. You have always had a way of supporting and motivating everyone, which certainly helps when one is in the trenches," Toney responded, while accepting Corbin's hand. They both took a seat.

"Do you want coffee or a soft drink before we get started?" Corbin asked.

"How odd," Toney thought?

"Back in the days when she first started, she would never have thought that the President of the company would be offering her a cup of coffee personally."

"No thanks Charles. I grabbed a fast bite about thirty minutes ago, so I'm fine, but please don't let that stop you from having something."

"No. No coffee for me. Not anymore. I barely touch the stuff," Corbin said as he shifted in his seat.

"What do you have here. I'm very excited about your success. You know, many people like to hang around for years on end long after it's there time to turn the reigns over to someone younger with more energy. I have been thinking about it for a while now. But, I had to make sure that if I did leave, the company was setup in a great financial position. These two deals may just put us in that position. Smart people leave while they are on top," Corbin rambled.

Toney sat there wondering where he was going with this.

"Well Charles, I guess I know where you're headed with this," she said to patronize him. "The two contracts that I picked up in Tokyo certainly puts Prophecy in a much brighter light. The Yamaguchi paperwork will net the company seven hundred million over two years and the Aoki Group is running a close second with millions over an eighteen month period. The terms of delivery for the first contract are forty percent in six months and the other sixty- percent over a period of one year. That gives our production-arm enough time for parts and labor to produce the products for Yamaguchi. They are expecting upgrades in software produced by Prophecy as well. Here are the areas in the Yamaguchi paperwork that were difficult to negotiate," Toney said flipping to the pages in question and pointing them out to Corbin.

They took a moment to read the points of interest slowly for complete understanding. Then Charles spoke up.

"These items aren't bad...not bad at all. When you consider the fact that there is Two hundred and thirty three million on the line. What about the Aoki Group's particulars?" Corbin said with a smile.

"Are you satisfied with this?" Toney said pointing to the Yamaguchi document.

"Absolutely," Charles said still smiling.

"Alright then," Toney shared.

"Here is the Aoki paperwork. Things are quite a bit different here. Even thought the contract does not have the same monetary value, the stipulations are quite a bit choppier. This group probably doesn't have the kind of investment moneys, as does Yamaguchi. But, it's still financially a great opportunity for Prophecy. This opens of our international markets without question," Toney said trying to assure her boss that she had made a wise deal for the company.

Silence fell upon the room again. Corbin became very quiet and focused. He read word for word each item. Finally, he looked up from the paperwork and put the document down in front of him. . He stood appearing to be in deep concentration and walked over to the tray of refreshments without so much as a word. Toney didn't know what to think. She followed his movement across the room and back.

"Toney. You couldn't have spent a more productive week anywhere in the world for your career or the company," he finally uttered.

"Thank you for personally taking this on. You could have just as well sent one of your underlings or had Bukura handle this. I'm not sure the outcome would have been the same with someone else handling this. But, being the perfectionists that you are, you had to do it yourself. And, what a masterful job you did," Charles said as he took his seat again.

"Thank you again for a job well done. You will be handsomely rewarded for it soon."

"Thanks Charles...I was only doing my job. These deals were much too large for me to leave it to anyone else other than myself. It was a pleasure in deed," she said as she stood to make her way to the door. Toney was lighthearted and very happy at the moment. All of her other cares and worries seemed a million miles away. She would have to think more about those other things later this afternoon, when she met with Babbitt.

Toney walked through her office and everything was in full swing. She passed June as she looked up at her and immediately back down at the keyboard of her computer. Toney acted as if everything was okay and entered her office closing the door behind her. It was ten till one. Toney focus turned to her paperwork for the next couple of hours. She fielded phone calls and office questions from the staff. It was a normal business day for all of them. Sonjia was busy trying to unload some of the work that Toney had completed, while juggling the office interruptions and the like. The new mail runner was becoming indoctrinated into his position. He had just dropped off the mail for the afternoon. Sonjia sorted each piece and efficiently took Toney her batch. More work that she could get off her desk. Toney began to read through each piece of her mail. There was a note from Cameron and an envelope with strange markings. The intrigue was too much for Toney, so the letter with the strange markings was the first of the last two pieces that she decided to open. It was one of those letters that you see in the movies where the stalker clips out letters from magazines as not to reveal the identity of the sender. The note said.

'YOU HAVE ESCAPED FOR NOW BUT LOOK OVER YOUR SHOULDER EVERYWHERE YOU GO BECAUSE I'LL BE THERE AND IT WON'T BE PRETTY'

Toney just sat there for a moment. Who was this idiot? Fear was his game and she couldn't afford to allow fear to take her over.

"If anything," she thought..."this is making me stronger and more determined to see my way through this mess."

"Oh my gosh…it's getting late," she said looking at her watch, it was already four forty-five so, she quickly headed out. She wanted to make sure that she was at Babbitt's office exactly at five thirty.

"Sonjia. I have an appointment out of the office at five thirty. I'll see you tomorrow. Oh, by the way, Grant and I will be at your family reunion in Cumberland Park on Saturday. We have a friend of ours coming in from Los Angeles. Is it alright if we bring him with us?" Toney said stopping briefly at Sonjia's desk.

"Of course Toney, the more the merrier. Besides if he's a friend of yours and Grants, he couldn't be all bad, right?" Sonjia said offering a comforting smile.

"I'll see you in the morning. By the way…your weekly conference call is all set for nine a.m."

"Thanks Sonjia," Toney said as she swiftly moved through the office and out of the door.

As Toney rode down Michigan Avenue, she thanked God for the opportunity to boost her career and the company that she had come to love. It certainly hadn't always been that way. She started thinking about Dick Negri again …

More and more disrespect oozed from Dick. But, Toney kept plugging away at her job. She was becoming more and more proficient. Her recognition from the Vice President of the company took Dick's attention off her case as he moved to strikeout at others closest to him. Finally, it wasn't only Toney that was his object. His new prey was Meagan. She had begun to show signs of incompetence of which proved to be an embarrassment for him. She didn't have the capacity to complete the terms of the tasks that were laid out before her. Dick found himself overloaded with both his and her work.

"Ugh, Toney can you take this on for me? Meagan can't get to it?" Dick said with his disposition that of a weakling with his tail between his legs surfaced.

"What is it Dick and when is it due? You know that I have a full plate. You still have me designing programs. That quota alone has me working more than ten hours a day. I would never mind helping, but we've got to reestablish the roles here and job descriptions, if you want me to get involved in the administrative side of things."

"Your title and pay warrants your getting involved," he snapped.

"Well now...let's see," Toney said as she paused.

"No problem, I will help anyone at anytime. But, may I ask you a question?" she said coolly.

"Sure. What is it?" Dick said seeming to ease up feeling that Toney was a pushover.

"What does Meagan's title and pay warrant? I've noticed that she is able to keep a clean desk, which indicates to me and everyone else that she doesn't have a whole lot going on. She can go to lunch for well over an hour each day...sometimes with you in tow. That she can leave every night at four or four thirty, while I am here most nights until six or six thirty, if not later. Something is terribly wrong here. And now, you want me to do her work and mine. I don't think so. She was your pick and I suggest that you deal with it. What I really think is that I should go to Human Resources and let you all have this job. I really don't want to walk out of here, because I love my job, but I have not been treated fairly and this has got to stop," Toney said in a low respectful tone.

"You do what you gotta do missy, but I need some help and you're the number two here," Dick said loudly completely out of control as he turned sour and walked away in a huff.

Toney stood there watching him when Jamie came from around the cubicle.

"You go girl! It's about time you told that mother fucker a thing or two. He's getting the glory from all your efforts and then he brings that bitch up here treating her like a queen. Well the war is on. Let's see what his next move is. The head honcho's love your last years shit, because you make them money. Dick's head will roll if you quit. Stand up for yourself girl. Get the recognition that you deserve. I can't wait to tell Tiff. She's always talking about me and now her ass has called off. It's probably that old man of hers. Anyway, let me know what happens, okay?" Jamie said turning to go back to work.

"Not a problem. Thanks for the words of encouragement Jamie. I've taken about all that I plan to from Dick. It will become a Mexican stand off and I'll probably lose, but I've got to start standing up for myself.

I've been here for over three years and worked my butt off, never complaining and letting him run over me. It's time to put up or shut up. I'll let you know," Toney concluded going back to work herself...

Toney drove past 484 LaSalle to find a parking spot. It was five twenty. She would be right on time. She parked and began here short walk back to Babbitt's office, fumbling in her briefcase to get the information that she had for Babbitt out. She wanted to be ready with all the things she needed when she got there. The corridor leading to his office was partially lit indicating that there were few people still in the building. There had been so many strange things going on that she was cautious even in this environment. She walked investigating every nook and cranny. Finally, she was in front of Babbitt's office and knocked as they had planned that she would. No answer. She waited a minute or so and knocked again. She saw a shadow through the glass part of the door coming toward her. She stepped back hoping that it was Babbitt. The door opened.

"Toney, you're right on time. Come in," he said stepping aside to allow her to enter.

"You looked stressed a bit. What's the matter?" Babbitt asked as he led her back down the corridor to his office.

"So much is happening Fin. It's been strange. I took that trip to the orient and was gone for seven days. Nothing. I mean nothing happened out of the ordinary. The moment I get back in my office today more of the same shit. I just can't understand it." She said appearing to be totally over it at this point.

"Now, now. That's what you're paying me for. I'm making some headway into this intermingled situation. I'm getting a little confused though. Who is Peter Beeage? And, Jimmy Belleu, Nick Sampson, Terry Conners, Holley, and Guy Gamble? All of these people have in one way or another been around you if nothing but by telephone frequently. All of them have had access to you and your movement of late. I have to get a fix on them before moving forward because without the process of elimination it could take much longer. I know that Holley and Gamble are tied to Surrant. But the others, who are they tied to and what is their relationship to you?" Babbitt asked as he moved forward from the reclined position that his chair fell into automatically.

"Let's start at the beginning. Peter Beeage is the husband of one of my friends who works in the same building as I do. What would he have to do with this?" Toney asked bewilderedly.

"What would he be calling you for, if he is just the husband of a friend?"

"I'm not sure. I've only met him on a couple of occasions. I can't remember him ever calling me. When did he call me?" Toney asked.

Last week. I worked with one of my connections at the courthouse and got a tap put on your office phone while you were out. I needed to see who was connecting with you in all regards. One is on your phone at your condo too. Beeage called your office last Thursday and sounded strained on the call. That's why his name made the list. So, what are your thoughts about him?"

"I barely know him. His wife is going through a lot on her job, so they would have nothing to do with me and my problems. Or, at least that wouldn't make any sense to me," Toney reported.

"What about Jimmy Belleu?"

"He's a sweetheart. He's my assistant's husband. And wouldn't harm a fly. He calls my office all the time to talk with his wife, Sonjia. There's nothing there," Toney said confidently.

"Okay. What about Nick Sampson or Terry Conners then?" Babbitt said as a measure of furthering the investigation.

"They work with Grant. They're Attorney's. Grant's having some problems with them at work, but not me. I don't think they even know about me for that matter."

"They've called your office as recently as Friday, asking your whereabouts."

"What? I wonder what that was all about?" Toney said bunching up her face.

"Maybe they were looking for Grant and thought if they could put their finger on me, that Grant might be with me....I don't know."

"Okay, so there's a possibility."

"What about the calls from today?" Toney added.

"It usually takes a day or two to get the reports. Why do you ask?" Babbitt paused from his line of questioning.

"Because I got a strange call this morning. The caller threatened me in a deep whispering voice. That's one of the things that I wanted to update you on. The other thing was this note. It came in the mail today. Someone's trying hard to frighten me, and if it weren't for you it might be working," Toney said handing Babbitt the envelope with the note inside.

Babbitt examined the envelope and then the note inside.

"Someone is working overtime to get to you. Phone calls, notes traveling to Jamaica. Breaking in your office, trying to run you down. That's a lot. They are in a lot of places at once, actually too many places at once. What about Holley?" Babbitt continued.

"She works for Surrant. It's normal for her to call me," Toney said.

"And Guy Gamble?"

"I absolutely have no idea who he is. I never heard of him. Maybe he's who's after me. I wonder who hired him to hurt me?" Toney said in a panic.

"Alright now…remember our deal. You are to stay calm and let me work through this, right? Now. You've given me a lot of information. I'll make my next move and get back with you in a couple of weeks. In the meantime, watch your step and remember that I'm never very far from you. You are my number one priority now and until this case is solved."

"Okay," Toney said sounding almost relieved.

"Are we finished?" she asked as a moment of silence fell on the room while Babbitt made some notes.

"Yes that's all for now. I'll be in touch," he said standing to begin their walk to the front door of the office.

"Will I be alright leaving here alone? It's dark outside," Toney said appearing to be afraid.

"Where did you park?" Fin asked.

"Half block down."

"This is downtown Chicago. There are still plenty of people on the street. You'll be fine."

"What about in this building? It seemed kinda empty when I came up here."

"Don't worry. It's real safe in here. There's security everywhere. Trust me."

"Okay, if you say so," she said stepping onto the other side of the threshold.

"I look to hear from you in a couple of weeks," Toney said as she began her departure.

"You will," Babbitt said standing in the doorway until Toney was out of site.

Toney got back down to the street safely, and to her car as well. Before she knew it, she was at home safe and sound and beginning to prepare for the next day. She took a bath, prepared a small snack and called

Grant. She had to hear his voice, before she turned in. It had been another full day.

TWENTY FIVE

After thinking things through, Grant started his own investigations on the shorter twins. The fact that they were pushing so hard in the Firm, had him suspicious about them. The other thing was that they always seemed to have their heads together plotting and planning, and that was bad enough, but the office incident had him especially puzzled. In almost six years of being employed at the Firm, nothing remotely like that had ever happened. Who were these guys? He was radically leery of them. They were much too bold to be so young, but their actions since they came on board were severely abnormal. He had learned over the last nine months that they would do anything to get what they wanted. If this was the case, it could become a lot more serious, as time moved on. The law firm that Grant had helped build, was very prestigious and well known…one could do a lot worse than to be named a partner in this firm and they knew it. It was a highly respected firm, and had been hired by nearly a fourth of the big outfits in the Chicago Land area to represent corporate concerns. Grant felt that he had put his blood, sweat and tears over past five years and ten months into the firm, because he believed in it. He had helped the firm attain the success that it now enjoyed, and these half-formed kids were risking its reputation.

"Mill. Do you have my itinerary ready for my trip?" Grant said as he opened his office door headed for Millicent's desk.

As Grant crossed the corridor he was one step away from running into Terry. Terry was returning to his office from the copy room holding a freshly poured cup of steaming hot coffee.

"Where you headed Grant?" Terry asked trying to appear innocent.

"Just on a short trip."

"When are you leaving?"

"Why? You want to try and take over more of my cases?" Grant joked.

"Now Grant. I thought we'd been all through that?" Terry smoothed over.

"You're right we have," Grant said trying to end the conversation.

"Well. When are you leaving?" Terry pushed on.

"Tomorrow night. Why?" Grant came back.

"Just wondering. I hadn't realized that you were travelling again so soon," Terry pushed.

"Should I check with you when I need to go?" Grant volleyed.

"Awwww.....come on Grant. I'm just trying to be a pal. Don't be so defensive," Terry struggled back.

"When you coming back?" He continued to push.

"Actually, I'll be back on Thursday at the latest. Why do you ask?" Grant surrendered.

"Just a question. Is it company related? You must have another big client you're trying to romance?" Terry continued.

"No it's personal. Now if I can please get back to it?" Grant said turning his attention to Millicent.

"Okay, okay. I hope your plans work out," Terry said with a smirk as he walked toward his office area.

"That faggot has some damn nerve," Millicent labeled.

"Why do you even bother to answer him. They have always got their fucking noses in everybody's business. And, you. You are way too damn nice and accommodating to them," Millicent scorned.

"Look, have you ever heard that you keep your enemies close? That's what I'm doing. It'll all be over soon. Something in my gut tells me that their days are numbered. They seem too antsy, when, if things were as they should be, they would just be working hard in a low-key manner like these other kids that have come on board. I wonder what they are really all about? Anyway, here are the flight arrangements that I need for you to make for me. Keep these plans confidential. No one needs to know that I'm going San Francisco on personal business. As far as everyone is concerned, I'm going home to see my mom. You got it?"

"Ten four boss. I'll get back to you in a few minutes to let you know the particulars," Millicent added.

"Thanks Mill," Grant said as he turned and walked back into his office. He immediately got back to work. He wanted to get as much done as he could before he left. He started thinking again. If he left on Tuesday night, he would have all day Wednesday to find out what he needed to know. Then, he could take the flight back at nine-ten on Wednesday night, in order to be back in the office on Thursday morning. It would be perfect. Once he got there, he knew he could make it happen. He would pass himself off as one of them. He could fit right in on campus, just using his experience from his days in college.

Ten minutes later, Millicent approached Grant in his office.

"You're scheduled on the seven twenty five flight out of O'Hare, tomorrow night on Delta. Your return from San Francisco, is as you suspected on Wednesday night at nine ten. Now, you won't get back into Chicago until after two in the morning. You sure about this? It'll be a rough trip. Then, you'll have to be here all day on Thursday without any sleep," Millicent said trying to look out for Grant.

"It'll be okay Mill. I can get some sleep later, once I know that the boys are taken care of," he said taking the information from Millicent.

"Okay boss, if you say so. The ticket will be over this afternoon," she reported as she left his office headed back to her desk.

PART II

Cameron was beside herself. And, she was tired of waiting on Summers. She had been trying to schedule a meeting with Summers for over a week and a half to talk about the position that he had put her in with April and he kept putting her off. It was obvious that he was determined to ignore her because everyone knew that he was awful at handling confrontations. They were also under the gun with several meetings that were being planned and had to be executed in the next few weeks as well as several large functions that had to be planned for next year.

"Cameron. I need for you to complete this request for proposal today. It should be out and at all of the major hotels in San Francisco by the end of the day, so if we get it to the Chicago Convention Bureau, they will handle it, right?" April said with authority, standing in front of her desk with her fluffy scooped neck sweater, hugging her large breasts and her tight fitting mini skirt, which was half way up her thighs.

In Cameron's mind, she went reeling, "first the blonde guy, who hadn't worked out and now this ding bat cheerleader type."

"How dare this little bitch give me orders. She can just do this herself," she thought as she looked at the request for proposal.

Cameron sat there just looking at April, rolling her eyes with her head vacillating between April and Summers' office, champing at the bit and waiting for an opportunity to get with Summers. She was enraged. This situation was simply ridiculous. Then, Cameron thought about the last conversation she had with Toney. Toney's words seemed to comfort her, and tended to calm Cameron down.

"This is just a job. I can do better than this," Cameron mumbled to herself, as she turned around giving April a view of her back without so much as a grunt.

April walked away pissed. Summers had created this situation. April was certainly in it for what she could get and as anyone would be which is why most of us come to work everyday but it really shouldn't be this way. She went straight in to see Summers. Actually April was assisting Cameron without knowing it. Cameron's plan was to piss April off and let her tell 'The Boss'. She wanted him to call her in for this. At least that would get her in front of Summers, which is what she had been trying to make happen. Then she'd let him have it. Ten minutes went by, then twenty. Still nothing. Summers wasn't' buying it. He wasn't as stupid as he looked. Thirty minutes later April came back to pick up the paperwork to complete it herself. Cameron had won that battle, but was still aching for a victory in the war.

Cameron picked up the phone to call Toney.

"Toney Chambers office, this is Sonjia, may I help you?" Sonjia said professionally.

"Hi Sonjia. It's Cameron. Is she in?" Cameron said sounding strained, which had become her basic disposition of late.

"Hi Cameron. She is just about finished with her Tuesday morning conference call. Will you hold?" Sonjia said looking at the big office clock over by Elaine Slant's desk. It was already five after ten. The calls rarely lasted over one hour and they had been going for one hour and five minutes.

"Sure, I hold for a moment," Cameron said sounding as if she really needed Toney.

A couple of minutes later Sonjia went in on Cameron's line again.

"Cameron, they're still going. Can I have Toney call you back, the minute that call is over?" Sonjia asked.

"Uh. Sure. I should still be here. If we miss each other, please tell her that I really need to talk with her today. Do you know if she got my note?" Cameron asked.

"I'm not sure. She took her own mail yesterday from the new mail person. She happened to be in the outer office when it was being distributed. I didn't see a note from you on Thursday or Friday of last week when she was in the Orient," Sonjia confirmed.

"It would have been delivered yesterday, I think. But, I'll ask her when I get her on the phone," Cameron concluded when they each said goodbye.

When Cameron hung up, Summers was standing there waiting for her to get off the phone.

"May I see you in my office?" he said without much to read on his face, which totally caught her off guard.

"You certainly may," Cameron responded with glee rising from her seat and marching off behind him as if she was looking forward to getting her day in court on a case that she was sure she would win.

Summers walked in taking his seat while he left Cameron to fin for herself. Cameron took a seat in front of him.

"Would you close the door please?" Summers said pulling out a file with Cameron's name on it and without looking up at her.

"Okay," Cameron said starting to feel uneasy. She cleared her throat, which she hoped would give her a measure of courage as she closed the door and took her seat again. She had to take this opportunity to read Summers the riot act about the office predicament. And, her courage began to surface again. It was now or never. No way would she answer to Miss boobs.

"Cameron. We've got a problem. It is apparent that you have a problem with the way I'm running the office. There's a reason why I'm the Executive Director and you're one of the Director of Meeting Services," Summers started.

Cameron interjected, "Ben, I've been with this company longer then you are anyone else who currently works here. I written procedure and policy. I've worked my fingers to the bone for this organization. And what thanks do I get? Last year you brought Patrik Gardner in here to reign over my department. He couldn't handle it, and now he's gone. You even asked me to train him, which I did for the good that it did. Now, you bring April in here with little or no experience, and you want me to train her and you've made her my equal. How can you possibly justify this? It just doesn't add up. I want to formally ask for a promotion to Senior Director of Meetings," Cameron said as she started to feel good about the fact that she could finally have this meeting.

"Cameron, I've heard you out now here me out. There will be no promotion for you. April was brought in as Director of Meeting Planning because she's a bright energetic young woman who brings some fresh blood and fresh ideas to the table. She has done an incredible job since she's been on board just over six months ago. Her promotion to Senior Director of Meetings will be announced tomorrow. You have forced me to make this decision after hearing about your attitude and state of mind over the last six months. You have not been acting as a leader. You've been acting like a spoiled child and that is unacceptable.

I should have gotten with you sooner, but that is my decision, and I have the approval of the Board of Directors. I didn't want you to hear it from someone else," Summers' said appearing to be determined that he could handle the fallout from Cameron's temper tantrum. As he suspected, Cameron went ballistic.

"You are promoting her to what? I'm in shock. How can you possibly justify that? You are a fucking loser. You've had it in for me since you came here. Nothing I do is good enough. Well, I think this stinks. It just stinks," Cameron said completely breaking down.

"Cameron, please get a hold of yourself. See? This is what I'm speaking about. This is the workplace and you have to learn to conduct yourself in a professional manner," Summers' said becoming alarmed at the state that she was forming.

Cameron became a mess. She was whaling and crying. Her face became a miscellany of positions. Dirty, confused, irate, bewildered. She was wildly becoming unglued. Summers became very concerned. He was afraid of the next phase.

"Cameron, are you all right?" he asked timidly.

She offered nothing, but sobbing. A few seconds later, she looked up from her tissue which, had been offered by Summers'. She had scant amounts of tissue stuck to her face in different areas. Her makeup was smeared around her face. Her eyes were as red as fire.

"I am leaving here," Cameron said looking at him as if she hated the very sight of him and getting up from her seat, rushing out of his office.

Cameron swiftly walked through the office with everyone looking at her in her wounded standing. Most of them could hear the yelling that had taken place. The entire staff within earshot of Summers office was in shock. Cameron had been a staple there for as long as many of the staffers could remember. They felt sorry for her because she had indeed worked so hard. Cameron opened her desk drawer to retrieve her purse and before anyone could expect, she was walking through the door.

Cameron was shaking uncontrollably. She wandered aimlessly through the streets of downtown Chicago. Not five minutes after Cameron left her phone rang.

"Cameron Beeage's office," the secretary answered.

"Hi. Is she in?" Toney asked.

"Uh…she's out at the moment. May I take a message?" one of the secretaries asked.

"Yes. Please tell her that Toney Chambers returned her call. I'll be in all day, so she can call me back when she returns."

"Ma'am. I don't think she'll be back today," the secretary whispered.

"Well…what do you mean? She left me a message that she'd be in all day. Did she get sick or something?" Toney asked becoming concerned.

"I can't really go in to it now, but she was very upset when she left," the secretary continued appearing to enjoy being a part of the circumstances.

"Alright then. If she does come back please tell her that I called," Toney said before hanging up.

Toney sat there for a moment before pulling out her phone book to look up Cameron's home number. 847.555.4811.

Toney dialed the number just knowing that Cameron hadn't gotten home this soon.

"Hello?" the voice on the other end of the phone said.

"Hello. Is Cameron there please?" Toney said fully expecting a no response.

"No, she's at work. Who's this?" the man asked.

"This is a friend of hers. Peter?" Toney asked.

"Yes. Who's this?" Peter Beeage responded.

"Hi Peter. This is Toney Chambers. We met last year here in the lobby of our building at work. Remember?" Toney asked.

"Yes, I remember," Peter said with a puzzled tone.

"I hate to bother you, but is Cameron at home yet?" Toney said as easily as she could muster.

"No. Cameron's at work. I was just getting myself ready to leave for the construction site. Did you try and give her a call at her office?" Peter asked.

"Well." Toney hesitated. "I tried to return her call at her office and they said she was gone for the day. She left me a message an hour earlier, that she'd be in the office all day and now she's gone for the day. I wanted to make sure that she was alright," Toney cautioned.

"Let me check into it. I'll give you a call back," Peter said, eluding to the fact that he was about to hang up.

"Oh Peter, you'll need my phone number to call me back. It's..." Toney began just before Peter interrupted her.

"I have your number Toney. Cameron gave it to me months ago as a go to person who'd be close just in case. As a matter of fact I called you early last week to see if you could go to see about her. Something happened on that damned job that had her all up in the air. But, they said you were out of the country, so I had to come in to town to see about my wife," he explained.

"Oh. Okay. Well, please get back to me and let me know what's going on with Cameron. She's a very special woman and a good friend, so I want to make sure she's okay," Toney said.

"Okay. I'll call you back," Peter said just before they hung up.

Peter waited for a second or two, took a deep breathe before calling for his wife. In the back of his mind he felt that Cameron had gone off on the deep end. He knew that she had been teetering on the edge with the April situation and that it was just a matter of time before she blew up. He carefully picked up the telephone to dial her office.

"Cameron Beeage's office. May I help you please?" the secretary answered.

"Yes. May I speak with Cameron please? This is her husband calling," Peter said in a strong voice.

"Just a moment sir," the secretary reacted.

Diane placed the call on hold immediately going to alert Ben Summers of the phone call. She didn't want to get in the middle of this sticky situation. The controlling factors were much larger than she or her position.

"Knock, knock, she rapped on the door lightly.

"Excuse the interruption Mr. Summers, but Cameron's husband is on the phone. What should I tell him?" she said timidly.

"I'll take the call Diana. Transfer it in here to me he said turning his attention to April who was sitting in front of him in a closed-door meeting.

A few seconds later the phone in Ben Summers office rang.

"This is Ben Summers, may I help you Mr. Beeage?" Summers said sounding as if he were in total control.

"I hope so. Can you tell me where Cameron is, sir?" Peter said trying to maintain his composure.

"I'm not altogether sure Mr. Beeage. She left the office about an hour ago and we haven't heard from her since. I hope she'll be back soon though. There's a lot of work yet to do here," Summers voiced without feeling.

"You mean to tell me that she just walked out …just like that?" Peter asked sounding more frustrated.

"Well, not exactly. We had a meeting one on one. She was being prepared for some of the changes that were to happen here in the office and she blew up," Summers continued.

"And, I take it that no one from the office cared enough to go after her to make sure that she was alright?" Peter said in an eerie voice that incorporated concern, rage, and disappointment.

"No sir. We thought she'd be right back. You know Cameron has been very moody lately, so we thought it was just another mood swing," Summers said in a presumptuous tone.

"Well thank you for not taking a good person's concerns to heart. You must be one hell of a person to work for…I'll tell you. No wonder my wife is so damned unhappy there," he concluded before slamming down the phone.

Summers smirked turning to April and saying to her, "No wonder his wife is such a bitch," as they both laughed it off and went back to what they were doing.

The next call Peter made was to his job to tell them what had transpired and that he'd be late or maybe, depending on what happened, he may not make it in today at all. The next call was to Toney to let her know what he found out.

"Toney, I'm on my way downtown. I've got to find her. She could be in a bad way," Peter hurried.

"Peter. Meet me in the lobby of our building…in what, forty-five minutes…an hour? I'll go with you," Toney said trying to console him.

"She'll be alright. She's a strong woman."

They both hung up and prepared themselves for whatever they found. They both knew that this had been coming on for several months. Toney turned her attention to her work, which was difficult for her to do. Cameron was such a good friend. In the early days when the Board of Directors leaned on her solely for the operation, she was so uninhibited and so much fun. This new group that had been brought in had a totally different way of doing business. She started to become unglued over the last eighteen months, which is when all of this first started.

Toney worked her way through six more items and then prepared herself mentally for the search. She had a few ideas of where she thought Cameron would go. She hoped that she was right.

"Sonjia, I'll be out for the next couple of hours. If anyone is looking for me and they can't wait for my return, you page me, okay?" Toney said making her way through the outer office and to the elevator bank.

Peter arrived about fifty minutes later with a wired look in his eyes. He was more than concerned. Cameron had never just gone off like this.

"Hi Toney. Do you have any place in mind that she might go?" Peter asked feeling ashamed that he had no clue.

"A couple of places Peter. Let's just take it easy and think good thoughts…alright?" Toney said in a comforting way as they began their trek.

"She likes Pizza. We recently went there just to get out of the building a few weeks ago. It may be what she needed. There's a pizza place just around the corner let's check that out first."

They walked and chatted about the situation. It had been getting progressively worse like many jobs have been over the past few years.

When they arrived at the pizza parlor…nothing. The place was buzzing with lunchtime patrons, but not Cameron.

"I have one more special place. If she's not there, maybe we should consider calling the police," Toney said.

Peter shook his head in agreement. He was not talking very much but the worry took over his expression.

"Peter, two blocks over is the Michigan Avenue beach. Cameron likes the water so, maybe she is sitting there thinking things through," Toney said. That's actually where we met a couple of years ago. We've both been so busy that we rarely get out of the building at all to go there even when the weather is good. But, maybe today, she decided to go there even though it's cold out today," Toney said as they kept walking.

"Maybe. I'll feel really bad if something has happened to her. She's been complaining about that damned job for over a year. I should have protected my wife and gotten her out of there before now," Peter said shaking his head and wringing his hands.

"Peter, let's not talk that way. Cameron will be alright," Toney said as they rounded the corner headed for the beach area. They saw a person seated on the beach bench but they were still too far way to determine if it was Cameron. As they came closer to the individual they both saw that it was Cameron. But she was much too still. They became very concerned and began to pick up the pace of their walk. When they arrived at the bench, Cameron was sitting there foaming at the mouth.

She was having some sort of seizure, which rendered her unconscious and in a very bad way.

"Peter you stay with her, I'll call an ambulance," Toney said as she ran back to the street to the nearest pay phone.

Toney was very nervous. She had never experienced anything remotely like this. By the time she got back to Peter and Cameron, the sound of sirens were vivid in the area. They had been dispatched quickly and for that Toney was grateful. Maybe her friend would be spared. Onlookers began to gather to see what all the excitement was about. Knowing Cameron, Toney thought of how embarrassed she would be if she were aware that she was the object of everyone's attention. She had never liked people who tried to get attention, and this time it was her who was the center of attention. As the paramedics worked on Cameron, Toney prayed, while Peter's held her hand. He was totally out of it. They wheeled her to the ambulance, as Toney and Peter followed close by. Peter climbed into the Ambulance with his wife, turned to Toney to mouthing 'thank you so much' as the door closed and the vehicle took off.

Toney felt sick inside, as she walked back to work. She vowed that she would never be that type of boss...Never.

TWENTY SIX

Grant arrived in San Francisco hoping that he could leave with some information that would help him understand more about the twins. He took advantage of his frequent guest points at Hyatt Hotels and checked in at the Hyatt Regency on Union Square. He had mapped out his plan for the visit to the campus of the University of California at Berkeley.

He ordered a small snack from room service and turned in. He had a big day ahead of him and wanted to be rested for it. As he lay there in the bed he remembered that he hadn't phoned Toney and that she might be worried when she couldn't reach him, so he picked up the phone to give her a call.

"Hello?" she said appearing to be rung out.

"Honey? Are you alright?" Grant said as he sat straight up in the bed.

"I'm fine, Grant. But, today has been very taxing. Cameron had an even tougher time today. It's a long story, one that we can discuss when I see you. I tried to call you about an hour ago, but I got your service. You had a long day too I see? Are you still going or are you at home now?" she said sounding half-asleep.

"You're right; it has been kind of a long day for me. I'm in San Francisco. I had some last minute business to take care of. I'll be back tomorrow night. I didn't want you to worry about me, so I'm checking in," Grant said on a roll.

"San Francisco? You didn't tell me that you were travelling this week. This must have been a last minute thing. You always like to have solid plans made for the moves that you make. Is everything alright?" Toney said seeming to wakeup somewhat.

"Oh sure, honey. Everything is just fine. Like I said, I'll tell you more about it this weekend. Remember that Brandon is coming in on Saturday. It'll be good to see that rascal," Grant said, cleverly changing the subject.

"That's right. I spoke with Sonjia about bringing Brandon with us to her family reunion and she was excited about it. Well honey, I'm tired. I need to get some sleep, so, have a safe flight back tomorrow. I'll talk to you then."

The next morning Grant got up, got dressed and went down for breakfast before picking up his rental car heading out for the campus. The weather was chilly, somewhere in the low forties, which was typical for northern California in the early fall. The nights were normally cold with the temperature warming up throughout the day. As he drove, Grant thought about the twins. There was something about them that was much too smug, much too devious. Thirty minutes later he arrived at the northern portion of the university campus. Right away it reminded him of his days in Boston when he was in school. A chill overtook his body thinking about some of the negative encounters he experienced during those days, simply because of the way he looked. That was sick he thought. Those kids never gave him a chance. After all, he was a very nice guy…so, it was their loss.

Grant parked the car and strolled over to some of the students who were headed to class. One after the other he asked around. Finally after twenty-eight people, Grant found someone willing to talk.

"Hey, man. I'm looking for Terry Conners or Nick Sampson, you know 'em?" Grant said acting as if he were a buddy of theirs.

"Those clowns graduated last year," the young man said.

"Oh, clowns? Why do you say that?" Grant probed.

"Do you know 'em?" the young man asked.

"Yeah. I know 'em. I just haven't seen 'em in a year or so. That's why I'm looking for 'em. Where are they now?" Grant pushed.

"I don't know and frankly, don't care. If you want to know about those two, find Chad Baines. He still goes here. He's a senior. He's around somewhere. Now…I've got a class to get to," the boy said as he walked away.

"Okay, okay. Thanks," Grant said walking at a much slower pace than the kid did.

Grant moved through the halls and through building after building searching for Chad not sure how to approach him or if Chad were a friend of theirs or someone they had used in their move through the school. One moment, Grant got close and then the illusive Chad slipped away. It was already lunchtime and Grant was getting hungry. He stopped at the campus pizzeria. He felt right at home there. After his order came up, Grant took a seat near the door. Little did he know, he had ended up exactly where he needed to be. Several kids came in for lunch. At eleven fifty Grant heard one of the girl's say, "Come on, Chad. I have to see that movie. Take me…please?" she pleaded as they waited for their order.

Grant's ears perked up. This was perfect. He remained seated and just observed as the group of kids collected their pizza and took a table across the room. Grant sat, watched and eavesdropped on their conversation. They spoke about this and that…what happened over the weekend after the frat party and what their plans were for the upcoming weekend. An hour later they got up to leave. Grant wanted to make sure that he capitalized on this favorable moment.

"Excuse me man, I wonder if you have a moment? I want to ask you about a couple friends of yours, Terry Conners and Nick Sampson. Do you mind?" Grant asked with caution.

"Who are you? The cops?" Chad asked.

"The cops? Naw. I'm a friend of theirs. I've lost contact with them. As a matter of fact I'm from Ohio, Dayton. Terry and I are old chums. I was trying to catch up with 'em is all," Grant said trying to fit in.

"Let me tell you…if you're a friend of those two, you're sad, man. Those two are awful. Everyone on campus was never so glad to see the day that they graduated and got the hell outta here. We really hated those two," Chad said looking like the end of the world was at hand.

"I know. They are awful. I'm trying to catch up with them to try and help em. I was a good influence on them in high school and when I left Dayton, they started up again. Hopefully I can get with them and help." Grant said trying to sound sincere.

"If I were you, I'd stay the hell away from them. They're bad news," Chad murmured.

"What did you say, Chad? They're bad news? Why do you say that?" Grant asked in a tone that appeared to be befriending.

"They would step on anyone or do anything to get what they want. They had some people beat up so badly while they were here just because the guys wouldn't cheat on a test for them. This guy is still in traction today. They say he'll be rehabilitating for some time. They hurt several people physically because they wouldn't do papers and shit for 'em. Several people went to the cops to try and stop them. The thing was, they're so slick with their shit that the cops couldn't lay it on 'em," Chad said looking both fearful and sad.

"What else did they do?" Grant inquired.

"They raped a girl and tore her body up so much so that they say she'll never have kids. But, she was blindfolded when it happened. They found some of Nick and Terry's pubic hair on her clothes. But, neither of them ejaculated in her so, their DNA was mixed up with five other guys' DNA, so they all got off on a technicality. But, it was Nick and Terry that did it. Man, those two terrorized the campus. And, as soon as they left, everything calmed down. Now tell me it wasn't those two pricks," Chad said as he began to pack up to leave.

"If I were you man, I'd stay a long way away from those assholes," Chad warned.

A few seconds of silence overcame the moment.

"Wow! I had no idea it was that bad. Thanks, Chad, I appreciate your candor. I'll take your lead and forget about them. I guess, I'll go back to Dayton and just plain forget about it," Grant said convincingly.

"Okay man…See ya later," Chad said as he and his petite girlfriend walked away.

"See this pretty little thing here? She wouldn't have been safe around here with those two bastards around. If you go near them watch your women that's for sure," he said as he held the door open for the girl and followed her through it.

Grant sat there stunned. These boys were dangerous. His mind instantly focused on the office break in. Neither of them had seemed real surprised at that situation. He wondered if they were in on it. He began to get very worried. Grant threw away the remnants of his lunch, because the information that he had just received, made him lose his appetite. He left the restaurant headed for his hotel to check out. He remembered that the tags on the truck, which was at the base of the door during the break in, had Ohio tags. Terry is from Ohio. The trail was leading back to Dayton. That's where he'd have to go next. But, for now he had found out some good information.

PART II

Brandon was packing for Chicago. He was excited that he would see his Grant and his ladylove soon. They were a very special couple to him. Brandon had high hopes that he would find someone soon for himself.

He hoped that the interview that he had in Chicago would be successful. He could be happy in Chicago, he thought as he moved around. There were just too many bad memories. Bradley was doing a stretch in the Los Angeles county jail for trafficking. Over the years, things had turned around for him and Bradley. It was as if Brandon became the big brother over night. He spent many days and nights pleading with his older brother to straighten up and to stay away from the guys that he found himself with over and over again. Bradley's only response was that Brandon was a faggot because all of his time was spent with his head in books. That thought had been planted in his head for years, so he was still struggling with the thoughts of being gay. As if that wasn't enough, Bridgett was hanging around with a drug dealer and from her actions, Brandon wasn't sure if she had started to use or not; even though he tried to probe the controlling factors. He was constantly cornering her about that too and to top it all off, Brandy had become severely lazy, not having any ambition at all. She really didn't want a lot out of life. He couldn't stand all the negativity. He wanted to leave Los Angeles for sure, and this just might be his ticket out.

He had promised Grant that he'd call with flight information for Saturday. Brandon picked up the telephone to call Grant's office.

"Mr. Parlarme's office. This is Millicent, may I help you?" Millicent answered.

"Hi Millicent. Is he in?" Brandon queried.

"No he isn't. He won't be back until tomorrow. May I take a message?" she asked.

"No, I'll call him at home. Thanks," Brandon responded indicating he was about to hang up.

"He's not at home either. He went to New York to see his mom," Millicent shared with him.

"Who's calling?" she asked fearing that she had given out too much information not even knowing whom she was speaking with.

"This is Brandon, his friend from Los Angeles. Is his mother all right? When will he be back?" Brandon asked voicing concern.

"His mom's fine, Brandon. He just went over for the day. Like I said, he'll be back on Thursday," she consoled.

"You want to leave a message?"

"Yes. As a matter of fact, I do. He's picking me up from O'Hare on Saturday, and I promised him that I'd call him with my flight information. Can you take it for him?" Brandon asked with circumspection.

"And tell him for me that I plan to stay the whole week now. Okay?"

"Okay," Millicent said as she continued to write.

Once Millicent took down the information with a quick verification back to Brandon, the call was over. Brandon sat there thinking about Grant and the mere fact that he was taking a trip in the middle of the week to see his mom. That was strange. He had a sinking feeling that something wasn't right, but he knew that Millicent didn't know him well enough to share any of Grant's information with him. He would want to help Grant if there was something really going on. He would ask the question when he saw his friend.

On Thursday morning Brandon reported to work as he did everyday. He was dismayed with his job because of a group of black men that he worked with. It was preposterous as he saw it that there was no camaraderie with any of the black folks there. They were all existing independent of one another and seemingly out to make sure that neither of them was more successful than the other. No support system or appreciation for the education that he had taken the time to get. Jealousy and envy were the cornerstone of each of their days, and he had had enough. As he walked in that morning he thought about the events as recently as Monday, Tuesday and Wednesday of this week. Daily, the comments and innuendoes rang out. Several of them were involved in trying to drive him out, and it was working.

"Hey, kiss up. How's that jailbird brother of yours? Any news on your sister? What about your old man? He still raking leaves? And, you want to act all high and mighty…please!" Keith Passmore chanted.

Keith knew several people who lived in the Crenshaw area, and once the connection was made, he volleyed each of them for as much information on Brandon as he could muster.

Brandon walked past him as if he hadn't heard a word. Later that morning, Keith and two of his cronies made their way to the third floor where Brandon was located. They walked the corridor quietly until they passed Brandon's office.

"Hey, man, you seen any fags lately? There are a couple of fags downstairs looking for a good time," Keith said just under a yell.

"I heard one of them say that they were looking for a gay black lawyer. Someone on the third floor. Maybe Brandon can help em out. What do you guys think?" one of the other guys chimed in.

Brandon started grinding his teeth. "What idiots," he thought. And, if the janitorial staff wasn't enough, Will Ulmer, one of the lawyers who had been with the firm for almost six and a half years, was trying to sabotage him as well. He hadn't liked Brandon from the first day that he arrived at the firm more than a year earlier. He was pissed off at Brandon because of his academic achievements and the fact that the firm brought him on board to be fast tracked through, and Will would have none of that. If he had to work his way up so did everyone else. So from the moment they met, it was on.

TWENTY SEVEN

Cameron was admitted to the mental ward of Chicago General Hospital. The early prognosis was in. She had suffered a mental collapse, caused in part by a continual buildup of stress and in part by the way she accepted and dealt with the betrayal that she had experienced. Her self-respect, among more serious things, was severely damaged. She had experienced a life altering moment, which would change her forever in one-regard or another. The plain and simple truth was that her psyche had been beaten down hour after humiliating hour, day after day and month after month. Summers wanted her out and couldn't make it happen any other way and get away with it, so he bided his time and inflicted his torture slowly.

Peter paced continually outside the hospital room where the doctors were running additional tests on Cameron, one by one in order to be sure of their findings. His wife's health status would depend on her mental strength at this point, and Peter couldn't be sure of that after the horrible clashes she had braved on her job.

"Doctor, doctor," Peter started calling out for the doctor that he saw leaving Cameron's room. He practically set out in a running motion toward the doctor trying to ensure that she didn't get away before sharing information with him regarding his wife.

"Pardon me, ma'am, I know that you may not be finished with your work at this point, but I need to have an update about Cameron. That's my wife in there, I just need to know what's what. How is she? What have you been able to find out about her status? She was in such bad shape when she was brought in here yesterday. She just gotta be all right, you know?" Peter said looking very concerned.

"Sir, I understand how you feel, but we're still running tests. We want to be sure that all of her brain activities are normal. She has suffered a slight stroke, but the brain waves indicate some damage from the stroke, and that could be a factor in her complete recovery. So, we'll get with you to give you an update as soon as we have something concrete to share, okay?" she said as gently as she could.

"I appreciate all that, but you've gotta tell me how it looks now. She's been in here since last night. You have to have some kinda update for me. I'm going crazy out here," Peter said almost pleading.

"Sir please calm down. We're doing everything we can," the doctor said just as she was being paged.

"Please excuse me sir. We'll get back to you as soon as we can, I promise," she said as she scurried down the corridor to answer her call. Peter slumped in his posture as he dragged himself back over to the area where he had been seated. He threw himself back into the same chair in the middle of the front row. He was losing it.

"Those bastards are dead on that damned job. How could anyone treat a wonderful hardworking person like Cameron like she's been treated? It's criminal," he said out loud.

"God, she's gotta be all right. She's just gotta be!" he continued out loud as he closed his eyes to begin a pray for her again.

Peter had made it his business to call the immediate family members to alert them of the situation at hand. He waited until the sun came up trying to allow them to sleep through the night, and one by one they arrived to be with Peter and they all waited together. Two hours later, a team of doctors approached Peter and the family.

"Mr. Beeage?" a doctor asked looking from face to face of the individuals standing there.

"I'm Peter Beeage. Do you have some information for us on my wife?" Peter said with uneasiness.

"Yes, Mr. Beeage. I'm Dr. Gillespie. I'm leading the team of doctors handling your wife's case. Right now she is resting comfortably. The patient has suffered a partial mental breakdown due to build up affecting the nervous system. This system literally affects each part of the body and particularly the brain and its activity. She'll be out of commission for several weeks and will begin to slowly get back to herself. But, she'll be able to go home tomorrow because there is really nothing more that we can do for her here in the hospital. We have prescribed a battery of medicines for her to take which will keep her relaxed as her body repairs itself. She may not get back to 100%, but we are hopeful for a near complete recovery. Until then, watch her carefully and at any signs of inconsistencies relating to her normal personalities, please let us know. Remember she will have to visit her doctor regularly to make sure she's progressing the way we think she should until such time as she can be totally released. In the meantime, the best thing for her is complete stress free rest and to be around loved ones and familiar surroundings. We want to keep her again overnight to make sure that she is completely out of the woods, but we feel good about the timeline of her release. Do you have any questions?" the doctor said summarizing the team's findings.

"Thank God," Peter said as his entire demeanor changed to relief.

"Thank you, doctors, thank you so much," Peter said as he and the others began to shake each of their hands individually.

Peter thought about how he and Toney found Cameron. He really thought she was dead when he first saw her sitting on that bench. He was grateful that Toney even knew where to look. He would have been lost without her and wanted to thank her for her help. Plus, he wanted to make sure to give Toney an update on Cameron.

"She'll be glad to know that Cameron can go home tomorrow," Peter said as he picked up the pay phone to call Toney.

"Toney Chambers office, this is June. May I help you?"

"Yes, this is Peter Beeage. Is Miss Chambers in, please?" Peter said with great anticipation.

"No, sir. She's out at the moment. May I take a message for her?" June continued.

"Yes. Please tell her thanks for helping me find Cameron. I'm still at the hospital and the doctors said that Cameron will be released in the morning. Ask her to call me tonight at our house. Tell her that I'll give her the particulars then," Peter rushed.

"Okay, sir. I'll give her the message," June reported as she continued to write on the note pad.

PART II

Grant made his way back to Chicago and into the office. He was tired, but he had gained a certain level of energy, which was difficult to explain. He was shaken a bit about the information that he had found out about Nick and Terry. They had terrorized the campus and nothing had been done about them. Now they had become his problem. What else had they done and how far would they go to get what they wanted? Their sites were set on a partnership in the law firm that Grant had worked so hard to help build, and he had to find a way to make them dispense of themselves. His next trip would be to Ohio, but that would have to wait until Brandon came and left.

"Mill. Did I miss anything?" Grant said softly as he dragged himself out of his office and to her desk.

"Hi, Grant. Man, you look like something the dog dragged in. I told you before you left that this would be rough on you. And, what a question, 'did you miss anything?' Hell yeah you missed something. Yesterday I walked past Nick's office and the door was slightly cracked. Neither Nick nor Terry saw me, so I stood out of sight and listened to their conversation. The two of them and one other man have been into some nighttime activities. I couldn't quite hear the whole conversation, but they've been terrorizing someone. I didn't get the name or anything, but these guys are for real. And, then they switched to you. They said they had already started rumors that it was you who setup the office break in a few weeks ago. The fact that you tried to make it look like you were blowing the whistle on those guys who were moving the stuff out of the office. They factored in the reality that you had some black blood in you and all so it would be easy to believe that you'd be robbing the hand that was feeding you. Nick said that they were going to make sure you go down. That you were the only thing standing in the way of them getting what they want. Terry said that he had made contact with two of your customers feeding them a line about your not being able to handle it and so on. What the hell you gonna do about these guys, Grant? I'm getting scared," Millicent said nearly shaking.

"Mill, don't worry. They'll somehow be their own undoing. I'm working on some things. On Monday, I'm headed for Ohio to see what I can find out, and then we'll see," Grant said, changing the subject and thinking in the back of his mind just how he was going to handle all of this.

"Uh, Mill, anything else happened yesterday?" he said thinking mostly of the work that he may have missed.

"Damn it, Grant, I almost forgot. Remember the girl that they busted for screwing in the copy room a few months ago? Well, that stupid bitch was busted again fucking in the last office to the right down that way," she said pointing in that direction.

"You know that office is unoccupied right now. She and the same guy decided to go in there to get their freak on again right here in the office.

What in the hell is their problem? Both of them are stupid. Why not get a motel room, if it's like that for them? But, noooooo. They have to do it right here in the damned office. And, guess who busted them?" Milllicent taunted Grant.

"Who?" Grant said with his facial expression reaching a height of anticipation.

"The old man. They said he was in the copy room and heard some noise. He went to investigate. When he opened that door, he went into shock. Brooke and Kit said they were in the area and heard him shriek. He fired their asses on the spot. That's some shit isn't it?" Millicent said loudly waiving her arms up and down in a way only Millicent could.

"Shhh, Mill," Grant said looking around to see if anyone else was paying them any attention.

"I've told you that you get way too involved and too doggone loud. You have got to keep it down...it's unprofessional," Grant said as he always did.

"Man. That's something else. I can't believe that they got a reprieve the last time and they did it again, Grant said as he walked away back into his office.

When he got back to his office he decided he wanted to talk with Toney. They hadn't spoken since Tuesday night. When he arrived back in Chicago it was too late for him to call her. He knew she needed her sleep and didn't want to wake her just to say hello.

"Hi, honey. How are you?" Grant said sweetly.

"Hey, good looking. I missed talking with you yesterday. Did you try calling me? I was beginning to get concerned that my private line was on the blink again. No rings in three days," Toney said teasing.

"That's incorrect, my love...it's been two days and I made sure to make your home number ring on Tuesday night," Grant retorted.

"You're right baby. I'm glad you're back. What was happening in San Francisco? It's not like you to take impromptu trips like that," Toney said sounding unsure of what was going on.

"It's very interesting and I'll fill you in when we have a quiet moment. Are you all set to entertain Brandon?" Grant changed the subject. He wasn't sure that he wanted Toney to know about everything that was happening. There was nothing that she could really do about this anyway except worry, so what was the use? He admitted to himself at that moment that he would have to tell her, but just not now.

"I am excited about Brandon's trip to Chicago. It's been a while since we've all been together. Did he call you to give you his flight information yet?"

"He called me earlier this week. Millicent took down all of the information. He'll be in around twelve thirty. That'll be a good time to go to Sonjia's event, right?" Grant answered.

"That'll be prefect. I'll let Sonjia know that we'll be there around two thirty then. She'll be happy that we're coming," Toney continued.

"How long is Brandon staying?" Toney asked.

"He'll be here until Wednesday. He has an interview with a firm downtown on Monday. He's trying to move here," Grant said as Toney heard him softly grunting and shifting in his chair.

"You alright, honey? You sound a bit tired. What time did you get in last night?" Toney asked sounding concerned.

"It was late. I can't sit too long when I'm this tired. Baby, let me get back to you later," Grant said.

"Okay. But, I've got to tell you about Cameron," Toney pushed.

"What about Cameron? How's she doing with that preposterous job situation?" Grant said seeming to wake up a bit.

"Cameron lost it yesterday. They promoted the cheerleader. She became Cameron's boss. Can you believe it? The next thing we knew, she went off and ended up spaced out and sitting on the Michigan Avenue beach in a strange state. I called Peter just to see if she was at home, because Cameron had placed a call to me and within five minutes. I returned her call and they told me that she'd gone for the day. I thought that was odd, so I called her house and when Peter answered, he knew nothing about her coming home early. He got worried and so did I. A little more than an hour later he met me in the lobby of the building and went for a walk to look for her. We checked out a couple of her favorite places. In the last place that I thought of, which was the beach, we found her. When we spotted her we knew immediately there was something very wrong. She was so still. I had to run to call the paramedics while Peter stayed with her. She was in a bad way," Toney explained.

"Was she alive?" Grant whispered holding his breath.

"Yes, but barely. Her breathing was shallow, and all the color had drained from her face," Toney said trying to hold herself together.

"But, when the paramedics arrived, they started to work on her right away, and her color got a little better before the ambulance took off. I'm not even sure which hospital they took her to. So, I'm waiting for Peter to call me with an update," Toney said.

"Well, I'll pray that she'll be alright. These damn jobs are a mess. Too many times the wrong people get promoted and their people skills suck. Their efficiency relates only to the bottom-line, and that's where it begins and ends with the people at the top. You would think that the philosophy would be to make your people as happy as you can and they'll produce for you, netting bigger profits. I just don't know what this is really all about. When I make partner, I'll never manage like that, you know?" Grant retorted again.

"I'm the same way, honey. When I'm President, I'll never treat people that way either. Never," Toney said.

They spoke for another few minutes and hung up.

Toney decided after speaking with Grant that she wanted to go to visit Cameron. She couldn't get the way Cameron looked out of her mind. She was almost lifeless. To think that a damned job could do that to anyone was astounding, she thought. Then, she sat back in her chair, as she started to think about the nonsense that she had experienced in the years before. It made her sick inside. She began to daydream again ...

The weeks rolled into months. Dick and Toney bumped heads constantly, but as ridiculous as he was he wasn't stupid. Toney had saved him on more than one occasion. As a matter of fact she carried her location almost single handedly. Toney kept pressing forward. She made a mental compromise with herself that she'd stomach Dick, because she knew that it was difficult for her to promote her social development to a point where it would rub off on him, so she did it for herself. He was forever an asshole, and she felt that he would be taken care of in time. In the spring two years later, Toney was transferred to Chicago. She had faired so well in her work in her D.C. job, that the vice president of the company requested that she be brought to Corporate to assist with some special projects that were to head up special plans for Prophecy's future. On the eve of her departure, Dick came in to her office to say goodbye.

"Toney, I know that we didn't hit it off at first, but I feel that we've grown together and have become fairly good for each other. Much like good friends. I'd like to wish you well. I have been interviewing for a replacement for your position, but you'll be difficult to replace," Dick said looking like a weasel.

"Dick, we can never be friends. Our standards are too far apart. I respect you as my boss. I even respect you for your knowledge of the business and your creativity, but not as a man. I have tried and tried hard to be a good employee for the company even through some very boorish times. We all have to work at something, and I thank God that I found my niche as early in life as I did, but you surely didn't make it easy for me and to be honest, in a way I thank you. I had to find out what I was made of, and that was a character builder. And, because I love what I do so much, I stayed here. So, it worked out for me. But, you never took into consideration how I felt when you embarrassed me over and over again, yelling at me out in public...talking to me any kind of way on a consistent basis...and just overall treating me like I wasn't even human. But, through it all, God saw to it that I was successful. So you see, there's no way that we could ever have been friends," Toney said as she turned back to packing her personal things.

Dick stood there for a moment and finally she heard him walk away. Her intuition told her that Dick wasn't going to make it. He was in for some hard times. He would have a hell of a lot of work to do to keep up.

'One more thing to do,' she thought. She walked over to Jamie and Tiffany's area.

"Thanks for all of your support ladies. You have no idea how much you both helped me through some tough times, and I love you both for it. I'll stay in touch with you both."

They all hugged. Toney picked up her box and slowly walked away and out of the building. When she got to the street, she turned to take one last look at her beginning. As she looked, tears streamed from her face.

She turned and walked to the metro. She hoped that Chicago was going to be good, very good for her.

Toney moved to Chicago. She found a little place about three exits from downtown off the Dan Ryan. With her raise, she was able to get a little plucker to get back and forth. She felt a challenge in her new position, but with the Vice President's backing, all of the corporate players welcomed her.

"So you're the wiz kid, huh? We've heard an awful lot about you all over the company," the man said.

"Hi. I'm Jim Surrant, Director of the Southern California remote office located in Los Angeles."

"Hi. I'm Toney Chambers," she said timidly.

"Well, I hope they get their money's worth," he said as he walked away.

Two years later, Toney was promoted again to the Director of the Chicago regional office. And, six years later, after mega successes and four more promotions, she was asked to the big summer Corporate meeting in Dallas. She was named Vice President of the company.

And, on her way back from Dallas, she literally bumped into Grant Parlarme, at O'Hare **...**

Toney shook herself awake from the trance, smiling, thinking of the first time she laid eyes on her fiancée. Her mind shifted once again to Cameron. She had received the message from Peter. She was happy that Cameron would make it, that she'd be home today and that she wanted to see Cameron. Today she was really busy, but not too busy for a friend. Cameron was one of the people that she had met during the first two years in Chicago. She would never forget how much Cameron had helped her get settled in. She would always be grateful to her friend.

"Today will be just as good a day as any," Toney said out loud as she stood to pack up her office. It was already two fifty five. She wanted to get out to the suburbs before rush hour traffic. That way she could be back down town before eight.

On her way to the suburbs, Toney had good thoughts on her mind about Cameron. She hoped that the unrealistic job predicament was over for her. She was too good at what she did to allow someone like Summers to get away with the way that he treated her. He really didn't deserve someone as good as Cameron. Thirty-five minutes later Toney was pulling into Cameron's driveway. There were seven cars surrounding the house, which indicated that Toney would be just one of the people who thought so much of this lady. Toney climbed out of her car and walked with purpose to the front door to ring the doorbell. Peter opened the door. Once he saw that it was Toney, he gave her a big smile.

"Toney, thanks for coming," he said as he opened the screen door to let her in.

"Hi Peter. I'm so happy that Cameron is going to be alright," she said as she walked in and immediately began to focus on the individuals who were in the room. Right in the middle of the people seated in the room was Cameron. She was drawn and looked weak, but at least she was alive.

"Cameron. Hi honey. How are you? I'm so glad to see you," Toney said moving toward her as Cameron's son moved to allow Toney to sit next to his mom.

"I'm better, Toney," Cameron said slowly, sounding strange to Toney.

"I'm much better, honey," she continued slowly.

"How are you?" Cameron said to relieve the focus from herself.

Toney thought that was good…at least she's able to think independently.

"I'm alright, Cameron. I miss you though. What do you think? You gonna be up and around real soon?" Toney coached.

"I hope so, Toney," Cameron mouthed slowly.

"I'm gonna try my best," she said even slower as if she was guarding her words.

They all sat there chatting about this and that, and a while later, Toney got up to excuse herself.

"Cameron, I'll be back to see you next week. Keep doing good, girl. And, I'll call to talk with you. If you need me you have all of my numbers. Please let me know if I can help you in any way," Toney said as she moved to the door.

"I appreciate all that you've done for me and my family, Toney," Peter said as he opened the door. "Cameron's going to be fine thanks to you."

"It was the least that I could do, Peter," Toney said as she took another look at Cameron sitting there staring out into space. It was as if she was only partially there.

Toney got into her car to begin her short trek back to downtown Chicago. As soon as she entered the Dan Ryan, a car appeared out of nowhere and was tailing her very closely. Toney changed lanes…the car swiftly changed lanes. Toney changed again…the car changed again. Minutes later the car began to ram her from the back. Five, six times. Toney was frantic. Who was this idiot? Was this part of the harassment that she had been experiencing over the past months? Suddenly after eight times, the car sped away as suddenly as it had appeared. It jumped off at the next exit. Toney was gripping the steering wheel so hard that her knuckles had become very light brown. "This has got to stop. I'm losing it…it's got to stop."

TWENTY EIGHT

Rumors in the West Coast office had cooled off over the past several weeks. Jim had not spent much time in the office. He was travelling part of the time and more recently, because he hadn't been feeling well. The last two conference calls had been held without Jim. He was in bed sick. Toney called him at home to see how he was after he missed the second call.

"Mr. Surrant, please," Toney said.

"He's asleep. May I take a message ma'am?" Amy their maid, asked.

"Is there a good time that I could call him back?" Toney pushed.

"Who's calling please?" the maid responded.

"This is his boss in Chicago. I know that he's not well, but I'd like to know if there is a better time that I could call him to make it convenient for him?" Toney said apathetically.

"I'll get Mrs. Surrant. Maybe she can help you," the maid finally decided.

After thirty seconds another extension in the house was added to the connection.

"This is Joanie Surrant. May I help you, please?" Jim's wife said sweetly.

"Mrs. Surrant, this is Toney Chambers in Chicago. I'm calling to see how Jim is coming along. We're concerned about him. Anytime he's not at work, it's clear to us that he's not well."

"That's kind of you. He's doing a little better. We expect that he'll be up and around in a few more days. The doctors haven't been able to diagnose the problem. They think it may be the flu. But, as recently as last night he said he was better; even though he was still talking a bit out of his head. Would you like for me to wake him for you?" Joanie asked.

Toney thought… 'Hummm…talking out of his head…why, that's not unusual for Surrant.' Then she snapped back into the conversation.

"No, absolutely not. I want to speak with him, but if he's asleep, please let him get his rest. He certainly needs it. If you could guess, when would be a good time to call him back, that would be great?" Toney asked in a concerned way.

"Try calling back in a couple of hours. Over the last few days he has been staying awake longer and longer, so once he's up for the first time today, he'll be awake for a little while," Joanie said appearing to be hopeful that whatever it was would soon be over.

"Okay then. That's what I'll do," Toney said as the hung up.

Joanie tipped into the room where Jim was fast asleep. She stood there for a few minutes just looking at her husband. He was a very complicated man who was now as sick as he had ever been in his life. Just as quickly as she tipped in, she tipped out.

Joanie went about her morning waiting for her husband to wake. Over an hour passed. She thought she'd be proactive by asking Amy to start breakfast. The smell of bacon and coffee would usually wake him, and she hoped that he would be hungry. His appetite had waned over the past week, and it was noticeable when Joanie saw him in the buff. An hour and ten minutes later, Jim was awake.

"Joanie? Joanie, I could use a cup of coffee," Jim bellowed through the intercom, clamoring for breakfast. Joanie was happy to see that he even had an appetite.

"Good morning, dear. Amy will be right up with a pot of coffee for you. How are you feeling?" Joanie asked.

"I'll be right up to help you get prepared for your day, honey. I'll be right there," she continued before he could even answer her.

Amy took the coffee and a breakfast plate with a very light offering.

"Good morning, Mr. S. How are you? You've been out of it for several days. The house has been too quiet without you running about yelling orders and such. How are you?" Amy said as she put down the tray and touched him on the shoulder indicating that he should sit up so that she could fluff his pillows. He followed through on her suggestion. A minute later, he was comfortable as Amy adjusted the tray, placing it right in front of him. She poured him a cup of coffee, took the top off of the food, which she had plated for him, and all in one motion, excused herself. A minute or so later, Joanie walked in. Jim had doctored his coffee to suit his taste. He had begun eating a few spoons of the breakfast.

"Hi, baby. How long have I been out of it? I feel weak but a little better than I did the other day. You going to church?" Jim said still hallucinating from the fever, pushing the tray back and adjusting himself in the bed.

"Church? Honey its Wednesday. You've been feverish and sleeping for over a week.

Believe me you look a lot stronger. Doctor Payne came out to examine you. He thought it was a complicated case of the flu, so he gave you a juices. He left this medicine for you to take whenever you were awake enough to take it orally. How are you feeling?" Joanie said as she sat on the side of the bed, sweeping his hair from his face.

"A week? No way. Are you serious? I have to call work. I wonder if they've found the money? What has Chicago said? The conference calls? I got to get up and go to the office," he said as he scooted to the end of the bed trying to get up and avoid the area where Joanie was sitting.

"Honey, you're not strong enough...."Joanie was about to say just as Jim stood and fell back on the bed.

"Ohhh," he moaned.

"What in the hell is this shit? I'm in pain," he said as he crawled back in bed.

"What did you say Payne came up with? The flu? I hadn't had any symptoms. How'd I get home, whenever it was when I was conscious? I don't remember shit," Jim said reaching down to pull the covers back over himself.

"I was about to say to you that you're not strong enough to be out of bed yet, except to go to the bathroom. You're weak because you haven't eaten in more than a week. Now, let Amy and I nurse you back to your feet. Okay?" Joanie pleaded.

"Ohhhh. My head is hurting. What choice do I have?" Jim moaned as he lay there completely helpless.

"Okay. Try to eat just a little more of this and please drink all of your orange juice. This is the stuff that'll get you back on your feet.

Jim followed orders for one of the few times in his life. Once Jim went through the ritual of eating and taking his medicine, Joanie apprised him that she had been in touch with Holley over the week.

"And, by the way, Toney Chambers called this morning. She seemed to be very concerned about you. I asked that she call back in a couple of hours. She should be trying to get back with you in the next thirty minutes or so. Will you feel like talking?" Joanie asked with great concern after the display that she just saw her husband go through.

"I guess I should at least talk to her. What day did you say it was?" Jim reflected.

"It's Wednesday," Joanie said again.

"That means I've missed a conference call. The last thing I remember is that I was working with Holley to get the missing funds located and that she was working with the controller to get him involved. What time is it? I really need to talk to Holley before I talk to Chambers," Jim said reaching for the phone.

"Okay, honey, you can talk on the phone but please don't try to get up without some help, alright?" she asked as she handed him the phone.

"Okay," he said dialing in to the office.

"Jim Surrant's office, this is Holley, May I help you?" Holley said sounding very strong.

"Holley, it's Jim," he said sounding very weak.

"Jim. How are you? Joanie said you've been out of it."

"Yeah. I obviously have. So much for that. Did you find the money? Chambers called her this morning. I'm concerned that she is calling me up to lower the boom. I have to know what you've found out." I..."

"Jim," Holley interrupted.

"Toney is only calling you because she's concerned about your well being," Holley said.

"Toney? When did you start calling her Toney? Shit. You think I believe that? No way. That bitch is out to get me and it doesn't matter to her that I'm lying flat on my back sick as a dog. I know I have to cover my ass. Did you find out where the rest of the money is?" he forced.

"Jim. We found nothing. There is no more money. Someone has taken the funds because there is no more. There is at least two hundred and twenty seven thousand missing," Holley told him.

"That's bullshit. That has to be wrong. I'm responsible and I know I didn't take it. What happened? How did we keep such poor records? This is awful," Jim said as he got the call-waiting signal on the other end of the phone.

"That's her. It's got to be her. I'll call you back, Holley," Jim said as he clicked onto the other line.

"Hello?" Jim said trying to sound extra sick.

"Surrant? This it Toney in Chicago. You sound awful. How do you feel?" she asked.

"Terrible, boss. I've really been through it. I haven't been awake for any period of time in over a week, or that's what Joanie told me. Something about a bad case of the flu. I hope to be up and out in a week or so. I've already missed one conference call..."

"Toney interrupted...No sir, you've missed two, but who's counting? The main thing is that you get back on your feet. Everything else can wait. Besides, Holley is doing a great job while you're out. She's been in on the conference calls and has filled me in on the items that I needed to know about. You're very lucky to have such a talented person at hand," Toney said trying to console him.

"I guess I am. How are things going? Anything that I need to know or do. While I'm recuperating, is there something that I need to think about?" Jim fished.

"Not a thing in the world, but about getting well. We'll take care of everything else. Okay?" Toney assured him.

"Well, okay if you say so boss. I'll talk with you soon," Jim concluded. When they hung up, Jim laid there just thinking about all that happened over the past five to six months. It was nearing the middle of October and he was no further along than he was earlier in the spring. He thought to himself all the things he'd do when he got well; he'd make strides on everything he touched, he assured himself as he dozed off to sleep again.

PART II

Grant and Toney were at O'Hare early enough to park and get a bite to eat. At twelve they made their way to the gate to meet Brandon. It would be a fun day. Sonjia's family was fun. They all loved one another and seemed to get along well. It would be just like being at home for Toney.

"There he is, Grant," Toney said sounding excited.

Grant stood to wave, making sure that Brandon saw them.

Brandon waved back and kept moving toward them.

"Man, that was a long flight. I'm glad to be on the ground again. We circled for over an hour as if the flight wasn't long enough," Brandon went on and on.

"That's just like a lawyer. You can really talk, man," Grant said as he moved closer to shake Brandon's hand and to hug him.

"How are you man? You look great. Now move aside and let me at the beauty," he said gently shoving Grant aside and moving to Toney.

Grant laughed.

"Grant, you are one lucky son of a bitch. Look at this beauty. Come here, girl, and give me a hug," Brandon insisted.

Toney blushed and moved over to Brandon.

"Hey good looking. Welcome back to Chicago," Toney said in a flirting fashion.

"Well let's get going gang. I understand you guys are taking me to some family reunion? I'm surprised at that. It's October in Chicago. Most family reunions take place in July or August. Who are these people?" Brandon said as they walked toward baggage claim.

"We are having great weather, and besides, they're untraditional. So, it might be real real nice now that we don't have to worry about the bugs and the heat."

They continued to chitchat about this and that as they strolled. They had a lot of catching up to do.

They picked up Brandon's bags and were on their way. They rode for twenty-five minutes before puling into Cumberland Park in Melrose. About three minutes into the park, Grant saw the group gathered around picnic tables. There were over a hundred people in the area. Playing softball and other games as well as playing cards and so on. The three got out to join in on the festivities. Toney and Sonjia saw one another at about the same time. They hugged as Sonjia welcomed them. Sonjia took them around to introduce them to everyone.

Brandon and Sylvia, Sonjia's cousin, were off to themselves for quiet sometime just talking.

"Where do you live Sylvia?" Brandon asked.

"Here in the Melrose park area," Sylvia said blushing.

"What about you?" she asked Brandon

"In Los Angeles. But I'm in town for an interview. I'll know more on Tuesday," he said.

"So, I take it you're not married?" Brandon said clearing the way.

"Nope. Not yet," Sylvia responded.

"What about you Brandon?" Sylvia retorted.

"No. I haven't found the right person at this point. Besides, we just met," he continued with a big smile.

"What kind of interview?" Sylvia asked.

"With a law firm in downtown Chicago. I'm an attorney."

"I sort of thought so…your being with Grant and all," she said.

"What do you do?" Brandon reciprocated.

"I'm a librarian. I love books and people, so I became a librarian."

They really appeared to be getting off to a great start together. At five, Grant, Toney and Brandon prepared to leave. Brandon and Sylvia exchanged information with a commitment to talk again soon. As they walked away from the gathering toward the car, Toney noticed a familiar car parked across from Grant's car. She saw the man seated in the car. He favored one of the men that she saw in Jamaica. That was strange. The man saw Toney peering at him, started his car and took off. His car had Chicago tags and looked ordinary. Toney chalked it up to her imagination.

After dropping Toney off they went to Grant's place to allow Brandon to unpack and get settled in. Grant and Toney had plans to take

Brandon to dinner, but that was cut short by Brandon's request just to stay in and prepare for his day on Monday. So they did. Grant did paperwork and Brandon took a nap.

At seven Grant and Brandon got together to prepare something to eat. They raided the refrigerator for whatever they could manage. It was just like their days in college. As they prepared the meal, they began to talk.

"So, Brandon, tell me about the challenges on your job and the reason that you're in Chicago interviewing."

"Man, you won't believe it. The African Americans on my job are pitted against each other. It's the same old thing, the crabs in a barrel syndrome. It's messed up. I was recruited out of school. You remember when you left, I told you I wanted to stay for a couple more years. I stayed three. So, when I came out I was hot stuff. But, I did get the offers that I thought I would from New York or Chicago. The best offer that I got was from Los Angeles. When I first arrived at the firm, I was mocked and ridiculed, because they had me fast tracked. A couple of the black lawyers that had to work their way up and had been there for four and six years respectively, were against my coming on board and being breezed by, as they put it. Man...you should have been there to witness some of the shit they did to sabotage me. And not only that, the so-called leaders in the firm turned many of the hourly people against me too."

By the time that Brandon finished telling him about all of the indiscretions that he faced, Grant was appalled. Just to think that your own kind would try and block you as well was disappointing to say the least.

On Monday morning at five o'clock a.m., it was misty and just turning a slight bit colder. Grant gave Brandon directions on how he was to get where he needed to be for his interview, while he headed for Ohio. It was less than a four-hour trip from Chicago. He wanted to get there as early as he could and be back in time for dinner.

During the drive to Dayton, Grant thought through several things that he was lucky enough to find out in the Bay area. He wondered how much more successful he'd be in Dayton. He was hopeful that the trip would be worth it.

Toney arrived at the office early that morning as well. She was hoping that she'd hear from Babbitt. She couldn't continue to hide the nerve-racking incidents that she was concealing from Grant much longer. Her day would be as full as ever, so she would pace herself to get through it all. At six thirty-five, there was a knock on the door of her office.

"Yes, who is it?" Toney answered concerned that it was an intruder at this hour. But, would an intruder knock? She asked herself as she rose to respond to the individual at the door.

"It's me, Toney. It's Sonjia," Sonjia's sudden solemn voice responded. Toney smiled, "Come in, dear. Come in."

"Good morning, Sonjia. Thank you for inviting us to your family's party. It was wonderful. Each of us enjoyed it, and as it seems, for all different reasons. It was wonderful meeting your folks. I see why you're such a lovely woman. Grant was happy to see me happy and well, Brandon was suitably happy with Sylvia. She's all he spoke about while we rode home. How are you today?"

"It was fun, wasn't it? Thanks for coming. Sylvia spoke about Brandon too. She was really excited. She's been looking for someone special. I hope they can get together."

"Uh," Sonjia hesitated.

"What is it Sonjia?" Toney's temperament turned purely business.

"It's June again. I didn't want to spoil your weekend so I didn't tell you on Friday.

She has been going around not only the office, but also the building talking about you and Cameron. Saying that you were somehow involved in what happened to Cameron. Toney, I recognize that it is your decision whether to let her go, but I believe that you should get her out of here. She's been warned again and again. She's no good for your reputation and what you're trying to do here," Sonjia concluded.

"I'll handle it, Sonjia. Thanks," Toney said as she stood to walk Sonjia out to her desk.

They each went back to work only looking up just before noon to take a break.

PART III

Cameron would be alone. Peter was on his way back to work. He had taken half of last week off trying to look out for his wife. But, now it was time to get back. He made sure to leave things easily accessible for her. She was so dear to him.

"Honey, you did pretty well with your breakfast. I have your meds right here on the table. I've also made you a sandwich for a snack. So, you should be all right until I get back home. Just watch television or sit out on the porch, okay?" Peter said making sure she was comfortable.

"Alright, Peter. Don't worry so much. I'll be fine. I'll be alright," Cameron said slowly.

"Okay, baby. I'll call you to check on you later," he said as he kissed her on the forehead and left.

It was two in the afternoon. It had turned out to be a pretty day. Cameron wanted to sit out on the porch to get some fresh air. She got up and got dressed much like she would if she were headed to the office. She took a seat in the corner of their front porch. She sat there with a million mixed up thoughts going through her head. She was worked up.

She really hadn't understood why she was in this state. She was still very confused. The next thing she knew she walked back into the house, got her coat and Peter's handgun and headed off to work. She was clearly out of control to herself but to the onlookers she was just one of the crowd. She got off the bus and caught the train headed for the city. Forty-five minutes later she was on Michigan Avenue headed for the building. She wanted Summers to tell her why he screwed her the way he did. Maybe today he wouldn't be so smug. Just as she arrived on the thirty-seventh-floor, she started to shake uncontrollably. She walked into her office with her eyes glaring. The receptionist immediately went into a petrified state. She was so scared that she couldn't react. As Cameron reached the area where her desk was located, she saw April seated in her spot. She became deranged taking out the gun. April looked up and before she could mumble a word Cameron shot her in the head. The staff started screaming. The loud sounds of the screams sent Cameron on a shooting rampage. She shot three more people. The next stop was Summers office, but before she could get to him, he came to her.

"What the hell is happening out here?" he said, walking into the open area. As soon as Cameron saw him, she shot him three times, dropped the gun and fell to the floor. She began to sob uncontrollably. It was awful. People started scrambling and running and others from the adjacent offices came running to see what they could see. It was a massacre.

The sirens and the crowds became uncontrollable. Each individual in the building who heard about the shooting made their way to find out who was shot. The news cameras were setup outside, and the crews were interviewing whomever they could. June had gone to lunch late and was headed back. She saw all of the activity and instantaneously got in the mix. Once she ascertained what had happened, she hurried up to the fiftieth floor to spread the news.

"Sonjia, is Toney in? Is she here?" June said in a state that was unusually pushy for June.

"What's wrong June? What has happened?" Sonjia asked, as she also became excited.

"Cameron has killed some people in her office. Please tell Toney that her friend has killed some people downstairs in her office."

Toney heard the voices outside of her office and rushed out to see what was going on.

"What's the problem?" Toney said moving over to June.

"It's Cameron," June said with her eyes filling up with tears.

"She's killed several people on the thirty-seventh floor. They say it's awful," June said starting to cry.

"Oh my God!" Toney whimpered as she ran out and into the hallway headed for her friend.

"This is crazy...it's really crazy!" Toney said over and over again as she paced waiting for the elevator to come.

When Toney arrived on the thirty-seventh floor, it was swarming with police. She tried to get through to her friend, but they weren't letting anyone through.

"Ma'am, this is a crime scene. No one is allowed in or out. No one at all," the officer said.

"But, the lady who shot these people is my friend. I have to get to her. She really needs me. She just got out of the hospital and she needs someone," Toney said pleading with the officer.

"Ma'am. I'm sorry. No one is allowed in or out."

Toney was upset.

"Poor Cameron. She doesn't deserve this," she said pacing in the little spot that she had.

A couple of seconds later the police brought Cameron out. She had a far away look in her eyes. She had her hands cuffed behind her back and was being lead to the elevator by two cops, one on each side of her. Toney stood there in shock. The paradox was so pervasive.

"All she wanted to do was work and be treated fairly, which should be embraced. But the arrogance of some people is embarrassing," Toney said as she walked away feeling as if she should have been able to do more.

When Toney reached her office everyone was buzzing about Cameron. Toney waited in the reception area, stopping briefly to recognize Lane who appeared to be shaken about the activities on the thirty-seventh floor.

"Lane, try to calm yourself. I know it's difficult but we have to make sure that we don't let what happened take us into a volatile situation," Toney pleaded.

"I know, Toney, but this kind of thing just doesn't happen around here. There have been too many strange things happening," Lane continued.

"You're right. They say things come in threes. So, I hope the break-in of my office counted," Toney said as she began to walk through the door to the outer offices. Just before she walked in she heard June talking loud.

"I think Toney had something to do with this predicament, too. Cameron is her friend. Plus Peter, Cameron's husband, called here yesterday to speak with her and now this. I tell you there is definitely some connection here," June said as Toney opened the door and walked in.

"June, may I see you in my office please?" Toney said as she continued walking past the seven individuals who were standing there listening.

"Uh, yeah. I'm right behind you, Toney," June said, walking with Toney and turning back to the others indicating that she hoped that Toney hadn't heard her comments.

Toney walked past Sonjia with June right behind her. She moved to take her seat behind her desk looking up at June. "Please take a seat."

"Alright," June said shakily.

"June, I have been fair in giving you the benefit of the doubt for weeks now. There have been several times that I have counseled you because I thought that much of you. Now, there is only so much unprofessional behavior that I'm willing to tolerate. As far as I'm concerned you have hit a brick wall. At this point, I would like to hear what you have to say for yourself."

"What are you talking about, Toney?" June said innocently.

"June, please don't play games with me. You and I both know what I'm talking about," Toney said in a rough way becoming irritated.

"I have just witnessed a horrible scene, and I do not have time for this nonsense. If there is nothing else, I'd like to ask for your resignation," Toney said turning emotionally cold to June.

"Toney, please give me another chance. I promise I'll keep my mouth shut. Please," June said starting to cry.

"I'm sorry. My mind is made up. Will you be submitting your resignation?" Toney forced.

Silence filled the room. Thirty seconds passed by. June stopped sobbing long enough to look through her tears to say, "Toney I am so sorry. I'm so very sorry."

June stood and began to make her way to the door. She turned to Toney and said again, "I am so sorry." Then she left.

TWENTY NINE

After the mild morning and the crisp sunny afternoon, it was turning very cold outside, somewhere in the twenties. A light snow was starting to fall. Most of the city was moving forward, having no knowledge of the horrible events that only a small percentage of the populace had braved. Toney was personally experiencing an apogee and had become an emotional wreck after seeing Cameron's face that afternoon. She knew that this individual had ventured to a different mental level now. She definitely wasn't the same person that Toney had befriended several years back. As a matter of fact, she couldn't believe the transformation. This display was a testimony to how much a human being could take before cracking. She went back to her office to sat quietly trying to try and collect what was left of her fragile psyche, because she herself had endured monumental injustices over the years, but chose to deal with them in much different ways. She thought that being conditioned had to have something to do with her ability to make it through. She sat there that afternoon stunned, until she began to daydream again ...

The successes that she had enjoyed were of God, and Toney knew it. She was so grateful for His power that obviously led her way. Toney often phoned Tiffany and Jamie at the Prophecy office in Washington, D.C. to make sure that the ties that they had developed weren't broken. That afternoon was taxing for Toney, so she took a break to call the girls. She wanted to catch up on things in D.C.

"Tiff. Its Toney. How ya doing girl?" Toney said after hearing Tiffany's very upbeat voice on the phone.

"Girl. This crazy ass man you left us with is sick. He's in way over his head. He can't keep up, and Meagan, she's outta here. I heard her telling some other people that he wasn't going to work the shit outta her.

A few days later she was gone. She just up and quit, leaving him holding the damn bag. So, I'm fine as long as he's getting what he deserves. What goes around comes around, doesn't it?" Tiffany scarped.

"You're kidding. I knew that he would catch it when I left. I was doing all the work, you know? But, old Meagan hung in there with him for a while, didn't she?" Toney said not sounding too surprised.

"Well, I believe he's on his last leg. He's been called to Corporate, and I think he's gone. He should be up there with you tomorrow. Let me know if you hear anything," Tiffany said sounding very pleased.

"The other thing is, I took his ass to EEOC. He's been talking to all of us in a foul way. I don't have to take that shit, you know?" She said.

"When do you go to court?" Toney asked.

"We've already been. I won. The company had to pay me one hundred and fifty thousand-dollar. I don't get it for a year...but, shit I can wait. That's why I know he's outta here. Man, life is good to me now."

"Tiff, I'm so happy for you. You've been through a lot over the years. You've also been a good friend to me and I wish you the best. I'll let you know what I hear, okay?" Toney said sounding very pleased with the information that she had picked up.

"How's Jamie?" Toney asked.

"That girl is off again today. Probably her old-man again. But, she's fine. I really miss you, Toney. I hear you're kicking ass in Chicago, so hang in there. You'll probably be the President of the company someday with your smarts."

"I'm sticking with it. I just get a little lonely sometimes, so that's why I called. Tell Jamie I said hello, okay?"

"Okay girl. I'll call you next," Tiffany said as they both hung up.

The next day, she saw Dick as he was walking up the steps to enter the building. He had his head down as if he were in deep concentration. The next thing she heard circulating was that Dick had been relieved of his responsibilities ...

"You just can't think that you can keep violating people and believe that your path will be paved with gold. Eventually you have to pay the piper," Toney said as she stood to leave for the day. She literally had nothing left.

As she walked through the lobby, many members of the press were still occupying the furthest portion of the lobby near the front doors of the building. She walked through the people who were ten to twelve deep picking up snatches of conversation as they also tried to make sense of what had transpired. She just wanted to get away from the madness. She walked through the garage in what had her feeling like it was suspended animation. She finally reached her car and slid in. Her ride home was eerie. She felt a cold chill run up her spine. Someone was after her, and it had to be all because of the position that she had. Cameron had killed people because of the position that she should have gotten. Toney had a huge capacity for many things, but somehow she just couldn't make heads or tails of this. It just didn't make sense.

That night, Toney couldn't sleep at all. All she could manage was to toss and turn. She was so restless about it all. She couldn't help but think that there had to have been more that she could do to help Cameron. She got out of bed and began pacing while she thought. She needed to hear Grant's voice. She thought about the fact that she had never even called him to let him know what had happened to Cameron. She never even told him about all the things that had happened. After thinking it through, she decided that she didn't want to tell him tonight. She'd call him in the morning and let him know about everything.

Grant was on his drive back from Dayton, Ohio. He was extremely disturbed about the information that he had uncovered. Those shorter twins were literally dangerous. At nine thirty he pulled into his parking space at the condominium. He sat there for a moment just reflecting. He had an uneasy feeling about this situation and knew that he had to manage it all before it ended up managing him. He had to bring Toney into the loop. He got out of his car and headed upstairs. As he put his key into the door, he hesitated because he saw lights on in his unit and he typically didn't leave lights burning. Was there someone there?

"Grant? That you, man?" the voice uttered sounding as if it was heading toward the front door.

Grant offered a sigh of relief as the voice continued, "It's me Brandon. It's me."

"Brandon, I literally forgot that you were here for a moment. How'd it go today? How was the interview?" Grant said changing the subject.

"I got the job on the spot. I'm moving to Chicago," Brandon said flashing a huge smile and extending his hand to be shaken.

"Astounding, man. It'll be great having you around. When do you start?" Grant asked putting down his briefcase and taking off his jacket while accepting Brandon's hand to shake.

"On December 1, 1998. I told them that I had to go back to tie up some loose ends and then, I'm all theirs."

"That's good news, man," Grant said looking wired.

"You look a little tight Grant. What did you find out?" Brandon asked with great concern.

"Plenty. I'm just too tired to talk about it now. But, tomorrow...I'll tell both you and Toney at the same time," he retorted as he picked up his briefcase and jacket heading for his bedroom.

It was difficult for Grant to sleep. He thought he heard little noises all through the night but, after checking, he found nothing. He was also concerned for himself, but only half as much as he was for his lady, his mother and sisters and even Millicent. These guys were notorious and there was no telling what they'd do to get him out of the way.

The next morning Toney followed her ritual and got out early. She thought about it and she was grateful that it was Friday. This had proven to be more than an eventful week, and she wanted it over. When she arrived at the office that morning, it was five-thirty. She checked her messages first and discovered Babbitt had called her three times in a row. He sounded pumped.

"Toney? You need to come to my office around nine tomorrow. I've got to see you. You should bring Grant with you. It's urgent," the message stated.

The second and third messages were even stronger and more pointed. Toney instantly picked up her phone to leave Babbitt a voice mail message that she would be there. She called Grant at home.

"Hello?" Grant answered

"Honey, I know you're on your way to the office but, I have to get you to go someplace with me this morning. I've also got something to share with you. It's really important," Toney said tacitly.

"I've got some news for you too. Besides, I can't wait to see you. It's been almost a week," Grant reacted.

"I'll be there at nine," Grant replied as they hung up.

The shorter twins were at it again. They had a plan that they had laid out for Grant. He would be out of their way soon.

Jim Surrant was feeling much better; although, he wasn't completely well. He decided to visit Chicago again unannounced. He was getting restless and wanted to see Diane again. She had shown him one hell of a time, and he needed to see her again. Beside, the last time he spoke with Gamble, he was tailing Chambers but hadn't really completed the job. He needed to speak with Gamble again before he left. His thoughts were that they could get together face to face so that he could get an update.

"Holley, sorry to wake you so early but, I need your help. Get Gamble on the phone for me. Call his cell number. He should be in his car in the Chicago area at this time of day," he said lacking luster.

"Okay, Jim," Holley responded in her normal manner trying to completely wake herself.

"Where are you at this hour?" Holley rambled.

"In the office. I know...it's only four am but I have a flight leaving at six thirty. I'm off to Chicago again. I should be back on Sunday. I have to talk with Gamble first. I need to let him know I'm coming. Also, tell him that I'm on United flight number one forty-two, and it arrives in Chicago at eight forty five a.m.. I should be at baggage claim by nine."

"Okay. I might as well get up and start moving anyway. I'll call you back in a little while. Okay?" Holley said sounding a slight bit irritated. Holley pulled her day timer phone book from her brief case, while grabbing her glasses to aid her half closed eyes.

"Let's see Gamble, Gamble..." she murmured.

As she dialed the phone, she stretched and yawned forcing tiny tears from the corners of her eyes. She had clearly not gotten enough sleep that night.

"Hello?" Gamble said sounding like he had just been disturbed.

"Mr. Gamble?" Holley questioned.

"Who's this? Where did you get this number?" Gamble asked appearing to be shocked out of the state that he was in.

"This is Holley, Jim Surrant's secretary. He asked me to phone you. He wanted you to know that he was on his way to Chicago. He wants you to pick him up at the United Airlines baggage claim area at nine this morning, Chicago time. He wants to meet with you as soon as he arrives. Are you available?" Holley followed up.

"Yeah. Let him know that I'll be at O'Hare at nine. I'll pick him up curbside," Gamble said.

"Okay." Holley said as they both hung up.

Holley phoned Jim back at the office and gave him the information that he needed. He immediately left headed for the airport.

At seven Grant and Brandon had gotten clearance from Marvin at the desk to go up since Toney had called their names down to the desk. They were on the elevator headed to meet Toney in her office at Prophecy's headquarters. They wanted to be there on time.

"Toney's summons was urgent. There has to be something happening," Grant said.

"What's been happening with you guys? I can see the strain in your face this morning. And, last night you really had me concerned. Plus while we were at the family reunion and dinner on Saturday you both seemed a bit jumpy. It was odd how neither of you seemed to want to discuss it?" Brandon said.

"There was some tension in the air. I couldn't put my finger on it if I had to but for my part, I've got some answers now...and both you and Toney will know soon enough. I hope that whatever is happening with her, she'll be ready to talk about it and get it all out too." Grant said as he stepped off of the elevator and walked to the door of Toney's office. The door was locked due to the time of morning. He casually knocked. No answer. He knocked again. Brandon saw a little doorbell on the side of the door, which was only visible to him due to his position. He pushed the button and few seconds later they saw a figure headed to the door.

"Good morning, honey," Toney said as she opened the door, while stepping aside for them to enter.

"It's too early for my staff so I normally lock my self in," she said as she stepped up to Grant to give him a quick kiss on the cheek.

"Hi Brandon," she said grabbing them both by the arm and leading them to her office.

As Brandon walked in, he couldn't believe his eyes.

"This is huge," he said out loud. Appearing to be in a stupor.

"What an office! I had no idea you were this large girl," he said giving Toney a thumb up.

"Awww Brandon. This is just an office," Toney said smiling, while taking a seat on the closest chair in the first sitting area and motioning for them to take a seat as well.

"Honey, what's going on here? You've been uneasy for weeks now. I haven't wanted to push you on it. You normally talk to me about everything in time. Now, you call me with this urgent request. So, what's the deal?" Grant said taking a seat next to her.

"You remember the accident in Jamaica?" Toney said starting in the beginning.

"Yes. What about it?" Grant asked.

"I don't believe it was an accident. And, that's only the beginning. There have been so many strange things happening," Toney continued.

"Like what?" Grant coached.

"Like my office was ransacked several weeks ago. Like Freddy being murdered. Like someone trying to run me down in the garage at my house. Like someone chasing me on the freeway," she said as she started to shake somewhat.

Grant eyes became big.

"First of all Toney, calm down. You mean to tell me that you've been going through all of this and you didn't tell me. Toney…I'm hurt and disappointed. You have been trying to handle all this by yourself. Honey what were you thinking?" Grant said as he sat there in disbelief.

Brandon chimed in, "Who could want to harm you like that? What is this all about? Do you have any enemies that you know of who would take that road with you?" he asked as an attorney would.

"My initial thoughts were that it had to be Surrant. But, some of this stuff…I just don't know." Toney said, as she sat there looking puzzled.

"Why did you want us here at nine? What is that all about? We should go to the police," Grant said talking charge.

"That's what I want to tell you honey. I've been working with a private investigator."

"A what? This just gets better and better. How long has this been going on?" Grant asked.

"About six weeks," Toney carried through.

"Okay who is this person?" Grant said sounding anxious.

"Your life has been in danger and you didn't tell me? I'm supposed to protect you. Do you realize that I love you? How can you have these things going on and not tell me about them?" he said sounding crushed.

"Grant, there was nothing that you could do about it. I didn't want you to get hurt too, so I tried to handle it myself. I hired someone who I thought would take care of all of it. Fin Babbitt with All About the Truth over on LaSalle. He's supposed to be the best and promised me that he'd get to the bottom of it," Toney said trying to calm Grant down.

"Babbitt? I've never heard of him. Who is he and where did you find out about him?" Grant asked.

"I got him out of the yellow pages. And, we have an appointment with him at nine," Toney said feeling sort of silly.

"The yellow pages? Well of all places...why didn't I think of that?" Grant said sarcastically.

Toney was surprised at Grant's disposition. She knew that he was angry with her, because of the method in which she handled this, but to be sarcastic was out of character for him.

"Grant, is there something else going on here?" Toney abruptly changed the subject.

"Well, I guess I should tell you now rather than later since we're both fessing up. I went to San Francisco, as you already know and to Dayton Ohio this week. There have been several strange things happening at work and the feelings that I've been getting about Nick and Terry have had me on edge. I decided to see if I could utilize my investigative skills to find out a little more about those boys. I had to see what I could find out so I would know who was right up on me everyday. And, what I found out will curl your hair. What time is the appointment again?" Grant said.

"It's at nine. Since you and Brandon are here, maybe we can grab a quick breakfast, and then head over to talk with Fin? What do you say? We can continue our conversation over breakfast," Toney said in a charming way, which she knew would turn Grant's disposition around.

"Well alright honey. But, you're still not out of the woods with me yet," he said as he stood to reach out for her.

They walked out into the outer office area. Sonjia was just opening the door and was surprised to see the trio headed out.

"Good morning. And where are you guys going?" she said playfully.

" Hi, Sonjia," Brandon said alertly.

"How's your pretty cousin?" Brandon forced.

"Oh she's fine. How are you doing? How did your interview go?" Sonjia asked.

"I got the job, so you'll be seeing a lot more of me around here," Brandon said confidently.

"Sonjia, I'll be back before noon. Okay?" Toney reported.

"Okay Toney. Are you alright Grant?" Sonjia observed.

"Oh, hi Sonjia. I'm fine," he said appearing to be preoccupied.

Over breakfast they had a detailed discussion, which enlightened everyone. They were all bewildered about the state of affairs. Neither of them felt that this had to go this far if in fact all of the incidents were all connected. They agreed that Babbitt probably could lay it all out for them. At nine they were walking into Babbitt's office. He was at the receptionist desk waiting for them. He looked like hell. He also looked worried.

"Toney, I'm so glad that you got my message. Who are your friends?" Babbitt said cautiously.

"This is Grant. You asked me to bring him. And, this is Brandon, he's a friend of ours from Los Angeles," Toney said as Grant and Brandon extended their hands to Babbitt.

Babbitt shrugged his shoulders and accepted the pair as safe as he turned to lead them down the path to his office. Once they were there, Babbitt insisted that they take seats.

"You'll be here with me for an hour if not more so please be seated," he directed.

"I can tell you this...you people are very lucky. The formidable components that have been artfully waging war on you are deadly," Babbitt began.

The essential elements of the case are...Jim Surrant has hired a thug by the name of Guy Gamble to shake you up Toney. So, some of the little stuff is his work. He has a reputation as a leg breaker. He's never done time, but has been on the brink of it many times. But, here's where it gets worse. You and your Fiancée," Babbitt said as he turned to Grant, "have been artfully toyed with and the fact that people around you Toney have been falling was meant to send you off on the deep end. If you fell, you would have taken Grant with you and therefore, he would have been out of the way for Terry Conners and Nick Sampson."

Grant grimaced. What the shorter twins had done had transcended the workplace. They had moved into his personal territory, which was the woman that he loved. Grant was furious. 'There was no punishment hearty enough for those sons-of-a-bitch,' Grant thought.

"You mean to tell me that Toney has had to endure this shit while I was the target? Babbitt, are you sure?" Grant asked manifesting an unstable posture.

"I'm as sure about it, as I am that I'm breathing. We are as thorough as one can get. Now, Surrant should also go to jail for his part in this. The activities that he and Gamble participated in are illegal too, but not deadly. So, all of my findings will go to the cops today, as a matter of fact they already have my preliminary findings. And, they will all be jailed," Babbitt continued.

"Toney, you know that there will be court appearances, right?" Babbitt asked.

Toney was sitting there stunned and saying nothing.

Grant added, "I went out of town this week and found out that both Nick and Terry have been on a terror trail. They have participated in some hideous activities and even murder, but no one has ever been able to prove any of it," Grant said.

"Well here's where it stops. I've got proof that they murdered Freddy Talbert. They were masquerading as two gay guys and lured him into a motel in South Chicago. That's where they murdered him and moved his body to the park. I've already spoken to Sergeant Billings at the Chicago Police and given him all of the evidence in that case. They should be picking up Nick and Terry this morning. And, as for Surrant, we have to alert the authorities in Los Angeles. They'll handle him for his part in all this."

"So, what you're saying is that it's all over?" Toney asked.

"Just about. Once the boys are arrested, then court but then...its all over Toney." Babbitt said as he reclined back in his soiled chair. He had broken another case and was happy to do it. Babbitt walked the trio to the door of the reception area. Toney hung back and spoke with Babbitt as the walked, "Fin, I can never repay you for what you've done for me. I feel safer and more confident now that you've solved this ridiculous mystery. It's appalling what people will do in the name of getting ahead. And to murder someone, that's ludicrous," Toney concluded as they reached the elevator.

"Please send me your bill."

"You're a nice lady and I was determined not to have you live that way. It was my job to get to the truth," Babbitt said as he offered his hand to Toney.

Grant dropped Toney off in front of the building at eleven fifteen. As they sat there saying goodbye, Surrant pulled up and got out of the drivers side seat of a car which was being driven by a man that Toney had seen before. He was at the Melrose Park, parked across the street last Saturday afternoon when they left the Family Reunion. She thought at that time that she had seen him before, but forced the thoughts away. She thought she was being paranoid. But, there he was again and with Surrant. It was all making sense now. She got out of the car to approach Surrant.

"What are you doing back in Chicago?"

"Just came back as soon as I was well enough to travel, so I could catch up. How are you Toney?" Surrant said.

"I'm great Surrant. Let's go up to my office. I'll bring you up to speed." Toney said as she aimlessly walked to the front door. She was livid. This son of a bitch had her followed and taunted. She wanted to make sure he didn't get away. She wanted him to go down and go down today. Grant stepped out of the car to try and get her attention as Brandon moved out of the back seat and into the front seat.

"Toney are you alright?" he bellowed.

"She turned to him, smiled and said…"Better than I've been in months," as she pranced through the door.

Once they were in her office she asked Surrant to take a seat as she excused herself for a moment. She stepped into the outer office and called the police.

"Sergeant Billings please. Toney Chambers calling."

Fifteen minutes later, the police were there.

"Ms. Chambers please," the lead officer asked.

Sonjia buzzed Toney, "Toney the cops are here."

"Please show them in," Toney said calmly.

"Jim, there is someone I'd like for you to meet," as she got up from behind her huge desk and strutted over to her door to allow the cops to enter.

"Officers, this is Jim Surrant and he's been a very busy little boy. He's all yours!" she said as Jim went to pieces.

Jim twitched as he sat there accepting what was happening. He still looked weak from his illness. Toney thought, as things moved in slow motion, that if Jim hadn't been such a son of a bitch, she would have mercy on him. Toney felt triumphant for herself and all of Surrant's victims and she was sure that he had many victims. She put her conscious to rest about the matter the moment that he was handcuffed and taken out. He alone was the responsible one. He had chosen his activities. And, besides there was still the question about the missing funds. She'd be ultimately responsible for it so, she had to replace him anyway or risk not doing her job.

Brandon went into the office with Grant. He wanted to be there to watch his friend's back.

"Good morning Mill. How's everything?" Grant said sounding very loose.

"Things are fine, I guess. The shorter twins have been at it again today. When I got in Nick was rambling in your office. Something tells me those fools are going to make a move today. I think they're going to Montrose today about taking over your main accounts. I over heard them again. If these ridiculous excuses for professionals worked as hard at getting their own cases as they do trying to steal your cases, they'd make a fucking million dollars on their own." Millicent said.

"Mill what have I told you about that language in the office? Quiet yourself," Grant cautioned.

"This is Brandon, my friend from Los Angeles. Brandon...this is Millicent."

"Hello Millicent. We've spoken several times on the phone. It's nice to meet you," Brandon said hardly able to get the words out before Millicent cut in...

"Hi good looking...nice to meet you to...Grant, we've got to do something about those boys. They keep too much shit going on in here. Everyone's talking about it."

"Not to worry my dear. It'll all be over soon," Grant said as he went into his office with Brandon in tow.

Nick and Terry approached Grant's office at twelve fifty.

"Grant, you got a minute?" Terry said.

"I'm busy right now but, I can come over to your office when I'm finish if you like," Grant said smugly.

"That won't do man. I got to speak with you right now. I'm taking over some of your cases and I just wanted to give you the heads up," Terry continued in a gruff manner.

"And, I'm taking over two of your cases. I decided that my name was on the two that I want," Nick growled.

"Oh, so you guys are just going to take my cases?" Grant said as he stood to make his way over to the shorter twins who were hovering outside of the door to his office.

Brandon stood along side of Grant.

"And who is this nigger supposed to be, your new body guard? I don't think you want to mess with us man," Terry said looking at Brandon.

"Why you gotta call the man names? You don't even know him. I'll tell you what, I suggest that we meet on neutral territory to discuss this matter at a later time. I'm not feeling too good about giving either of you anything. And, I know damn well you ain't coming in here to take the files," Grant said knowing that any minute the cops would be there to arrest these jerks.

"We'll talk about it this afternoon, when the office closes. We'll have to get it all straightened out then. Don't try to sneak out of here either. You're not doing those cases any damn good and the firm needs to move on them. Montrose is in the loop on this," Nick said as the shorter twins walked away.

"What the hell was that?" Brandon said.

"Those guys got balls. They just came to your door and demanded your cases. If they'd do that, they'd do anything." Brandon continued.

"That's what I've been trying to tell you. These guys have killed before to get what they want, so to try and take these cases is nothing to them. That's why they have to be stopped. No one else will have to be hurt by these pricks. In a few minutes the cops should be here to sweep them up like the scum that they are," Grant said as he took his seat again shaking his head.

Just before one o'clock, two detectives and two uniformed police arrived.

"Are Nick Sampson and Terry Conners in, please?" Detective Hendericks smoothly asked.

"Yes sir. I'll get them for you," Beatrice the receptionists said nervously.

Buzz.

"Mr. Conners there are four gentlemen here for you and Mr. Sampson. Will you come to the reception area please?" she announced nervously.

Terry surfaced from his office, while Beatrice phoned Nick. A couple of seconds later, Nick surfaced. They were both looking cocky as they went to the front to see what this was all about.

"I'm Nick Sampson and this is Terry Conners. What can we do for you?" Nick asked.

"Sir, you are both under arrest for the murder of Fred Talbert. You have a right to remain silent...." the officers said as they cuffed them both. A crowd was forming to watch the dramatics.

"Murder?" Terry scoffed.

"You'll never be able to prove it," Nick said confidently and struggled to gain control of the situation.

They were both led out of the office.

Grant and Brandon walked to the front after hearing the buzz that had ensued. Millicent had gotten the news late, but rushed to the front to catch the end of the action.

"I knew your asses were up to no good. You just can't trust people like you. Get your asses outta here and let decent people work. This is no damned place for the likes of you," she roared loudly.

"Mill, what am I going to do with you? You've gotta stop talking like that. Please." Grant scolded her as he and Brandon walked her back to her desk. This would be just another day for good old Millicent.

Later that afternoon, Grant, Toney and Brandon met for dinner at Vidi's. They wanted to celebrate today. Their lives would finally be back to normal. As they sat there discussing the events of the day, they heard restlessness around them about a tragedy on the news ... the restaurant patrons watched the television over the bar. Grant's building had exploded. There had been sixteen people killed. Grant was in shock. They believed that the twins had sent someone to do their dirty work again. Grant promised Toney that he would contact Sergeant Billings about the matter.

THE BEGINNING...

It was finally spring and one could smell the flowers in bloom. It was to be a joyous day. Grant and Toney had a fabulous visit with their folks over the holidays. They would all soon become family. She was optimistic, at least for now, that the bad events were over. She realized that life brought along the bad with the good, but she hoped that she had managed the many, many negatives and that she and her future husband had earned a smooth time for a while.

Exactly one week earlier, Corbin announced his premature retirement and his replacement. Toney took over the helm of the company. Corbin was confident that the talent, dedication and morale fiber that this young woman had was what Prophecy needed to take it into the new millenium.

Finally, Toney understood why she daydreamed so much. She had to put her entire legacy together in her mind. She understood most of it now that the complete puzzle was together. The last piece was the wedding. As Toney got dressed that day, she pondered all of the events of her life and especially the last year. There had been many things to manage. She thought that things would never be the same after the terrible episode with Cameron. That was the most devastating and life altering situation that she had ever witnessed. She was still hurting for Cameron and people like her, who were good hardworking people. But, she realized the obstacles that had been placed in her path helped her to sustain herself over the years and that one had to condition themselves in any way they could. The fact that many of us do not have "the look" that Corporate America wants, prepared us more than it did those who had the so-called look. We are conditioned for the fight and realize that the war can only be won, if we pick the right battles.

Vanessa is now living with Bi-Polar disease and managing it with the help of the specialist that Toney sent to her.

The mere fact that her blessings had been constant, she could only be thankful that she was having today as her beginning. In two hours, she and Grant would be married. Vanessa, Sonjia and Tiffany were on hand and would be her brides maids. She was surrounded with love and attention, which was all she had ever really wanted in life. Brandon was the eager best man and had recently asked Sylvia to marry him, so there would be another wedding soon. So, he found himself, after all of the ranting and raving about his sexuality, as a man in love with a wonderful woman. He just needed the right person to fulfil him as many of us do.

Cameron was still suffering, but she was released in her doctor's care after the horrible shootings. Jim Surrant was diagnosed with the AIDS virus and sentenced to five years. Guy Gamble was sentenced to fifteen years. Nick Sampson and Terry Conners were charged with the bombing of Grant's building and are serving life in a maximum-security institution with no chance of parole. Sonjia Belleu followed Toney upstairs to the fiftieth floor. Millicent is still with Grant in his new position as Senior Partner of the law firm.

As Toney walked down the aisle that beautiful day, she was walking into the rest of her life. She looked through her veil at the site of the most perfect man that she would ever get to know. He was all hers and she was all his. She vowed to herself that she'd never keep anything else from him again. Then, thoughts of trivial things that she had allowed to upset her in her early days in the workplace, were one by one remedied. As she rose...they became even more profound and her character and strength rose to combat them. Periodic indiscretions would always be there...but, she learned that the higher the level that one aspired to, the higher the stakes would be. But, one has to fulfill themselves completely or only live a partial life. That was never who she was. God had given her a talent that she felt a burning passion to cultivate.

Outside the church a glorious day was developing...it was time for the birds to fly north for the summer. As several leaves fell from the roof, one could see two ravens perched on the steeple of the church. They had rested long enough and flew off to continue their journey home.